SK HORTON

THE CAPTURED

HEIR OF EARTH
AND SKY BOOK TWO

aethonbooks.com

THE CAPTURED
©2025 S.K. HORTON

Aethon Books
www.aethonbooks.com

Cover by Steve Beaulieu. Print and eBook formatting by Kevin G. Summers.

Published by Aethon Books LLC.

ALSO BY S.K. HORTON

HEIR OF EARTH AND SKY

The Concealed

The Captured

Want to discuss our books with other readers and even the authors?

JOIN THE AETHON DISCORD!

To Brooke and Claire:
My extraordinary girls. I can't wait to see where your wings will take you.

CHAPTER 1
CATE

"Oof." Every muscle ached from hitting the ground yet *again.*

"Come on, Cate. Give me more than that." Daniel's eyes gleamed in the butter-yellow sunlight of late summer as he taunted, motioning me to pick myself up for the tenth time that morning.

When I didn't immediately rise, he started toward me. "You alright?"

I gave a disheartened nod to reassure him. We were working on Caelum powers today. I'd been trying to use the surrounding energy to push air but ended up frustrated by my lack of progress, and instead used my annoyance to propel it. Unfortunately, this only led to a rebound effect, which sent me onto my sore tailbone.

"I'm not going to have to report you to Alana for borrowing your own energy?" He raised his brows, two perfect raven-black wings arching over thick lashes.

"No." I slanted him a glare. My relationship with Alana swung the pendulum from mother-like figure to drill sergeant. Since The Great Battle with the Embers two months ago when I'd drenched the mountainside, I hadn't been able to conjure even a drop of dew. Alana scolded me frequently for using emotions instead of the surrounding energy to undertake magic. It literally zapped my own power and nearly killed me that day on the battlefield. But I'd had very little success without thrusting anger or fear into whatever skill I worked to master. Well, *master* was too strong a word. Perhaps *attempt.*

I stretched my sore limbs, still sitting. "I'm trying not to."

Rather than rising, I eased the rest of my body to the ground, the prickly grass at the castle's north lawns cushioning my head. Exhaustion had set in. I'd given too much of myself, failing to utilize the energy that supposedly circled everywhere. If only I could feel it. Being in America instead of here until turning eighteen made what should have been second nature into something awkward and nearly impossible.

"Cate." Daniel's voice sounded worried.

"Hmm?"

The grass bristled as Daniel edged next to me. He tapped my forehead until my eyes crept open to serve him another glare.

"Ah. There she is. Come on. Get up. You've got more in you."

"Nope. You are quite mistaken, sir. I'm done for today." I *did* have a modicum of reserve left, but the constant failure, more than fatigue, sent my shoulders nestling deeper into the turf.

"Sir? Don't you mean *Your Highness*?" He flashed me a lopsided grin, one that threatened to turn my already weak knees into jelly.

"What? We're the same rank. There is no way I'm *Your-Highness-ing* you." Daniel might be the Terran prince, but since my father was the Caelum king, I held the title of princess and King Aldridge's only heir.

He leaned in, his mouth hovering over mine. "Are you sure?" Those bright-blue eyes I once mistook for glacial glimmered with warm mischief. He knew I had trouble resisting his kisses. Taunting me was truly an unfair tactic.

I swallowed thickly and croaked, "Yes." I only reliably sensed the energy when he came close. It floated around us like drifting butterflies, just out of reach. I longed to feel the tingle—the rush that always shimmered across my skin with his touch. He moved closer. A buzz reverberated in the millimeters between our lips. It would be so easy to give in, but I still had something to prove.

The vibrations intensified, and my focus honed on the current. The pads of my fingers gently nudged against Daniel's chest to keep him from closing the distance. "Not yet," I whispered. The energy deepened within me, filling the drained reserves. My palms itched, and I thrust out in one swift motion. Air rushed through the small space between us, expanding and gusting, sending Daniel launching several feet away.

His mouth hung open, the astonished expression entirely worth the loss of a kiss. I'd actually done it. My body pulsed with invigoration. Whether it was the joy of success or the absorption of surrounding energy, it didn't matter. The exhilaration of not being exhausted after using magic charged through my veins.

"Back home, boys have to learn that no means no," I teased.

"Noted." Daniel stood and rubbed his backside with a grimace. "Well done. Let's go again."

My excitement waned at the proposal. The only reason I had been able to use the power was because our proximity allowed me to feel it. I could throw my arms around him now, but somehow that seemed like cheating.

We squared off ten feet from each other. The air fell silent. I searched for any sign of energy but could neither sense nor conjure it. I took a step toward him, then another. A pause. Was that a butterfly whisper of something? Another quick shuffle. A quiver, but not enough to harness. Three more steps. Now I could reach out and touch him. He'd stood his ground, watching my moves with interest. With focus, the vague buzzing turned audible. I fluttered my eyes and probed for the feeling. The air pulsed against my open hands. My lids flashed open, and I shoved. Just enough wind to ruffle Daniel's hair.

He laughed. "Good. You won't win any battles by mussing up a hairstyle, but it might come in handy."

"Be nice!" I cried, then rushed him with palms out and shoved him the old-fashioned way. He barely budged.

"Seriously, great improvement today." He took my hand and cradled it near his heart.

I hadn't told him my headway was dependent on his closeness. If I confided my secret, it would only add an extra burden to his already full plate. But he was smart; it wouldn't be long before he figured me out.

We headed toward the towering blue spires of Caelum Castle.

Adjusting from poor student to princess was still a work in progress. Since my biological mother, the former queen, died from complications of my birth, the place lacked a feminine, homey touch. Not that I knew what a castle should feel like. Probably not *homey*, but the barren glass walls needed something. My room back in Oregon could never be considered sterile. The thought of worn paperbacks, sitting lopsided on my shelf, family photos pinned to the memory board over my desk, and the ruffled curtains leading out to the backyard of rhododendrons and tulips sent a pang of homesickness into my belly. Everyone eventually has to advance past their childhood home, though most don't move into a magical castle. With a grumpy king for a father.

Alana met us on our way, gray bun bobbing along the path, her ever-severe black attire incongruent among the greenery.

"We've had a breakthrough," Daniel called as we approached. "She actually knocked me down." He laughed, the sound filling me with guilt rather than pride for cheating.

Alana searched my face. I studiously avoided her knowing eye. "Is this true, Catherine?"

Her adamance that I shouldn't use my emotions to fuel my powers never wavered. She wasn't wrong—it left me drained and vulnerable. I imagined she wouldn't take keenly to my Daniel problem, which would leave me defenseless when he wasn't around.

Daniel answered for me, "Absolutely. I think she's getting the hang of it."

"We were just going back for a bite to eat. Need anything?" I dragged my gaze from the horizon, now noticing Alana's downturned expression. "What's wrong?"

"We've had a report. Your father would like to speak with the two of you." Her heavy tone, inconsistent with her usual steady countenance, sounded alarm bells in my head.

My insides lurched. If the king wanted to speak to both of us, it likely wasn't great news. He typically preferred to exclude Daniel from our talks. Even though he saved my father's life during The Great Battle, his distrust of Daniel's father, King Dryden, ran deep. And for good reason. We were supposed to be allies, but none of us could forget how the Terran king plotted to use me for Terra's gain.

Disturbing scenarios of Ember fires or raids tumbled through my brain until my thoughts turned to Lucas with sinking foreboding. No one had heard from him since he left two months ago to sway the dragons to our side. I'd been expecting a message for weeks.

King Aldridge sat in the strategy room, surrounded by counselors and generals. Unease trickled down my spine. He hadn't gathered this many advisors together for several months. We'd been in relative peace since the last conflict and expected more of the same after killing a third of the Ember's soldiers before they could retreat. Not bothering to brush the mud from my skirts, I marched inside.

"Catherine. Daniel." He nodded to each of us. "Have a seat."

A round conference table stood at the center of the space. In contrast to the rest of the castle's bright atmosphere, the room's windows were covered with thick curtains for privacy, the sconces along the walls casting dim, bronze-tinged light. I slid into a tall-backed chair, recognizing Baron Graftonberg, or "Jowly" as I'd secretly dubbed him when we'd first met, because of his ruddy jowls that wobbled when he spoke. General Griffin sat to my right, a serious, sandy-haired man with graying temples. His posture and aura shouted *military*, no matter what world you came from. Several other new and familiar faces were seated around the table. They all held something in common—a grim expression. None met my gaze. Alana stiffly perched next to my father.

"I'm afraid I have some bad news," the king said.

My stomach tightened, thoughts spinning in a circle of dread.

"Lucas has been captured."

CHAPTER 2
LUCAS

It's been forty-seven days since they threw me in the pit. Five since food and water were delivered. The marks I'd scratched on the stone wall served as a constant reminder. Rationing became second nature—this stretch without sustenance longer than any yet. Only a withered apple and a few swallows of liquid remained.

Whenever the Embers left, I wondered if they would ever return, though why keep me alive all this while if they weren't going to use me for something? For some reason, my mind kept returning to the brief time in history class back at university in England. The topic had been World War II and a single phrase imprinted in my brain. *Prisoner of War.* We don't use that term here, but we should. Funny how through the portal there are rules for prisoners, even if they are sometimes broken. Pretty sure the Embers wouldn't care about treaties and rulebooks.

I let myself dream of a simple life in Britain. Of higher learning, parties, a shelf full of cereal, and cute girls living across the hall. But there was only one beauty that captured me. *Cate.* In a roundabout way, she was to blame for my predicament. She'd fallen for my rival. I couldn't compete with the brooding prince. Their doe-eyes for one another sent me on this foolhardy journey to sway the northern clan of dragons to support our cause against the Embers.

A suicide mission.

I'd been reckless and cocksure, eager to rid Cate from my head, yet at the same time needing to do something—anything for her. Did I really think to win her back by bringing home a flock of dragons to Caelum? Not consciously, but forty-seven days in a hole brought on some painful self-reflection. I'd made so many mistakes, the first believing there had been an ounce of chance for success—for either Cate or the mission to turn the dragons into allies. My thoughts turned to that fateful day I departed from Caelum.

Fifty-eight days ago

I tightened the straps on the specially designed saddle for Molly, her gray-green belly flinching. She hated the contraption. Long-distance travel required extra storage for items to make camp, which the leather saddle provided. I'd volunteered for this task to find the main dragon lair in the north and change their opinion of our enemy. Although the dragons didn't always play a major part in the war between the kingdoms and Embers, whenever they showed, the odds drastically flipped against us. Humans were no match for such creatures. Molly, though young and small for her species, was still the length of a whale and stood nearly forty hands. Her fire could blast over ten meters.

I'd found her years ago in the woods as a fledgling, starving with an injured wing. I'd given her my meager lunch and departed, suspecting her parents would return at any moment. Something about her soulful golden eyes sent me back the next morning with meat from the kitchens. She hadn't moved. Still not convinced that her mother wouldn't come for her, I made her a bed of leaves and left the food.

Every day I'd revisit, spending more and more time, finally gathering the nerve to stroke the orange patch below her chin and examine her injury. Her wings, surprisingly strong with a leathery surface, were a marvel of physics capable of carrying a dragon into flight due to the wings' sheer size. The bones were hollow and, unfortunately, broke easily. She allowed me to set the fracture and splint it, though fire had shot out of her nose, scorching the surrounding vegetation and nearly roasting me in the process.

She gained strength, and after a time, followed me back to the castle. My father was King Aldridge's favorite knight, and I suppose the other men indulged me because of it, welcoming her into the stables. We ended up building Molly her own structure because the horses proved jittery with her in the barn. I'd thought about giving her a more regal dragon name, but her sad eyes reminded me of my beloved childhood hound. Molly and I have been tight ever since.

The saddlebags bulged with food, water, and camp supplies. Bittersweet feelings colored my departure. Cate lay in the infirmary recovering, and I ached to be with her. But if I stayed, I would only be in the way. *A third wheel.* The expression I'd heard in England never sounded so fitting. After all, Cate had stopped an entire battle to save her prince.

Once successfully leading the Embers' dragons away, I had circled back on Molly. From the air, I'd witnessed her anguish at seeing Daniel and her father covered in flames. The deluge of rain she'd conjured nearly unseated me. The prophecy had come to fruition. Cate was our savior.

Though she'd never be mine.

"You ready, Molly?"

I sensed her reluctance, her talons scraping into the dirt.

"I know. We usually try to avoid the others, but this time we have to convince them. They can't keep popping up and burning down swaths of the city."

She trembled.

"They're not going to burn *you* down. You're one of them. It'll be fine."

Fine. I kept telling myself. I'd completed dozens of missions for the king. Was always away more than home, yet somehow this felt different. For one, I had no idea where the dragon lair was located, and two, I hadn't any clue how to persuade them to fight for our side. Communication between Molly and I was easy—instinctual. I sensed her feelings, and she usually understood the gist of what I told her. Truthfully,

I talked more than she likely grasped, but she seemed to enjoy my company, and right now, I needed a friend. Even if it came in the form of an adolescent dragon.

But other dragons? I hoped between the two of us we could get the message across. Molly, the real hero at The Great Battle, convinced the creatures that fighting was too risky and led them away. I remember sensing the flashes of relief as they left, which made me believe they didn't truly want to fight, especially if they might incur injury.

My foot found Molly's stirrup, and I mounted, the quick movement counter to my reluctance. I'd said goodbye to Cate, studied the maps, and packed my gear. King Aldridge had made it clear that failing was not an option in his usual uncompromising demeanor. Not exactly the pep talk I'd hoped for, but the king wasn't known for his inspirational thoughts. I shouldn't have expected anything more.

Nothing left to do but leave. Alone. Not even a stable hand to see me off. I'd jokingly made Cate promise to throw a parade in my honor when I returned, but now I'd settle for a couple of salutes and a "good luck."

I nudged Molly with my heels. "It's time. Let's go."

Her wings whooshed into motion, and we lifted. The cool morning air rushed across my cheeks as we headed north. I snuck one last look at the blue glass castle sparkling in the sun. She was in there somewhere. It took discipline not to turn back.

"I'll see you soon, Cate." My words swept away in the wind. No one was listening anyway.

CHAPTER 3
CATE

At my father's words, my pulse ratcheted. *Lucas is captured.* When my breaths bottomed out, I turned my focus on avoiding the tailspin into a full-fledged panic attack. *Calm down, Cate; think.* Something else was happening here. As much as Lucas was like a son to King Aldridge, and a best friend to me, his kidnapping wouldn't bring this many advisors together.

Father steepled his fingers. "I've brought all of you here to inform you that I'm going after Lucas *personally*."

"Are you mad? Why would you do that?" Jowly exploded, his cheeks seesawing with each word.

"Because they've asked me to join a peace treaty. If I arrive in person, they'll let Lucas go and we'll return home together. If we resume the war or I don't show, they will kill him." Father gazed at each member of the group, his expression neutral.

"Surely it's a trap," General Griffin spoke up, his inflection more statement than question. "They've never been interested in peace before." He ran a hand through his cropped salt-and-pepper hair. "We all like Lucas, but it's not an even trade—a boy for the king."

"It might be a trick. But we're going in prepared. That's why you're here." King Aldridge leaned forward, placing his forearms on the polished wood table. "We need to plan our own surprise. If they don't want an agreement, then we spring an ambush."

"How about Princess Catherine?" Jowly asked. "Hide her somewhere close and she can drown them."

"Absolutely not," the king's firm tone belied no argument. "You're willing to put my daughter, my only heir, in danger? If something happens to me, she must remain safe."

Baron Graftonberg's already red face shaded purple. Apparently, he wasn't aware I hadn't been conjuring any storms lately. I wondered how many at this table knew my failings.

"She's not ready," interjected Alana.

Great. Now everyone would know of my inadequacies. But to my surprise, she didn't share the mortifying details.

"Well, when will she be?" The baron slammed a fist on the solid wood. "It's time we eradicated these demons for good. Kick them when they're down instead of meeting for a tea party."

Daniel's palm went to my knee, squeezing lightly. I swallowed through the tightening in my throat and didn't meet Jowly's thunderous gaze.

The general spoke up, "The Great Battle was a victory, but we can't discount the number of men we lost. Even if the princess was ready, we *aren't*. It'll take careful planning and organization to win the war. A peace treaty will be in both our interests."

Heads nodded around the room. Baron Graftonberg scowled, seething in silence. The relief of knowing I still had more time to train loosened my muscles, which had coiled into tight knots along my shoulders at the thought of going into battle again so soon. One day, if we were ever to rid ourselves of the Embers, I'd be key in the strategy. Fortunately, we've learned that fire isn't an effective weapon in a downpour. *Unfortunately,* nobody else in the kingdoms of Terra and Caelum possessed this power. Although these days I couldn't even dampen a sponge.

Daniel's warm fingers lightly traced my kneecap as he spoke, "How much time do we have? Terran soldiers would be useful in an ambush if the Embers aren't cooperative. I'd like to speak with my father."

King Aldridge's blond beard twitched at the set of his jaw.

Terrans had notoriously been our enemy until forced into allying with us to fight the Embers. "Actually, I hoped you'd say that." Even though my father agreed, his voice rang with resignation. "As much as we dislike relying on King Dryden, we could use the Terran abilities. The treaty is in two weeks, so the timing will be tight."

I tended to agree with my father's reluctance. Terra's king could never be trusted, and would no doubt manipulate any opportunity.

"I'll go at first light tomorrow. That will give me time to speak to my father and gather soldiers. I presume we'll want those specializing in camouflage?" Daniel asked.

Although the Terrans were known for their ability to channel energy from the earth, it manifested in many forms, each person with different strengths. Some were renowned for their power to grow plants, often useful for hiding in the forest or constructing traps among greenery.

My father nodded once in assent. "We leave in seven days, so be sure you're back in time."

"One more thing," Daniel added. "I'm going with you."

"No," I blurted without thinking.

"What's that, Catherine?" Alana asked, her silver-gray eyebrows raised in warning.

With Lucas captured, and Father leading this mission, if Daniel went too, then everyone I most cared about would be in danger. "It's too risky. He should stay." My eyes focused on the king's. I didn't dare look at Daniel. "He's too important to our relationship with Terra. We can't lose him."

"That's all I'm worth around here?" Daniel's voice turned brittle. He crossed his arms, removing the hand from my knee.

The desire to protect him at all costs overpowered logic. "It's your worth that makes me want to keep you safe." He would hate me interfering—treating him like a child. Guilt warred with fear for his safety. An apology would have to come later. "Father? What's your decision?" Placing it in King Aldridge's hands should work in my favor. After all, he wasn't exactly Daniel's biggest fan.

"You've proven handy to have around on occasion." My father's lips turned up in the barest of smiles, referring to Daniel saving his life by shielding him from an Ember's blaze. Daniel still bore the scars snaking up the right side of his body. "I'm sorry, Catherine, but if the prince wishes to come, I won't stop him. Anyone disagree?"

I searched the faces at the table, but their eyes averted from mine. "Fine," I gritted out. "But you better bring him back safe."

"We'll be okay," Daniel said, then lowered his voice for only me to hear, "I'd think you'd want my help to save your prized Lucas."

"What does *that* mean?" I hissed.

"Eh-hmm." Alana cleared her throat. "You two can take it elsewhere or assist in the planning of this mission. Stop wasting our time."

Fantastic. Scolded for having a spat with my boyfriend in front of the most influential people in Caelum. My face flashed heat, both from embarrassment and simmering frustration at Daniel for volunteering. Not to mention insinuating something untoward in my relationship with Lucas. At least Alana included him in her chastising—he deserved it more than me.

His jealousy *was* understandable. Once upon a time, Lucas and I did have a *moment* together. A kiss brought on by stress. Unfortunately, I'm pretty sure it meant more to him than me. The air at our last awkward goodbye had lingered with unsaid feelings that I tried to squash in order to not hurt my dear friend. Lucas had known I'd chosen Daniel, and it hadn't been easy for him. I wished I'd said something to make it better. But there had been nothing but goodbye.

And now he'd been kidnapped. My stomach squirmed with more guilt. How much of his decision to leave was due to my inability to bridge the gap in our friendship?

The rest of the meeting sped by—the plan coming together rapidly. I contributed little, as tactics weren't my forte, but once my focus returned to the task, I ferreted pieces of knowledge away like a squirrel storing acorns.

Afterward, Daniel motioned for me to walk out with him. *Good.* Because I wanted to speak to him too. Once we were out of sight, he pulled me through a door and flipped on the lights. We'd entered a storage room. Buckets, brooms, rags, and a shelf stacked with tools and various cleaners lined the space.

"I'm sorry," we both blurted simultaneously.

"That shot about Lucas was low." He bit his lip, regret etched along his brow.

"It was." I paused. "But understandable." I hadn't confessed the kiss, wanting the past to be left alone. Daniel and I *had* been broken up at the time, after all. Our relationship had already been through enough, and I needed him on Lucas's side. Now wasn't the right moment to tell him… perhaps never.

"No—he's a good guy." Daniel grimaced. "I probably need to get used to having him around. Lucas has certainly helped us out of a few scrapes."

"And I'm sorry I railroaded you with my father. It's just…"

He tugged me to his chest. "You're afraid because everyone you love will be in danger." His breath tickled my hair and I melted into him.

"That sums it up." I resolutely stepped away and poked him in the arm. "So, you better come back safe."

"I promise." He placed his hand over his heart. "But first, Terra, to get my father to provide some soldiers. You can lecture when I return." He grinned.

I poked him again. "Count on it, Prince."

He closed the gap between us, his grin morphing into something more suggestive. "Will you send me off with a token to remember you by?" A lock of dark hair fell rakishly over his brow.

"Like one of my ribbons?" I asked, smirking.

I leaned against the wall behind me, the plaster cool along my back in contrast to the heat radiating from him, his chest now inches away.

He loomed over me and bracketed his arms on either side of my head. "Something else," he whispered, hovering before his lips crashed into mine.

He kissed me as if he were making up for all the ones we'd lose when he was away. Like he couldn't bear to leave, despite his flippant tone in the boardroom. I brought my hands up to his jaw, angling for more access, then took a moment to catch my breath before my lips returned to his. We clung to each other, the energy oscillating a frantic rhythm until we slowed, languid, and beautiful, savoring each touch, his fingers trailing down my neck.

"I'll miss you." His thumb brushed feather-light along my collarbone.

I fought the tears springing to life behind my eyes. I wish he hadn't volunteered for this assignment, but his willingness to support my father, to put himself in danger, made me love him even more. The secret of requiring him by my side for my power simmered beneath the surface, making his return all the more crucial. I couldn't let my reliance on him sabotage the mission.

I forced a wobbly smile. "Be safe." I've never wanted those words to be truer.

CHAPTER 4
DANIEL

Raven picked his way among the boulders and loose stones strewn over the path. A half a day's ride from Caelum Castle, and this, the third mudslide to traverse, considerably slowed our pace. I trusted the stallion's footing; we'd been together for five years, our special bond never letting me down, but galloping across this terrain would be too dangerous.

Cate's torrential downpour two months ago during The Great Battle had spread even this far, damaging the trails. The sheets of water she'd produced were no typical rainstorm. I didn't know the number of kilometers the storm covered, but from the looks of things, quite a distance. Hopefully, not all the way to Terra. The main thoroughfares had already been cleared, and I'd heard no reports of impassable roads, so I chose a shortcut through less well-known routes, perfect for a single rider. Soldiers had wanted to accompany me, but I preferred a bit of solitude for the three-day journey. Whenever possible, I avoided an entourage.

The life of royalty meant constantly being surrounded by people—advisors, guards, servants. I'd seen it with my father. The more sycophants attached, the more orders he could bark, boosting both his ego and pathologic need for control. The result produced my deeply introverted personality. Not until escaping into nature did it feel like my lungs fully expanded. Because of the king's ability to sense emotions,

I'd learned at an early age to block them. Some probably thought I was as cold as him—most of the time they'd be right. Years of carefully constructing walls around my feelings had left a hard empty shell.

A felled log blocked the path ahead. "You can jump it, boy." I tightened my knees at Raven's girth, his muscles contracting to sail over the obstruction. We slowed to a trot to conserve his strength. We still had several days' journey to go. "Nice work. We'll rest in a while, okay?"

My thoughts wandered back to my father. Was he a *bad* king? I often pondered this question, as one day I'd fill that crown. His power lust certainly wasn't an admirable attribute. But he'd built a talented army, one that for the most part kept the Terran people safe. He wasn't a complete villain, but King Dryden dealt in the gray zone more frequently than I would prefer.

He loved his family while maintaining a narrow view of acceptable behaviors. When we performed to his exact specifications, he praised us, but that meant striving only for his will, never our own. Being a girl, fewer pressures were coerced on Mya, though it still wore on her. While I'd been away these last few months, the king's unwanted attention had likely turned to her. She'd always been the favorite, much to my annoyance, but I should ensure she'd held up under the strain.

Father had not been pleased I'd chosen to stay in Caelum with Cate, which won't help my request to assist with the peace treaty. Knowing him, he'll turn it down just to spite me for leaving. My absence wouldn't last forever, as duties in Terra couldn't be completely abandoned. After the battle, Cate and I hadn't been ready to separate. We'd wanted—no—*needed* a chance to explore our connection. I'd nearly lost her due to my disastrous secret-keeping and an idiotic need to please my father. Only time would solidify her trust in me again.

It had not been easy letting my guard down for her. Years of shuttering emotions left me ill-equipped for relationships. Learning to share my feelings, trust her, and let her into my complicated head hadn't been a task I'd been able to master overnight. Thankfully she understood my struggles while I marveled at her patience. The irony that Alana persistently badgered Cate about shutting down her emotions while I battled with the contrary hadn't escaped me. Sometimes it seemed as if life worked against us.

Yet, I could never give up on her. Just thinking of Cate embarrassingly made my insides go soft. Her goodness and openness were completely different from the oppressive atmosphere at Terra Castle, and it had attracted me immediately. The way the light caught the gold flecks in her green eyes, her unguarded smile, how she touched my arm as if to reassure me everything would turn out okay, was addictive. The energy humming around her was like we were opposite poles of a magnet—constantly drawn closer and stronger when combined. The sense of relief when those magnets clicked together felt more right than anything in the world.

Raven halted, jerking me aware of my surroundings. A landslide with boulders, massive dirt piles, and several downed trees, their roots spraying toward the sun like giant dying blooms, blocked our way. We traveled on a path cut into the side of a small mountain, and the rubble's height obscured the trail beyond. I could move the whole lot myself, but it would be easier to go around. The boulders would take the most time—long hours I couldn't spare. If Cate were here, I'd probably do it, just to show off my powers. *Ugh—I'm such a prat.* Six days to travel to and from Terra, convince King Dryden of our plan, and assemble a group of soldiers left no space for delays, including ego-boosting endeavors.

Climbing might lead to more rockslides and potential danger. I could only hope this colossal mound was smaller than it first appeared. I slid off Raven and led him by the reins through the sloped underbrush. Manipulating the energy to push the leaves and branches from our path barely registered, now second nature after years of practice. We trekked through the forest in this fashion for twenty minutes, still keeping the landslide in sight. Gradually, the slope became steeper, forcing me to grasp at roots and limbs for support.

Rocks and gravel filled the incline, and soon I shifted to crawling on hands and knees. The arduous process took even more precious time. If we ever reached the trail, we'd have to travel in the dark to reach Terra. The mud and stones forced us south near a cliff, and our progress halted again, the avalanche now completely blocking our path. If alone, I'd repel down the mountain, but leaving Raven wasn't an option.

I scanned the landscape for the best place to cross. We'd need to backtrack to gain more ground uphill. Attempting passage this close to the drop would be too risky. Sweat clung between my shoulder blades despite the cooling autumn air as I started back the way we came.

It was going to be a long night.

Another twenty minutes in the wrong direction led us to a relatively flat area with a few still-standing trees among the rubble. The other side wasn't visible, but at this point, we were left with no other choice. We'd have to tread carefully to not disrupt the unstable shale.

"Come on." A tug on the reins and Raven readily followed. He hadn't sensed danger, which I took as a good sign, as his instincts often beat mine.

Raven's cumbersome body naturally shifted more rocks and dirt than me, his hooves scrambling with every step, stretching my already-taut nerves. We progressed slowly while I constantly checked and rechecked the solidity of the earth, sometimes using energy to counterbalance and strengthen it. Finally, after skirting an enormous tree root, safety came into view. Another fifty yards and we'd be home free.

The trail would eventually fork, one way leading to the main road, the other continuing on the shortcut. I still had several hours of daylight to decide which path to take. With my thoughts on home, my focus drifted, just for a moment.

The debris shifted beneath Raven, then me. I tried to shore up the instability, then everything happened at once. Raven faltered, the ground rushed out from under my feet, and a rumble sounded from above. I shielded us with energy to deflect blows from plummeting stones and branches. The powerful avalanche carried us downhill, half-buried in a tumbling, terrifying journey, my body whipped about like a rag doll.

My heart hammered against my ribs, and I forced myself to relax and concentrate. The earth would work with me, but in my panic, our connection had severed. How many times had I practiced keeping focus on the energy in training? How was it failing me now?

I searched for something to grasp, but only sky shone ahead. Which could only mean one thing: a sheer drop. I pictured the earth rising, cracking, and piling in great heaps. Rich, dark soil beneath the surface shifted and mounded, but it wasn't enough. My body careened over the barriers, my flank jamming against the created ridges, sending me curling into a protective ball.

The mountain roared around us, the sound almost as horrifying as the descent. I gasped for air, the breath knocked from my lungs while I desperately emitted my feeble shield, now nearly useless against the onslaught, the pain and disorientation too much for me to navigate any sort of power. The cliff edge loomed—my last thought before everything went black.

CHAPTER 5
LUCAS

Footsteps sounded above. Maybe they'd finally decided I wasn't worth the trouble and had come to kill me. Not that throwing me in a pit and occasionally sending down food and water would qualify as *trouble*. I'd been as docile as a house cat. What else could I do? Climbing out of this hole was impossible, which left me with few options. Although shouting insults held the potential to be mildly entertaining.

Perhaps I'd change tactics.

"Hey, flame-face!" I yelled. "Did you hear about the fire at the cobbler's?"

No answer.

"No? Many soles were lost."

Was that a grunt? Well, not my best work. Not sure I would respond to that one either. "I'm not saying I dislike you or anything, but if you were on fire, I'd pull out the marshmallows."

Still nothing. And a worse joke than the last. Even I hadn't known what a marshmallow was until Cate explained it to me a few months ago. *Cate*. Why'd everything come back to her? I let my mind drift to leaving Caelum Castle and Cate behind.

Fifty-seven days ago

Molly and I headed northeast, the warm early summer air pleasant high above the trees and farmlands. Solemn in her task, she flew with purpose. After a while, she loosened, enjoying the weather, the anticipation of a new journey, and the wind buffeting her wings. She playfully swooped and banked, which used to make my stomach sink, now exhilarating and free. Funny how an animal will turn your mood around when no human can.

I laughed and whooped. "Faster, Molly!"

She obliged with a barrel roll and dive that sent us plummeting.

This time my insides did drop. My knees shook from squeezing to maintain their hold on her slippery scales.

"Okay. Slow down!"

She didn't listen. It was like she was playing chicken with the ground, and I knew which one would win if she failed to stop. "Mollyyyyy!" I plunged my cheek against her neck, the wind slicing across my already chapped face.

At the last moment, she straightened out, her belly rustling the golden, tall grass in the field that stretched before us. She lifted her wings higher to catch air and slowed to a stop, her sides heaving from exertion.

"Now you've gone and tired yourself out, huh? Trying to unseat me. What kind of a best friend is that?"

I could almost hear her smirk.

"You're right. I suppose we are entitled to a bit of fun." I slipped off the saddle onto the spongy ground. My legs wobbled, and I steadied myself on her firm side before giving in and collapsing into the soft meadow.

I can't even handle a friendly dragon. I prayed our encounter with the others would be quick, diplomatic, and most importantly, on land. I pictured tea, finger sandwiches, and my grandmother's china. What a sight that would make.

"Molls, can you hold your pinky out while drinking tea?"

She snorted a puff of smoke. I doubted she understood, despite her annoyed reaction to my question.

"All right. Back to business. Let's have lunch, then be on our way. We'll stop at Quorum tonight." It was the last border town before Ember territory. Molly would have to hide outside the city to avoid attention. No one trusts a dragon these days.

After some dried fruit and nuts—man, I missed that cereal back in England—we continued our flight at a more sedate pace. We'd still make it to Quorum on schedule. I could squeeze in a pint, a warm meat pie, and sleep in a bed for the last time in a while.

The village came into view just past the treetops. "Pull up here." Unlike most Caelum cities, a tall stone barrier circled its perimeter. Quorum's proximity to the enemy forced them to utilize any extra defense possible. Guards paced the top of the wall, and I maneuvered Molly into the forest to hide. I'd have about a kilometer walk into town, but keeping her safe was well worth the effort.

"I'll be back in the morning. Meet you here?" I placed my hand on her neck to better communicate. She tilted her head to slide my fingers into her favorite scratching place, behind her jaw where leathery skin met gray-green scales. I rubbed her for a few minutes, then turned toward the road past the trees I'd spotted from the air, which led to the gate.

I had visited Quorum several years ago, and at that time it had been less heavily guarded. The Embers were relentless in their attempts to take over our lands. The town would be a feather in their cap, giving them a new settlement without all the work required for construction.

I trekked down the road, the heavy iron gate closed ahead. Sentries flanked the entry inside, evident through the thick bars. I approached warily, making sure to keep my hands visible.

"Evening, gentlemen."

The two guards regarded me without comment, their expressions blank. After a few moments of silence, the shorter man with an unfortunate, absolutely enormous nose spoke, "State your business."

"I'd love a warm meal and a soft bed for the night." I flashed them a friendly smile, which usually worked with women, but had spottier reactions from the male gender. Big Nose glowered. You'd think they'd be happy to have someone spend money in their town. I'd rather lay low, but flashing my credentials with the king's seal might become necessary. Although many liked King Aldridge, as with every leader, there were always those who opposed him. The farther from central Caelum, the less likely subjects extolled the king. Those who observed him in person—the man, not the crown—grew to understand his deep love for our kingdom and were quick to offer support.

The taller guard's expression softened. "What are you doing way out here? Not many visitors to these parts."

Good question. I hadn't expected an inquisition.

"You got papers?" the first sentry barked. "No one gets in without papers."

"Why? You been having trouble?"

"None of your business," he sneered. He moved closer, the sheen of sweat flocking his forehead coming into focus. His sour breath goaded me to step back, but I held my ground. "Papers?" His meaty hand jutted through the bars.

I wasn't sure what he referred to; presumably, the townspeople had some sort of identification, or letters for those doing business here. I hadn't heard of requiring documents for travel within our borders. Apparently, I wouldn't be flying under the radar. I dug out my credentials from the king, which proclaimed my knight status and commanded assistance at my discretion from any Caelum citizen. *That* oughta go over well. I handed it to the tall guard, ignoring the outstretched hand of his grumpy partner.

"He's clear." The sentry nodded and moved to pass the decree back.

But Big Nose was too quick. He snatched and scanned the document, his beady eyes narrowing. "The king's man, are ya? Well, don't expect to recruit any of us. We've enough problems on our hands, with little help from the lot o' you."

I interrupted before he could continue, "I don't want anything from anyone. Just plan on spending a bit of coin and filling my belly."

The friendlier guard moved to open the gate. With obvious reluctance, the other man handed me my papers and stepped aside, making me wonder if I should have spent the night with Molly in the woods. I hoped to gain some intel. Someone here might know the location of the dragon lair or which areas overflowed with Embers. It was worth the risk. The townspeople couldn't all be as bad as this guy.

I slipped through the opening without a backward glance and onto a cobbled street. Stone buildings lined the road with brightly colored painted wooden signs hanging from their awnings. I passed a feedstore, ice cream shop (dessert—yes!), several clothing establishments, and finally came upon a pub.

My first impression of the Lucky Horseshoe met my expectations as a typical outer-rim establishment: food—likely greasy, a pint—probably bitter, patrons minding their own business—more like pretending to, and dark décor, complete with sticky wood floors. I refrained from the temptation to slide unnoticed into a rear booth, given my mission to gain information. A central table sat empty, and I pulled out a chair with a scrape and settled in. Eyes landed in my direction then the buzz of conversation resumed.

A middle-aged man with curly hair smashed beneath a wool cap and wearing a white apron approached. "What can I get ya?"

"What's good?" I asked. Typically, the pub staff knew what to order for an out-of-towner like me.

"I've got meat pasties, bangers 'n mash, shepherd's pie, all the usual." He plucked a pen and pad from his pocket.

"What kind of meat?" Once I'd had an unfortunate drundle pastie. Wouldn't make that mistake twice.

The server rolled his eyes. "It's wumbeast."

Glad I asked. Not my thing—too gamey. "I'll have the bangers, thanks."

He nodded and disappeared into the back. The front door opened with a thud, the setting sun streaming into the dark pub momentarily blinding. The outline of a stocky man shadowed the entrance. Once the door slammed shut, his bulbous nose showed itself in the dim light—

the guard from the gate. I fought the urge to hunch over the table and shield my face. This is *not* what I needed. He sat at a nearby booth and leaned in to speak to its occupants. Hushed whispering passed along the room. Occasional muffled words, such as "Aldridge" and "swine" carried through the space.

Fantastic. Looked like any hopes of friendly intel gathering would be impossible. The guard turned to stare at me, a challenge gleaming in his eyes. I wanted to smack the smirk off his face, but starting a bar fight wouldn't do me any favors. The real question was why so many opposed the king?

The server returned with my drink. The glass slammed hard on the table, beer sloshing everywhere. "Food'll be awhile. Delay in the kitchen," he grunted, then stomped off.

"Wait. Sir?"

He turned slowly, his glare making me want to sink deeper into my seat. The guy outweighed me by at least ten stone.

"Could I talk to you for a moment?" My voice cracked to my annoyance.

"You gotta problem?" He hooked his pen into the front of his apron pocket, leaving his hands free.

"No—no problem here. Just hoping to chat." I attempted a grin, although suspected it was more a grimace.

"Didn't I just say we were behind?" With that, he stalked away.

"I'll talk to you, buddy," someone called from across the room. "Love to give you a piece of my mind."

Well, that was one way of finding out what was bothering them. Although, I hoped to escape this town unscathed. Letting them air their grievances could be risky.

"You're the king's man?" he shouted. I could barely make out who was talking through the hazy low light, his outline even larger than the server. They grow 'em big in the country apparently—not a good sign for me.

"I am. Would you like me to pass on a message?"

What he said next would've sent my mother straight over with a bar of soap and a switch, no matter the man's age and size. But seeing as my mum wasn't here, I chose to skip past those parts and concentrated on the sentiment. "Well, I see that you're angry, gentlemen. I have the king's ear. Perhaps we can put our heads together and do something about whatever's bothering you."

"That's just it. You should already know," someone said. "But since you've abandoned us, it might be new to you. We have to fend for ourselves these days."

"You need more protection," I said, staring through the shadows in the direction of voices.

"Oh, we've asked. We've *begged*," another replied. "But there's only been denials in return."

We pulled every soldier possible to protect the capital and for the battle deemed the last stand. Many didn't make it. Our resources were thin, and we hadn't allocated men back to places such as Quorum that needed our backing. The number of Embers was the real problem. They never seemed to run out of fighters, and there weren't enough Caelumites to go around.

"What sort of trouble you been having?" I asked.

"Not your business," Big Nose barked. "Come on. This guy isn't going to help." He stood and left, banging the door behind him.

In a span of a few minutes, the pub emptied, leaving me alone with my half-spilled pint. Off my game, I usually showed more finesse. So much for gaining information. Maybe someone in the ice cream parlor would be willing to talk.

The server arrived to an empty taproom, his expression turning thunderous. "You've driven away all my customers! Get. Out." His already ruddy cheeks flashed crimson.

I held up my hands. "Now wait a minute. I'm the only paying customer here, *and* I'm a good tipper. What's the harm in giving me my meal?" My stomach rumbled, echoing the sentiment as I set a stack of coins clinking onto the table.

He tromped into the kitchen without a word. As I debated if I should settle for dessert for dinner or wait it out, a girl stepped from the back with a steaming plate of food. Around sixteen, her fair hair, pink cheeks, and snub nose bore a resemblance to the waiter.

"Sorry about my da." She set the meal on the table with a shy smile.

"Sorry about clearing out your restaurant," I quipped.

She shrugged. "It's nice to have a quiet night for a change."

"Can I tell you something?" I cocked my head.

"Um—I guess so?" She hesitated, glancing back at the kitchen.

I lowered my voice, "I'm on a mission. A secret one." I gestured to a chair. "I could use a little help."

Her lips parted and one slim hand went to her chest. "O—kay..." She dragged out the word and sat perched at the edge of her seat.

"I'm hunting for something." I leaned in closer and peered behind both shoulders even though we'd established the room had emptied. Laying it on too thick? Perhaps.

Before I could ease up on the intrigue, she bent forward, eyes widening. "For what?" she whispered.

Would this girl know anything? The likelihood seemed low, but she was the only one talking. "Dragons." I paused for effect.

Rather than impressed, her brow creased in confusion. "Why would you do that?"

"To convince them to fight for us."

She let out a guffaw, uncharacteristically loud for her small body. "Hilarious. If you want my help, tell the truth."

Apparently, first impressions of this meek girl weren't entirely correct. She seemed to be warming up to me, which might work to my advantage, or she's more stubborn than appearances. I raised a brow. "My heroics in The Great Battle haven't reached Quorum yet?"

One side of her lips curved in a skeptical smile. "Heroics? Don't think so. What's your name?"

"Sir Lucas Bradbury, at your service. I actually *own* a dragon."

She huffed a laugh. "As much as I hate to admit it, I *have* heard of you. Everyone knows about the knight who rides the only dragon in the realm allied to our side. That's really you?"

"Yup. Molly's her name."

"Molly? Couldn't it be something more dignified, like Ophelia or Gretna the Great?"

"Gretna? No." I leaned back in my chair and crossed my arms.

She narrowed her eyes and tilted her head in a *sure about that?* gesture. "Fine. So, Molly loves her name so much you think you can convince the other dragons to work for us? Maybe we call them Rufus and Penelope."

This girl's a regular comedian. *Rufus.* "Since we're on the subject, what's yours?"

"Grace. Also not good for a dragon."

"Nice to meet you, Grace." She was more interesting than anyone else around here, but we needed to get down to business. I tapped the table with my palm. "*Any-hoo,* I'm looking for the lair. Any idea where it's located?"

"Why would *I* know?"

"Because you live a lot farther north than I do. Border towns sometimes come by information not available in the capital. And because one overhears things working in a tavern." I raised my brows.

"They might be in the Purple Mountains, but that's just rumor." She waved a dismissive hand.

The Purple Mountains loomed hundreds of miles northwest. I'd have to cross two other ranges and skirt the Embers' main settlement. Enemy encampments infested the landscape between here and there.

"Sounds like a suicide mission to me," she said.

Grace wasn't wrong. "Maybe. So, what's going on around here? Why does everyone hate King Aldridge?"

"Your guys rounded up a third of our men to serve not too long ago. Didn't give them a choice. We heard our entire company was slaughtered." Her tone slumped at the end, gaze shifting to the scarred table.

My devil-may-care attitude dispersed like the fizz in stale beer. "I'm sorry. There were too many losses in the last battle."

"And the thing is," she continued. "Quorum has a big problem. We needed them."

"Problem?" What else brewed in this small town? Intuition told me their unfriendliness wasn't only about their issues with King Aldridge.

"I shouldn't say."

I waited for her to continue. Silence often produced better results.

Her face crumpled. "If we ever *do* get any back, and people find out, they'll be ruined."

"Them?"

"You have to promise not to tell." She leaned in, her eyes wide.

"I won't," I assured her. I *might*. Depends on what she divulges.

"The Embers are taking them. One by one, the Embers sneak in and they just… disappear."

"Who?"

"Girls," she whispered. "My age. Like me. And I can't shake this feeling that I'm next."

CHAPTER 6
DANIEL

A hawk's caw rented through the stillness. I pictured it slicing through a breezy, bright sky, searching for its prey over a meadow of swaying grass. But instead of the air wafting softly, it felt oppressive and heavy. My eyes creaked open to meet darkness. The kind where the clouds are so thick every star and moonbeam were shadowed. I shifted my head and pain lanced through it, throbbing reverberations echoing through my skull. It jumbled my thoughts; snatches of memory hovered and floated like wisps of smoke.

The effort of breathing felt as if five Terran soldiers sat eating a banquet on my chest. My limbs were cemented, yet my mind still struggled to grasp what should have been easy to process.

The avalanche.

I was buried alive.

Panic seized my muscles, spooling them tight. Labored breaths slammed against ribs, my heart rate accelerating. Small spaces inevitably sent me reeling—the sensation of being trapped, the walls sliding ever closer. It's why I hated the dorms back in England. But this was no tiny room—crushing debris piled onto my torso and limbs. A nightmare surfacing into reality. My mind focused in and out of its surroundings, grasping at anything to calm myself. I was Terran after all. My power stemmed from the earth. The rational part of me hadn't yet caught up with the fear.

What about Raven? I listened, but there was only silence, further dampened by the packed soil around my ears. Using the surrounding energy to move the rubble would be possible if only my head would stop pounding. Though would it trigger more landslides? I could be teetering on the cliff's rim for all I knew, and any motion might topple me or Raven over the edge.

The dirt shifted near my foot with a breathy snort accompanying the movement. *Raven.* The relief knowing he lived felt like half the mountain had already lifted from my chest. We had been together for years, and I couldn't imagine life without him. Not to mention the guilt for putting him in this situation.

The news bolstered my energy, and with slow, tedious maneuvers, I began the process of shifting the surrounding earth. After focusing, I sensed my depth, with most of my body a mere one to two feet below the surface, although my legs sunk deeper. As I manipulated, light peeked through debris and finally, my head pushed through. The sun sat low on the horizon, a red-half globe spraying orange and pink across the cotton-like clouds. *The day is lost.* I must have been out for more than a few hours. Reaching King Aldridge with Terran soldiers in time would be a miracle if I ever made it out of here.

Several meters from my position, the cliff's edge loomed, though its exact location was difficult to gauge with a large boulder blocking my view. The enormous rock likely prevented me from tumbling over the bluff.

Raven knelt several feet away, one of his hind legs buried. He whinnied softly.

"It's okay, boy. We'll get out of here."

With renewed effort, I shifted the soil from around my middle, the energy pulsing. The Terran in me absorbed the earth's power, making it in some ways restorative once I'd been able to rid the panic clinging like spiders spinning a web. Not that I'd want to repeat the incident any time soon. The second my legs were freed enough to attempt movement, I bent each knee in succession. Sore, but workable.

My ankle gave out as I stood, pain shooting up my calf. I collapsed again, scooting to Raven, who watched with hollow eyes, foot still lodged. It took a few minutes harnessing both manual labor and the earth's energy until his limb came free. Crawling rather than walking through the wreckage was easier, with Raven hobbling behind across the avalanche's wake.

"We're quite a pair, aren't we?" Both of us lame, battered, and bruised. I focused on one task at a time, trying to avoid thinking about how this mission to Terra now seemed impossible, especially in the waning light.

When we reached solid ground, I gingerly stood, testing my ankle. Not fractured, but a bad sprain. A gnarled branch nearby would have to serve as a walking stick. Raven, however, fared worse. He could barely put any weight on his hind foot and his proud head hung low. My hands smoothed over his dusty coat, ensuring nothing had punctured it. I sensed his relief at my touch, though pain radiated from him.

"Looks like you're going to have to sit this one out." I hated leaving him, but I didn't have a choice. I'd send someone for him with a cart.

"You have to stay here." I brushed his nose, and he put his forehead to mine. Sadness emanated, our connection together so strong his emotions covered me in thick melancholy. With effort, I limped away, casting a single glance back. He'd laid down in the scrubby weeds where I left him. My gut wrenched to see him helpless and alone until his rescue, which couldn't happen until I made it out myself.

North, up the hill, and through uninhabited land would lead me to civilization. I tried to picture the maps I'd studied, now buried somewhere under the avalanche, but was unsure how far I had traveled. The trail lay a few hundred feet away, giving me some sense of direction. However, I was pretty sure it went east for a long while before it reached a town. I would have to bypass it and continue north, where farming communities were closer to the main road—the one I should have taken instead of this cursed shortcut.

After hours of stumbling through the forest in the dark, my ankle swollen to the size of a melon, I came upon a fenced clearing. Waxy moonlight crept from a cloud, dimly illuminating pearly gray shadows and ghostly shapes.

One of which moved.

I crouched behind bushes and inched forward to better visualize the figure. It was only a horse grazing in the meadow. The dark silhouette of a barn loomed in the distance.

A house must be nearby. I'd lost everything in the landslide—my pack, the king's seal, and anything that might identify me as the prince. My finger still bore the signet ring, although doubtful a Caelum farmer would even recognize it with equal chance he'd run me off his land *because* I was the prince. The alliance only went so far. Deep-rooted mistrust between the two kingdoms remained. I could put my faith in the farmer, or for the good of the people, *steal* the horse.

The fence was an easy vault. The landing, however, shot pain through my ankle, nearly collapsing it. I regained my composure and moved ahead. Crickets chirped in the distance, my hobbled footsteps soft on the spongy meadow. The horse stood unbothered by a stranger approaching. I sidled up beside it, finding no bridle as a lead. The muzzle appeared gray in the moonlight. Upon further inspection, the horse was female, with a shaggy coat and swayed back. Well-fed, her belly swelled disproportionate to her knobby legs. The old mare probably hadn't startled because she didn't hear my advance. *Great.* I'm apparently so desperate—or stupid—I'm stealing the most ancient mare in all of Caelum.

The barn stood several hundred yards away, perhaps housing a more agile mount inside. If nothing else, there would likely be a saddle and reins.

"Come on, girl," I whispered and patted her rump.

She didn't budge. A bit more of a slap, followed by a push, gave similar results.

I huffed in exasperation and headed toward the barn without her, remembering at the last moment to creep silently the final few steps to the doors. From this vantage, a two-story farmhouse came into view, separated from the stable by a small meadow and road. No light emitted from the windows. *Safe for now.*

In desperate need of oil, the door creaked and squealed, echoing in the night air. I winced and proceeded through the cracked opening. The high windows were worthless in providing moonlight, too small and not well positioned. Even after allowing my eyes to adjust, blackness prevailed. The unnerving stillness pricked the hairs along the nape of my neck. No sounds of rustling hooves or breathy snorts. I felt around the nearby walls for tack or anything useful. After nearly impaling my eye with a pitchfork, I came upon the distinctive, cool metal shape of a lantern under my fingertips. Matches were still in my pocket, fortunately not buried with my pack. Lighting it would be risky, but the household across the way slept.

The lamplight illuminated the space, its rays an unfortunate beacon through the upper windows. Stalls lined the barn, and with a quick inspection, they all sat empty, apart from a gray-bearded goat curled in the corner of one enclosure. I snuck quietly to not wake the beast, but while observing the creature, instead of watching where I stepped, my foot toppled over a feed bucket. The metal clanged and skittered along the plank floor. With a bleat, the goat jumped to its feet and butted the stall with a reverberating thud. Hooves stomped and its cry intensified to a heart-thumping, cover-your-ears screech. I spotted a bridle and reins hanging along one wall, snagged them, then snuffed the lantern.

After slipping through the door, I peeked over my shoulder at the house. One window shone brightly as if a sleeping cat opened a single eye to spy on its prey.

I surged forward, using the earth's energy to propel me toward my decrepit escape animal, ignoring the pain lancing through my leg.

"Here we go, Bertha," I murmured softly. She just *seemed* like a Bertha. "You've gotta channel your inner colt and run like the wind." The bridle and reins slipped easily over her head, and I hopped onto her back. She'd never jump this fence, and the only gate I'd seen was near the house. My heels dug into her wide girth with a sharp sting to my ankle, and she loped forward. When we finally reached the exit, I dismounted to open the gate. A figure, silhouetted by yellow light streaming from the window, stood on the house's porch.

"Hey!" a man's voice called out. The sound of dogs barking soon followed.

I ignored them, and rushed onto Bertha, praying she would kick it into another gear. Whether she didn't like the noise or just enjoyed the freedom outside the paddock, her pace did speed considerably. Without an injury, I could outrun her, but beggars couldn't be choosers. Or don't look a gift horse in the mouth. There was probably a more appropriate cliché regarding thieves not prospering, but the canines were now at our feet, snipping and barking. A pack of hunting dogs typically weren't vicious, but nevertheless, would track and alert the owner to our location.

An arrow whistled past my shoulder and embedded in a nearby tree with a high-pitched *twang*. The man presumably used it as a warning, not wanting to hurt his horse or dogs. But one never knew. He might be doing old Bertha here a favor.

The gallop of hooves rang out over the yipping. Glancing behind, two men astride able-bodied horses pursued. There must have been another paddock where the livestock that literally hadn't gone out to pasture resided. The cold metal of a sword glinted in the moonlight. My own weapons lay buried on the mountain somewhere. The choices narrowed to just one.

Surrender.

CHAPTER 7
CATE

Sometimes I felt like Rapunzel in my tower room in Caelum Castle. As the highest suite in the palace, it boasted its own elevator, only accessible with a special key. Stunning views of the lands to the west and the ocean could be seen glittering on the far horizon on a clear day, especially if someone used the telescope on the balcony. I longed to visit the sea, dig my toes in the sand, and feel the cool water rush over my ankles. Instead, I found myself trapped in the castle, drowning in war plans, training, and talks of Cate saving the world—if only she could pull it together and figure out all this magic stuff. Okay, I wasn't actually trapped, just figuratively. Spoiled princess much? Perhaps.

The room still reminded me of the battle two months ago, the Ember I'd strangled with a lamp cord, and the soldiers dead in the anteroom. The fields below had started to sprout with new green growth, but the charred swaths hadn't yet vanished completely. A black reminder of the number of deaths that day. The number of people I couldn't save.

I wouldn't travel to the sea. Instead, I'd work to understand this world's power so I could help our soldiers defeat the enemy again. If only the energy came naturally without Daniel's presence. And now he'd traveled to Terra to convince his dad to support the peace treaty. Persuading King Dryden of anything was laughable. Daniel would need some sort of carrot to sway the king. If there wasn't something in it for Dryden, then he'd never come to our aid.

That's what I *should* have told Daniel before he left. But he found it hard to accept his father's true nature. I needed him to figure it out himself without me pouring salt in the wound. Because it was a wound. Daniel wanted so badly for his father to be a better man. The kind of dad he could look up to, and sometimes, he wasn't ready to believe King Dryden was a lost cause.

The old-fashioned silver clock ticked to four in the afternoon. I was supposed to meet Alana at sunset, and still had several hours to wait. I'd scream if I remained in this room a moment longer. Maybe I could catch my father between meetings.

King Aldridge's office door stood open. He frowned at papers while hunkered behind his desk and caught my eye when I hovered in the doorway. A brief smile flickered, and he ushered me in, motioning to close the door.

"So, what's new?" I asked, keeping my voice light while taking a seat in the leather chair across from him.

"Other than planning a trap and making sure we're not ambushed in six days' time?" He glowered and tapped his pencil on the tabletop.

"I know there's a lot at stake." I worried my lip. "Thank you for rescuing Lucas. He'd do anything for you and this kingdom."

The king sighed. "I'm aware. He'd do anything for *you* as well."

Heat crept into my cheeks. "For the good of the country, of course."

He nodded knowingly. "Of course."

No one wanted to talk guy troubles with their father. Especially if he was king. It didn't seem real that next week he'd be gone. Daniel too. The three most important people in my life would be in grave danger.

I still didn't completely understand what motivated the Embers. Their insatiable bloodthirstiness and hatred toward the two kingdoms infused their every action. Did they have enough cunningness to pull off a trap, or even devise the treaty at all? The idea must be driven by self-preservation and a need to regroup. Or I underestimated them, and we were sending my father and Daniel into peril.

"You think the Embers are actually interested in peace?" I asked.

"I'm not sure. We hit their numbers badly in the last battle, but we lost quite a few men too. They may still have the advantage."

"How is that possible? Why are there so many?" Alana had mentioned we'd taken out a third of their number after I'd disabled them with the storm.

"You understand we live longer here, correct?"

I nodded, not sure where he was taking this.

"For both Caelumites and Terrans, longevity comes with a price. Conceiving children is difficult and having more than one unusual. We treasure every child. For some reason, the Embers don't have that difficulty. With each passing year, more of their offspring grow into fighting age. Patience will only serve their cause."

"They're just biding their time." Peace might last for ten to fifteen years, but it wouldn't be long before they overran us.

"Fortunately, they have little discipline. They want better land, and want it as quickly as possible. They've destroyed the forests up north, leading to drought. You witnessed it when you first arrived through the portal."

I remembered the dry, cracked earth we traveled across. Lucas had told me every year less and less rain fell.

"They are a selfish, impulsive people," he continued. "Their lack of conscience and self-control led us to imprison them in the first place, and their eventual banishment. Some are more crafty than others. If they find a shrewd leader to corral the masses, they would be dangerous indeed."

As if they weren't bad enough already. "But how will we ever be rid of them?"

"Nobody can agree on an answer. King Dryden wants every man, woman, and child killed."

My hand flew to my mouth. "That's horrible."

"I'm open to suggestions." He stood and pulled the rope to signal his assistant. "Enough morbid discussion. I've been preparing a present for you. It should be ready soon."

Niles, my father's clerk, stepped into the room. "Sir?"

"Tell Charlie that Catherine and I will arrive shortly, then send up a tea tray."

The man exited with alacrity. We might not be in England, but some of their traditions Caelum still couldn't shake. The king ordering tea made me want to giggle, but since I admittedly adored those tiny triangle sandwiches and scones, I kept a straight face.

"What are you up to?" I asked. "Tell me more about this present."

"All in good time." His mischievous smile wasn't one I'd seen before. *Intriguing.*

The tea arrived, and we chatted about his life at the castle when he was a boy, my childhood, and our favorites on the tray: berry scone with clotted cream, smoked fish and pickled onions, and a delightful buttery biscuit in the shape of a bird. Since my arrival, the king had set aside time for me most days. Sometimes we discussed the kingdom and war strategies, others we tried to fill the eighteen-year gap, forming a tentative father-daughter relationship. Loosening his stiff demeanor didn't come naturally, but occasionally I'd see a glimmer of affection or humor. He felt more comfortable in the role of king than father, and the effort meant everything to me. It wasn't easy for either of us; I missed my adoptive parents back in Oregon and couldn't help comparing parenting styles. A daughter was a new experience for him.

We exited the castle, and he turned toward the barns—clearly, jewelry wouldn't be the surprise, as I'm pretty sure he wouldn't be hiding diamonds in between the hay bales. Just as well, I preferred something more useful. Although his gift of my mother's favorite tiara before the ball in Terra would be hard to top.

We reached the mews with its rough-hewn wood and screened windows, and my breath caught. He'd promised me a bird some time ago, and I thought he'd start with a simple sparrow. The mews only housed birds of prey—I'd hardly dared to hope for one. Blade, my father's falcon, nested here when not perched by his side. The connection the two shared was special.

A man exited the small building with a brown bird, roughly a foot tall, on his arm. A few bands of black striped its wings and long tail feathers. "Your Highness." He nodded in a quick bow of sorts.

"Charlie, this is my daughter, Catherine. And I see you've brought the gift. She's a beauty."

Charlie also gave me a small bow. "I've been training this little girl up for you, Your Majesty. She's a sweet thing but loves to eat. You'll have to watch her, or she'll snip at your fingers. Too eager for a treat."

The bird cocked her head, aiming black eyes in my direction. "Is she really for me?"

The king nodded, and I threw my arms around him, forgetting both the audience and that I'd never hugged him before. He tentatively patted my back in return.

"She's beautiful. Thank you." I took a step back, awkwardness creeping in. "What type of bird is she?"

"A kestrel," Charlie said. "It's in the falcon family. Slightly smaller than King Aldridge's peregrine."

I moved closer. "Does she have a name?"

"I think the princess should name her own companion, don't you?" the falconer replied. I'd been so preoccupied with the bird I hadn't noticed the kind face of the man holding her. Curly, dark hair streaked with gray framed weathered cheeks from years spent outdoors.

I examined the nut-brown creature with her creamy breast and spotted and striped wings. She reminded me of my favorite coffee back home. As a special treat, Mom would take me to the coffeehouse down the street from our shop, and the barista would paint delicate leaves in the foam, almost like feathers. "I'll call her Mocha."

Confusion crossed Charlie's face. They had coffee here in Caelum, but none of the fancy specialties Portlanders loved. "It's after my favorite drink. I'll figure out how to make one, then you can try it."

He smiled. "Whatever you'd like, ma'am."

In America, ma'am was usually reserved for a woman of a certain age. But British monarch rules applied here, and ma'am was perfectly acceptable for an eighteen-year-old princess after first addressing her as Her Royal Highness or Majesty. All of it was still weird, and I often squelched the impulse to tell everyone to just call me Cate.

"Oh, no. What time is it?" Adjusting to the lack of computers and phones where it seemed impossible to forget the clock had led me to being tardy nearly everywhere I went.

"A little after six," Charlie replied.

Late *again*. "I'm supposed to meet Alana. I'd love to start working with Mocha, but I have to go."

Father and I started toward the castle. "You know," he said, "I've heard from Alana that your progress is lagging."

Heat crept up my neck. I wanted so much to make him proud. "It's a slow process."

"I'm hoping your falcon will help establish a stronger connection to the Caelum energy. We've taken for granted the things that ensure children here form a natural bond. Sparrows for little ones, classes in school, parental guidance. You've missed all that."

Life would have been so different if I'd grown up in the castle. I imagined Lucas and me playing with Molly, friends practicing magic together, and actual tutoring for royal duties instead of muddling through. It would make things easier for me now, but I wouldn't change my upbringing. My adoptive parents shaped me into the person I am today, and I cherished their love.

The king and I separated when he entered the castle, and I continued to the east lawns, my pace quickening. Butterflies sprang to life. Alana's stern but fair countenance still elicited nervousness before every lesson. She would not be happy with my tardiness.

"Catherine!" Alana's voice rang out. "You're late. Again."

She stood several yards away, near a towering tree. "I'm sorry. I was with my father." Maybe playing the king card would keep me out of hot water.

Her dark eyes glittered. "I need you to take our training more seriously."

She didn't seem to understand how hard I already tried. "But—"

"King Aldridge wouldn't need to put himself in danger if we could count on you." Her height, shorter than mine, suddenly seemed to tower.

My throat tightened, and I blinked back hot tears. It *was* my fault. *Everything*. If Lucas hadn't left to avoid me, he wouldn't have been captured. The kingdoms hovered in peril, and if I could only master my power, they'd be safe. Our whole survival balanced on my shoulders.

I wiped away my tears with determination. "Let's get to work."

CHAPTER 8
DANIEL

Whether it was the sound of a familiar voice, the dogs nipping at her legs, or the horses at our heels, Bertha chose that moment to halt in her tracks. My balance, already off from peering behind me at the men with weapons, faltered, sending me flying over the old nag's head. A horse hadn't unseated me since grammar school. My pride ached more than the shoulder I'd landed on.

One man dismounted and strode forward while I attempted to scramble to my feet. The glinting sword tipped to my chest, and I fell backward again. "Thief," he barked. His black eyes flashed in the low light of the moon, his stocky frame holding a stance that suggested more than mere familiarity with a dirty fight. I'd hoped for someone closer to Bertha's age living at the farmhouse. "Why'd you go and steal my Hurricane?" he asked.

His what? Oh, he meant Bertha. I stifled a grin. "Sir, if you'd let me up, I can explain everything. I planned on returning her to you."

"Sure, you did." He motioned for me to stand. I attempted to not favor my screaming ankle; a weakness shown just might give them one more reason to make good use of their weapons.

The other man, taller and younger, still wearing a blue-striped nightshirt that fell open at the chest, stepped forward with a lantern, illuminating our faces. "What are you going to do with him?"

The stocky one's eyes narrowed. "I want to see what he has to say." He lowered his sword and turned his attention to Bertha—no, *Hurricane.* "You alright, girl?" He examined the horse with tenderness while the other man eyed me, knife drawn. Finding no harm had come to her, he said, "Get to talking."

"You might find this a bit hard to believe…" I began. Their hardened gazes didn't leave mine. I proceeded to unravel the story, including my identity, the mudslide, and that I had to reach Terra quickly for important business.

"I lost everything in the avalanche. But I do have my signet ring." They continued to watch me skeptically. "I promise. I'm the prince." I raised my hands.

The two men exchanged looks, one of them rolling his eyes. "You believe this guy?"

I slid off my ring and offered it. "Here. Take a look."

"We don't need your ring, Prince," the shorter man said. "We know it's you. We're not some backward Terran farmers. Newspapers arrive here in Caelum. I've seen your likeness more times than I'd like."

Newspapers. My father had banned them in Terra around ten years ago, proclaiming they promoted unrest. Yet, apparently, King Aldridge held no such compunctions. His more progressive stance may have saved my life.

"Great." I sighed in relief. "So, you'll help me."

The guy in the nightshirt raised an eyebrow. "I don't remember saying that." He glanced at his partner. "Why should we help this Terran dictator?"

My father's rule leaned authoritarian, but autocracy seemed a bit harsh. Though I had a sneaking suspicion that Cate would be appalled if she knew King Dryden banned newspapers. She wasn't a fan of my father and some of his other practices. Neither was I, though perhaps I'd had my head in the sand too long. After a while, one eventually became desensitized to what had become normal. I certainly didn't want to reign like him. It was time to start considering the types of changes I'd make. Not that King Dryden was going anywhere soon.

"*I am not* my father," I said. "I'm working with King Aldridge on a special joint mission and need to get to Terra quickly. Can I borrow one of your mounts?"

The Caelumites exchanged yet another look, a silent conversation passing between them. One shook his head while the other shrugged.

The stocky man spoke up, "Well, you can't have Hurricane here. She's special."

That came as a relief. She's a certain kind of special all right, but not the type I'd be looking for if I wanted to arrive at the castle sometime this century. "I wouldn't dream of taking her from you. She seems quite comfortable here." I patted old Hurricane on the rump. Pretty sure she side-eyed me in return.

"Fine. You can have Jester." The taller man motioned to a robust, dappled-gray gelding. His eyes narrowed. "But I want him back. With interest."

The name Jester gave me pause, but he at least appeared healthy, his coat shining in the lantern light, muscles rippling. A huge step up from my prior mode of transportation. We proceeded to the farmhouse where I signed paperwork stating the horse would be returned and outlined the additional compensation. They supplied me with food and water, directions to the main road, and advice on a few unfriendly places to steer clear. Once again, I was on my way to Terra.

Pink and orange painted the eastern sky in broad pastel strokes. Dawn had come all too soon. I could almost forget about my delay under the cover of darkness, but the light reminded me of the gravity of falling behind. Jester showed himself as strong and tireless, and I pushed him as hard as I dared. Although we'd crossed into Terran territory, it would be midday before my arrival. This meant I'd have to convince my father, rally the best soldiers, and depart, all before nightfall. Even then, we would be a day late. Hopefully, the king would be in an agreeable mood. Unfortunately, I couldn't recall the last time anyone characterized him as *agreeable.*

Why had I even attempted this mission? Deep down, I'd wanted to prove my worth to Cate and her father. Present myself and Terra as team players, and returning empty-handed wasn't an option. I worried our tenable relationship both with each other, and the two kingdoms might not withstand more missteps. She'd forgiven me, or at least she said she had, though I still felt the constant need to make up for my errors. Not from signals she had given—merely, my own guilt churning daily.

"Let's go, Jester. There's a bucket of oats and a bed of hay for you when we get there."

The sun shone high over Terra Castle as the gray stones overlaid with meandering green ivy loomed on the horizon. *Home.*

My last days here were tortured, consumed with Cate and my horrible mistakes. Then came the certainty I'd never see Terra again while fighting in The Great Battle. My actions were reckless, putting my life in danger over and over, knowing I wouldn't come back to this place if the kingdoms fell. I hadn't even been sure if I wanted to return when I believed Cate was lost to me. A battle where there had been everything to lose, yet nothing if I didn't have her. If things had gone differently that day… it couldn't be born. It would have been my fault for bringing her through that portal.

"Absolutely not," my father's voice thundered.

It had taken me an hour to gain an audience with him. Apparently, he'd chosen to demonstrate his apathy by ignoring me, presumably related to his annoyance that I'd been in Caelum these months with Cate. After first arranging Raven's rescue and the return of Jester, I barreled past the guards outside his office and ordered several advisors to leave. Their startled gazes reminded me they expected the subservient, orderly prince, not the half-crazed, covered-in-dirt person who charged into the room. A change of clothes might have been prudent, but it would only waste more time.

"Father. Hear me out." I stood, not willing to sit passively across from him, with the expanse of his polished desk widening the chasm between us.

"Why would you want to make peace when now's our chance?" he demanded. "We should be planning an attack. Had I known you'd be snuggling up to Aldridge and plotting this spineless mission, I would have yanked you home two months ago." Father warred to keep his features even, but they betrayed his annoyance, his pale skin mottling along his sharp cheekbones.

I focused on keeping my own temper in check, careful not to forget the king's secret talent of reading emotions. Since I too inherited the trait, I could feel his anger washing over me in hot waves. Mostly, other's moods pinged softly at my brain, like a mildly annoying *rat-a-tat-tat*. But my father's wrath boiled dangerously under the surface, heating my skin. Bubbling deep, I also sensed his fear. He didn't want to lose me. Or lose his power *over* me. A treaty shared with Caelum would strengthen the kingdoms' bonds instead of pitting us against one another, though he was never happier than when at odds with someone else and planning their downfall.

I blew a breath out slowly. "Remember, we've suffered losses just as they have. I'm not sure the people could stomach more war right now." I paced, my careful footsteps muffled against the plush carpet. "Plus, if they double-cross us, we might be able to take out some key members of their regime. But the plan requires Terran powers."

"The answer is still no." He stood. "Get yourself cleaned up. We'll visit over supper. Perhaps you can share some Caelum weaknesses. Your time there better prove more useful than just mooning over the girl."

"Yes, Father." A cold sweat sprung in tiny droplets across my back. I'd failed. His mind was made up, and once set, unmovable.

When I wandered into my room, the bath had already been drawn. My clothes hung in the wardrobe, untouched for the last several months. Everything just as before, as if I'd never left. I sunk into the steaming water, my ankle soothed and a touch less swollen, and scrubbed at the grime.

My choices were few. I could remain here, then send a message to Caelum that King Dryden would not be assisting in the plan. I'd eventually return, tail between my legs, because I couldn't bear to stay away from Cate. But would she feel the same after this debacle?

There was the option of defying my father. Venture back on my own, then travel with King Aldridge to the rendezvous point with the

Embers. Without Terran soldiers, the chance of failure would drastically increase. They might not even attempt the peace treaty lacking King Dryden's help.

The buttons of my jacket felt stiff as I changed for dinner, my fingers clumsy and numb from the shock of failure. Before we ate, I should find Mya and my mother. My sister would kill me if I didn't seek her out before the meal. No doubt someone had tipped her off I was home. Surprisingly, she hadn't barged into my suite while I dressed.

I found them in my mother's favorite sitting room, both reading, my sister's feet curled beneath her on the sunshine-yellow chaise. I'd missed them, and a pang of regret twinged for not writing more often or visiting earlier.

Mya glanced up from her book. "Bout time you showed up." She pretended to go back to her novel, but the turned-up corners of her lips betrayed her.

My mother stood to embrace me, her emotions enveloping me in warmth—happiness, relief, and love. I was never sure what she saw in my father; her pure heartedness always shone in contrast to his blackened one. I could only guess the king had changed over the years.

Soon Mya piled on for a family hug. Mother's tinkling laugh rang out. "So good to have you home."

"Yeah. I suppose we'll take you." Mya pinched my arm before flouncing back to her seat. "So why grace *our* presence? Cate wizen up again and dump you?" She grinned.

Mya liked to tease, but I knew she'd always take my side. She adores Cate, but was quite put out with her when she left a few months ago without letting me explain. Mya had been certain she would have straightened the whole mess out herself if given the opportunity. Her impressive persuasiveness might have saved us both a lot of grief.

"I'm actually here to get Father's support," I said.

Mya wrinkled her nose. "For what?"

I glumly proceeded to explain the circumstances. They both interrupted several times, mincing out the details. Mya peppered me with questions about Lucas's whereabouts, making me wonder if he'd caught her eye while visiting the castle at the last council meeting. I made a note to pursue this if he was ever freed. If Lucas returned her feelings, it would funnel his attention away from Cate. Ashamed to admit it to myself, I still wasn't confident enough to dismiss him as a rival for Cate's heart. Although, I wouldn't want Mya with anyone who'd rather have someone else. *Ugh.* My father was rubbing off on me—meddling with other people's personal lives.

"Daniel, are you even listening?" Mya's voice rang out.

"Um… yes?"

She sighed. "I *said,* how long ago did you speak to Father?"

"Little less than an hour. Why?"

"And he expects you at dinner." Her dark brows raised.

"Yes…"

Her eyes tipped in that sly look I recognized all too well. She straightened, placing her feet on the patterned carpet, then leaned forward. "I doubt anyone around here knows why you've come or the king's response to your request."

"Probably not." I shrugged.

"Sooo…"

I think I knew where she was going with this but wanted her to spell it out. "So?"

"Sneak out. Gather some men. I happen to know Dev is in the barn as we speak."

"Dev's here?" We'd been best friends since leading strings. As the son of the Duke of Earlington, he often had duties elsewhere. Perhaps my luck was beginning to change.

Mya twirled a lock of hair, her lips pursing. "I'll distract Father, come up with some excuse why you aren't at dinner, and give you a head start. He won't even know you're gone until tomorrow. If you only choose a select few to go with you, with a good cover story, he may not notice they're missing."

It wasn't a bad plan if we could keep it a secret. We could leave under the guise of a scouting mission with Dev as the lead officer. It might not get back to the king if I stayed out of sight and let Dev gather the men for me.

I glanced at my mother. She'd been listening quietly and now her expression was unreadable. If she told Father, this plan was over before it started. Even if she kept our secret, would she be able to tamp her nervous emotions during the meal so he wouldn't know anything was amiss?

"Mother?" I asked, realizing I needed her approval. Mya should not have discussed this idea in front of her. Now we'd put her in the middle, something we tried never to do. Mya chewed her lower lip, seeing her mistake.

My mother twisted her skirt between her fingers, the only sign of indecision. "I think you should do it."

CHAPTER 9
LUCAS
FIFTY-SEVEN DAYS AGO

Grace's terror-stricken face struck like a hammer. It somehow convinced me that she actually would be taken next by the Embers. It also tapped into my knight-in-shining-armor tendencies, pushing me to protect her and this town.

I couldn't believe we hadn't heard of young women—really just girls—being captured. And in how many other villages was this happening? Our backward society had led these townspeople to keep it a secret, claiming they would be ruined—no man would want them after being unchaperoned with the enemy. The stupid part was that their fears would likely be substantiated. Men wouldn't claim those girls as wives if they ever returned. They'd go through hell as a prisoner only to come home viewed as pariahs.

My recent time in England had been an eye-opener regarding women's abilities and rights. Cate was correct about our male-dominated tendencies. I'd been more prepared than many here to see women as equals because I grew up in a household where my mother was respected. I also spoke with people who traveled through the portal before it closed eighteen years ago, which helped me understand the differences in our societies. Previous British travelers led the kingdom in softening women's standards, but not enough to change the entire kingdom's views. Closing the portal all that time ago in order to protect Cate set us back.

I had to keep my focus on the mission given to me by the king. As much as I wished to help Grace and the townspeople of Quorum, I could only do it after I completed the job at hand. *If* I completed it.

I wanted to reassure her. But something told me words wouldn't placate her fears.

"How many have they taken?" I asked.

"Fifteen over the last year." She slumped in her chair and crossed her arms.

"Really? What's being done to stop them?" I thought of the burly men in the pub earlier.

"We have guards watching the walls, patrolling. But it isn't enough. The Embers keep getting in. Last month my friend went to bed, but in the morning she wasn't there." Tears pooled in her wide doe-eyes.

"How do you know it's the Embers and these girls aren't running away?"

"We've caught a few in the act. Saved one. But the others…"

She focused on a scar etched in the table, tracing it over and over with her finger. With her attention turned away, I examined her while taking an overdue bite of food. Her hair drifted somewhere between brown and blonde, with wisps escaping a long braid trailing down her back. A faded blue dress with sprays of tiny yellow flowers and a rather ugly tan apron over the top hung several sizes too big. She inherited height from her dad, but a slight frame made it unlikely she would stand a chance against an Ember.

"Are you armed?" I tried to make out any bulges in her skirt that would indicate a hidden weapon, seeing none. Though as large as it was, she might have an armory under there.

She looked up in surprise. "No. Women aren't taught to fight."

The border towns' limitations on females were worse than expected. "Would you like to learn?" I grinned.

She gave a tentative smile. "Are you offering?"

"Looks like it." I stood and pulled my dagger out of its sheath. "Does your dad have any of these lying around? You could stash it in your apron pocket and put it under your pillow at night."

"We have a few. I know there's one in the shed he wouldn't miss."

"Good. Make sure it's sharp. Now, stand up. I'm going to show you a few moves."

She arched a brow. "Are these moves to help me against the Embers, or are you just trying to impress me?"

"Grace," I deadpanned. "My moves *always* impress."

She stood, laughing, her cheeks glowing pink. I took her through some basic fighting maneuvers, showing her to angle the knife upward to reach the heart under the ribs. "Won't do much good to injure. Go for the kill."

She nodded, her lips a thin line of determination. The blade slashed toward my chest, and I hopped back, toppled over a chair, and barely missed being struck by her parry.

"Whoa, there. Don't maim the teacher."

She smiled impishly. "You're King Aldridge's famous knight. I think you can handle it."

"Okay, time to hand it over." I stretched out my palm, then sheathed the dagger after she returned it.

I'd picked an excellent student. Why did so many men underestimate women? She had every intention of assassinating any enemy that came within twenty yards of her without batting an eye. In fact, after this lesson, I had better avoid angering the girl.

I assigned her a few more tactics to practice, then decided it was time to retire to the inn for some sleep. Molly and I had a long journey ahead of us to the Purple Mountains to find the lair.

"Next time I see you, I expect to hear tales of how the Embers are too scared to travel to Quorum because their secret weapon makes a mean bangers and mash but slays anybody that messes with her."

She waved a small goodbye on my way out the door, suddenly shy again. Grace hid a lion underneath her kitten exterior. As she grew, she'd learn to use it. Hopefully, the fierceness would emerge before it was too late.

The Royal Inn's sign spoke of a bygone age, its colors of red, purple, and gold dulled with time. The blue shutters hung askew, one missing altogether. However, when I passed through the door, the wood floors shone with polish and the faded jewel-toned rugs appeared spotless. The lobby deserted, I strode across the room to ring a bell that sat atop a desk. A man arrived promptly, dressed in a tidy navy tunic, tarnished brass buttons trailing down the front.

"I'd like your best room, please," I said, then amended, "with the most comfortable bed."

The sandy-haired man with small wire-rimmed spectacles perched on the end of his nose handed me an old-fashioned key and directed me up the stairs and to the last door on the left. Although sparse, the orderly space gleamed, the bed neatly made. I collapsed into it and groaned in pleasure at its softness. After tossing my boots across the room, I snuggled in deep. Well… did something more manly than *snuggle*. Whatever that was.

Shouting disturbed my otherwise peaceful slumber. Darkness showed through the crack in the curtain. Why did it always seem drunks were the loudest in the middle of the night? I shoved the pillow over my head and turned over. Voices still penetrated the cushion. I could just make out, "Let's find him," and "…invading our town."

My eyes shot open. Were they talking about me? I hadn't made any bosom buddies here, but this hostility seemed a bit drastic. I sat up and struggled to locate my earlier abandoned shoes. Listening more intently, I heard the word, *Embers*.

My thoughts immediately turned to Grace, the instincts in my gut swirling.

I took the stairs two at a time. Outside, several men stood pointing and talking over one another. They mentioned the Lucky Horseshoe, so I rushed past them to the tavern. A knot of people clustered in front, gesturing, and examining something on the ground. A gap near a smaller villager opened, and I slid through.

A male dressed in rough brown clothes lay in a pool of blood, a knife protruding from his chest. His sightless eyes stared upward.

"Is he from here?" I asked.

"He's one of them," a man replied.

"There must have been more than one," another said.

"How do you know?" I asked, trying to read their worried faces, digesting that "one of them" meant an Ember.

The smaller man answered, "Because she's missing."

The guy adjacent elbowed him. "Shut up, Stan. This is no one's business but ours."

"Who's missing?" *Please not Grace.*

Silence.

"Come on, guys. Maybe I can help." I jostled my way closer to the center of the pack, steering clear of the oozing scarlet puddle.

Stan spoke up, "The girl from the pub. They live above the Lucky Horseshoe. Her room is empty except for a shattered lamp and some blood."

Goosebumps traveled in a wave up my arms, snaking across my neck. So, it was Grace. And she fought back. The Ember at my feet was proof enough. These men were correct—there had been more than one, more than Grace could handle with her rudimentary lesson with me hours before. I should have stayed longer. Taught her about ambushes. How to escape from a chokehold. Anything. The knot in my stomach grew. Instead, I'd been more concerned about a feather bed and a good night's sleep.

"Any idea which way they headed?" I scanned the area for clues.

"Nope. We'll take care of it," said a man with unruly eyebrows slashed into an angry scowl. "You don't belong here, King's Man."

"I may be the best chance you've got. I'm a trained tracker, and my dragon is hiding in the woods as we speak."

Before they could express disbelief regarding Molly, the man who I recognized as the owner of the tavern stepped forward. "Give him a chance. Let's tell him what's been going on. Grace told me about him. Before… before we went to bed. He's that knight. The one with the dragon."

I blinked at his change of attitude, though he must be out of his mind with worry for Grace. He'd likely do anything to get her back, even trust the likes of me.

They recounted much of what Grace already shared. Teenagers were being snatched under their noses without a trace. Someone once spotted a kidnapped girl and her captor headed north, but they vanished by the time they pursued them. The dead Ember before us was the only other sign they'd been here.

"We don't have enough men to guard the walls properly," one said, shaking his head.

"Yeah, no thanks to you," another muttered, glancing at me, his mouth twisted.

Before they could advance further into the blame game, I interrupted, "I'll track from the air. Meanwhile, create a search party. This blood is fresh. They can't be too far."

"You really have a dragon, man?" Stan asked, his expression shadowed in disbelief.

"I do, and I better get going before it's too late."

Grace's father grimaced, making me regret my bluntness. The poor man must be caught in a mixture of grief and shock. Especially since they had no leads to the whereabouts of the previous girls who disappeared.

"We'll find her," I assured him.

Let's hope that was a promise I could keep.

CHAPTER 10
DANIEL

It didn't take me long to pack a few items, wrap my mending ankle, sneak through the kitchen for provisions, and head to the barn to track down Dev, where Mya had spotted him earlier. However, the stable showed no sign of him. His horse stood patiently in a stall, indicating he still roamed somewhere on the castle grounds. I should have checked first in his usual guest room.

Dev and I had grown up together, his father, the duke, a close ally of King Dryden's. His family visited so often they became "regulars" in one of the east-wing suites. His sister, Emily, had tagged along on our adventures when we were kids until she grew into too much of a proper lady. Everyone believed we would marry someday, and it seemed easier to let them, rather than be badgered by matchmakers. Perhaps we would have married if I hadn't met Cate. Not because of some deep romantic love, but because Emily and I were friends, and it would have been convenient. Now that I'd experienced genuine love, the word *convenient* left a bitter taste, like eating a piece of fruit turned rotten in the middle: decent enough on the outside, but unpleasant after digging deeper.

When Cate found out about our arrangement she'd unsurprisingly been angered by the whole affair. To make matters worse, unbeknownst to me, Emily had developed feelings for me. The torrent of tears and insults she'd hurled when she discovered I'd fallen for Cate

had been a nightmare. *Women.* How was I supposed to know our betrothal had become official in her mind if she'd never told me? The pang of our broken friendship still smarted. Fortunately, Dev hadn't held me accountable, as he too believed the engagement contrived. Emily failed to confide her true feelings to anyone.

After stashing my pack in the back to avoid suspicion, I used the rear entrance and servant stairs to reach the east wing. I tiptoed through my own home like a burglar, hoping no one would notice. *Not suspicious at all.* I slowed my pace and attempted a normal walk, which came out more like a pirate swagger, when I crossed paths with a maid. *Nothing to see here.* My father's eyes and ears pervaded every corner, leaving me perhaps more paranoid than needed, but I couldn't shake the dread in my gut that told me secrecy was imperative. It felt as if I'd never get to the east wing. Why was this castle so enormous?

I finally reached Dev's room and knocked. No one answered. So, I opened the door.

There stood Emily, mouth open in shock, half-dressed in her corset and tiny pink lace underwear. I'd seen more of her when we swam together in the river when we were eight. But things have changed since then. Several things…

"Daniel," she cried out, which startled me enough to cover my eyes. Cate better not hear about this.

"I-I'm sorry," I blubbered, trying to contain a nervous laugh. Man, I was a total prat. If Emily didn't hate me already, this would put her over the top. "I thought Dev would be in here."

"His room is *next door*. Why would he be here?" she cried.

Was it? I'd gotten mixed up. This castle really was too big. And what was she doing here, anyway? "I didn't realize you'd come." I turned around so I wouldn't be tempted to peek through my fingers.

"Same," she said. "My mother assured me you haven't been here for months. That you defected to Caelum to be with the princess."

I couldn't see her, but from her tone, she hadn't decided to put forgiveness into practice yet. Perhaps in about a thousand years. "Well. I—uh, just stopped by." It seemed I had to give a reason for visiting my own house. It had better be a good one because I didn't want her reporting to my father that I was up to anything nefarious. "I wanted to catch up with Dev. I thought I'd skip the meal and spend time with him before he went on that scouting mission."

"What mission?" Her voice turned sharp. She always could sniff out our schemes.

"Oh, you know..."

"No, I don't. He's dressing for dinner."

Is he? I needed to catch a break and get out of here fast. It'd be nearly impossible to reach Caelum in time, as it was. "Maybe there's been a mix-up. I'll go check." I couldn't spare precious moments in attempting to smooth everything over with her now. And I'd just made the situation worse. *Fantastic.*

"Nice seeing you, Emily." Ugh—not *seeing* you. "I mean—you know what I mean. I gotta go." As quickly as possible, I slipped to the next room over, the doors identical. The castle needed a numbering system like an inn.

Thankfully, Dev greeted me at the room's entrance, his cravat untied around his neck, sporting a peacock green jacket, magenta waistcoat, and a grin stretched across his face. He always was a bit of a peacock. I'd missed the old bird.

"Daniel! *This* is a surprise." He grabbed my shoulders and pulled me into a bear hug.

"Good to see you, too." My voice muffled against his silk-clad shoulder.

After inviting me in, I relayed the plan in hushed tones, all too aware of Emily's presence next door. Dev, never one to shy from danger, even if he was the heir to a Dukedom, immediately approved. We discussed which soldiers to gather and agreed I should stay out of sight until departure. The fewer people who knew my involvement, the better chance my father wouldn't catch wind of it.

Dev packed and thankfully changed into travel gear—that blinding outfit of his showed like an oversized pheasant during hunting season. Our meeting point established, he departed while I waited in his room, pacing the floor.

We hoped to locate twenty-five men within the hour. It didn't sound like much, but these guys were elite soldiers, trackers, and specialists in Terran powers. Hugo used the energy for strength. He'd come in handy in a fight, or if boulders or tree trunks needed to be moved around for shelter or barricades. Erikson led a group of expert camouflagers. We'd need them to execute our strategy and remain hidden during the treaty, so no one would suspect additional soldiers were present. Peters would communicate and gather animals. A smattering of others were some of our best fighters. The tricky part for Dev would be contacting them in the limited time.

The hike to the rendezvous point in the woods turned out uneventful, though well over an hour had passed, and Dev still hadn't arrived. Our timeline continued to shrink. King Aldridge would soon believe I'd deserted the mission. I couldn't just meet Cate's father at the treaty, bypassing the return to Caelum, because who knows if he'd leave without us or decide the scheme too risky lacking Terra's help and abandon the idea altogether. The longer we took, the less time we'd have to prepare. Approaching before the Embers to set the trap was paramount to the plan. Arrive too late, and it would compromise the entire operation.

I waited at The Tree, well known to both of us, located about two hundred yards into the woods behind the stables. It was perfect for climbing, had evenly spaced, sturdy branches that reached taller than any others, offering a bird's-eye view. As kids, we pretended to be kings of the forest, with The Tree as our castle. We tried to make Emily our servant, but she insisted on being a famous knight who saved the land from all evils, until she became too old for such things and transformed into a boring princess, more worried about her curls than deterring danger. Perhaps a telling predictor for our non-future together.

Cate could never be boring, even if she *was* abysmal at tree climbing. She considered dressing and acting like a princess the dull part. As much as I loved her desire to save us all, I wished she didn't bear that burden. Amazing how something that drew me to her was also the part I wanted to shield her from. Now *I* played the part of the protector, not the king. Yet, somehow, with her, it fit. I didn't need to be the savior, I already had one.

The team finally arrived with an even count of two dozen. Before I saddled up, Dev took me aside. "We ran into your father in the stables."

My stomach dropped. "He saw you? Did you talk to him?

Dev's frown deepened. "Unfortunately. We told him we'd heard Embers were gathering up on High Basin, so we were going to take a look. Fortunately, he only caught sight of about ten of us. The rest were already around back."

"It could be worse. Do you think he suspects anything?"

Dev's eyes cast downward. "I do." He lowered his voice even more, "He asked about you. Kept badgering me like an interrogation."

"Did it make you nervous?" Dev wasn't aware of my father's ability to read emotions.

He huffed out an awkward laugh. "Well, yeah. Sorry, man, but when the king turns those all-seeing eyes on you, it's impossible not to sweat."

And there it was. My father knew.

CHAPTER 11
CATE

Alana's demands came fast and furious. Her tactics shifted toward stick instead of carrot. She'd either become so frustrated with me she couldn't hold her temper or wanted to discover if being the bad cop would motivate. The only person who'd ever tried this method with me was the Terran dance instructor, Mr. Hayworth, which only led to frustration, tears, and more clumsiness. Except these stakes were higher than avoiding toes during the waltz. Not that old Hayworth would believe such.

She first tasked me to blow a twig from a boulder twenty yards away. I'd never come close to achieving such a thing unless Daniel was nearby. Reality had set in. Daniel wouldn't always be around. Times such as *now*. I wondered if he'd given her a report before leaving. She might think I wasn't putting in effort, when in actuality… I was a complete flop without him.

Let's just say the twig stayed put. The grass didn't grow. The sky didn't open up into a downpour. No mist, humidity, or single drop of dew coalesced. She scowled, commanded, shook her head in dismay, and threw her arms up in defeat.

"This isn't working," she said.

Nope. Not even a little.

"You need the boy." It wasn't a question. She *knew.* "Or at least *you* think you do."

She had me there. But why wouldn't I believe it? Experience proved it.

"Imagine him here." She gestured around. "Close your eyes. Remember how the energy feels when you touch him."

My cheeks heated at the instruction. Surely, she meant touching his arm or something. Instead, my mind jumped straight to his kiss. The feel of his hands in my hair. His chest against mine and the heat between us. The scrape of stubble against my neck. My lids flipped open. My face must have flamed lobster-red at Alana's knowing glare.

"Try again and blow the twig," she said.

I went back *there*. This time, I focused on the warm buzz that always surrounded us. Usually caught up in the moment, I often missed it when we were together. I imagined feeling the energy then pushed the vibrations out so they expanded and billowed. The waves increased, undulating at a higher frequency. The sensation rushed around me, picking up speed until my hair whipped against my cheeks and the gale crashed forward. My eyes were wide open now, and I watched the piece of wood skate off the rock, leaves swirling about. Even a few gray strands had escaped Alana's tight bun, flying about her astonished face. Exhaling deeply, I let everything relax, and the wind stilled.

"That was better," she said stoically.

I smirked. Yup. *Better.* Still playing bad cop, was she? Instead of depleted and exhausted from using my own power, my body bubbled with vitality and anticipation.

Before she could say anything, I turned my attention to the grass beneath her feet. The earth's humming, likely always there for Terrans like Daniel, became not only audible but somehow tangible. The roots deepened, each a tiny tunnel in the dirt, soaking the nutrients, the damp. They expanded and pulsed until the green shoots slowly moved upward. Small, reed-like stems swayed in the light breeze, the sun's warmth inviting them toward the sky.

Next, a tangle of ivy-colored grass wrapped around Alana's ankles, extending up her calves. Soon the power waned. Whether it was my influence over it, or the energy itself, I couldn't be sure. The humming silenced—the connection lost.

Alana strode away without a word.

She left me standing in the meadow, speechless. Wait. I did good. I did *great*. What was her problem? I hurried after her in the direction of the castle.

"Where are you going?" I asked, reaching her side. "I thought we'd talk about this."

"You're here, aren't you?"

She totally knew I would follow her. My fingers clenched into fists, nails digging half-moons into the flesh of my palms. I'm annoyingly predictable. Chasing after her like a puppy wanting praise. But I *did* want accolades. Balloons. Ice cream sundae with three cherries on top. The works. This was big. Bigger than anything I'd been able to do, even with Daniel nearby.

We sat side-by-side on a bench, and I waited for her to speak. The one thing I had learned about Alana is that everything happens on *her* schedule.

"I've been telling you for months to dampen your emotions," she said, twisting the gold ring on her finger.

She had. Over and over. It had been torture. Instructing a teenager to not feel anything was like asking a bird not to fly.

"I might have been mistaken." She stared into the horizon.

Really. This was an interesting development. "How so?"

"You love the prince." A statement, again, no question in her tone.

Secret's out. I nodded.

"Your love heightens your awareness of the energy, doesn't it?"

"It's Daniel himself. Or so I thought. But maybe it's my feelings, not just him," I admitted. "In my world, sometimes people say being in love makes it seem as if everything is in technicolor."

She raised a brow, not understanding my American reference.

"Brighter and happier." Not that I'd experienced love in Oregon before meeting Daniel. "Maybe it enhances my senses or something."

"Perhaps. The key is to be sure you aren't drawing from your own feelings, which will drain you. Instead, use them to help find the energy. Can you understand the difference now?"

"I think so." I turned toward her, uncomfortable heat crawling up my neck. "You knew that Daniel's closeness had been helping me?"

"I suspected. But you should have told me. We might have come to this conclusion earlier and progressed further."

She was right. In my cowardice, I didn't want to admit that Daniel was a crutch. I should be able to stand on my own. Girl-power and all that. I'd have to change my mindset from crutch to bridge. He'd be a helping hand until I figured it out by myself. An uncomfortable sinking in my stomach settled. The truth? I *liked* him standing by my side. Going it alone was scary. I straightened my spine. Scary but necessary.

"I thought… that I wasn't enough if I couldn't do it by myself." I toed a clump of grass at my feet.

Alana turned to me, her usual stoic expression softening. "I've made it harder on you. I'm sorry for that. You've not been what we expected—no one, not even me, predicted that you wouldn't feel the energy. I won't lie and say it hasn't been a disappointment."

I swallowed the lump rising into my throat and returned my gaze to the lawn.

"But, Cate, you are also so much *more* than we expected. I shouldn't have been hard on you today. Your heart is huge and so full of love that you'd give your life to save this world. You nearly did. That's why I've tried so hard to separate your emotions. Because I want to protect *you*. The prophecy rests on your power, but I believe it's also about the person that you are—will grow to be. Rain won't unite the kingdoms. *You* will."

Alana placed her hand on my thigh, palm up. I took it, blinking away the burning behind my eyes. "It's a lot of responsibility," I said.

She squeezed my fingers. "You're ready for it. I don't tell you that enough." She chuckled sardonically. "Although, perhaps I never have. As you've probably gathered, it's not my way. But I sensed you needed to know I believe in you. Thank goodness the prophecy didn't come for some overly confidant male who thought he'd rule the world with his power. It's time for change, and I couldn't be happier that it will rise from someone with your character. Your strength is a stream, quiet and deep. When it's time, you'll roar like a river in a storm."

She let her words soak in, both of us sitting in silence while the sky darkened to twilight. The stars bloomed into existence across a navy and indigo canvas, reminding me how small we both were. Each star on its own did little to dampen the night, but when joined with others, had the potential to light the universe.

Alana instructed me to meet her again at sunrise. She departed to the castle, while I wandered to the mews to say hello to Mocha before dinner.

Charlie greeted me softly when I entered the dimly lit building, sawdust swishing underfoot. He provided gloves, meat, and showed me how to pass treats to avoid a finger being nipped. Mocha was housed in an enclosure near the rear.

She sat on her perch; her laser eyes focused on me. When I drew out a treat, her head bobbed in anticipation. I held it out and tossed it lightly above her strong yellow beak. She snatched it from the air and gobbled it, sidestepping across the wooden bar and chirping for more. The food rapidly disappeared in this fashion until we both appraised each other in silence. I crept closer, holding out a hand. She allowed a gentle pet on her back, but I didn't dare go further, wanting to earn her trust first.

The Caelum people usually had a special connection with birds, a unique bond or understanding of sorts. It felt like a lifetime ago when I first arrived and became lost in the woods. A giant worm attacked me —although Daniel later insisted it was just being friendly; I still wasn't buying that version of the story—and a flock of ravens came to save me. He'd maintained they'd come because of the Caelum in me, which, skeptical as usual, I wasn't ready to believe. And unfortunately, so far, Mocha acted like a nice bird who liked treats, nothing more.

Not willing to give up, I decided to return tomorrow, then the next day. I should try to find the energy again before returning to my suite, but conjuring images of Daniel abraded my already tender heart raw. I missed him, a phantom limb I kept reaching for that left my chest aching. I really needed to figure out my powers pronto. Imagining myself making out with Daniel in the middle of a battlefield conjured a ridiculously impractical image. I'd get my head lopped off while lost in fantasy land.

It was almost time for dinner, my cue to say goodbye to Mocha. My father didn't enjoy the pomp and circumstance associated with entertaining his allies, though he held a standing once-a-week meal, a several-hour affair, including tonight. The rest of the days, he ate in his office or with me, or met with a small group of advisors. He expected me to dress and act the part of the princess at these events. In reality, he'd instituted the weekly meal to give me a platform to interact with other prominent members of the kingdom.

I *hated* those dinners.

Introvert extraordinaire, awkward by nature, and not raised as a princess, often led to a crash-and-burn situation that made the battle with the Embers seem like a campfire. Small talk was my nemesis, and this would be the first event without Daniel. There he was again—acting as my crutch.

Come on, Cate! This was the time to shine. Show my personality, talk about more than the weather, and not insert my foot firmly into my mouth. I pulled back my shoulders and marched inside to dress into a ridiculously fancy gown.

The dining room's dazzling chandeliers sparkled over a meticulously set table of crystal and gold that stretched the length of the space, at least twenty feet. It had taken a few months, but I finally got the hang of which utensil to use. My cerulean-blue silk skirts rustled as I crossed the room to my father, still standing off to one side conversing with General Griffin. The king eyed me and leaned in to speak, angling his shoulder to block my view.

Secrets. Again. The general faced away from me, so he wasn't aware of my approach. I edged closer to overhear.

"That's correct, Your Highness. Not a word from Bandit's Hole either."

Bandit's Hole. We'd stopped there when traveling from Terra. "Not a word about what?" I asked. Father's pinched expression gave me pause, but I stood my ground. "General?"

The military man's face remained stoic. He glanced at my father for approval, who delivered a resigned nod. "Our scouts haven't seen Daniel and the men he promised. They're late."

The king crossed his arms and glowered. "I suspect they're not coming."

CHAPTER 12
LUCAS
FIFTY-SIX DAYS AGO, 3 A.M.

Molly lay fast asleep, curled against a pine-needle-covered knoll, oblivious to my approach. Domestication obviously led to the dulling of her natural defense instincts. Anyone could have been traipsing through these woods—someone who would relish the chance to slay a dragon.

"Molly," I hissed.

She didn't stir. "*Molly!*" A little louder. Nothing.

One shouldn't wake a dragon from a deep sleep by shaking them unless one wanted to be tossed fifteen feet in the air by their startled reflexes. I found a long stick and nudged her. She still didn't move. Unease swept across me like the chill of the first fall breeze. Her back rose and fell in a steady cadence. I'd never had so much trouble rousing her. After progressively heavier pokes and jabs with the stick, she finally drowsily raised her head.

"Molly. We've got to go. Wake up."

Her lids drifted closed while her massive head sunk.

I tossed the wood aside and rushed toward her. Something wasn't right. Heedless of who might be lurking in the forest, I flicked on my portable lantern to examine her. An object crunched under my foot as I approached. A swing of my light revealed a pile of bones at her feet. She must have found dinner. That same uneasy feeling sent me closer.

A mound of purple, spotted, round berries sat near the remains of some sort of animal.

Dappleberries. When carefully distilled by experts, they made an excellent sleeping drought. The concentration depended on the soil's composition, ripeness, and other variables, meaning one would never attempt to eat the fruit in the wild because a single berry might give a slight buzz or be so potent, you'd never wake up. The berries, stacked in a neat pile, would have been impossible for Molly's talons to have arranged. Upon further inspection, purple smeared across the creamy white of the carcass remains.

She'd been poisoned.

Before I could draw my knife and switch off the beacon of light, something hit me on the head from behind.

Something big. And hard.

I wobbled dizzily, sinking to my knees. Instinct guided my fall into a roll, grasping for my dagger as a club reverberated the earth where I'd been moments before. I rolled again, popping into a fighting stance. A man—maybe two?—stood with the weapon, while my vision swam in doubles and triples. I was in no shape to fight. I couldn't even tell which person was real. Maybe it was all my imagination, and I would wake up in that feather bed at the Royal Inn. But my head ached too much for a dream.

"Woah, buddy." I swayed. "I'm not here to hurt you."

"The feeling isn't mutual." His gravelly voice was quieter than expected.

Every muscle in my body ached to collapse. This mission had hardly started, and I was tired. So. Tired. It felt as if *I'd* eaten a handful of those berries. The head injury played with my thoughts, taunting me to give up. But I needed to fight. For Molly. For Grace. And Cate… always for Cate.

"Your type doesn't belong here. And your dragon friend, too." The man appeared to be a mountain roamer with long unkempt hair, beard, and soiled, torn clothes. Until he drew out his sword, gleaming in a beam of moonlight filtering through the trees. I took a step back. If his shiny weapon was any indication, he wasn't just someone who enjoyed the solitude of the forest. He was a deserter. My vision cleared enough to identify the Caelum emblem stamped into the hilt.

"I'm no Ember," I said, hands held aloft.

"Right." I could see his skepticism through his narrowed eyes, past his bushy brows and unkempt hair. "No one would approach a dragon unless they were crazy or had an alliance." He raised his weapon.

Explaining my allegiance to King Aldridge wouldn't help. As a deserter, he was wanted for treason, which would render me an enemy as either a Caelum soldier or an Ember.

"Know anything about the girls missing from the village?" I asked, changing tactics.

"If you think I had something to do with that, you'd be wrong."

"Another disappeared tonight. The Lucky Horseshoe's waitress."

He grunted, an ambiguous sound that could have meant, *Good. I only gave the service one and a half stars and the drundle pie was inedible,* or *That's horrible, she's a nice girl.*

"Yeah. Grace. You know her?" I took a second tottering step back, keeping my hands raised. "I'm trying to find her. Listen, I don't care why you're here, or why you have that sword. I just want to take my dragon here to track down the girl. Look at my boots. Embers don't have access to that kind of craftsmanship." It was true. I might be a tad vain when it came to my butter-soft riding boots. The even stitching, the polished shine. A *masterpiece.* They were my cousin's handiwork, the best cobbler in Caelum, who also crafted King Aldridge's footwear.

Molly let out a steamy snore.

"Doesn't look like that thing is going anywhere." He nodded toward her, the sword tip lowering.

Molly might sleep it off, or she could be drifting closer to permanent sleep, a thought that made my stomach swoop. Either way, she wouldn't be flying anytime soon. I needed an antidote. I could picture it in my mother's thick book of herbs and remedies, the one with random snatches of paper spraying out as makeshift bookmarks, but the name wouldn't come. "You don't happen to have the antidote on you?"

"Neemroot?" He snorted.

Of course. *Neemroot.* Found in mountain crags over three thousand feet elevation. None would grow here. "I'll have to go into town to the apothecary." Standing took monumental effort, and I couldn't imagine trekking into the village and back. "Don't suppose you'd run that errand for me?"

"You're lucky I'm not going to kill you both."

He had a point. I slowly slipped my hand into a pocket for my money pouch, pulled out some coins, then threw the remains of the bag at his feet. Fortunately, I didn't keep all the money in one place, but this hefty sum was much more than the trip to town was worth.

The man bent, keeping his gaze on me, picked it up, and peered inside, his dark eyes widening. This guy would not do well at the gaming tables with a face that readable. "I'd need more," he said, closing up the pouch.

A poor bluff. If he truly lived out here in the woods, it was more money than he'd see all year hunting and trapping. "The rest when you come back." I jingled the coins in my hand. I couldn't let Molly die from this scoundrel's poison. At the thought of losing her, another wave of dizziness swum inside my head. And Grace… she'd probably be long gone, but I had to try.

He tugged on his voluminous beard. But I knew he'd take it. "The apothecary won't be open at this time of night," he said.

More delays, though he was likely correct. "Wake up the owner."

He grunted and pocketed the money pouch as he walked away.

Was that a yes? "I'd appreciate a rush job, mate. See you in a bit," I called. Hopefully, I'd reserved enough for it to be worth his return with the Neemroot, though he might keep what was in the pouch and never be seen again.

I knelt next to Molly, shaking away the negative thoughts. The knobbly skin on her jaw smoothed under my hand like sealskin when it trailed across her snout. I rested my head against her side, which rose and fell in easy movements, my limbs collapsing beside her in relief. She slept soundly and unlabored. I needed to watch for threats, but my body betrayed me, falling into a dreamless slumber.

A sharp jab to the hip awakened me to a leering Mountain Man, his boot poised to kick again. I jolted upright, clawing the sleep from my groggy brain. Once more, I'd put us in danger. As the cobwebs cleared,

I realized this guy already had the opportunity to kill me in my sleep if he'd wished. My shoulders relaxed slightly.

"You on a suicide mission? You're lucky I'm such a nice guy and didn't slice you open for your money." The man rested his raised foot back on the ground.

His words reminded me of my true assignment for the king, eons away from being accomplished. Guilt stirred uneasily in my stomach, both for derelict of duty, and neglect of my own safety.

I stood, legs now steady, and although my head still throbbed, the dizziness had abated. Molly slept on, oblivious. "You get the antidote?"

"I got it." He held out his hand for the coins.

"Neemroot first, then I'll pay you the rest."

Huffing, he dug out a brown paper bag and passed it over. Dried crushed fragments lay inside, their fragrance sending me to my mother's herb shed. She kept it stocked due to the occasional village overdose of dappleberry elixir, typically produced by an inexperienced apothecary. "Right. This looks good." I handed over the coins.

"Not sure how much the beast needs. I bought what they had." He gave an apologetic shrug.

Mountain Man was turning into a real bleeding heart. Frankly, I had no idea either, but too much wouldn't be toxic, so I'd give her all of it. "Thank you for your help. If there's anything else I can do for you, say the word."

"Just keep this meetin' quiet." His gaze averted downward, suggesting secrets better left unsaid.

I nodded. "Will do."

He trudged farther into the woods without a goodbye. He'd gotten me into this predicament by poisoning Molly, but since she was the only dragon not siding with the Embers, it was tough to put too much blame on the guy. He was likely a traitor and deserter, but some conscience must still rattle around in there for him to return with the medication.

I bent next to Molly, her breathing remaining steady. Prodding her awake to get the Neemroot into her mouth proved to be a task, but eventually, she opened her jaws wide enough for me to pour the substance onto her tongue. The bitter taste alone helped the drowsiness, but I held her snout, urging her to swallow, chasing it with a gulp of water from my canteen.

It took around an hour for her to rouse enough to eat some dried meat. Her sleep-clouded golden eyes gradually turned brighter, and she finally stood with a wobble and paced the small clearing. The sun's light filtered through the trees, indicating we'd lost hours. Finding the Embers would be near impossible, but at least in daylight, they might be easier to spot, provided they hadn't hunkered into hiding to wait for nightfall.

"You ready, girl?" I patted her side, then slid my arms around her neck for a full hug.

She nudged me with her nose, then lowered her belly to the mounting position. After placing my pack in her saddlebags, I hopped up, and she rose to the skies. She wouldn't be winning any races this morning, but since our goal was to meticulously search, it didn't matter.

"We're trying to find someone, a girl with a couple of Embers," I told her.

She shook her head in protest.

"I know. We don't usually go looking for them. But it shouldn't be many. We can handle them."

We searched well past the sun setting against the western mountains with no sign of Grace. We circled the town, then headed north, weaving back and forth. Still no evidence of the Embers. We did come upon a search party and landed to talk with them. They'd found nothing.

"No tracks?" I asked.

"There are too many around the city walls to follow." The man shielded his eyes from the sun to speak.

It had been a while since it rained, making the likelihood of muddy footprints low. There were enough leaves and grass I'd think careful inspection might lead to tread marks or broken twigs. Presumably, none of these men were expert trackers.

"We're heading home." One patrolman slung his pack over his shoulder, accepting the loss.

The thought of Grace held captive by those monsters spurred me on. "I'll keep searching. Come on, Molly."

And so, we did. For days, flying farther and farther north, exhausting us both. We finally admitted defeat and traveled back to Quorum to report our failure. With heavy hearts, we entered town together. News had passed of Molly, so there was no need to hide her. Telling Grace's father that I hadn't found her would be one of the hardest things I'd done in some time.

The Lucky Horseshoe stood closed. Knocking on the thick wooden door felt like the pounding of nails into Grace's coffin. I swallowed thickly as footsteps shuffled from inside.

CHAPTER 13
DANIEL

We pushed our horses hard away from the castle to the confusion of those who hadn't been informed of the full mission brief. We'd have to stop at some point to tell them the king hadn't exactly approved of this operation, but a head start was certainly a silly thing to waste. The men deserved a choice. And they'd have one… just not at this moment.

Several roads led to Caelum, with a few off the beaten paths, one of which was my "shortcut" on the way here, which we'd obviously avoid. The northern route wound longer and passed through the forest—riskier with unpredictable wildlife, not to mention more opportunities for an Ember ambush. The main road would be fastest and ordinarily the safest, if King Dryden's men weren't chasing us down.

Psychoanalyzing my father was a challenge. Which way would he think I'd choose? If he thought me oblivious, then we would travel the easy road. If he thought I knew he was tracking us, then he'd believe I would pick the forest route for evasion purposes. Though if he knew that I knew, would I still pick the forest or… The whole thing made my head hurt.

The fork approached, and I slowed my mount. "Hey, Dev. Which way?"

He shrugged one shoulder. "You're closer to the king than me."

Maybe, though I often wondered how close we really were. He was ruthless. So ruthless, he'd likely send soldiers in *both* directions.

"Shall we make it more fun for him?" May as well have him suffer. He hated the forest, preferring the confines of his stone fortress. That is, if he didn't hole up in the castle and have his men bring me in, awaiting the contrite return of the prodigal son. Only one way to find out.

"The woods?" Dev asked.

"Definitely."

We traveled several kilometers until we reached a clearing. I halted the group and asked them to gather. Nerves fluttered to life at the thought of telling them the truth. I imagined them leaving in a trail of angry voices back to Terra to report to the king.

"Thank you all for agreeing to come on such short notice. We chose each of you for your special abilities, which are crucial for our success. Frankly, you're the best at what you do."

The two dozen men grouped in close. Hugo, the largest, with his misshapen nose, broken on more than one occasion, stood at attention. He might have a quick temper, but loyal to the end, that one. Erikson, the camouflage expert, was a full head shorter than his best friend Hugo. Someone small crowded in the back. Every time I tried to peer around the others, only a glimpse of a uniformed elbow or shoulder would appear, which made me wonder if one of my father's spies lurked in our midst.

I strode through the knot of men. The person shifted behind someone else. A quick change of direction allowed me to catch an arm.

But *she* was no soldier.

"Mya. What are you doing here?" I tightened my grip reflexively.

Her eyes, so similar to mine, held my gaze defiantly. "Can we talk about this in private?" she asked.

I shouldn't harangue Mya in front of my men, but my temper blazed. She deserved some embarrassment and to be sent home with her tail between her legs. She *deserved* to be put in her place. Father would surely notice her absence.

My sister had jeopardized everything.

"Fine," I gritted out. "Pardon us, gentlemen." We didn't have time for a brother-sister spat with the king following, yet she always got her way. Here we go again.

We traipsed through the grass to a copse of trees. "You shouldn't have come," I said.

She didn't shrink under my glare. She never did.

"You need me." She poked my chest.

"Excuse me?" I loved my sister, but her specialty thrived in ballroom battles rather than actual fighting. Cate would claim this pronouncement sexist (a word she introduced to me—multiple times), but it was as true as a drundle is clumsy. Mya had never trained to be a soldier. She'd only be a hindrance.

"I have a secret," she said.

I rolled my eyes. "Is this about Lucas?" I suspected she had a thing for him, but pretending to be a Terran Elite to help save him went too far.

"No. Of course not." She looked down and left, a sure sign she was lying. I usually sensed untruths unless someone knew to mask their emotions. Mya was used to being around our father, so she was somewhat adept at it, though she couldn't hide her tell. Her bravado wore thin, her nerves, now palpable, rising.

"I can help because," she lowered her voice, "I have a power I've never told you about."

Doubtful. "Being able to eat the most pastries at breakfast doesn't count."

She scowled, anger coming off her in waves. Annoying her was too easy.

"I can sense emotions," she whispered.

I huffed out a laugh. I should have known, but secret-keeping rose to a new level at our house. I'd kept the same information from her and my father about myself. Apparently, it was genetic. Both being an empath and our secretive nature.

"Doesn't change anything," I said. "You're not welcome on this mission."

"But… I can help. I'll be able to tell if the Embers are lying!"

"So will I."

"What? No, you can't." She shot one of those disbelieving looks that only a sister could have perfected so well.

"I have the same power. We just never told each other."

"Really? Why?" She blew a stray piece of dark hair out of her face that had escaped her bun.

"I didn't want Father to find out," we both said in unison.

"So," I crossed my arms, "we don't need you. Time to go home."

"Two is better than one?" She crinkled her nose and gave me hopeful puppy eyes.

"Nope."

"Can you—you know—influence the emotions?" She circled her finger in the air.

"What do you mean by *influence*?"

"Like calm someone down when they're angry. You can do that, right?"

"Uh—No? Don't you think I'd have tried that on our lovely father by now?" How in Terra did she do that? Wait—was she doing it right now? "You can't make me do stuff—can you?"

"Not really." She smirked. "But an idea starts to sound better if happy thoughts are projected simultaneously."

"You are NOT coming," I shouted.

"Sure about that?" she waited, holding my gaze.

She wasn't *that* good at manipulating emotions—I still felt the bite of anger, though she had a point. Her ability could come in handy.

"Plus," she said. "Father's following you. If I run into him on the way home, he'll realize he's on the right track."

"You could throw him off the scent."

"He's the master at lie detection. And you really want me in these woods by myself?"

I sighed. She had me. "Fine. But you're going to stay put in Caelum with Cate." I didn't want her with us because I wanted her safe, not because I didn't enjoy having her around. She'll cause me to lose focus, worrying about her constantly.

"Sure." She ambled toward the soldiers. "Whatever you say."

With Mya showing up, we'd already lost time, but the men

deserved to be told they might be committing treason. The extra moments to explain would be worth their trust.

"As I was saying," I told the soldiers, glaring at Mya, "there are some things you should know before we continue. Anyone who wants to turn back, I won't hold it against you."

I proceeded to describe the peace treaty and our concern for a trap, then finally King Dryden's unwillingness to support the operation.

"We could use your help. Peace would allow our communities time to regroup and prosper without all the Ember skirmishes or the anxiety of a large-scale attack. We'd use the time wisely and plan the next battle on our terms."

"What about Princess Catherine?" Hugo asked. "Can't she just wet 'em down, then we go in and clean up?" He ground his fist into his palm.

Now we trudged in muddy waters. I couldn't give away Cate's secrets, but they also needed to be told *something*.

"Cate almost died using her power last time. We're still investigating and want to be sure she's safe. A treaty would allow more training."

"Is she okay?" asked Peters, concern deepening the lines crossing his forehead.

It touched me to see a Terran soldier care about her, the Caelum princess. "She is. Alana's been preparing her."

"If it gives her more time, I'm in," Peter said.

"Me too." Hugo crossed his arms.

One by one, they all agreed. I exhaled a long-held breath. "I promise I'll take full responsibility with King Dryden. Do whatever I can to ensure you won't be in trouble." They probably believed I had sway with him, which twisted the guilt sitting in my gut.

"As will I." Mya stepped forward.

I tried not to roll my eyes. "Everyone, Princess Mya. If you hadn't noticed."

They nodded and jostled one another at her name. These guys were too aware of a woman in our midst for my liking. Surely none of them were dumb enough to try anything with me around. She grinned, batted her lashes, and the men were putty. This was going to be a long trip. That is, if we avoided the king.

"Let's go."

CHAPTER 14
CATE

After tossing and turning all night worrying about Daniel, morning finally arrived. My father's accusation stung, insinuating that he wouldn't show. After Daniel saved his life, he could at least *try* to have a little faith.

The fancy dinner last evening went as expected. Despite my intentions to act as a proper royal host, I barely conversed, nibbling tastelessly at the food, worried. I did that. Worried a lot. Considering all that had happened, I'd had few full-blown panic attacks. And who wouldn't be a worrier if you were the enemy's number one target? But sometimes, and this is where I needed improvement, I spun in these loops. The same thoughts circle around and around, leaving me immobilized, even though most of the time, I can't do anything to change the problem.

For example, Daniel's delay. The scouts were already looking. Molly was with Lucas, so I couldn't commandeer the dragon for a search and rescue mission. Waiting was the only thing left to do. I hated feeling helpless. I'd thought my princess status would gain more action, but alas, everyone still discounted the thoughts of a teenage girl.

At least King Aldridge began trusting me enough to join the strategy meetings with General Griffin and the others. Misogyny in this kingdom ran rampant, though hopefully, my gradual influence would wear them down.

I dressed quickly, eager to check with the sentries to see if Daniel had arrived overnight. Every person I passed knew nothing of his whereabouts. Same with the guards—no sign of him. Thoughts raced around my head like an Indy car. Was he hurt? Did King Dryden refuse? Had Daniel changed his mind? And lastly, although I tried to push it away and have more faith, had he decided I wasn't worth the effort? I didn't really believe that one, but the intrusive thought kept pressing its way forward.

I wound through the castle to King Aldridge's office. After knocking softly, Father waved me in. General Griffin stood near the oversized desk.

"Any sign of him?" I didn't need to specify. Daniel weighed on all our minds.

"No," the king replied.

I perched on the chair across from my father, and the general joined me. Breakfast lay out on the sideboard, a plate of untouched food in front of the king.

"We can only wait one more day. Our trap won't work if they arrive before us, and we're cutting it too close already," Griffin said.

"You'll still go without the Terrans?" I asked.

"I should speak to Princess Catherine in private." My father gestured for Griffin to step out.

"Think on it," the general said with a pointed look to the king as he walked out the door and shut it quietly behind him.

My spine tightened in apprehension. It didn't sound like he wanted to enjoy a lighthearted breakfast. My knotted stomach couldn't handle food anyway.

Once we were alone, he tapped his fingers on the desk, then leaned into his oversized chair. "I know you want to rescue Lucas."

Butterflies swarmed in my belly. "Don't you?"

"Of course. We're working on alternative plans without the Terrans. But we have to face facts—traveling to the meeting point at a disadvantage is foolish."

Left unspoken was the risk he'd be taking if not fully protected.

What would happen to the country if its king were taken? Or worse, killed?

And selfishly, what would happen to me?

And then there's Lucas. If we saved him, I would demand Father give him a desk job. Did they have those here? Maybe my personal butler? Daniel wouldn't approve—I could picture his scowl if *that* ever happened. Bottom line: I needed every person in my life safe. It wouldn't be possible until we were rid of the Embers—a burden that lay squarely on me.

"I made progress with Alana yesterday," I said.

"I heard." He took a bite of toast, chewing slowly.

"Instead of Daniel, take me?" I'd rather risk my own life than have others fall in my place.

"You're too much of an asset when you finally gain full strength. To lose you now…" He cleared his throat. "We need to keep you safe."

"Maybe rescuing Lucas should wait. We can't risk losing you either." I hated saying it. Even thinking about abandoning Lucas left a sour aftertaste—a betrayal of our friendship.

"I'll decide by the end of today," he said. "If I go and something happens to me, I'm placing Baron Graftonberg as regent until you meet the criteria to rule."

"It's one year?" Father had once explained the law to me. It was established in the twelve hundreds with the early settlers. The Caelumites instituted the decree to ensure a new immigrant couldn't attempt a coup before understanding the new kingdom's way of life.

"I'm afraid so." He picked up his fork as if to take another bite. He held it there, then placed it back on the table.

"And regent?" I'd read enough British history to understand his meaning, but questioned it anyway.

"He'll be in charge, but you'll be involved in decision making."

"The baron," I deadpanned, picturing his wobbly cheeks as he lectured me about some perceived wrongdoing. "What about General Griffin? At least he respects me."

"The general isn't a member of the aristocracy. He's not eligible, according to our laws."

"You know, in America, I can join the army at eighteen." I folded my hands in front of me, ready to further my case.

The king didn't blink. "Join, yes. Lead, no. There's no time to amend our covenants before I leave. That would take a vote by the entire aristocracy."

"This whole country is antiquated." I shook my head in disgust.

He scowled. "Not as bad as Terra."

True. There were so many things I'd love to change, but moving too fast would risk losing the people's confidence.

"But the baron. He *hates* me." My voice rose an octave.

"Untrue. He's loyal and a strong leader. If we decide to proceed with the mission, this will be a trial run." He leaned back in his chair. I couldn't tell if he feigned being unbothered in order to reassure me, or wasn't actually worried. "It'll only be a couple of weeks," he said.

"You won't change your mind?" I slumped in defeat, knowing the answer.

"I've already spoken to him." The resolute set of his jaw signaled decisiveness.

"Of course you have," I mumbled under my breath. Why would anyone around here consult me?

He stood. "We have much planning. Why don't you go work with Alana?"

I left, choosing to return to my room and stew. The balcony held a telescope, and I searched for signs of Daniel. The last time I gazed through the lens it had been during The Great Battle. Using it brought the scene back to life. The fires, the charred bodies, how the Embers had outnumbered us five-to-one. The desperate miasma collecting to form the rain that would nearly kill me, draining myself to save them. I now understood the difference between using the energy around me rather than my own. But I'd do it again if I could. Drain every drop of myself just to stop the Embers once and for all.

Alana met with me mid-morning after a renewed determination and a decision to quit sulking. "You made progress yesterday. I thought you'd be eager to continue and start early," she scolded.

When I didn't reply, she said, "You're worried about the prince."

"Yes. I worry. You should know that by now. I. Worry. Way too much." I immediately wanted to take back the words. She didn't deserve to be the recipient of my frustration. Subconsciously, I'd put Alana into a therapist role. She may be wise, but what did she understand about anxiety? Always calm, I'd seen her as something to aspire to. I needed to focus on being a better *me*, not turning into someone else entirely.

She sighed, the line of her mouth softening. "Are you willing to try today?"

It hurt to think she might believe I'd make a half-hearted effort. "Of course."

"I'd like you to produce dew," she commanded.

No luck. I truly tried, but conjuring Daniel's image led to distress rather than inspiration, my pulse ratcheting, panic barely held at bay. I toppled a leaf off a log with a breeze—a *faint* breeze, although not sure if Mother Nature didn't help me out on that one. Alana finally took pity and sent me away. My intentions were there, but I couldn't follow through. I trudged toward the mews, the guilt of failure still aching in my chest.

At least Mocha seemed pleased to see me. I dragged a chair into her enclosure to commiserate together. She hopped to me, eager to find out if I'd brought treats. Today, for the first time, she read my mood. Instead of begging for food, she sidestepped along the perch next to my shoulder.

"I know, girl. Why is life so complicated?"

Mocha nuzzled my cheek. The soft down of her neck dusted against my skin, and I tilted into her. She chirped quietly in my ear. Sadness emanated as she brushed her feathers across my face.

A connection. I'd finally done it. Or *she* had. Ironic, my despair is what sparked the bond. "You're trying to make me feel better, aren't you?" I laughed and pulled away when she hit a particularly ticklish spot.

"We'll be okay, won't we, Mocha."

After picking up lunch, then checking for reports of Daniel—there were none—I entered my father's office. "Made any decisions?"

He sat back in his chair. "We have."

I wasn't sure which verdict to root for. Both held horrible consequences that could mean never seeing Lucas or Father again.

I swallowed, my throat tight. "What did you decide?"

He watched me gravely. "We're going without the Terrans."

CHAPTER 15

LUCAS

FIFTY-THREE DAYS AGO

Grace's father, whose name I learned was John, ushered me inside the Lucky Horseshoe. Guilt weighed every step as I crossed the threshold. We stood awkwardly in the entry appraising each other. Just as well he didn't offer me a pint. I wouldn't be here long.

"You didn't find her." His voice came out hoarse as if he hadn't spoken in a while. His red-rimmed eyes spoke of another cause.

"We didn't. I'm sorry. There's no sign of them." I wanted to lie—to give some sort of hope—but that would be more for my own conscience than to ease his pain. He didn't need placation, rather the truth in its stark finality.

John stepped back, collided with a chair, and collapsed into it, his face falling into his hands. "I didn't hear them," he whispered. "I sleep in the room next to hers. How could I let this happen?"

"Don't blame yourself." His grief cut me, sharp as a soldier's blade, and I took the seat next to him, feeling unsteady. I'd seen men die. Even witnessed their families mourn, though I hadn't ever been given the job of notifying the next of kin, something I never wanted to repeat. We sat in silence at the scarred wooden table. He attempted to process the horrific news, while I tried to give comfort solely with my presence.

After a time, I spoke, "I need to go to the Purple Mountains. I'll continue to keep watch for her."

John lifted his head. "I don't know why any Caelum man would go there. The beasts…" he trailed off and gazed at the table, losing focus.

"The Dragons?" He'd heard they were there too?

John stood abruptly. "You should go."

I should. He needed time to grieve. But—what did he know? "John?"

He strode to the door and opened it. "Thank you for trying."

He wasn't willing to share, at least not right now. "You're welcome." As I passed, I placed my hand on his shoulder. He shut the door softly behind me.

While in town, I gathered supplies. I'd already lost so much time, and spending the night at the inn wasn't a luxury I could afford. The feather bed didn't even appeal to me anymore. The thought that Grace had been taken while I slept in comfort turned my stomach.

We set off heading northeast. Even though we'd already searched the first few kilometers, I instructed Molly to fly low just in case we saw any traces of Grace. We found nothing and flew well into the night until my lids drooped and Molly's wings flagged.

Moonlight illuminated a clearing in the woods, the perfect landing spot. I dismounted, then circled the area to check it was secure before unpacking our gear. Traveling alone increased the risks. As much as I'd love to always stay aware of my surroundings, my body wouldn't cooperate. Neither would Molly's. Dragons were a bit like cats—they loved their sleep. Thankfully, Molly typically slept light, except when dosed with dappleberries, of course.

The sounds of men shouting in the distance startled me awake. Molly's head rose and she swung it in my direction to be sure I'd roused. We had two options: pack up and get out as fast as possible—no one could catch us from the air—or sneak up on them and discover if whoever was out there held Grace prisoner.

I crawled toward Molly and gathered our belongings. "Find a place to hide. I'm going to take a closer look." Flying atop her low enough to see if they had Grace could put Molly vulnerable to arrows, especially her wings. And if the voices belonged to Embers, flaming projectiles would be guaranteed.

I crept through the woods, listening for movement. Sound had carried with the wind, and it took me nearly twenty minutes to find their campsite. Three men sat around a fire eating breakfast, one stoking it with orange flames extending directly from his palm. A tent stood closed on the other side of the camp, but otherwise, no sign of Grace. The inside of the shelter held the answer, but it would be difficult to examine the contents and remain undetected. If I circled around, I'd have a better chance of peeking into the tent's opening.

Slowly, I doubled back, creating a wide berth to approach from the east. When the campsite came into view through the trees it stood deserted, fire still blazing. The hairs on the back of my neck rose. An abandoned tin cup lay on its side, the dark contents spilled into the dirt.

A twig snapped behind me. I whirled around to find two Embers ready to attack. Adrenaline pumped through my heart's chambers, my entire body pulsing with nerves. I conjured a gust of wind, forcing them back and any fire they might wield. Using their momentary surprise, I slipped one of the daggers from its sheath strapped to my leg. My defensive wind stalled with the motion. The taller of the two, with shorn dark hair standing on end, shot toward me.

I dodged, throwing my knife simultaneously. The mark hit, lodging straight through the chest. My next blade slipped out easily. The other Ember, his narrowed eyes trained on me, pulled out his dagger. Secretly pleased—I'd rather deal with a weapon than fire any day—we circled one another. I adjusted my steps to edge closer to the tent to discover if Grace hid inside. So far, I hadn't heard her, though she could be gagged or drugged. If the latter was the case, a quick escape would be impossible. I'd have to either kill or incapacitate. As a seasoned soldier, this wasn't new, but I'd be walking a razor's edge with an enemy who killed without conscience.

Just a couple more steps to the tent. The man lunged, and I evaded his clumsy maneuver. The Embers lacked my speed, their only real power being fire. Most of their lands lay barren due to uncontrolled blazes. I wouldn't want to call anyone dumb, but let's just say they have trouble with impulse control. It might cross his mind to be careful not to burn down the whole forest, but no guarantees.

I cocked my arm, ready to propel my dagger with a gust of wind. Something caught it and wrenched my hand behind my back, the knife falling useless to the ground. A cold blade slid against my throat.

The third Ember.

"What are you doing way out here?" asked the man in front of me, still poised for attack.

"I don't want to fight," I said, wincing as the knife nicked my Adam's apple. "I left the army a while back and am out here on my own."

"A deserter," the one behind me said, his voice laced with interest.

"Yep. That's me," I lied. "Came to see if you'd left anything good behind. Didn't mean to disturb you." I swallowed carefully. "Maybe you could lower that knife just a touch?"

"He killed Masters." The Ember tilted his head toward his friend with my dagger protruding from his chest.

The steel at my neck burned hot—any slight movement would brand my skin permanently. "I was just defending myself." The sinking feeling of knowing I wouldn't be able to persuade them with words descended like an egg falling from its nest, hope cracking into pieces. My only way out?

Fight.

I bashed my head backward, breaking my captor's nose, wrenched myself free, then slid my sword from its sheath. Before he could react, I'd sliced through his neck. A blast of wind sent the other Ember reeling backward. My sword ran him through before he realized the end had come. He joined his friends on the dirt, motionless.

Sick to my stomach, I gathered my weapons. I had to check the tent but wanted a moment to collect myself. I cleaned the blood-soaked blades with leaves the best I could, as if able to somehow wash the blood from my conscience, then shoved the steel away, keeping a dagger out in case of more attackers.

I hastened to the shelter and lifted the flap. "Grace?"

The tent was empty.

CHAPTER 16
DANIEL

We rode nearly without incident the rest of the day. However, while stopping for a quick dinner break, limkins descended on us. Mya of course thought the furry creatures adorable, but they'd stolen enough from me over the years that I was immune to their golden eyes and long lashes. Mya offered one a stone fruit, bringing on a whole gaggle of them swinging from the trees, swiping packs, and anything they could get their paws on. She stopped laughing when one plopped onto her head and yanked a gold comb out of her hair, pulling out plenty of strands in the process.

We managed to recapture most of the important stuff by bartering with food. But no amount of coaxing could convince the limpkin to return Mya's comb. It stared at her with those big eyes, blinking its enormous lashes that rivaled court ladies and refused.

"Come on. We're wasting time," I said.

"Mom gave that to me." She scowled and pointed to the creature in an overhanging branch.

"And she can get you another. Let's go."

We galloped away, glad to be rid of the limkins, though night arrived far too early. Clouds covered the moon and stars, sending us into near-complete darkness. The path was circuitous and veered off in different directions multiple times before we would reach Caelum, making it impossible to traverse in the shadows. We slowed our pace.

Even if we had chosen to take the main road, traveling at night would always be dangerous. Even more so in the forest when the nocturnal animals came out to hunt. My grip on the reins tightened at every rustle in the bushes.

"Next clearing let's make camp," I called out. The last thing I needed was a big cat pouncing on one of us. The horses also required rest given how hard they'd been pushed today.

After dismounting, we started building the fire, both for light and protection. I'd seen Lucas with a portable lantern that didn't require flame, which would come in handy tonight. The Caelumites were ahead of us in technology, an annoyance that burned at my pride the longer I'd spent there with Cate.

"Mya. Over here," I called. She laughed with Peters on the other side of the campfire. "Make your bedroll next to mine." There had better be more than makeup and dresses in that bag of hers. She drew out her bedding, proving me wrong, then set one of the portable lanterns next to it.

"Where'd you get that?"

She shrugged, rather smugly if you asked me. "I have my ways. I'll leave it between us in case you need it."

I should stop thinking of Mya as just my baby sister. Maybe she *could* prove to be resourceful.

Before the sun peeked through the trees we were packed and ready to move on. I mounted my horse, wishing he was Raven. It would be a relief to receive word of his safety, but I likely wouldn't hear until after we'd negotiated this peace treaty.

"Think we're safe from Father?" I asked Mya.

One side of her mouth turned up. "Not really… What do you think he'll do if he finds us?"

King Dryden was capable of any number of atrocities. He might threaten to hurt our crew, knowing we wouldn't let him punish them.

Soft, he'd call us, before blackmailing us to return to Terra. His training often consisted of transferring his power into me. I'd done this to Cate to help her learn to dance, but with the king—he used pain. A buzzing and tingling under the skin that kept increasing until you wanted to rip yourself to shreds.

The hairs on my arms rose remembering the last time he'd executed this form of punishment. When Cate left for Caelum after discovering our duplicity, he'd been angry and took it out on me. I had loathed myself so much at that point, I'd almost welcomed the pain as if it would absolve me of my mistakes. It was the first time he'd incapacitated me, leaving me broken, confined to my chamber for two days so no one would see what he'd done. I couldn't have gone after Cate even if I'd wished to. My shattered confidence convinced me that I didn't deserve her. It was Dev who urged me to write the letter explaining my mistakes, then delivered it to the soldier who carried it to Cate in Caelum.

I didn't know if King Dryden had ever touched Mya. I'd always thought of her as the golden child, an expert at not raising his ire. She'd never said anything if he had. Then again, too many secrets had been kept between us. Something that needed remedying. After all, we were on the same side.

"I don't know what he'll do," I said finally. "Try to get us to go home by whatever means necessary I 'spose."

"You ever wonder what kind of ruler you'll be?" she asked. "Before Cate, I thought you might follow in his footsteps."

Cate, coupled with my short time in England, challenged me to see things at a different angle. Regardless, I would have never turned out like my father. It hurt to think Mya once believed that, though not too surprising—we'd drifted apart. I'd thought I was the big brother protecting her, always shielding my emotions from Father. But I'd sheltered everything from her too.

"I'm still figuring that out. He won't be my role model. I know that much." My thoughts drifted back to our relationship. "Hey, Mya?"

"Yeah?"

"I'm glad we're spending time together."

She grinned up at me. "Me too."

"But you're still staying at Caelum Castle." I launched my horse into a canter now that the sun had risen enough to illuminate the trail. And because I wanted the last word.

At midday, there was still no sign of Father. Far ahead, a herd of animals blocked our path. Perhaps cattle? Big, whatever they were. As we approached, their features came into focus.

Drundles. They traveled in herds, mean as wild boar, slow and clumsy until they wanted to defend their territory—then they'd attack faster than an angry hornet. The creatures must be migrating south to a different water source.

We slowed our horses and Dev rode up beside me. "How many?" he asked.

"Not sure. Hundreds?" The sight was incredible. I'd never seen so many at once, lumbering across the trail. Impossible to estimate their actual number as they disappeared into the forest on either side of the path, a wall of gray, wrinkly hides. They were notoriously grumpy creatures and extremely difficult to kill. Harpoons were the best bet, but none of us carried one. We'd never make it through safely.

"I guess we wait it out?" Dev asked.

The rest of the group pulled up behind. "Take a break guys," I called. "And keep your distance."

"Don't have to tell me twice," Dev mumbled.

We sent Hugo down the trail as a lookout for approaching Terran soldiers or Embers. The rest of us dismounted, easing off our horses, and shaking stiff legs from the hard ride. Dev and I sat on a log, and Mya joined us.

"So," I said to Dev, breaking the silence, "your sister still hates me."

"Pretty much," both Mya and Dev said in unison.

"You've talked to her?" I leaned over Dev to view Mya's expression, which was barely contained laughter. At my glare, her hand reached up to hide her grin. She never cared for Emily, who excluded her from our games when we were younger, then later her group of friends. Now that I thought about it, I wondered what I'd seen in the girl. I should have been way more protective of Mya. This trip seemed to be highlighting all my faults.

"Don't worry," Mya replied. "She keeps it together in public. She doesn't want anyone to find out you hurt her, but you should know," she smirked, "she's telling everyone that *she* terminated your betrothal before you went to England."

"She broke things off with me, did she?"

Dev chuckled. "So she says."

If that made her feel better, it was fine. I should have cleared things up with her long before bringing Cate to Terra.

Before I could respond, Hugo galloped toward us. "The king!"

A quick glance at the herd of drundles revealed a steady stream ten hides wide, with no end in sight. Our only other option would be to skirt around them through the dense forest, which would make it difficult to stay together. Father might take out some of his best men in a chase to soothe his pride. I surveyed the group. They deserved more than being hunted by a narcissistic king.

I stood and held out my hand to Mya. "Ready to talk to Father? Or..." I let my arm drop. "Maybe he doesn't know you came? You could hide."

"Oh, he knows. We should do it together." She grabbed my palm, hers as slick as mine, and I helped her up. We trudged down the trail, and with each step, I could feel Mya's nervousness radiating from her, just as she could likely sense mine.

"Wait here," I called to the troops as they started to follow. Dev couldn't have chosen a more loyal group, but I'd gotten them into this mess. It was up to me to clean it up.

King Dryden rode in front atop his favorite stallion, the tallest horse in the stable. A green cloak embroidered with finely stitched ivy flowed behind, gold braid trimming his uniform. All he required was a crown to announce to an Ember assassin his royal status. I shook my head at the vanity. He may as well have worn a target.

Mya and I knelt, waiting for him to signal we could rise.

"You've disobeyed me," he said. "An act of treason." He glowered while we continued to kneel. A rock dug into my knee. Not an auspicious start.

"There's a group of Embers up north at Canyon Rock. We were just checking to see how many had gathered," Mya said.

I inwardly groaned. He'd know she wasn't telling the truth. He *always* knew.

"Don't lie to me, Mya. Tell me how your brother convinced you to participate in this goose chase?"

He finally let us stand, allowing Mya a chance to gather her thoughts. Of course as the favorite, he wouldn't believe her capable of taking it upon herself to be disobedient. Mya rarely got into trouble. She didn't want to lose her status as Golden Child.

"Well?" he asked.

"I came on my own," she said, raising her chin. "And if you had sense, you would have supported this mission from the start. Everyone wants peace. Everyone."

Finding it difficult to hold my face impassive, I could hardly believe she stood up to him. I silently cheered her on, yet a frisson of worry at what he might do kept me wary.

"I know you don't want to help King Aldridge," she continued, "but it would send both our kingdoms into a tailspin if anything happened to him. Terrans would worry Caelum couldn't mount support to fight the Embers without a leader. I know," she sighed, "you guys hate each other. We *all* know. But Daniel's doing the right thing."

I could not believe Father let her defy him this long. I would have been fileted, quartered, drawn, then burned at the stake by now.

The king dismounted. My entire body tensed. He was going to transfer power to her—his own special brand of torture. Mya's nerves jacked, sending my own sky-high. I scrambled to think of something to protect her.

"She's just repeating what I've said," I blurted.

Mya elbowed me in the ribs. "Hush," she whispered.

Father's brows furrowed as he stared me down. "I never doubted you were the instigator of this insolence. The question is, how should you be punished?" He looked over my shoulder. "Along with the other traitors with you?"

CHAPTER 17
CATE

Insomnia. I don't recommend it. Awakening from nightmares to peer at the clock only to find a mere thirty minutes had passed, readjusting the pillow over and over, moving the blankets off, then on again. Miserable. I couldn't miss Father's departure by oversleeping. One last goodbye. No—not goodbye—those words were too painful. I just couldn't let him leave without wishing him well. Not that whatever I did or didn't do would make any difference to his safety. The feeling of helplessness twisted in and out of my broken dreams.

The sun had not yet peeked over the horizon when I stumbled into the stables, bleary-eyed. "Any word on Daniel?" I asked a groom.

"No, Your Highness."

Anxiety over what happened to him ate at my insides. If King Dryden didn't agree to assist in the operation, Daniel must know he's welcome here, even if he returns empty-handed? I should have made that clear before he left. Now I'm wondering if he doubts me. Doubts *us*. The horrible scenarios that might explain his absence circled endlessly: an Ember ambush, eaten by crocodiles (did they have those here?), or simply choosing to stay in Terra. With Emily.

Father stood at the end of the barn with a few other Caelum soldiers, including General Griffin. Alana patted a horse nearby, presumably also here to send them off. She waved me over.

As I approached, I noticed she wasn't wearing her typical black dress. Instead, she was garbed in an olive-green tunic and leggings. Why did *she* get to wear pants?

"There's been a last-minute change," Alana said.

"I know, Daniel didn't make it. We're having to take up the slack with more Caelum soldiers."

"That's correct, but I was meaning that General Griffin and I are both joining the group."

My hand flew to my mouth. The general didn't surprise me, but Alana? What about my training? One more person I cared about in danger. I wanted to argue. To insist she stayed. But that would be selfish, and they needed her more than me.

"Take care of Father." I surprised her by wrapping my arms around her waist in a hug. "And yourself."

"I will." She patted my back rather stiffly, as if she hadn't had human contact in a long time.

"Practice while I'm gone. Clear your mind of all those tumbling thoughts and you will master your powers. I expect you'll greet us with a rain shower when we arrive home."

I smiled and pretended to have heard encouragement instead of expectations. "Better bring your raincoat." *Like, maybe in the next century.*

I strode over to Father and hugged him, too. I remembered a time when he insisted that princesses never showed their emotions in public. But he squeezed me back and kissed me on the cheek. He'd come a long way.

"Be safe," I whispered.

"You too."

"Me? I'll just be here. Hanging out." I pulled a face.

"I still worry about you. Suppose that means I've taken to this fatherhood thing."

Despite the morning chill and dire circumstances, warm fuzzies enveloped me. "The only thing you need to worry about is Baron Graftonberg annoying me to death." I tried to smile.

"Cate. Show some respect, please."

"Fine," I mumbled, the blanket of father-daughter goodness evaporating. What did he see in that guy, anyway?

"Sir," General Griffin interrupted, "we're ready."

The king nodded and turned to leave the stable.

Butterflies stirred and my arm hairs climbed upward. "Wait." The feeling that something bad was going to happen itched under my skin. He pivoted back, and I ran into his arms.

"I love you." I had never said it. Hadn't even been sure I'd felt it before now. But the thought of losing him…

"I love you too," he said, his voice scratchy. "You'll see me soon."

We broke apart and I saluted, not sure what to do with all these messy feelings. "I'll hold down the fort."

He sighed at my American colloquialism. I shouldn't have annoyed him, but awkward me didn't know any other way.

The band of twenty left me waving broadly in a rather unprincess manner. Next on the agenda: practice, as I'd promised Alana. Yet my feet took me to Mocha. We greeted each other like old friends. She enjoyed a neck rub and cocked her head for better access.

Footsteps approached. "You've bonded." Charlie watched us fondly.

I smiled up at him. "I think we have."

"It's about time she flies with you."

I'd been looking forward to the day I could trust her enough to fly and return to me. She'd practiced on a tether with Charlie but hadn't yet been given free rein. Anything to get my mind off… everything else.

We exited to the field outside the mews with Mocha perched on my glove-covered hand, a pouch slung over my shoulder containing treats. She snatched up an offered piece, and I laughed. "Don't get too excited and distracted when you see the live version of that out there. You ready? Come back to me when I raise my arm, just like Charlie taught you."

He unclipped the leather leash. Mocha flapped her wings, flying higher and higher, soaring over the field. My heart lifted as if I were up there with her.

"She loves it," I called.

"Don't let her go too long. Put that arm up and signal her home," Charlie urged.

Mocha spotted me and glided downward, landing safely on the glove, gentler than expected. She gobbled the proffered treat, and I showered her with praise. She preened under my approval.

We tried a few more times, letting her fly longer with each attempt. She acted proud as a strutting male peacock, fluffing her feathers and pushing out her chest. I could sense her happiness. Not exactly sure how, but I did.

"Good job today," Charlie said after we'd deposited her in the pen. "Next, we'll try messages back and forth between us."

"Really? Like a homing pigeon?"

He chuckled. "Don't let her hear you call her a pigeon, but yes."

After grabbing breakfast, I traipsed outside again to train. Years ago, I took piano lessons, then never wanted to practice because I wasn't naturally gifted. The constant struggle took the fun out. If I had stuck with it, I might have enjoyed it because, as Dad always said, everything worth doing takes diligence. I should *want* to work on my powers, but I felt talentless—ironic because I actually possessed the one skill nobody else had… if I didn't turn out to be a one-hit-wonder. That or I'd nearly die every time I used it like at The Great Battle. I might not be so lucky again.

After multiple attempts to clear my mind, I detected the energy and was able to grow a dandelion, start a gentle breeze, and even produce a dew drop on a leaf. It wasn't as dramatic as when I imagined kissing Daniel, but I avoided those thoughts. Today it would only derail my concentration.

I stayed until sundown, mostly focusing on feeling the surrounding power instead of using it. Getting used to the ebbs and flows, how the sunlight affected it, and the plants absorbed it. I thought of chemistry class and wondered if the energy consisted of all the molecules floating around that we couldn't see. I should have paid more attention to Einstein.

When I rounded the corner near the stables to access the back entrance of the castle, the sun dipped below the horizon, leaving a pink-orange glow. Still in tune with the energy, the power bloomed more vibrant than usual. Alana had always insisted sunrise was the best time for detecting it, but sunset worked too. I rolled my eyes at my absent teacher, who demanded I wake up way before any teenager had the right. Except, something felt different. Almost… joyful?

Daniel.

The air buzzed; the same sensation I'd become accustomed to experiencing when near the prince. I searched the courtyard and found him and a group of soldiers riding up the hill. I ran to meet them, heedless of an undignified approach. Daniel slid from his horse, which I barely registered as not being Raven, before he wrapped his arms around me.

"I'm so sorry we're late." He squeezed me nearly too tight, almost desperately.

"Daniel," a female voice called. "Hate to break up this reunion, but…"

I gaped at Mya standing near us, a smirk displayed across her features.

"Cate. Good to see you," she said.

I had no idea why she'd come—and dressed as a man—but I was happy to have her. Two women in pants in one day—maybe there was hope for my jeans yet.

"You too. Welcome to Caelum Castle," I said, remembering my manners.

Dev stood next to her, his height towering over Mya's petite frame. "We ran into a few issues."

Daniel rolled his eyes. "Yeah, just a few."

"I saved the day," Mya interrupted, her dimples showing.

"You might have." Daniel heaved a sigh, and I now noticed the black smudges beneath his lashes.

I linked my arm around his. "Father left this morning with a group of soldiers and Alana. If you come inside, I can show you the maps. I know the route they planned. That is, if you want to catch up with them?"

"That's why we're here." Mya had a bounce in her step, much more refreshed than Daniel.

"Not why *you're* here." Dev came up beside Mya and jostled her with his elbow.

She raised her brows at him. Dev shook his head and looked at me as if to say, "You believe this?"

I didn't, actually. Mya and I weren't particularly close. I hadn't seen her since I left Terra Castle in a rainstorm of my own making after I thought Daniel betrayed me. I always wondered how much she'd known. If she'd been an accomplice with her father.

"Let's look at the maps so we can get back on the road," Daniel said.

"I don't think so, Big Brother," Mya shot back. "You've hardly slept in the last six days. We should spend the night, then we'll be ready to travel tomorrow. You'll catch up to King Aldridge within a couple of days."

The Caelum group had already left a day later than planned, which meant they wouldn't dawdle. But Daniel's fatigue, based on the amount of his weight leaning on my shoulder, told me a break would be best.

"Mya's right," I said. "I'll have someone show your men to the guest quarters. And you three, let's have dinner brought into my father's office. We can eat, review the maps, then bed."

"Who am I to argue with not one, but two princesses," Dev said, hastening to the castle.

We convened in King Aldridge's study. Dev descended on the food. Daniel seemed almost too tired to chew. I tempted him with a few of his favorites, including venison sandwiches laced with creamy herbed cheese, and juneberry tarts, the kind that left purple juice and custard cream dripping down your chin. He swallowed a few more bites at my urging. After they'd memorized the route, Dev and Mya retired to their rooms, while Daniel remained slumped in his chair

"I'm sorry we missed the deadline," he mumbled. "You must have been worried. I figured you'd be mad."

"Why would I? I knew you would do everything you could to not be late." In truth, I'd run the gamut of emotions, with anxiety topping the list. "Must have been some trip."

"I should tell you about it."

Curiosity piqued, but he looked so exhausted that I stood and held out my hand to help him up. "Another time. You need to rest."

I pulled him to me. The energy around us pleasantly hummed. He placed a gentle kiss on my lips, which spiked the buzz, turning it into something more. I gripped tighter, needing the closeness, the solidness of him in my arms. He trailed hot kisses across my skin, each one erupting a delicious shiver.

"I missed you," I whispered.

"Thank you for trusting me. I don't deserve it." He traced fingers along my neck where it meets the collarbone, my exposed skin tingling at his touch. "I try not to make the same mistake twice."

I slid my palms into his hands. "Come on. I'll walk you to your room."

I meandered toward my suite, wobbly after depositing Daniel with a steamy kiss. His exhaustion would have endangered the mission if they continued their journey tonight. He needed sleep. Still, I couldn't shake the niggling feeling that I'd pushed him into the wrong decision, and they might not make it there in time, putting Father, Alana, Lucas, and the others in further danger.

CHAPTER 18

DANIEL

A pounding on my door woke me from a dreamless sleep. The moon still shone through the windows I'd been too exhausted to cover the night before. Dev waltzed in, the sconces from the hall illuminating his figure.

"Everything okay?" I rubbed my puffy eyes.

"The rest of us have been packing up supplies. We let the prince get his beauty rest, but it's time to go."

I should feel embarrassed they were working without me, but gratitude for the extra sleep was all I could muster. I didn't detect annoyance from Dev, so it was my own hang-ups over not wanting to seem entitled rather than any slight.

In the courtyard, Cate stood surrounded by my men, handing out packages wrapped in twine, presumably breakfast for the road. She tucked them into saddlebags, and I could tell they were as charmed by her as me. Hugo's face turned pink at something she said, her long honey-brown hair catching the moonlight and drifting across his arm when she reached over to slide a bundle into his bag. She was so beautiful. My heart kicked up at the sight of her, yet ached at the thought of leaving.

Mya also helped organize, thankfully dressed in a gown and cloak, rather than a soldier's uniform. I assumed she would attempt to cajole me into letting her go with us this morning. Fortunately, she'd gained some sense. The two heirs to the Terran crown together on a dangerous mission—pure lunacy.

I had to admit, she saved us from Father yesterday. Just when it seemed he would drag us home and throw everyone into the dungeon, he'd had a change of heart. Mya must have influenced his emotions, otherwise the king would have never conceded. Or, as I'd suspected my entire childhood, she was the favorite. I shook my head, wondering how often she'd wheedled her way with me. I had braced myself to be steadfast this morning, but it appeared she was actually acting responsibly, and we wouldn't have to argue.

She glanced up from her task and smiled at me. *Ears burning, Mya?* I strode over to the group.

"Looks like we're almost ready," I said.

"No thanks to you, sleepyhead." Mya grinned, her dimples catching the attention of several soldiers.

I ignored her comment. "Thanks for not putting up a fight about not going with us. Cate could use a friend."

"No problem," she said.

Cate strolled up beside us. "What's no problem?"

"Mya staying here with you."

"Of course she can. I'll take care of her."

Not what I'd meant. If anyone needed taking care of, it was Cate. Her anxiety, coupled with her father, Lucas, and me all in danger, weighed heavy. She'd tried to explain her anxiety once to me as a hamster wheel of thoughts that kept spinning. Unfortunately, I'd never seen a hamster, or its wheel, which led to a detailed description of the creatures and their cages. I found it quite appalling, both for her and the rodent.

"Can I speak to you alone for a moment?" Cate asked me.

I glanced around. The crew would have to wait a few more minutes. "Sure."

She led me away, but not before Dev shouted, "Hurry it up, lover boy," which led to cheers, flushing Cate's cheeks a lovely shade of pink.

We turned the corner of the castle, out of sight of the unruly soldiers.

"I want to say goodbye. In case…" she trailed off.

"Stop that thought. You'll see me soon." I kissed her forehead.

"I have to tell you something." She pulled away.

My stomach flip-flopped. Those words were never good news.

"I need you to come back."

It was nice to hear, but hardly earth-shattering material. "I will, I promise. Try not to worry." I'd adjusted my vernacular with her to avoid saying *stop* worrying. It frustrated her as an insurmountable task.

"No, I mean, I need you for my training."

I'm sure the surprise showed on my face. And it was a bit hurtful, as I hoped she needed me for more than that.

She opened her mouth, then closed it, biting her lip. "I'm better at my powers when you're with me. Actually… I can hardly do anything unless I'm thinking about you. Or near you."

Her gaze fixated on the dirt path. I detected embarrassment and anxiousness rising from her, though I still couldn't puzzle out exactly what she meant by needing me.

Cate took my hands. "Let me try something."

We stood in silence, her cool fingers wrapping around mine. Cate's eyes closed. Nothing happened. I searched the ground for growth, strained to feel a breeze, but all stood still. Eerily quiet. Until a tiny drop of rain hit my forehead. Then another. A fine mist drifted over us, barely enough to dampen hair. It was the first time I'd witnessed her creating moisture since The Great Battle. It took effort not to whoop with enthusiasm, but I waited until she was done. I monitored her breathing, the pulse at her neck, the subtle flush of her cheeks beneath the wet sheen, to be sure she wouldn't faint.

"I'm good," she assured me, opening her eyes and seeing my concern. "In fact, amazing." A wide grin spread across her beautiful face.

I, on the other hand, grew uneasy. For the first time, I had doubts about going on this mission. What if she truly couldn't use her power unless I was there? She was our greatest weapon, and if this plan went south, I might not make it back. I'd always assumed that if I was killed in battle, life would go on without me—that it wouldn't change the outcome of the war. My safety now mattered more than it had mere moments ago.

"I thought I could do it," she said, seemingly oblivious to my internal struggle. "Thank you, Daniel. For being there for me. I don't know what I'd do without you." She kissed my lips softly. "I love you. Be safe." Her hands slid down my shoulders, then gently pushed against my chest toward the courtyard. "You have to go."

"I love you too." I leaned in and kissed her one more time before wheeling toward the others.

The pit in my stomach grew. Something about this whole mission felt off, and it wasn't just the teetering extra weight she'd added.

Mya and Cate stood arm in arm as they watched us leave. Cate had experienced too many goodbyes as of late. A pang of guilt resounded when I thought of my sister. She'd spent far too much time without an older brother. When we returned, perhaps she'd like to stay with Cate and me in Caelum for a while. At some point, I would have to return to Terra for at least part of the year. Dread lowered my shoulders. I'd think about that another time. Besides, there were more pressing matters.

The meeting place, located farther north, halfway between our kingdoms and the Embers' main encampment, would take seven days if traveled at a careful pace with reasonable rest. King Aldridge had departed a day late, leaving them six. Since we were another day behind them, it meant pushing our horses more than I'd prefer with minimal breaks and short nights.

I'd become soft during the peaceful time at Caelum Castle following The Great Battle, and now I was unused to multiple days in the saddle. We had a long trip in front of us.

Around five, Dev pulled up next to me. "We could use a quick breather."

The breakfast Cate sent had long since worn off, leaving us tired and hungry. We'd given the horses a moment at a stream hours ago, but that had been the extent of our rest.

"All right. Everyone take fifteen," I called.

My bones creaked like an old man when I dismounted my roan gelding. He didn't fit as well as Raven—didn't anticipate my movements. We pilfered through our bags for a snack and gulped from waterskins. Most of the men paced the clearing, not eager to sit again until after sunset. A soldier hovered near the tree line, catching my focus. Not smart to wander off alone.

He backed away from something, hands held up in surrender. I nudged Dev's arm and pointed. The man froze, but the foliage obscured whatever frightened him.

I drew my sword and signaled a few to follow. We formed an arc, curving behind where I assumed the threat hid in the brush. The trees thickened, continuing to block my vision as I crept as fast and noiselessly as possible.

A break in the vegetation revealed a massive spotted tree leopard, crouching, and ready to attack. When the soldier came into view, my blood turned cold.

Mya stood in her borrowed uniform wide-eyed, still attempting to back away from the big cat. Big was an understatement. Tree leopards, roughly the size of tigers, typically made their home well north of here. I'd only seen one once. Notorious for their surprise attacks, usually only the carcass of whatever it had eaten, human or animal, was found. I didn't have time to be angry at her for following us, or to even consider a rational plan, except to lure the predator from her.

I snatched up a rock and threw it into the forest. The cat's head followed the sound, but it remained in place. When that failed to work, I took off into the trees, making as much noise as possible to lead it away from everyone else.

I was fast. One of the swiftest in Terra, plus I could manipulate the brush to bend at my will, clearing the path. But outrun a tree leopard? I'd certainly never had the opportunity to put it to the test.

My ears strained to hear the animal behind me. Like any good cat, it loved a chase. Even if the toy was human. Climbing obviously wouldn't help. Water wouldn't work either, as they were known to enjoy a romp in the river. I might be able to communicate with it and ask it to stand down as Cate had done those months ago with the wolf. Although, considering the speed it pursued, this seemed unlikely.

Peters. We'd brought him along solely for his skill with animals. I'd taken off like an idiot trying to save the day instead of following his lead. And where did it get me? Running through the forest with a giant cat on my tail.

My muscles stretched as I pushed them to the limit, my nearly healed sprained ankle twinged, and all the while I concentrated on thrashing the vegetation back into place as I passed. The sounds of the beast crashing through the brush remained too close for comfort. Blood pounded on my eardrums and cold sweat dripped down my spine, the realization that running was futile setting in. I could try to lead it back toward the others, which would be risky, as the whole point of this goose chase was to keep them safe. Peters hadn't been one of the soldiers to follow us into the woods, but surely, he'd be searching now.

I circled back, listening for any signs of the group. A felled tree lay ahead, its branches extending in every direction. The panther's paws thumped steps behind. Climbing over or going around the limbs wasn't an option. The leopard would be on me in moments.

I braked and turned to face the animal, praying it wouldn't keep charging. It gracefully halted and crouched, muscles at its haunches rippling under a shiny coat. The stance reminded me of Mya's favorite barn cat preparing to leap onto a mouse. Dappled sunlight gleamed off its thick, black-and-orange fur with golden eyes trained on mine, every powerful muscle tensed in anticipation for the kill.

"I don't want to hurt you." I suspected the feeling wasn't mutual. Connecting with the leopard would be tricky. It came down to dominance. This cat stretched bigger and moved faster than me. It would have to decide whether to give deference to me or not, probably based more on a whim than anything concrete.

It growled and paced, only a few steps between us. Carefully, I sent a gentle rumble into the ground, the energy responding and pulsing beneath the earth. The leopard paused, never taking its eyes off me. Now that I'd stopped tearing through the forest, I could focus on sensing the cat's emotions. They reminded me of when Cate missed lunch. What did she call it?

Hangry.

Not good… and it was well past dinner time.

CHAPTER 19
LUCAS
FIFTY-TWO DAYS AGO

I trudged to Molly with a mixture of defeat and thankfulness to be alive. I hated war. Hated the Embers for putting my back against the wall time after time to kill or be killed. And I hated that they tore apart families like Grace's, and all the others who'd fallen by their hands. The destruction they'd caused on the land resulted in climate implications and would take hundreds of years to recover. If ever. I'd heard about the depletion of rainforest on earth, of particular interest to Caelumites as much of the same occurred here. I'd read more about it when in England—the melting icecaps, the hurricanes, the heat. We didn't have the same pollution problems, although the fires led to unclean air, and the loss of forests had started to take its toll. The Embers must be stopped. I wished that didn't equate to killing them, but it was all anyone could do for our survival.

Molly bounded happily toward me, but soon sensed my mood. She placed her head on my shoulder and sighed a steamy breath, the hair curling at the nape of my neck from the humid heat.

"Thanks, Mol." I leaned into her. "No sign of Grace. But I took care of 'em—they won't bother us."

Our supplies didn't take long to pack up. I'd gone through the Embers' camp, pilfered a few things, and gathered their weapons. Molly and I once again headed northeast toward the Purple Mountains. We flew over swaths of burned forest, arced around known

Ember dwellings, and found safe places to camp near streams which allowed time for both of us to hunt and forage. Days passed without incident. Molly's dive-bombing antics had long since tired, and we grew weary of the trip and the constant threat of enemy territory. We still hadn't come upon any dragons.

The air turned crisp. Elevation had slowly crept up on us. The mountains at the far north rose in four tiers, with plains or forests between. The first, the Reds, relatively short, held Ember encampments in the valleys between it and the next incline, the Blue. The Purple Mountains earned their name from the shadow cast over them by the final White Range.

The White Mountains towered so tall they'd never been crested. Too high for even a dragon to cross, the air simply too thin and cold. No one really knew what the other side held as they stretched across the northern borders of our lands from east to west.

I once dreamed of becoming an explorer as a child, though now I understood the loneliness of that life, far from family and friends. I longed to share a cup of coffee with Cate or a scone with my mother by the fire. A bowl of her stew could warm a man to his toes, the best in the village with her expertise in herbs. I pictured her laugh, her gray-streaked chestnut hair dancing around her face as if it sensed her joy. I hadn't seen her since before leaving for England to find Cate. Homesickness panged through my chest, and I vowed she would be my first stop after returning.

The Reds finally rose in the distance, the other mountains framing behind like solemn adults watching over their children. We camped in the shadow of one of the larger peaks. Fire or drought had destroyed much of the land, but we managed to find a clump of trees and brush, tucking ourselves beneath them.

"We're getting close, Molly." I stroked under her chin the way she liked it. "You ready to meet some more dragons?"

I could sense her resignation, lids drooping over her golden eyes. One would think she'd want to connect with her own kind, but her entire life the only association with them had been fear and anger from the humans she'd grown up with. Including me.

"You can do it." I counted on her to help with communicating, but trepidation trembled beneath my fingers. She curled around me, and I nestled into her warmth. "Love you, Mol."

She responded with a soft sigh. The guilt of putting her in danger gnawed at my conscience. If anything happened to her, I'd never forgive myself. Eventually, the rhythmic motion of her breathing lulled me to a restless sleep with dreams full of vengeful dragons chasing us into a wall of flames.

The next morning, we doubled back so Molly could gain the height necessary to cross the first mountain. Waiting in the valley below could sit an Ember dwelling, and we wouldn't know until we reached the other side of the peak. If we remained high, it shouldn't be a problem as long as they didn't spot a rider atop Molly. To my knowledge, the other dragons hadn't trusted the Embers enough to let them astride.

Far below, around a hundred hut-like structures dotted the landscape, smoke extending from crude chimneys. Many Embers had formed these smaller settlements, breaking from the larger group in the west, because of the scarcity of resources from uncontrolled fires.

I tucked deep into Molly's neck. "Keep going, girl." We banked farther east to avoid flying directly over them and hoped to cross over the next range before nightfall. It wouldn't be safe to camp in this valley, but it was a long trip for Molly. Not only were the mountains tall, they were wide, with multiple crests between us and the nearest landing point. We climbed higher and higher. My cloak and scarf might as well have been flimsy paper against the biting wind. Molly's wings pumped harder, but the gale made it seem as though we were at a standstill. Snow started to fall, whipping against us.

Below, a ledge in the cliffs appeared as a relatively flat place to land. "Let's rest," I called, squeezing my knees and directing her downward. She dove, the wind catching her wings, increasing our speed like a descending arrow. She pulled up just in time, and we skidded across the slippery surface, banking hard into the icy wall of the mountain.

"Maybe we can wait out the storm." We huddled on the ledge, using the wall to partially shield us from the tempest. Poor Molly's head drooped in exhaustion. I found some dried meat, but she only nibbled at it.

"Come on, Mol, you gotta eat." I shoved some more toward her. She chewed slowly and gazed south. Toward home.

"I miss it too." I leaned against her. Her usual warmth wouldn't penetrate the cold, and I shivered. She obliged with a steamy, warm breath. We'd have to be careful, because if dragons became cold enough, they could lose the fire within their bellies, which made me wonder why the others had chosen the Purple Mountains. Perhaps their nests were at the base rather than the upper elevations.

Instead of slowing, the snow increased, beating upon us as a full-fledged blizzard. With visibility roughly a meter in front, our only option was to wait. Molly tried to warm me with her breath, and I worried that each exhale drew out her inner warmth. We had to get off this mountain before we both froze to death.

"I don't know how much longer we can delay," I shouted through the storm.

Her resolution to fight came through strong, the determination echoing in my head. She didn't want to be turned into an icicle any more than me.

I fumbled for rope in the saddlebag and tied myself to her, wrapping it around her belly and over my legs. I already wore every stitch of clothing I'd brought in layers for warmth. Nothing left to do but take the risk.

"I believe in you." I hugged her and leaned low across her neck.

Molly pushed off into the abyss. I knew we had to fly higher to pass over the peaks, but they weren't visible through the snowstorm. Muscles contracted and heaved beneath my knees as Molly fought against the raging winds. We tipped and tossed, wavered, and flew higher leaving my chest burning in the thin air.

One moment we couldn't see anything but white, and the next the sun shone, the sky now that ice-blue only seen on the coldest of winter days. We'd flown above the clouds and out of the storm. The Blues weren't visible below, but that meant we were above them and could safely fly. In the distance, the Purple Mountains towered like icebergs peeking out of a stormy sea.

"We made it!" I patted her in relief. She was exhausted, but able to glide as a momentary respite. Finally, when I decided we had flown far enough, Molly dove into the valley between the two ranges. Numbness took over, and I barely felt the ripping winds from the plunge. The blizzard hadn't traveled to this side of the mountain, so aside from a few clouds and fog, visibility improved. The air turned warmer, the ground below a patchwork of grass, dirt, and snow. We soared lower, and I could feel Molly's relief to glide rather than fight the storm, her breath exhaling in a long sigh beneath my knees.

And then they came into view. In the eastern distance—dragons.

CHAPTER 20
DANIEL

The tree panther and I remained in a standoff. Me: wondering if it would decide I'm more trouble than I'm worth. Cat: wondering if I was tasty. I sent another reverberation through the ground. It backed off a few steps and snorted.

"That's right. Go find something else to eat. There's a herd of drundles back that way." I gestured south.

Apparently drundle wasn't to its taste because it crouched into the pounce position, a low growl emanating from its throat. I steadied my sword.

"You don't want me to use this." Nor did I want him to use those giant fangs. I felt 75 percent sure I'd move my blade faster than it, but one-in-four odds of becoming dinner didn't suit me.

The leopard gradually lowered its backside to the ground, cocking its head to the side appraisingly. Swirling emotions rose from it at an ever-changing pace, though I sensed some level of relaxation from the panther. I slowly blinked. I'd read once that to a cat, blinking showed a sign of trust. The yellow eyes returned my gesture.

I wanted to shout in relief, and instead, lowered my sword. "I'm gonna leave now." The felled tree blocked an easy exit, so I awkwardly sidestepped around it. His watchful gaze followed every movement.

Finally, I turned the corner and almost ran into Peters. *Now* he shows. I touched my index finger to my lips and gestured from the leopard toward camp.

"Why did you run?" he whispered. "They love a good chase."

"I was trying to get it away from Mya."

His gaze fell to the dirt, and he shook his head, the ponytail at the base of his neck swaying. Whether it was due to my stupidity or Mya's was anybody's guess. He probably had serious doubts regarding the heirs to the throne. Well, let him. He wasn't nearby to help, so what else was I supposed to do?

"I'm surprised," Peters interrupted my thoughts.

"By what?"

"I've never heard of a tree leopard this far south. Not his usual territory."

"Maybe he's lost?" The cat seemed perfectly capable of figuring out where to go, then again, what did I know?

"I'm not sure." He crinkled his broad brow. "Something feels off. The drundles, now this. I'll keep an eye out and give you updates."

We regrouped, and I groaned at how low the sun hovered on the horizon. More time lost. Mya sat next to Dev on a boulder chatting as if she hadn't a care in the world. My blood pressure rose with every stomp toward them.

She smiled up at me sweetly. I narrowed my eyes at her to convey, *Don't be messing with my feelings,* which of course I couldn't say aloud. Families needed their secrets. Even from best friends like Dev.

"How did you get here?" I asked.

"I followed you. After you left, I made a quick change, wrote a note for Cate, and hopped on my horse, which I saddled early this morning. While you were sleeping, I might add. It wasn't hard. We studied the maps together last night."

"At least you didn't involve Cate in this nonsense. What are you going to do when Father finds out?"

"I'll figure it out." She shrugged, then stood. "Don't send me away. You need me."

Her words soured my stomach. More like *Lucas* needed her. "Well, I can't ship you back now. That panther is hangry."

She wrinkled her nose. "What?"

"Hangry. It means hungry—and… never mind. Let's just go." My anger boiled near the surface, which I'm sure she could sense. More conversation would be useless.

We rode a few more hours, cutting off into a main thoroughfare for easier riding in the dark. Cate had given us portable flameless lanterns that helped guide our way. The night passed uneventfully, as did the next day. We found signs of King Aldridge and his crew but had not yet caught up to them.

One morning Mya and I rode next to each other a distance from others. "So, what do you hope to gain by endangering both of the Terran heirs at the same time?" I asked, finally able to keep my cool enough to have a civil conversation with her.

"No matter how careful we are, Father will outlive us. Don't you think?"

I snorted. "Probably. Out of spite."

"Exactly." She smiled weakly. "I'm tired of being on the sidelines. I love a pretty gown, but I want to be more than the belle of the ball. Why can't I be both?"

Of course, she was more than her looks, but the risk of being here untrained outweighed any "help" she might provide. At this point, telling her was useless. When—if—we made it back I'd set her up with self-defense classes, maybe even military strategy.

"I have an overwhelming feeling that I need to be here. I don't know why. I just *know*."

Was she some kind of prophet now? My sweet and frivolous sister was either delusional or had more depth than anyone credited her. "Ever happened before?"

"I don't think so. Not like this. I've been directionless, honestly. This is the first time I've felt any real purpose."

"So, what's your plan? When we get there, I mean."

"Stay hidden but be close enough to influence their feelings if things start to go south. Maybe I can turn it around. Change their minds." Her shoulder inched up in a half-shrug that didn't exactly exude confidence.

"Like you did with Father on the way to Caelum?" I had to both admire and fear her for that ability.

"One can hope." She fingered the reins nervously.

"Does it work all the time?" Now that I'd gotten over the shock of it, this talent intrigued me.

She scrunched her nose. "I can only smooth their emotions one way or another. Agitate or calm, that kind of thing. If their mind is made up, it usually isn't helpful."

Wasted on the social scene, her power could prove useful in the future. Although King Dryden would only be too happy to use her to his advantage. Which would, in theory, be to Terra's benefit. What our father wanted for the kingdom and what I thought best often didn't match. Mya must have felt the same by keeping her skill a secret. "Can we make a pact?" I asked.

She arched a single brow in skepticism, a skill that apparently wasn't genetic as both of mine always rose together. She might suspect I'd attempt to use her as Father inevitably would. "We tell no one else about our powers. No. One." I wasn't sure who she'd inform, but I wanted her to know her secret was safe.

"Agreed." She held out a hand to shake. I didn't take it.

"And..." I extended my arm, not quite touching her. "You never use your power on me or Cate."

She dropped her hand. "But you're so fun."

Heat crept under my collar. How many times had she manipulated me?

She laughed. "Deal."

We shook and I knew she must feel the waves of relief billowing from me like steam from a kettle.

Peters rode up beside us. "Something is off with the animals."

We slowed to let a group of deer pass over the road, the fifth such gathering in the last couple of hours. I'd never been in this part of Caelum. The wildlife was plentiful with colorful birds sounding overhead, jackalopes bounding this way and that, and wumbeasts scurrying into burrows. At least there was plenty to eat for predators other than us. I was always able to weakly sense a creature's emotions. It didn't come easily, and usually only occurred when they had strong feelings toward me. This was Peter's strongest gift. "Off how?"

"They're spooked about something. And why are so many headed south?"

They did seem to be moving in the opposite direction as us. Apprehension buzzed under my skin. A flock of birds careened overhead. "I guess we're going to find out."

We smelled it before we saw anything. The acrid stench of smoke. Another accidental forest fire from the Embers, or something more sinister? We still hadn't caught up to King Aldridge. Did the treaty happen early with both parties arriving before the agreed time? They shouldn't be that far ahead of us. We were on track to reach the meeting point tonight, on schedule, after riding hard for days. Fortunately, we hadn't experienced any more major mishaps.

Dev rode beside me. "I don't like this." His horse whinnied and balked, demonstrating his unhappiness with the haze.

"Me neither." But there was nothing else to do except keep going. My gut churned with nerves, and my skin crawled with an uneasiness of something bad waiting ahead.

I sensed Mya's worry next to me. Her eyes held panic, and for the first time, she must be realizing the possible consequences of her decision.

The smoke thickened, blanketing us in a hazy brown fog. The air stood still, which would keep fires from spreading too swiftly, but left us traveling through the miasma. Wetted cloths wrapped around our mouths and noses served as makeshift masks. We all carried fire-resistant drundle cloaks in our bags and readied them for use, draping them across our saddles for quick access.

The meet-up point was still several kilometers away when we came upon the fire. It blazed through the trees and blocked our path. King Aldridge's whereabouts were still unknown.

"Does this mean the treaty is off?" Mya asked.

It certainly appeared that way, though we needed to find Cate's father first.

I sent Erikson up the tallest tree, far enough from the blaze to not be burned, and hopefully where he could see something. A breeze now shuffled the leaves, indicating the smoke may have cleared farther up.

"The whole place is blackened to a crisp," he called. "Wait, I see them!"

"Where?"

"They're inside a circle of fire."

My heart sank. We would have to find a way through. The Embers had leveled the meeting location so there would be nowhere to hide. All our schemes of a trap were now burned to ash. We'd planned to use Erikson to obscure us behind greenery for a surprise attack. Now, anything green would draw attention rather than conceal.

"The Embers," Erikson yelled. "They're headed toward the king.

"How many?"

"Too many."

CHAPTER 21
LUCAS
FORTY-EIGHT DAYS AGO

"You think they saw us?" I asked Molly as we landed on the partially frozen turf. "Yeah, I'm not sure either." As usual, I talked to myself as much as Molly—it felt reassuring to converse.

"Let's wait here and see what happens. Rest up." We did need the break after the mountain storm, especially Molly, though what I didn't mention aloud were the nerves gnawing at my insides like an angry wumbeast. This is why we'd come. To convince the dragons to take our side; at the very least not join with the Embers. Yet even after all this time on the road, I still hadn't figured out how we'd go about it. I sensed Molly's apprehension—her haunches tight, head drooping. Perhaps she felt my nervousness and we fed off each other. Not for the first time, I wished we could have a real conversation. A proper strategy meeting right about now would be in order.

The dragons in the distance circled nearer. Coincidence? Unfortunately, not. They loomed closer and closer. The time had come, prepared or not. I stood next to Molly, hand on her back in mock reassurance, and waited for them to arrive.

Three landed, tufts of grass spraying under their talons, while a few others circled overhead. All were larger than Molly, with several breeds represented. One shared her green-gray scales and orange patches beneath the wings, breath coming in bursts of steam. A rusty-red colored beast with sharp, spikey spines crowning his head and extending in a lethal trail down his back stood next to the first. The last was blue-gray and the largest, though somehow the least terrifying with smooth, seal-like scales so small they blended in a seamless weave. This one, a female—not sure how I knew, but I did—had enormous wings and an oval head devoid of sharp projectiles, somewhat like a winged brontosaurus I'd seen pictures of in books. She appeared to be the leader, standing in front of the others with cat-eyes an unusual deep brown. She approached us with surprising grace for her size, towering overhead.

I stood my ground as the two dragons bent their faces together. Molly shook her head, a human trait she'd learned. How much could she really understand after growing up without her kind? Were memories triggered from when she was a baby? The big dragon stomped her foot and flapped her wings, hovering just above the ground.

Molly tipped low, an indicator I should climb on her back. Prickly unease wrapped itself around my middle. Barely waiting for me to secure myself, she rose. We met the other dragons above and followed them east.

"They want us to go with them?" I asked her, ready to give the signal to reverse course and bolt back over the mountain. The dragons had done nothing to harm us, yet the unsettling feeling that we were flying into danger persisted.

Molly's head bobbed in affirmation. We flew for several kilometers, passing more dragons than I'd ever witnessed. They used to assist people at Caelum Castle up and down the steep cliffs, but I was a young child when they defected to the Embers, and my memories were vague. Riddled with caves, the Purple Mountains, as it turned out, provided perfect dragon dwellings. They roosted on ledges, sunning themselves in the afternoon light. Little ones played, swooping and diving, leaving me with a pang of sadness that Molly had missed out on this companionship.

The dragons banked toward the mouth of an enormous cave, yawing huge, the recess inside only shadows. The large dragon, Big Momma, as I started thinking of her, soared and landed inside the entrance. We dropped to the ledge but didn't enter, probably by her order because Molly made no move to follow the larger beast.

We waited. And waited. The others stayed outside, circling sentries guarding their prisoners. Sweat dripped down my back, even though the air remained crisp, leaving me clammy. Molly shifted from foot to foot, impatient, her jittery nerves on display. I slid off her back since it didn't appear we were going anywhere anytime soon. This seemed to give the creatures outside some peace of mind because one landed near us and proceeded to eat some kind of large rat-like creature. Maybe Molly *was* better off with me instead of here. She'd turn her nose up at eating rodents.

Big Momma returned and ushered us to follow with a flick of her enormous tail. The gaping hole in the mountainside stood wide and tall, able to fit numerous dragons inside. The shadows deepened, forcing me to fumble in the saddlebag for the portable lantern. Alcoves cratered the walls, their recesses inky, my light reflecting off the eyes of others watching, otherwise hidden in the darkness.

We traversed the uneven, rocky surface until reaching a dead end. Big Momma circled so that our backs now faced the wall. Other dragons emerged from the shadows, my light not reaching far enough to illuminate their full number. One stood in front of the rest, similar to the beast we met earlier, with the rusty color and sharp spines poking out like a bramble bush. I shone my light on the dragon, which gleamed off projectiles laddering down his spine and spraying from his face in the shape of a deadly lion's mane. He reminded me of a red version of a poisonous lionfish, a drawing of one I'd once admired framed in King Aldridge's library. The king favored anything represented by the big cats, fancying himself as Richard Lionheart, the long-dead English King.

This particular dragon-lion, now deemed Leo, loomed above as if it wanted to trample, then impale my head onto one of his spikes. I swallowed hard, resisting the urge to step backward. I couldn't retreat if I wanted to with sheer rock ascending behind. His golden eyes glared down with contempt.

I took a deep breath, then started to explain our mission without a clear idea if he could understand me, using my charming smile, honeyed words, and bowing several times on shaky legs, extolling all the virtues of dragons. I'd prefer to think I was smooth as a knight returning home from a victorious battle, but suspected I more resembled the court jester. He let me talk… and talk, all the while staring down as if he wanted to skewer and roast me over a pit for his next barbeque.

Molly finally jostled my arm to make me stop talking. Quiet descended—the only sound came from the whistling wind outside the cavern.

Molly trembled, then proceeded to communicate with short head bobs and wing motions, once nearly knocking me over. Her motions were exaggerated, overcompensating for her anxiety or their lack of understanding, not sure which. Then, she stilled.

Silence.

A dozen slitted dragon orbs peered at us like a gang of ruffians ready to pummel a posh gentleman in an alley. I hoped they would listen as the group did at the battle outside Caelum Castle. Had those dragons returned here and relayed the story? Or were they elsewhere, and these creatures hadn't heard the tale of war and death brought on by the Embers? Unlike with Molly, I couldn't decipher their feelings. Apart from menacing body language, their emotions were elusive.

This faction may enjoy the freedom of doing as they pleased, much like the Embers, rather than following the more civilized Caelum playbook. I might have underestimated their desire for free will, and I already knew the dragons believed they didn't possess it under our rule. If they hadn't witnessed the terrors the Embers were capable of, they would have no reason to care.

The eerie quiet persisted, leaving me holding my breath in anticipation. Nothing about this situation felt right. Molly agreed. She tipped low so I could mount. We were going to make a run for it. A rock wall stood behind us. And in front—a wall of angry dragon hides.

I catapulted onto her back just as a burst of fire erupted from the dragons. Molly took them by surprise and shot forward through the flames, toppling several beasts. The heat rushed into my lungs, the scorching temperature sweeping my breath in a burning wave. She furiously flew out of the cave like a mouse escaping a cat's pounce.

A glance behind revealed our head start wouldn't last. A flight of dragons emerged from the cave, Leo in the lead, Big Momma on his wing.

"Come on, Molly," I shouted. "Faster!"

I could now sense their anger and in turn, Molly's despair and fear. She believed the mission futile, which by now was pretty obvious. My stubborn streak wasn't ready to accept whatever torture they had in store for us. And neither was Molly.

I gripped her sides tighter with my knees as she attempted an evasive move by nose-diving toward the ground. They clung to our tail, easily maneuvering as Molly leveled inches from the dirt. We swerved and dodged to no avail. These dragons were bigger and faster than her. Virtually no tree to hide amongst, the expanse spread out in a flat tundra flanked by the mountain ranges, our only hope turning to cross the Blues and lose them in the clouds or snow. Instead of the raging storm we crossed earlier, only calmness remained above. The peaks shone glossy in the sun, a blanket of new whiteness, clean and innocent, as if nothing ominous ever took place the day before.

A perfect canvas for our blood.

"Up and over, Molly," I urged.

The dragons no longer just flew behind. They surrounded us on all sides, Leo at our right flank. We were pinned in. Big Momma's wings edged closer, steering us toward the spikes protruding from Leo's massive head.

"They want us to land," I shouted. Every muscle in my body coiled so tense it felt as if they might tear at the jerky movements.

Molly had other ideas with another nosedive, but Leo, too quick, shifted below and head-butted her flank on the descent. Molly screeched, a deafening high-pitched scream of terror and pain, one I'd never heard in all our days together.

Already descending, we plummeted into a tailspin, Molly's wings half-collapsed protectively against her side. I desperately gripped her spine and neck, holding on as if my life depended on it—which it very much did. I attempted to manipulate the air to slow our fall, but there was no time. I'd never witnessed Molly so out of control. We careened toward the earth at blistering speed. Fear took hold. My body, convinced these were my last moments, braced to die in a heap of broken bones on the tundra.

At the last moment, she spread her wings to break our fall, the pain when they extended palpable through our connection as if it were my own. She'd given up on escape. We hit the ground hard, my teeth knocking together. She keened again, the sound ripping me in two.

I slid from her back and rushed to unbuckle the saddle she hated, heedless of the group of dragons literally breathing fire down my back with steamy breaths, ensuring no path to escape. I could draw my sword, but there was no hope of defeating them, and I'd rather tend to Molly.

She rolled on her side after I'd removed the saddle and bags. The gash between two of her armor-like scales bled in rivulets down her side, already pooling into the dirt. I grabbed a shirt out of my bag and applied pressure to staunch the flow. Several of Leo's needled spines spanned at least a meter, but it was hard to tell how deep it had punctured her flesh.

Leo snorted a fiery breath and stomped his foot, his impatience evident. One moment I tended to Molly, the next I was lifted into the air, great orange talons digging into my side. Thoughts raced—Molly's safety, the dizzying height we'd already reached, and attempts to decipher the intentions of the angry dragon.

Big Momma bent over Molly, far below. I couldn't tell if she planned to care for her or hurt her. As an adolescent dragon, I could only hope they'd take pity and admit her to their clan. But what of me? All Leo would have to do was let me go at this elevation and I'd smash like a bug. I doubted my ability to manipulate the wind and slow my descent would be feasible at this height. He might take me as a prisoner to one of the many caves, or worse yet, deliver me to the Embers.

We climbed higher and higher; Molly now as small as the toy dragons my father used to carve for me when I was young. He'd met his fate from an Ember when I was fifteen. I had the sickening feeling I would soon join him.

We crossed the Blues, the snow sparkling in the sun as if nothing bad could come on such a beautiful, cloudless day. Leo crossed the

Reds, then descended on the other side, banking west toward a village at the foot of the mountains.

He circled over the huts and screeched to announce his arrival. Although the village appeared tiny, several hundred Embers poured out, including men, women, and children. I'd seen a few Ember females, but never their kids. The enemy kept them safely tucked away in their northern territory.

We were still several meters above the ground when Leo dropped me into a ring of Embers, who jostled to gain a better look at the dragon's prize. My shoulder and ribs ached from the unceremonious landing, and I scrambled to my feet, raising my hands above my head. No reason to expedite my demise by reaching for my sword at this point. Several whispered amongst each other, although I wasn't sure what they were debating. Death seemed certain. Perhaps they were choosing the mode of execution.

They were a motley crew—clothing rags as much as anything. Embers typically didn't take the time to dye the cloth, making it from the kuro plant which could be boiled down, dried, and loomed into a scratchy, drab tan fabric.

I caught a few snatches of words, including, "His boots." They'd saved me earlier in this journey only to betray me as a man of means now.

One of the whisperers, a slim man with a face weathered from the sun, or perhaps years of proximity to flames, came forward. "Take him to The Camp," he commanded while gesturing west.

Before I could brace myself, Leo had me in his talons. The Camp, otherwise known as Ember City, was the original colony site where hundreds of years ago, we'd banished them far north, away from our lands and people. It'd grown into an enormous city, though I'd never been. A place no one hoped to ever visit. Reports of crowding, dirtiness, constant eruptions of fire, and barren terrain had traveled through the grapevine from those lucky enough to have witnessed it and escaped alive.

Leo flew for several hours, me dangling in his grasp. Devastation manifested as swaths of incinerated forest, with gaping holes marring the landscape. A stretch of earth extended ahead, only a few remaining trees, charred and black, standing like gravestones marking the past.

The Camp must be getting close. They'd destroyed everything around it over the years, yet we continued to fly with no city in sight, only the vast wasteland. No wonder they wanted our territory. On and on we flew, my face mercilessly chapped in the wind. Leo's talons uncomfortably pinched into my sides. My feet turned numb, dangling as if I were a puppet hanging from strings. I kept picturing Molly and the blood streaming from the wound that she'd received from the very dragon who transported me.

Finally, a sea of wood and stone structures came into view. Leo banked around the outskirts, the city itself too crammed for a dragon of his size to land. Ember sentries stood at attention, swords hung at their sides, bows strapped to their backs.

The dragon dropped me again, and I landed with a thud, this time having the presence of mind to tuck and roll. The men signaled, and one jogged away, likely searching for someone in charge. If that person even existed. The Embers were notoriously unorganized and unwilling to accept leadership of any kind.

"So, how's everyone doing today?" I asked the remaining men, who glared at me in silence. "Sun's out. Nice day for a dragon ride, thanks to 'ole Leo here." I gestured to the creature who guarded my back, making escape an impossibility. Once again, I fell into my casual, friendly demeanor, my go-to when nervous. Acting as if everything would work out made me believe it. Although, my racing heart told another story.

The Embers remained silent, probably unsure what to make of me.

"So nice, in fact," I continued, ignoring their lack of response. "It would be an excellent day for a walk. I could just amble on out of here. Be on my way. Less work for you guys, ya know?" My wobbly legs might not be up to the challenge, but I'd fake anything to get out of here.

"Shut up," a squat Ember with a mean set to his jaw replied. Both his body and face were square-shaped, as if someone had built him out of wooden blocks.

"Just making friendly conversation. Sheesh." I shrugged at them dramatically, palms up as if to indicate it was no big deal. They didn't agree.

The square man approached, drawing his sword and sending the tip to rest uncomfortably against my side, where dragon claws had already punctured the skin. "I said, be quiet."

The steel point was enough to shut me up until a giant of a man with an entourage of more giants arrived. His hair was dark and trimmed short, unlike most of the scraggly Embers. Wearing a well-fitted tunic (still brown), and trousers, one might call him handsome with his chiseled jaw (if one liked that sort of thing), and rather arresting blue-gray eyes. The others looked to him with deference.

"Rowan," Square guy nodded once. "The dragon brought him in. He's dressed too nice to not be someone important."

I cursed my vanity and the shine still evident on my boots. "I'm no one. Stole these." I lifted up a foot. "Saw 'em and had to have them. The poor guy didn't know what hit 'im."

Rowan smiled congenially. Not something I'd ever witnessed from an Ember. "And where do you hail from, sir?" he asked, more formal than I'd expected.

"South. In Caelum. But I couldn't stand the war. Thought it was awful what they did to your people—bannishin' you way up north just because they're jealous of a power they don't have. I've been wandering these last few years."

I wasn't sure how much they could communicate with Leo, but if they found out I came astride Molly, it wouldn't be long before they put two-and-two together and discovered I was the Caelum knight who persuaded the dragons to leave The Great Battle.

"Is that so?" The leader smiled again, but it flickered away. "Search him."

After a rough forage through my pockets, they discovered the letter sealed from King Aldridge, declaring me as a knight of the realm. My name, also printed on the paperwork, gave me away. If they knew anything about who the king favored, and I suspected they did with their history of spies, they'd figure it out soon enough.

Someone handed the paper to Rowan; the crinkling sound as good as a death march. When he scanned it, a slow smile crept onto his lips. "Put him in the pit."

CHAPTER 22
CATE

Everyone had been gone several days, leaving me alone in Caelum Castle. Mya's note rustled in my pocket, and I pulled it out and read the words that made my insides clench with worry for the twentieth time.

Cate,

I'm sorry to abandon you, but I have left to catch up with Daniel and the rest of the soldiers for the peace treaty. It's difficult to explain, but I have a feeling that I'm meant to be there. Please don't try to follow me. I know what I'm doing.

—Mya

Daniel will be furious. She'll likely serve as a distraction rather than a help, and when I'd found the note hours later, she would have traveled too far to fetch. I liked Mya well enough and had hoped we'd use this time to get to know each other better. With Lucas missing, and my father, Alana, and Daniel on the mission, this left me with nothing to do but worry.

Determined to be productive, I marched down to the offices to find

Baron Graftonberg in the conference room holding a meeting… without me. My mouth fell open on finding a gathering of important landowners and gentry rising from the round table and shaking hands.

"Princess Catherine," he said smoothly. "I'm afraid you just missed a boring business meeting. Nothing for you to worry about."

"But I'd like to join," I said, equally pleasant, matching his false tones.

"Gentleman? We're all finished here, aren't we?" His gaze met the others in the room, who had already started for the door, a few sending me apologetic glances.

"Next time, I'll be present," I said.

"Of course." The baron smirked and resumed shaking hands with the guests as they exited past me.

When my father returned, I would renew my campaign for a different regent. Instead of harping at him in front of others, I tromped to the mews to work with Charlie and Mocha. We'd been making progress on message delivery while standing across the meadow from one another. Today we'd practice with one of us out of sight, forcing the falcon to search.

"Good girl." Mocha landed on my gloved arm after a few passes back and forth, this time with a paper attached, and I unwound it from her leg. Her gentleness still amazed me when she allowed us to tie and untie items easily. The note from Charlie read, *She's doing great. Time to let her rest.*

I tucked Mocha into her enclosure, making sure she had plenty to eat, then gave her an extra nuzzle through the mesh wall.

North and I had formed an afternoon ride routine. Anticipating the exercise, she nickered and danced at my arrival. I'd taken to wearing legging-like pants specially developed for riding beneath my skirts. This allowed me greater freedom and protected the skin on my thighs if I chose not to ride sidesaddle. I only rode conventionally when I could be sure the king wouldn't catch me in the act. A painful shard caught in my chest at the thought of Father. I missed him already and wished I had worked harder on our connection before he left. The infancy of our relationship and the awkwardness of new fatherhood led to a tentative, tumultuous bond. One that needed more time to fully meld.

I mounted my black mare after stroking the white star on her forehead. "Let's go get these boys out of our heads."

We cantered out of the stable yard, and I headed down the mountain, entering the trees to avoid the field where The Great Battle took place. It held an ominous air, even with the new growth of grass. Back in America, I never heeded superstitions or intuition, but now I paid much closer attention to the emotions that places and individuals produced. My dad in Oregon used to tell me I had a good sense about people. It took time to realize he was right, and now I knew to trust myself. The field dredged up emotions that could be related to bad memories or the ghosts of the souls lost that day. North sensed it too, or at least my uneasiness, projected with a skittishness in her usual smooth gait.

The forest beyond was lush and cool in the otherwise warm late summer heat. We loved this area outside the castle grounds, our rides taking us here almost daily. She wanted to jump fallen logs, and I gave her free rein to frolic where she wished, while I enjoyed the wind plying strands of hair from my braid, whipping across my cheeks.

We stopped at a stream at the bottom of the mountain. North nearly always brought us here, a favorite place to stop and refresh. She bent to gulp the cold, clear water while I dismounted and prepared to join her.

I knelt to scoop my hands into the icy pool. A shadow crossed the surface, a wavy reflection of someone—a guard? My dagger was sheathed at the waist, and I bent lower toward the stream to camouflage reaching for it with one hand.

I spun and leapt to my feet, ignoring the water now at my ankles. An Ember stood with a sword much larger than my short, though deadly knife. I calmed my breathing but could do nothing for my thudding heart.

"What are you doing way out here by yourself?" I asked.

The man had the same general air about him as most Embers—bedraggled, bulky, and mean, with the same coarse brown clothes they all wore.

"Now, Princess, you think I'd come without backup? You're so naïve, coming here day after day, none of your little protectors around. We knew the king would leave you here at the castle. Alone."

A fireball flashed from his free hand, catching my skirt ablaze. Plunging it into the stream, I expunged the smoking fabric. He laughed, the sound grating.

"I wouldn't be so quick to chortle over there, buddy. I may look helpless, but I've killed more than one Ember." Okay, only two, and they both haunted my dreams, but pretending to be brave helped quell the shaking in my limbs.

He whistled. Not the kind of noise showing disbelief, or when a boy disrespects a pretty girl out his car window, but the shrill sound of alerting others. Goosebumps that had little to do with the icy water at my feet spread across my arms and traveled up my neck.

I had to make my move now, or risk being overtaken by whoever lurked in the woods. I wobbled up the bank, my shoes sloshing, skirts heavy from the dunking, my feet sliding on slick stones. North followed, her steady presence anchoring me.

The man watched with a lidded stare, seemingly unconcerned with my movements. "Sure you want to leave the safety of the stream?" His lips widened into a smile, displaying a gap between his front teeth.

I glared. "I can make rain whenever I choose. No matter." Would he call my bluff? Even if I was able under this pressure, it took a few minutes for the water to coalesce. A good old-fashioned jab and run is what I had in mind.

"Then why haven't you?" He edged closer—exactly what I wanted. I needed the proximity for my plan, which must be executed ASAP before his gang arrived. With each movement near to me, my skin felt a little tighter over my bones. I'd been working on this with Hugh during our latest hand-to-hand combat class. It would be harder with a heavy, wet dress, but still my best shot of survival.

In one fluid motion, I rolled forward and slashed his legs with my dagger. Hopping to my feet, I leapt onto North, not waiting to finish the job. My best chance of escape waited at the castle where plenty of guards patrolled. North raced through the woods. Shouts and thundering hooves echoed behind. We knew the forest better than the

Embers, and North weaved through brush and jumped over logs as she'd done countless times. Soon we'd reach what I liked to call my secret tunnel—a path entrance completely hidden by brush. Once through, branches draped over the trail like a hidden cocoon. It took me weeks to find the passage, and it provided a straight shot to the castle. An arrow whizzed by my head, sending me crouching over the mare's neck. North weaved and dodged until we reached the tunnel and crashed through the bushes. I glanced behind—no one was close enough to see the opening.

We finally approached the field of The Great Battle. For once, we raced across instead of skirting the space, betting the Embers would stay hidden, and hoping they too were superstitious about the land that had been the site of their recent downfall.

We entered the stable yard safely and I spotted a guard. "Embers! In the woods," I shouted. Following my direction, he raced to rally more men to chase them down.

I led North into the barn, her sides heaving with exhaustion. "Good job, girl. Couldn't have done it without you." I walked her to her stall, shooing away the groomsman. "Did you hear what he said?" I wiped the lathery sweat from her neck with a cloth. "*We knew the king would leave you here.* They came for me, knowing how chaotic the household would be with the peace treaty elsewhere. Doesn't sound like they're interested in peace, does it?" North bumped me with her head. Saying it aloud made the realization hit, my legs turning wobbly.

"If they had plans to ambush me, what does that mean for Father and Daniel?"

CHAPTER 23
DANIEL

We'd walked into a trap. Our tactics to outsmart them failed. The meeting date wasn't until tomorrow, yet the Embers had come in numbers, ready to weaken us, anticipating our move with a countermove.

"Do you see a way in?" I called to Erikson, still perched in the tree. The blaze scorched hotter, but we had to help King Aldridge. We wouldn't abandon him now.

"There's a bit of a gap over there." Erickson pointed west.

We donned our drundle coats and raced in the direction he'd indicated. The fire burned less strongly here, though we would have to navigate flames no matter where we crossed. Mya rode up beside me, and the irrational thought of sending her home even after we'd come this far flashed. That or find a place to hide her away, but I feared for her safety somewhere I couldn't protect her.

"Stay close to me or Dev," I told her, then raised my hood and galloped into the blaze.

We dodged felled trees, one collapsing mere feet from our path in a spark-filled crash. The wind blew the flames in unpredictable patterns. More than once, I brushed burning debris from my horse, who did his best to evade the perils. Mya stayed on my flank, deftly maneuvering her mount. I'd forgotten how accomplished a horseman—horsewoman, she was.

We finally reached the charred clearing. Roughly five hundred Embers were positioned at one end, while King Aldridge and a much smaller group of Caelum soldiers waited on the other. I spotted Lucas across the way, surrounded by the enemy, standing with ropes binding his hands and feet, his expression mutinous.

The Embers crossed the field at a methodical pace. The man in front stood taller than most, but unlike the others, he was clean-shaven with close-cropped hair and an air of authority. They'd never had much of a leader before, which aided in keeping them at bay, but there was something about him that sent an extra jolt of unease into my gut.

We rode up beside the king's men, and I wound my way to Aldridge's side.

"Sorry we're late," I said.

"It would have come to this no matter what." The king glanced over at me. "For Cate's sake, I wish you'd stayed home." His emotions were nearly always in check, but now they rolled freely as the tide. Fear and regret washed over me in painful doses.

"This doesn't look like a peace treaty." I scanned the army across the charred field.

"Indeed, it does not." Aldridge rode forward. "Hold until I signal," he called back.

"It's a trap," Mya whispered beside me.

"Uh-huh," I murmured. "Can you do anything?" At this point, changing their leader's mind bordered on last hope, but we were out of options.

"I'll try." She followed their movements, her mouth a tight line of concentration.

Cate's father headed to the center of the clearing alone. A risky move, but if we drew our swords now, any chance of negotiation would be lost.

The Ember leader rode out in front to meet the king. I could see them speaking, but they were too far to make out the words. King Aldridge's horse danced with unease. They appeared otherwise calm, though it was hard to tell if an agreement was being reached. I couldn't read the emotions of the Ember, whether due to the distance or because he was just ice-cold. As the seconds ticked by, I fought the urge to ask Mya if she'd made any progress, knowing it would be unproductive to interrupt her concentration.

The tall Ember's arm shot up without warning, and masses of his army unsheathed their swords and surged forward. Chills of dread shuddered across my skin. The king wheeled toward our protection while we prepared for battle. Adrenaline crashed over me in waves, readying my body for a fight.

Mya's face turned ashen. She held a dagger and was otherwise unarmed.

"Dev," I called, "take her out of here." I would have liked to do it myself, but couldn't abandon Cate's father. We needed Dev too—needed every person on our side. Mya's safety was too important to keep her here, so we'd have to do without him. I trusted Dev more than anyone.

"Got her." Dev nodded.

I thought she might fight me on this, but Mya turned her horse and galloped away with Dev toward the blazing forest, fear trailing behind.

The king rejoined us just in time for the crash of swords. Flames erupted from the nearest Ember, sending me lurching in my saddle. If they kept using fire, riding would prove more of a liability than battling on foot as they were known for aiming at the horses to dismount their opponent. I slashed through a man before he could conjure more fire, my speed quicker. Flashbacks of The Great Battle reminded me to check King Aldridge's location. He fought valiantly with others nearby, including Hugo. Several of us showered stones, dirt, and rubble into the mass of Embers. The Caelum soldiers used their winds to blow ash, temporarily blinding the enemy.

More Embers rode into the battlefield through the circle of flames. I slid off my horse and nudged him away. My sword clashed over and over, some slashes hitting their mark, others glancing off opposing steel. A rhythm settled, dodging fire, spraying debris, then swinging my sword as our adversaries grappled with dust in their eyes and batted away stones. I'd trained for this, starting as a young boy with a wooden weapon and combat instructors. Hours upon hours of maneuvers and contests with other apprentice soldiers and knights had led to muscle memory. It hardened me to the killing, though later, in the quiet, I'd remember each death blow.

If only they would stay in their territory. No one wanted this war. But they'd burned their resources, changing the climate in the process, and now we killed for survival. To protect our homes. To save our friends and family. And with each slash of the blade, a part of me was left behind on the battlefield.

I momentarily gazed across the clearing where Lucas was still trussed up like a pig, unable to move. Using wind powers on that side would only blow the fire toward us, so he waited helplessly, watching the battle. They must have brought him as a show of power. If we lost, I shuddered to think what they'd do to him. He caught my eye and shook his head, tilting and rotating, as if to indicate something surrounding us. More men? Dragons? Whatever it was, it didn't bode well. We were outnumbered already, yet still making headway due to the skilled group we'd assembled.

King Aldridge fought ten yards away. I shot up a wall of dust and ash, cloaking myself to reach him. Eager to relay Lucas's warning, I miscalculated how near an Ember stood in my path. While we jostled against each other in the whirlwind, his hand sent a fiery brand to my neck. I pushed my powers into him as Father had so painfully instructed. The man's blue eyes grew wide, stunned at first, then radiated agony. I stepped from his loosening grip, then slashed my sword, saving him from the pain I'd already inflicted. I hated seeing their eyes. Watching them was imperative in battle, often tipping me to an opponent's next move. Later, they would haunt me.

When I reached the king, I pulled him a few yards from the nearest fighters, signaling several guards to watch over us, then relayed the warning from Lucas.

"You think there are more?" He glanced around the periphery.

"I do, and I'm worried they're working on surrounding our fighters so they can capture you. I'm just a bonus they didn't expect."

His green eyes, similar in shape and color to Cate's, fell. "We'll have to leave Lucas." His gaze met mine again. "I'll sound the retreat."

The moment he reached for the whistle around his neck, more Embers flowed onto the battlefield. A trap within a trap. They'd brought just enough men for our team to think we might take them, engaged us in battle, then crept in from all sides like fire ants marching to the remains of a feast.

The king's whistle blew shrill three times, signaling withdrawal. I searched for an escape through the circle of blaze but saw none, and the inferno didn't slow the enemy with their flame-retardant skin. I checked on the king, making sure to stay close. Bringing him home safe was of utmost importance. A slight break in the fire to the southeast suddenly became visible—our best chance.

"That way." I motioned to Aldridge. Hundreds of Embers still lay in our path. And what of Mya? Had she and Dev made it past the converging enemy in time to escape? I surveyed the charred landscape in search of their return to warn us, but there was no sign of them.

Alana stood in the center of the field, a tornado of ash whirling about her, aided by her dual powers of earth and air. She was a one-woman army, the force of her gale growing, sending everything into its path flying. The Embers tried to keep a wide berth, but the new soldiers crowded against them, pushing their comrades into the hurricane. Glimpses of her through the melee showed her drundle cloak tossing and turning, feet planted firmly against the torrent. She was the eye of the storm, but not completely shielded from its wrath.

An Ember became swept up in it, his boots sliding out from under him, carried by the circular force. The debris and rocks pummeled him, but he still managed to throw his dagger. Somehow, it cut through the winds, maybe because he'd made it close enough to the center.

The tornado stopped, the gusts ceasing into a dead calm, the rubble dropping in a sudden shower. In the center lay Alana, facedown and unmoving, a knife in her back.

Everything inside me went numb. I'd seen comrades fall in battle before. But Alana. She had seemed almost immortal, a constant guiding hand for both our kingdoms. I put a palm on King Aldridge's shoulder. "Alana's down."

His features turned hard as flint. "Come. We must get out."

I did my best to shove aside the ache in my chest for Alana, fighting toward the perimeter of the fight, every strike powered with desperation. The king used his wind while I raised the ash. I cleared the way momentarily, but more Embers always filed into our path. We soon realized the debris obscured our vision too much to be worth the effort, slowing our progress. Escaping as quickly as possible became the priority.

They were closing in on all sides. We fought, both nimble from our power and years of training. Soon, the Embers erected a wall of fire surrounding the remaining soldiers in the battlefield.

"We have to break through," I yelled. "Follow close."

I raised my hood and ducked my head, knocking away Embers with my shoulder, my sword, anything to escape, hoping I'd made a trail large enough for the king to follow. I glanced back to see him on my tail.

"Keep going," he shouted.

The fire wall blazed directly ahead. More enemies surely stood beyond it, the ones erecting the inferno, and likely many more between here and safety. We were dangerously close to becoming trapped.

I lowered my head, readying myself to duck through. It wasn't just a little campfire, but wider and taller than any soldier present, blazing white hot. It stole my breath, the heat scorching my uncovered cheeks the closer I approached. The burn on my neck from the Ember earlier flared. Speed was my only option. I dashed through the incinerator, so hot it felt as if my heart would explode from its rapid pulse. On the other side, I was met with a different wall. I'd bulldozed into the men sending up the flames, a barrier of muscle. The closest Ember grabbed me by the arms, two others stepping in front to close the gap in the fiery barricade.

"Cowards," he said. "You lot are running away?"

The man towered over me, built like a rugby player, making me feel almost childlike.

"A little unfair, don't you think?" I cocked my head up at him. "We just wanted the peace you promised."

He smirked and painfully tightened his grip on my upper arms. "And we wanted your king."

It appeared he didn't know I wasn't a Caelum soldier, my cloak hiding my Terran uniform. The man certainly hadn't realized he held the prince. My body was battered, burned, sweaty, and exhausted. I took a moment, letting the earth's energy flow back into me. I didn't have long—this guy would kill anyone too lowly to bother with holding hostage.

I let the power build, then expelled it into him with a quick blast. Similar to the man earlier, he froze in shock—because that's what it felt like—a giant electric shock. I didn't take the time to kill him. He'd be incapacitated for a while. Instead, I searched for the king. Even in the fray, he should have been close.

But he hadn't made it through the fire barrier. Indecision tore through me. What were the chances of making it past the enemy again and fetching King Aldridge? Before I could contemplate further, more Embers swarmed.

I dodged and parried, sliced and stabbed, and ultimately, after breaking through, ran. I sprinted away, slowing briefly to search behind. No one else appeared. Was I a coward? Deep down, I knew that turning back meant certain death. I had Mya to think about. And my duty to Terra.

It felt wicked. Self-indulgent. Shameful. All the things I didn't want to be. Yet I still ran, knowing my report would be valuable. My life valuable to the Terran people. To my sister. And to Cate.

Cate. Her father and Lucas both lost to her. Would the Embers keep them alive as a bargaining tool? Only time would tell. As my feet pounded in the opposite direction, I vowed I would return and somehow free them. This battle may be over, but the war raged on.

I pushed through the fire surrounding the clearing, evading flaming branches and underbrush, then trekked toward the location of where we gathered before we entered the fight. There hadn't been time to discuss a meet-up plan, and I could only hope to find Dev and Mya nearby.

I finally reached what I thought was the right place, the landscape now changed due to the spreading fire, a mosaic of charred vegetation and flames. A man too large to be Dev stood in the distance, his drundle cloak half torn away, revealing a Terran uniform. When he turned, he saw me and waved. Hugo's face materialized when he lifted his hood. We joined one another and chose to wait a few more minutes to see if any others made it out. He hadn't seen Dev or Mya, which didn't stop me from searching, my blood now cold, even in the heat of the fires.

A few more stragglers arrived, both Caelum and Terran soldiers, a patchwork of burns marking their cloaks. No King Aldridge, Lucas, Dev, or Mya. Erikson made it, breathing hard, his arm hanging limp, bleeding from a wound near his bicep.

"We've got to... get out," he managed between breaths. "They're coming."

I tore a sleeve from my uniform and used the material to bandage his wound, my hands fumbling, trying to work fast. "Tell us on the way. Let's go." I headed south, glancing back one more time. A collection of Embers burst through the fire and approached, with presumably more to follow.

"Ordered to track us," Erikson said.

We broke into a run, six of us in total, a bedraggled group struggling to find our usual speed. Erikson lagged, slow from blood loss. The thick smoke was suffocating, but at least we headed away from the fires.

Through the haze, I spotted a figure. *Dev.* I whistled our special signal, which mimicked a Terran Redbird, a call we'd used since we were kids. He saw us and changed directions to join. While we ran, I kept glancing over to see if Mya accompanied him.

Dev came upon our group, panting. "I'm sorry," he huffed. "They took her." He stopped and placed his hands on his knees. "I tried." He shook his head, the anguish plastered over his features. "Mya's gone."

CHAPTER 24
LUCAS
PRESENT DAY

The defeat of King Aldridge and the Terran and Caelum soldiers had been inevitable. A horrible scene I helplessly watched, tied and abandoned at the edge of the battle with no one but several guards between me, my friends, and my king. I had seen them assemble—thousands marching for two days. I'd overheard snippets of a meeting point, without realizing we journeyed to a summit between the Embers and Caelum. They dangled me as bait, and must have lured something else more valuable than me, though I wasn't sure what that incentive might be.

We all knew Embers couldn't be trusted. King Aldridge more than most. And Daniel mixed in the fray, sticking with his future father-in-law? Even after observing the capture of my king, the nausea in my stomach swirled with the thought of Cate and Daniel together. I shook my head. *Disgusting*. I watched my comrades fall, yet I still couldn't stop the jealousy.

And they did fall. So many of them. Even Alana. The smoke, the chaos, the blood, all came rushing back. The binding on my wrists stung raw from the struggle to free myself and join the conflict. What would become of the kingdoms? This would surely lead to war.

Our only hope was Cate.

I'd walked about half a day's journey after the battle with several more to go, my arms tied behind my back with a rope lead attached to an Ember like a dog on a leash. King Aldridge was presumably among us, though I had yet to see him other than when we left the battleground when I'd witnessed the enemy tying him up. I'm not sure how many prisoners they captured, or if most were killed.

The Embers would probably throw me back in the pit if they didn't kill me first. After all, what did they think to gain by keeping me alive now that they had King Aldridge? If my faith lay at the feet of King Dryden, I had no hope. For once, I could almost feel grateful for Daniel and Cate's relationship. Their bond might be the only thing stopping Dryden from invading Caelum instead of rescuing us. Daniel had escaped the battlefield, I'd seen him slip through, but I couldn't be sure he made it completely out. Rowan had sent trackers to hunt the fleeing soldiers.

I trudged through the terrain, much of it already scorched and dying, toward the Embers' main encampment. A ramshackled city, I'd seen parts of it after they'd released me from the hole and dragged me to battle. The pit reminded me of my hunger, which gnawed at my insides. Fatigue from dehydration made each step more difficult. When we finally stopped to make camp, I watched for weaknesses, with a better chance of escaping out here than after they deposited me in solitary. The men gathered around fires in circles of twenty to thirty, placing prisoners inside each ring.

I craned my neck to see who else might be captured. A couple of Terran soldiers in their green uniforms were in the next group over. Still no sign of the king. No other prisoner entered my circle. If I tried to escape, it would be on my own. The best opportunity would come when most of the camp slept. With any luck, the guard on duty would be drowsy after the battle.

A collection of Embers had been tasked to track game during our march, which now roasted over the fire. Their organization was better than I'd witnessed in the past on scouting missions. My stomach rumbled at the heavenly smell of cooking meat. The belt looped around my middle had already been tightened by several holes to account for the lack of food in the last six weeks.

I turned to a man near me, the friendliest appearing of the lot. He had enormous ears sticking out from his head, and a couple of missing teeth beneath wide lips. "Hey, mate, you think I could get some of that?" I nodded to the fire.

"If there's any left, maybe."

"Don't 'spose you guys want to carry me if I collapse from hunger tomorrow. We've still got a long way to go." I didn't mention that it might be easier to leave me for dead to avoid giving him any ideas.

The man grunted and otherwise didn't respond. When the food was ready, I'd ask again to plant the seed before they devoured it all. Waiting patiently became torture, my stomach eating itself from the inside. Finally, they tore into the meal bringing out flasks and bread from their bags.

"Buddy?" I said to the man with the ears. "I may look skinny, but what's left is pure muscle. You don't want to carry this." I would have patted my chest, but my hands were still tied behind my back.

He rolled his eyes, then collected some leftovers from a few nearby men and set the food directly before me.

"Uh… need a little help here. Can you tie them in front?" I pivoted my body away from him and wiggled my fingers.

He checked with his comrades, and several nodded in affirmation. "He's not going anywhere," one of them said.

The blood rushed into my fingertips when the knots loosened, tingling and warm. I flexed them, finally able to relax my shoulders when my arms were brought forward. It could've been a chance for escape, except two Embers gripped my biceps, fingers digging in, while a few others watched. Not to mention the hundreds occupying the campsite. A better opportunity may come later.

They'd just tightened the bonds again when a commotion erupted several campfires over. Shouting ensued, and a scream rang through the air. A *woman's* scream. My first thoughts zeroed on Grace, but what would she be doing out here?

A riot broke out near the uproar, still fifty yards away. Men jostled to gain a better look. The surrounding group loosened, leaving me to wonder if my best chance to flee might be now.

A stocky guy, who had held me moments before, called out, "Hold your positions." He painfully gripped my shoulder, smart enough to know chaos bred conditions for escape.

After a few minutes, order was restored. Most rounded their campfires, heads together, mumbling to one another about whatever just happened. Many sat back down, giving me a clear view of Rowan with a girl dressed in a Terran soldier's uniform. Her long dark hair hung halfway out of its binding at the base of her neck. Although Rowan had a tight hold on her, she strode with her head held high as if she were a princess being escorted through a crowd of peasants instead of a prisoner, wrists tied with the same coarse rope as mine.

The two continued in our direction until they reached our circle. A gap opened so that Rowan and the girl could step inside. She appeared near my age, a young woman, with piercing blue eyes and a pert nose. I winced. I'd seen those eyes before. The Terran princess was in our midst. More fodder for trade for our rivals. More leverage. At least this meant we might gain the assistance of King Dryden.

Rowan shoved her toward me. She stumbled, then righted herself. Loudly, he addressed the group, "No one touches the girl. She's too valuable." The men's side-eyes told me they weren't used to holding back with women, which further turned my stomach. Mya shifted closer to me, her only indication of fear.

Rowan stepped forward and leaned in close to my ear. "I'm putting her with you because I know you'll sound the alarm if anyone lays a hand on her." He gave me a pointed look. "Correct?"

I'd protect her against these brutes, though if he asked something of me, I intended to get something in return. "I want better conditions when we arrive. Food, blankets, a bed. Look at her," I glanced at Mya, then back at him, "she won't last a week in the pit."

"Fine." He didn't hesitate, which made me wonder if I could have asked for more and if this fit into his plan all along.

He left without additional comment, leaving Mya and me standing inside the hostile circle. I sat near the small discarded pile of food, gesturing with a tilt of my head for her to join me. "Have you eaten?"

She shook her head. "Not really hungry."

"Tomorrow will be the same as today. You need to keep your strength up."

She shrugged and reached for a torn piece of bread, brushing the dirt off the crust. Her hands were already tied in front.

"I'm Lucas, by the way."

She looked up from her food with a quizzical half smile. "Yeah, I know. We danced together a few months ago at the ball?"

Had we? I'd been so preoccupied with Cate, I must have forgotten. I recognized her, of course, and vaguely recalled a few polite conversations between us. "I could never forget a dance with the princess," I covered. "Wasn't sure you would remember me. I'm just a lowly Caelum knight."

She cocked her head. "Not so lowly, if I recall. You're friends with Cate. She's been worried about you."

My traitorous heart jumped. "You've seen her?"

"Just before I came." She said it offhanded like it wasn't important.

"And how is she?" Couldn't she see how desperate for information I was? A morsel of intel on what Cate ate for breakfast that day—anything.

"She's fine. Worried about you, like I said." She took a tentative bite of bread. I watched her chew, waiting to see if she'd elaborate. "Not sure here is the best place to talk about it." She raised her brows.

The gossipy princess had to remind the seasoned soldier about discretion. My starvation for contact and news had led to carelessness.

"Have you seen Daniel?" she asked. "I thought I heard someone say the prince escaped, but it was hard to hear."

"I saw him retreat from the battle. After that, I don't know what happened. But I haven't found him. What about King Aldridge?"

She shook her head. "I'll keep my ears open."

We finished our meal in mostly silence, our minds elsewhere. With two of us, the odds of escaping tonight turned unlikely. I'd had plenty of training in stealth, but who knew if Mya would step on every loose stick, let her feet crunch on gravel, or trip over an Ember on the way out of here. Though I certainly couldn't leave her.

My thoughts hitched. Why not? I didn't owe her anything. Definitely not her brother or King Dryden either.

She lay down closer to the campfire, her hair spread out on the dirt, gleaming in the firelight. Her proud countenance withered, body curled in a ball, vulnerable. I sighed, resigned. She was my charge, whether I liked it or not.

The next morning, we rose stiff and cold. "You'd think Embers could keep a fire going all night," I whispered to Mya. Every time I had rolled over, I scanned the area. At least three men in our circle had always been on guard—no opportunity to sneak away, especially with the extra risk of taking Mya.

She stretched, raising her still-tied hands above her head. A breeze blew her half-fallen hair into her face, a few leaves clinging to the strands. She fumbled to reach behind to resecure the locks. "Can you?" She wriggled, unable to grasp the hair band.

"You want me to tie it back?" I didn't have sisters, let alone experience with hair.

"Please. It's driving me crazy." Her blue eyes held something beneath the surface. Mirth? Embarrassment? Beguile? No—not beguile. Couldn't be that.

"Um, sure, I'll try."

She turned. A thin leather ribbon wrapped around most of her black hair, strands escaping on either side. I untied the cord, letting the locks fall into a thick curtain. It felt soft. Softer than one would think after sleeping on the ground. I picked out a few leaves, then did my best to gather it all together and tie it, my own hands hindered by their bonds. "There, better?"

She faced me again and smiled. The full power of it stunned—a light in the gloom. It had been so long since I'd seen anyone smile without a mocking or sinister edge that it took me aback.

Soon we were on our way again. We marched for miles, surrounded by Embers and tethered with a rope leash and a cranky Ember holding the far end. I hadn't caught sight of the king, but it was nice to have Mya as a companion. I sent warning glares at any lecherous glances tossed her direction, repeatedly announcing loudly that I would report impropriety to Rowan.

To pass the time, she described her family, careful to keep anything important safe from prying ears. I told her about my parents—my mother, a specialist in healing herbs, and my father, killed by an Ember five years ago. I hoped to not meet the same fate. The time passed without any opportunity to escape, yet still more enjoyable than the day before, if one could call marching for endless hours enjoyable.

The night passed much the same. Mya scooted closer to me for heat and protection. She wasn't a complainer or prone to panic, which I appreciated. She seemed to take things as they came and adapted.

We finally arrived in the Ember's main settlement, known as The Camp or Ember City. A congested maze of shanty-like structures, most sharing walls and sometimes roofs, populated the outskirts. A peek inside one revealed dirt floors and a single room with pallets for beds. No wonder they wanted our cities. I hadn't been prepared to see the masses of people crowded together. Their burned lands failed to provide enough food, and they projected the hollow look of hunger as we trudged by.

"They're starving," Mya whispered.

I nodded and swallowed hard, not able to hold the stare of a child who had missed too many meals.

As we marched closer to the center of town, structures turned sturdier and slightly more spread apart. Actual streets with a mix of stone and wood buildings lined the central part of The Camp. These were the more prosperous Embers. Though who knows what propelled them to this status.

Our guards stopped at a crude building constructed of brown stones with thick mortar set in a jigsaw-like pattern. They started to lead Mya inside while my leash jerked in the opposite direction.

"Wait," I called. "We're supposed to be together."

One of them shrugged. "Why?"

So none of you Neanderthals accost her, was my first thought. Instead, I replied tersely, "Because Rowan said."

The largest of the group, a beefy man with his hair pulled into a knot, shot me a look of disgust. "You're going back to the pit. She's got a cot ready in here. Or would you rather her go with you?"

That was not the deal I made. Dread clutched at my chest at remembering the days and days of solitude, less than ten feet of space… and very little food.

For the first time, Mya's wide eyes reflected terror. I shook my head. "You don't want to come."

"Don't leave me." Her voice rose shrill.

"Mya, trust me. Go with them." I wanted to vomit. She couldn't trust me or them. I had no idea if I was making the wrong decision. The pit was dank, isolating, cramped, and so horrible it sent shudders laddering down my spine at the thought of returning. With winter coming, it would only get colder—probably my death sentence. I wouldn't let her die there too.

They pulled her into the building, and I stared after her before I too was yanked forward. "Take care, Mya," I whispered, hoping it wasn't the last time I'd see her.

CHAPTER 25
DANIEL

"What do you mean, she's gone?" I asked Dev, my pulse pounding in my ears.

"They took Mya. A group ambushed us while we waited for you. I tried to fight them off. They argued about keeping me prisoner too, but in the end, they must have decided I was too much trouble. They hit me over the head and left me for dead." He gingerly touched the back of his scalp. His usually fastidious clothes were torn, littered with dirt and dried leaves, burn holes scattered in the wool cloth. "I woke up a few minutes ago with this massive headache and no sign of your sister."

Hugo raised a finger to gain our attention. "We need to get moving."

I jerked my head toward him, incredulous. "We have to find Mya."

Hugo took a deep breath, expelling it noisily. "With all due respect, sir, we don't have a prayer. A thousand of them, and just a few of us, with injuries. We have to go. They're moments from locating our position, and they'll capture or kill all of us. We'll come back for her—for all of them."

I looked to Dev, the reality of needing to be a soldier instead of a brother sank in. "Maybe you should decide," I told him, putting my trust in my oldest friend. "I'm not impartial. She was under my protection, and I failed. I'd send us all to our deaths because, as you well know, bad odds have never stopped me."

Dev hesitated, indecision and worry flashing across his features. He hadn't witnessed the army. Hadn't seen Alana go down, and his guilt wouldn't let him make a rational choice, either, even though I wanted to pass that burden to him.

"We'll come back," Hugo interrupted. His eyes made a silent promise to do whatever it took to find Mya, but only when we were prepared.

My shoulders sagged. "Let's get out of here." My feet remained planted, despite the words. They echoed in my head, like a nightmare. I couldn't decide if it was cowardly or wise to let Hugo make the call. I told myself that he possessed the objectivity I lacked, though my conscience screamed to find Mya.

"Daniel." Dev placed a palm on my arm, seeing me stare over his shoulder at the horizon behind us. "Hugo's right. We'll return when we're ready."

His reassurance helped ease the knot in my belly. Returning now would only get me killed or captured.

One last look, and we headed away from the fires at a quick pace. Shouts echoed in the distance while a steep slope slowed our progress. Erikson stumbled, and I caught him before he tumbled down the hill. The blood loss had rapidly taken a toll on him. The remaining unburned forest allowed reasonable cover, but the Embers gained on us, their voices louder. Erickson's sides heaved in exertion. He wasn't going to make it, and his diminished speed endangered the rest of us.

"Camouflage," he said with effort.

His skills were renowned in Terra—the reason he was chosen for this doomed adventure in the first place. He was right. Hiding until nightfall was our best bet, as long as the fires didn't spread. "You have enough energy?"

He nodded, gulping air.

The group headed west to a knoll tucked into the ravine. "Kneel here," I commanded the Caelum soldiers.

"Like sitting ducks?" one asked, his expression more perplexed than angry.

"You'll see, just stay put."

Erickson, Hugo, Dev, and I quickly went to work. All of us possessed the ability to use the earth's energy to grow vegetation. I manipulated a nearby bush, lengthening its spindly branches to overhang the bowl-shaped cavity where the Caelumites sat. Erickson searched for anything that could be transplanted as cover. The others encouraged weeds into tall, tangled growth. I rushed over to Erickson who dragged a sapling, roots still intact. This is why he was the best. It took skill to extract something that large without damaging each thin rootlet.

"Hurry," Hugo urged. He formed a hole, and we set the small tree into it.

Erickson's skin had turned gray, his breaths shallow.

"Can you do it?" I asked.

He nodded.

"Everybody in," I said. He followed, nearly collapsing as he sat. His eyes flickered closed, face narrowed in concentration. The branches grew over us, leaning in and forming an additional canopy. Erickson cut off nutrients to areas, causing scattered leaves to brown and curl at the edges so the shelter didn't appear out of place with the struggling vegetation nearby.

At last, he leaned on me, his energy spent. The makeshift tourniquet on his arm soaked red with blood. It would need changing soon, but for now, silence was imperative.

It wasn't long before we heard them.

Steady, methodical footsteps tromped down the hill. The number of bushes surrounding our makeshift bunker should divert them around us, but the real question was whether they would investigate further. We'd camouflaged in such a way to make it difficult to notice the dip in the ground where we huddled. If they came too close, they'd fall right into the hole where we all crouched, holding our collective breaths.

The thumping pounded closer. I fought the childish urge to shut my eyes like I was hiding under the bed, remaining alert, my sword ready. The tree leaves overhanging my head rustled. Someone stood nearby.

A pause. Silence.

Then footsteps. Dry brush crunched, followed by the sounds fading away. Someone in our group exhaled, but no one dared move. My body ached from holding it still for such an extended period, each muscle strained from the earlier conflict screamed to stretch.

Long minutes passed and finally, we loosened our stiff positions. Our hiding spot was cramped but effective.

"We should stay here until nightfall," I whispered. "They might come back or there may be more." The dark would arrive with its own dangers, but avoiding capture remained our greatest concern.

As the adrenaline faded, the exhaustion of battle and the pursuit afterward wore on our bodies. Erickson fell into a deep sleep slumped against me. In order for us to all return safely, he'd need to recover some of his strength. There were seven of us in all, with the addition of Dev: Hugo, Erickson, and me, as well as three Caelum soldiers. We'd introduce ourselves to the Caelumites later because, for now, silence remained paramount.

"I'll stay on watch. One of you guys?" I whispered to the nearest Caelum soldier.

A gangly man with his knees scrunched to his chin from the cramped space volunteered. I wondered how many others had escaped. Perhaps King Aldridge managed to elude the Embers and was out there hiding like we were, waiting for the cover of darkness to move. The chances were small, but for Cate's sake, it settled my nerves to imagine him safe.

CHAPTER 26
CATE

At the east lawn, dew clung like tiny crystal balls to threads of grass. They coalesced under my concentration into larger drops, sliding down the blades of green in sparkling rivulets. Bringing moisture together that already sat on the turf came easier than conjuring it from the air, though I had yet to form a large enough crystal ball for predicting fortunes. If I possessed that particular talent as Alana did, I would constantly be drawn to it.

I took a deep breath to focus more clearly on my task. I'd worried all day and night about those at the treaty. Expelling them from my thoughts to work on my powers wouldn't change their fate. Worrying wouldn't help either, but telling my brain didn't stop me.

Before I could fully concentrate, shouts rang out in the distance. A cold shiver skipped down my spine. Embers? Did they have enough men to attack here and ambush the others? I raced to the stable courtyards. As I approached, one of the grooms shouted, "She's here."

"What happened?" I asked the nearest worker.

"A group returned, ma'am. Prince Daniel among them."

I couldn't contain my smile from spreading. "Where is he?"

He tilted his head toward the castle. "Inside. You just missed him."

"The king?"

His eyes shifted away. "Not yet."

The door to the castle flew open as I sprinted up the steps. Daniel stood, emotions crossing his features like conflicting seasons. Relief, love, exhaustion, and anguish. I ran, shortening the distance between us, and threw my arms around him. He smelled of smoke, grass, sweat, and the sharpness of blood. I pulled away.

"You're hurt?" I searched him, his filthy uniform still intact. No obvious injuries other than a red burn blistering his neck.

"I'm fine. It's been a long few days."

"Who's with you? Lucas?"

He shook his head. "A few Caelum soldiers, a couple of Terrans, and Dev."

"That's it? Where are the others?" I grabbed onto his sleeve, not letting him enter inside.

Exhaustion slowed his every movement. Even his words dripped with lethargy. "It's a long story." He slid his hand into mine and pulled me to the door.

Butterflies fluttered in my stomach as we entered the castle. He led me past room after room, climbing several flights to his bedroom, each footfall thudding heavily on the tread.

"You're going to sleep? Without talking to me?"

"Two things have kept me going: seeing you and stretching out on that bed. Sit next to me. Leave the door open if you want. I'm too tired to worry about propriety."

I selfishly wanted the whole story, but he obviously needed care. I'd never seen him this exhausted. Servants should be summoned, though I couldn't leave without one question answered. "My father?

"We were separated. I don't know." He put his head in his hands. "I'm sorry."

The news crushed against my chest, the weight of it almost too much to remain upright. After a few shallow breaths, I said, "Wait for me. I'll send some things up."

I needed a moment to collect myself. Ensuring Daniel received the proper care would allow me to turn my attention onto something other than my father. My eyes fluttered closed as soon as I crossed into the corridor, unable to stop myself from imagining him in the hands of the enemy. I sagged against the wall, my mind spinning dangerously into panic mode. There wasn't time to fall apart. People needed me. *Focus on something else, Cate.* I swallowed hard, searching my brain for a distracting gruesome statistic, which ironically almost always centered me. *Six people per year die of shark attacks.*

I repeated it as if it were a mantra while rushing to the head housekeeper's door to have her send food and a footman to assist Daniel. She had already arranged assistance, with two of the soldiers being sent to the infirmary.

After seeing everyone was taken care of and confirming Daniel's story that only a few made it back here, I headed upstairs again. He'd changed into clean clothes and was sitting up in the bed eating a sandwich. For a prince, he sure was partial to some bread, meat, and cheese slapped together.

"Where'd you go?" he mumbled with his mouth full. Apparently, princely manners didn't always apply to him either.

"I sent someone up to help. You looked about ready to collapse, and I knew you'd regret crawling into that bed with those dirty clothes." I wrinkled my nose. "We'd have to burn the mattress."

He took another large bite and nodded. Patience wasn't something I excelled at, even though I'd had plenty of practice. Finally, he finished eating and set the plate aside, making room for me to sit next to him. The story unfolded, each moment more horrific than the last.

"You think they took my father?"

He brusquely pushed the dark hair off his forehead, rubbing his brow. "It's likely. He was right behind me. I was clearing the way for us until," he paused, looking down, "until I turned around and he wasn't there. He might have escaped, but I haven't seen him."

My eyes burned. One tear slipped across my cheek. I didn't bother to brush it away. "You think he's dead?"

"I imagine they'll try to get some information out of him first. Bring him back to Ember City."

My body felt like it would collapse in on itself, a hole forming in my chest so wide the entire kingdom might get sucked in. "Torture. You mean torture."

Daniel's eyes grew watery. "Yes." He pulled me close, and I sobbed into his shoulder, the pain cutting deep and sharp.

After a few minutes, I wiped my tears to hear the rest, the ache still pounding beneath my ribs. "Lucas and the other soldiers? Alana? They're all missing?"

He described Lucas being led away, ropes crisscrossing his body. Then he broke the news of Alana's downfall.

"She couldn't still be alive?" I scraped my palm across my brow, fresh tears blurring my vision. How could everything have gone so wrong?

His voice was grave, but firm, "I don't think so."

Yet again, I'd taken someone for granted. She'd pushed me, annoyed me, and mothered me at a time when I had none. Now she was gone. Just like all the other mother figures in my life. Tears streaked my cheeks. "I'll miss her," I whispered.

I crawled farther onto the bed, leaning against the carved headboard, and rested my cheek on his shoulder. "What are we going to do?"

"We'll send search parties out to look for anyone that might have escaped and needs help."

"Like Father?"

"Yes. Let's exhaust the possibilities first, then worry about fighting to get them back."

Just the thought of another battle turned my blood cold. And who would lead the soldiers? Everyone I trusted on Caelum's side was gone.

"It'll take time," he said. "We can't rush. We'll build an army that's ready to defeat them."

My throat clogged with tears again. "And time for me to figure out my power."

He circled his arm around me. "We'll figure it out together."

In the meantime, the Embers either held those I loved hostage, or it didn't matter how long we deliberated because they'd already been murdered. I suddenly sat up straight. "Daniel, where's Mya?"

His stricken face said it all. "Taken."

I gasped. It was too much. My head collapsed into my hands, and I took a few deep breaths. "We'll get her back. We have to," I said, forcing more confidence than I felt.

"I know." His voice sounded hollow. Broken.

I took his hand in mine and traced the lines of his palm. We sat together in silence, mourning our losses and second-guessing our decisions. There wasn't anything we wanted to say, though I knew our thoughts mirrored each other.

How did we get here? And what were we going to do to get out of it?

CHAPTER 27
LUCAS

Several men escorted me on my leash through the streets, heading outside of town toward the pit. I dragged my feet, weary from travel, and exhausted from the last several months. The worst expanse of my life, and my skin crawled at the thought of returning. I felt both helpless and reckless, not caring if I lived or died. The more we trudged, the more my decision solidified. I would not let the Embers put me back in that hole. I'd wait until fewer people were around—once we were farther out of the city and my odds would be two against one. Except *I'd* still be tied up.

I studied my captors, one beside me, the other holding the rope in front. He favored his right leg—perhaps an injury from battle. The other, pretty ordinary, was a couple of inches shorter, but outweighed me by a few stones. A homemade tattoo in black ink wormed up his forearm and under his pushed-up sleeve.

Up ahead, the road cleared. A few more yards, and I'd take my chance. I planned to use my leash as a noose for one of them if it didn't burn through before cutting off his airway. As we continued, the city sounds and the bustle of soldiers returning from battle faded. Now was my opportunity. My muscles coiled, ready to spring forward, grab the rope, and wrap it around the man's neck.

"Hey!" called a deep voice.

The Embers turned and straightened their sloppy stances. "Sir?" Tattoo Guy asked.

I swiveled to see who spoke. Rowan stood several yards away, his brow furrowed. "Where are you taking him?" he asked.

"Back to the pit," the man with the rope said, although his tone was less confidant than the insistence of earlier.

Rowan advanced a few more steps. "I told you to keep him with the girl. Has he given you any trouble?"

"No, sir." They both shook their heads.

"He'll behave because he knows he's protecting the princess. We'll get some work out of him. Send him out with the others tomorrow."

Apparently, I was being upgraded due to good behavior. All thanks to Mya. If Rowan hadn't shown up, I would either be dead or dumped in the pit. Because attempting escape would never qualify as not being a troublemaker.

We entered the stone building toward the center of town where I'd left Mya. The accommodations would definitely not be up to princess standards. Several hallways of jail cells stretched before me. Most held men dressed in the same coarse clothes as the Embers. Impossible to tell if they were from Terra or Caelum, stripped of any uniform they might have previously owned.

Toward the end of the corridor, a room was set apart by a closed door—perhaps an office for the guards on duty. Next to it was a cell larger than the others with iron bars crossing the front. Still small, but spacious compared to the pit. A cot sat against each wall, faded blankets draped across. We entered the empty cell, and the tattooed Ember cut the rope away, sneering with jagged teeth.

"Thanks." I grimaced back. Pins and needles rushed through my fingertips from the rapid blood flow returning. "Where's Mya? Aren't I supposed to be watching her?"

He ignored my question and sauntered out, slamming the door behind him.

"Hey," I yelled. "Someone!"

No response. I banged on the bars and kept shouting. What had they done with her?

"Shut up down there," a man shouted.

"Have you seen a girl?"

"Dark hair," someone else responded. "They took her to the back."

My pulse quickened. The worst happened already. These men were animals. I paced the room, hating the feeling of helplessness. I should have never left her. Should have taken her to the pit. I slumped onto the cot, head in hands.

Footsteps sounded in the corridor. "I'm going. No need to push," Mya's angry voice rang out.

She came into view, head still high in that I'm-better-than-you princess stance. They'd taken her clothes and provided her with a sack-like brown dress, a dark strip of cloth wrapped around her upper arm. When she spotted me, the haughtiness morphed into a bright smile.

"They brought me back," I said. "Looks like we're bunking together."

They shoved her inside, and I caught a flash of fear before she could pull on her mask of bravery.

"Mighty improper of them, isn't it?" I smirked to lighten the mood.

She cocked her head, then re-donned the haughtiness. "Quite. I'll be sure and file a complaint. Or, since I will have been thoroughly compromised, you'll just have to marry me." She meant it as a joke, but her cheeks bloomed rosy at her own suggestion.

"Nice," I played along. "Does this mean I get to be a prince like Daniel? That guy's always trying to show me up."

Her lips tilted up enough to know this conversation was a welcome distraction. "He's good at that." She sat on the cot across from me. "When we were kids, I loved archery. I would practice every day. One time, our father came out to the field and had us both shoot. I beat Daniel by quite a margin, but he couldn't stand that I might be better at this one thing, so he spent hours shooting arrows every day after that. He made a special target, carried a bow with him everywhere, that sort of thing."

I snorted. "Yeah. He likes to win, all right." Talking about Daniel wasn't helping my mood, but it did seem to improve Mya's.

"Now that I think about it, I wonder if it had to do with Father. He took Daniel aside and spoke with him, but at the time, I was too excited about winning to pay much attention. Maybe it was Father who made him do all that practicing."

I didn't know King Dryden well, but it wouldn't surprise me that he controlled Daniel to that degree. "How old were you?"

Mya paused to think, brushing a strand of dark hair behind her ear which inexplicably reminded me of how soft it had felt. "I was eight. Daniel ten."

A bit harsh on a ten-year-old. Those lessons from the king started young. But pity for the prince wasn't something I was ready to conjure just yet.

"Do you think he'll save us?" Mya twisted the corner of the rough blanket between her fingers.

The question took me aback. She didn't know if her own father would come for her? Our chances plummeted lower than expected. "You'd know better." I leaned against the wall and crossed my arms, schooling my features to shield her from the sinking feeling in my belly.

She proceeded to inform me how he was against the peace treaty, which I also knew nothing about until she filled me in, and how she convinced her father to concede and not throw her, Daniel, and the soldiers in a dungeon for disobeying. "And now I'm captured, and Daniel is out there somewhere, and…" Her eyes turned glassy and darted around the small room, now focusing everywhere but at me.

"It's gonna be okay," I told her. "We haven't seen your brother, which leads me to believe he got away. Otherwise, they'd lock you up with him instead of this improper union." I gave her a cocky grin. "Unless, of course, their idea of torture is to annoy him to death by putting us together."

She cracked a small smile. "I hope you're right."

"I'm always right." If only that were true. Although, I did have a sense about things. For instance, I knew the dragon mission would be a disaster, yet I blocked my intuition because I abandoned self-preservation due to a stupid broken heart. Deep down, I also knew something would happen to Grace. Maybe not that night, but her conviction had certainly convinced me. And now… I had to get Mya out of here—or protect her until someone else could take over because the sense of foreboding about this place hung dense as smoke from the Embers' fires.

Daniel's stubbornness and self-assuredness would force him to return for his sister. Let's hope he kept Cate out of any plan they might have because—and this I felt deep in my bones—the long game for this peace treaty ambush wasn't to trap a knight, a princess, or even a king. It was to draw out Cate. Their intense belief in the prophecy, almost like a religion, made them fanatical in their quest to find her and break it.

I only hoped King Aldridge made it out. Because if the Embers held him somewhere, it was a good bet his daughter couldn't be convinced to stay away.

"You're quiet all of a sudden," Mya said.

"Yeah. I guess I'm tired. Should we take advantage of the high-quality cots they provided and get some sleep?" I patted the scratchy blanket. Light still shone through a tiny window near the ceiling on Mya's side, though the sun would set soon. A little more rest wouldn't be a bad thing.

Mya yawned. "You mean you didn't sleep well on the cold ground surrounded by the enemy these last few nights?"

"I've gotten used to it, but no."

She lay down, tucking her feet under the blanket. She didn't bother removing her shoes. Probably a good idea to stay prepared for anything.

"In the pit?" she asked.

"Hmm?" My mind had already wandered as soon as my head hit the cot.

"Was it bad in there?"

I rolled on my side toward her. "Not a great topic for a bedtime story." The despair I had felt. The hunger. Not something I wanted to relive or burden Mya.

She shifted in her bed rather violently. "Ugh. My kingdom for a pillow!"

And there she was. The princess. Mya had put on a brave face, but she'd been coddled her entire life—entitlement had to come out sometime. She wasn't wrong. Our cots swayed in the middle, their only redeeming factor was that they kept us off the floor. A pillow would help.

"Goodnight, Mya."

A sigh. "Night."

Despite the missing headrest, I slept better than I had in nearly two months, probably because it was the first time the cold earth hadn't seeped into my marrow. An Ember rudely awoke us, jiggling a stick across the bars.

"Let's go. Boss says to put you to work."

Mya roused, her hair a messy dark halo around her head. He escorted us outside where a group of prisoners waited, their legs shackled. Someone secured metal cuffs onto my ankles, but let my hands stay free. They led Mya in the opposite direction, unchained.

"Hey," I called. "We're supposed to stay together."

"She'll be fine. She's with the other women," the guard said. "Don't want to ruin those pretty hands with what you'll be doing."

"Could I go with her?" It sounded better than whatever they had in store for me.

The man snorted. "Not likely. You'll see her safe and sound in your little cell tonight."

I watched her go while the Embers gathered more men from the prison. As usual, she acted confident, even in her sack of a brown dress they'd provided her.

A guard rudely shoved me ahead. "Let's go."

We walked in a line, the chains chinking with every step. "Detour through the square," one of them called. "I want blondie here to see something."

The nearest Ember jostled my ribs. I must be blondie. The bedraggled group marched on until we arrived at a courtyard of sorts. None of the streets were paved, so there were no cobblestones, statues, or fountains that often denoted a town square. Stone and mud buildings lined all four sides. In the middle stood a cage, stretching taller than wide with a person standing inside. We approached, the man coming into focus. Dried blood crossed his temple and cheek, one eye bruised and puffy. Even with the deformity, it was easy to make out his identity. Caged in the square like an animal.

King Aldridge.

CHAPTER 28
DANIEL

Cate and I met for breakfast the next morning. I slept well past sunrise, nearing noon, making our meal more of a brunch.

"I've arranged to meet with Baron Graftonberg after we eat." She popped a bite of scone into her mouth, licking a bit of clotting cream from her lips.

The baron was one of Cate's least favorite people, which led me to wonder why we were meeting with him.

"My father left him in charge." She toyed with the eggs on her plate, seeming almost embarrassed by the predicament King Aldridge had left her in. Graftonberg was a pompous jerk, which made me question the king's judge of character.

"I'm glad Dev made it back," she said. "Should we invite him?"

"Nah, let's fill him in later. The baron will probably dismiss him as unimportant, anyway."

She gave a half snort. "Even though Dev outranks him as a duke's son."

"A *Terran* duke. Graftonberg's never been known to hold back his opinions of Terrans."

"True. With him in charge, we'll be lucky he doesn't align with the Embers just to see your kingdom burn."

An exaggeration, but one likely not too far from the truth. Unfortunately, we needed him on our side. We needed a whole army.

I ate with gusto, making up for lost time, noting Cate ingested next to nothing. On our way here, we'd focused on escaping the scorched countryside, not taking the time to hunt, knowing a bounty lay in front of us. A gnawing hunger to arrive home—to leave the killing and fires behind us—led our small band of soldiers here. I gave Dev, Hugo, and Erickson the choice to return to Terra. Loyal, they stayed with me. They missed their families, Erickson with a toddler at home, but I was glad they remained. The injury on his arm had already demonstrated a partial recovery. I'd be calling on the three of them to fight again. Just the thought of another battle forced my plate away, the memories of smoke filling my nostrils.

The baron had taken up residence in the conference room. He sat in King Aldridge's usual position at the round table, papers scattered in front of him, and a tea cart within arm's reach. A younger man with a ruddy complexion and a bored expression slumped next to him. I glanced at Cate, but she held her face impassive. A wave of disgust from her at both the men wafted over me. And I don't think it was from the messy shortbread crumbs and jam-spotted paperwork.

"Thank you for meeting with us." Cate took a seat before he offered, and I followed her lead. We already talked through what to say, so her words were no surprise. "Baron, one of the things I admire about you is your discretion. I'd like to call on that now. Can we agree?" She folded her hands in front of her.

I was proud of her impressive command of the room, something that didn't come naturally to her.

"I'll hear you out," Graftonberg said.

"No. You'll give your word." Cate stared at him.

"Fine." Graftonberg picked up a pen and fiddled with it, scowling.

"And Roy?" She turned to me. "Sorry, Daniel, this is Roy, the baron's son. I don't believe you've met."

"Nice to meet you." I forced a smile. Cate's feelings were not friendly toward this man, and I wondered what he'd done to earn her ire.

Roy, blond, and a little older than me with the genetics that indicated he'll have his father's jowls in a few years, met my stare with the same disinterested hooded gaze, then turned to Cate. "Sure. Let's hear it."

"As you may have heard, King Aldridge did not return last night with the others. Neither did Alana or General Griffin. They were ambushed. The treaty didn't go well." She steepled her fingers.

The baron gave Cate a stony glare. "Which is exactly what I knew would happen, and I said as much in this room three weeks ago."

"You were correct. And now we have to get them back. Daniel thinks the king may have escaped, so we should send out search parties. I took the liberty of assembling several groups. One left last night, and the other this morning. All were instructed to be discreet, but we still need a few more. There is no reason to alarm the country at this point."

"Your father left *me* in charge. You mean, no reason for the people to know the regent is running the kingdom until the last possible moment."

I could feel Cate's frustration grow. "No, that's not it." She struggled to keep her voice calm. "I propose we search for the king for one week. In the meantime, we'll devise a plan to retrieve him so there won't be chaos in the streets."

"Princess. You think Caelum will go into pandemonium because your father's gone? I can assure you that I am more than capable."

"Yes. To serve as my regent. Of course."

He inclined his head. "Of course." It didn't take special powers to detect his animosity and dismissal of Cate. She deserved a leader who respected her, and Graftonberg obviously never would.

"I agree with the search parties. We will wait to inform the people as you requested. As far as retrieving your father? That's a lost cause. I have no intention of losing more men. You wanted peace? Well then, let's have peace."

Cate stood, her chair nearly toppling. "You can't mean that. He's the king," her voice rose.

"And he put me in charge." He leveled her with a glare. "I'm thinking of the people instead of you. You're just an emotional girl who wants her daddy back. No one wants war."

"But they want their leader returned." Cate leaned forward on the table.

"Do they?" Graftonberg tilted his head. "I guess we'll have to wait and see."

I wanted to defend Cate. Honestly, I wanted to punch this guy in the jaw so hard his jowls swelled, but that wasn't what Cate required right now. She needed to prove that she could run this kingdom. I stood with her to show my support. "Yes, we will see, won't we," I said as civilly as I could manage. "Roy." I tipped my head and followed Cate out.

We paced ten steps and Cate stopped, clenching her fists. "Ooooh. I hate that man! Can you believe him? He's not going to authorize an army because *he* wants to be regent. He's happy to have Father out of the way."

"Let's go somewhere more private. We'll formulate a plan. At least he agreed to continue searching for him. Who knows? Maybe King Aldridge will come riding in tomorrow."

She interlaced her fingers with mine. "I hope so. But you don't really believe that, do you." It was a statement, not a question. I ached from the pain that emanated from her.

"Keep the faith a little while longer." I squeezed her hand. "Dev might have some good ideas."

Urging her down the corridor, I knew she wanted to return and give Graftonberg a piece of her mind, but she followed. In the king's office, we filled Dev in on our meeting while sitting in plush leather chairs that flanked the coffee table.

Dev's disgusted expression said it all. "I'm fairly accustomed to ladder climbing sycophants—my father wrote the book. The best thing to do is to pretend we're going along with him." He crossed his ankle over one knee.

"Let him believe I would abandon my father?" Cate's voice hitched.

"He's one of those types that thinks women are weak, and men should be in charge, right?"

"It's almost like you've met the guy. And his sniveling son," Cate said.

"He's so full of himself, he'll believe you've decided that his plan is best. But we'll beat him when the time comes."

"I was detecting some serious distaste from you about Roy," I said to Cate. "What's he done besides being Graftonberg's son?"

She averted her eyes. "Nothing you need to worry about."

There was a story there, but I let it go. Maybe she'd tell me later when she wasn't so worried about her father.

"So," Dev said. "Bottom line. If King Aldridge has been captured, as of now, Graftonberg won't rescue him. We either find a way around or…"

"We're relying solely on the decision of King Dryden to help," Cate finished.

Dev's attention flipped between us. "I don't love those odds."

CHAPTER 29
LUCAS

King Aldridge straightened his posture, stepping from the iron bars as he saw us approach, too proud to stoop in pain, his dark blue uniform marred with torn strips across his back from a flogging. Blood caked his sandy beard. The Embers hadn't treated their rival king well, displaying him as some sort of sick trophy. Why they had even kept him alive, I could only conjecture—leveraging land from Caelum for starters. Cate had to be their real target. Although I doubted they would give up the town square's newest ornament anytime soon. I'd actually been lucky when they threw me in the pit. They could have locked me in a cage.

As we passed, I met the king's gaze. I nodded once to indicate I saw his predicament, though careful not to attract attention to either of us. Did he see in that nod the promise to do whatever I could to save him? That my allegiance hadn't faltered? Guilt sat heavy, knowing my supposed release factored into his imprisonment.

"Hurry up."

Someone shoved me to exit the square with the rest of the prisoners, leaving King Aldridge behind. I marched in the line of men, chains clanking the whole way out of town. We finally came to rows and rows of tilled ground. A crude irrigation system with connected pipes on wheels and holes punched in the conduits hung over the dirt. A river sounded in the distance, presumably the source of water.

The climate had turned to late summer. Any crops that grew here over the spring were likely harvested already. The soil would need preparation for cold-weather vegetables such as kale or gourds. A haphazard pile of hoes, rakes, and picks sat nearby, and the prisoners headed toward the stack.

"Terrans in the rear," one of the Embers commanded.

They unhooked us from each other, leaving the thirty-centimeter chain shackling each person's ankle. The lowly Caelumites without power over earth were assigned to the hard labor of breaking up the dirt while the Terrans tenderized the ground. If they weren't the enemy, I'd provide wind for windmills, but they didn't deserve the benefit of electricity.

We toiled all day until the sun rode low on the horizon. Other groups of prisoners from a different jail worked elsewhere in the fields, the distance too far to speak or evaluate if I recognized any of them. A few breaks with water from the river and a handful of nuts were our meal. No wonder they didn't feed me much in the pit. The Embers had a food problem—as in not enough of it. The land was tired and scorched. Most were illiterate, with few possessing the patience to learn. I'd heard there weren't even organized schools. The lack of education played a part in their failure to rotate crops, knowledge of planting seasons, and irrigation. Apparently one of them, or a particularly helpful prisoner who wanted dinner, had put this crude system into place.

A whistle sounded, and the more experienced quickly closed the gaps in our line. A thin man in a worn tunic stood next to me. "How long you been here?" I asked.

"Shh. They don't like talking," he whispered. "Over a year," he added.

"You do this every day?"

He glanced behind to see if anyone was watching. "Mostly. Sometimes I help build houses or haul dirt. Doesn't matter. It's always hard labor."

"Better than the pit, but not by much."

Creases crisscrossed his face, a tan deepening his skin from excess sun. Is this where I'd be next year? I wanted to spend time with my mom, buy a house of my own, and maybe one day get over my infatuation with Cate and settle down. This guy probably had dreams, too. Maybe even kids at home.

"I'm Lucas. Thanks for the intel."

"Bex." He reached to shake my hand, his palm cracked and dirt-caked, but a guard wandered close, and his arm dropped.

We trudged back to our jail, the only sound the clinking of chains and the scuffling of boots in the dusty earth. I wasn't certain if I was relieved or worried that they didn't take me past King Aldridge again. When we arrived, they let us rinse our hands and face in a trough.

"Wouldn't mind a bath or shower. You guys ever heard of showers?" They hadn't, unless any of them went through the portal to England to search for Cate. *Showers.* They truly were the stuff of legends.

"You bathe in the river once a week," a guard said.

They apparently weren't familiar with the saying that every Caelum mother pounds into their boys: cleanliness is next to godliness. Cate and I once argued if the phrase originated from her homeland or mine. The Embers had provided me fresh clothes in jail and had let me clean up after I'd exited the pit, but that had been the last time I'd bathed.

Mya was sitting on the cot when I arrived. A pleasant warmth crossed through my chest at the sight of her. I had become more attached, perhaps… more protective of her than I'd realized. Her brow furrowed. "You alright? You're filthy."

"I'm a farmer now, didn't you know?" I kept my voice light—always subconsciously trying to make things easier for her. "Where'd they take you?"

She scooted back on the bed to lean against the wall. "I babysat children all day. Wild, disobedient four-to eight-year-olds. I had to carry around a water pouch to put out the fires." She fingered a hole in her skirt. "I was a little late on this one. Sparks flew everywhere."

"So, is it some kind of school?"

She sighed. "I wish. It's crazy and disorganized. We watch the kids the entire day, and my only instruction was to stop them from killing each other or from starting too big of a fire."

"Who else was there?"

"Other prisoners, also some teenage Embers who weren't much help. The other captured women are housed on the far side of town together. Apparently, they wanted to keep a better eye on me, so they put me in the jail."

My thoughts turned to Grace. "The other girls. Where are they from?"

She shrugged. "All over. Not much time to talk. They did seem afraid. Something is going on here besides babysitting."

I leaned forward and softened my voice, "They're kidnapping girls for some reason."

"Kidnapping?" Mya's sculpted brows lowered.

"How many are there?" I brushed past her question.

Her face clouded as if she just realized how low our enemy would stoop. "I'm not sure. I'll see what I can find out tomorrow."

"Look for a girl. Her name's Grace. She's around fifteen or sixteen?" I proceeded to tell her the whole story. How Grace had been stolen from the town under my nose.

"But why would they go to all that trouble just for a babysitter?"

"True, it's not like there's an abundance of food here." My stomach growled at the mention of it.

"Ugh. Don't remind me." She clutched her middle. "I'm so hungry. We had cabbage soup at midday. Light on the cabbage."

It wasn't long before someone slipped trays under the bars with a meager helping of potatoes, a small cube of unidentifiable cured meat, and a few carrots. It tasted horrible—unseasoned and dry, yet we scarfed every morsel.

"I'm going to imagine this is Hildy's, our head cook's roast. With a side of fruit tart. Flaky. Buttery." Mya closed her eyes.

My imagination wasn't nearly so strong. Shoe leather was more like it.

"What would you eat if you could?" she asked.

I didn't hesitate. "My mom's stew. And a hunk of her bread. Generous amount of butter, of course."

One corner of her mouth quirked. "Of course."

We finished eating in silence, lost in our own memories.

"I wonder if I'll ever have one of those tarts again," she said.

"We're getting out of here. Don't lose hope. Your father's too proud to let you stay in enemy hands."

"I guess." She didn't sound convinced, which did nothing for my confidence.

"Let's do some intel tomorrow. You find out about the women, and I'll talk to the guys."

She sat up straighter. "We'll be spies."

One probably should be incognito to be a spy, not in prison chains. But sure. "Yup. Totally." I had a hard time keeping a straight face.

"Ooh. I'll be good at this. I've had years of training."

I gave her a skeptical look. "Really? Dryden's secret weapon or something?"

She waved her hand dismissively. "Of course not. Father doesn't trust a woman with anything. I'm talking about ballroom gossip. I'm excellent at ferreting out the truth. One wrong flick of the fan—I'll be all over it."

"You do realize there won't be fans, right?"

She smirked. "You too? Men. Always underestimating me."

Aww. Now I've offended her. I didn't want to hurt her feelings. She might have a point, though. She very well could be a brilliant operative. I certainly liked her spunk. "You'll make an excellent spy. I look forward to hearing your report tomorrow."

She lay down, sliding under the covers. This time, she took her shoes off first. "Yours too. May the best spy win." She turned to the wall.

"I wasn't aware this was a competition."

"And that's why I'm already one step ahead of you."

CHAPTER 30
CATE

The week passed slowly awaiting news of Father. Every time a set of scouts returned, we rushed into the courtyard only to find disappointed faces. I didn't want their condolences. I'd heard too many, "I'm so sorry, Princess," from the men, their voices ringing with defeat. They had given up.

So had I.

The Embers had captured King Aldridge, and whether they'd left him alive was anyone's guess. Each day I hoped for a ransom note, or conditions for his release, but there had been nothing except silence.

The only bright side was the return of some of the horses, including Dev's, found on a scouting mission. A small smile had crept on my face at his delight in seeing his companion uninjured. For Daniel's sake, Raven hopefully remained safe in Terra after being rescued from the landslide site.

Dev's words about relying on King Dryden echoed in my head, *I don't love those odds*. We didn't have much choice—at minimum, he should be informed of Mya. Daniel had been restless all week, knowing his father must be told, though not wanting to go to Terra until we were certain of King Aldridge's fate. He'd been working out his excess anxiety with Dev, both of them clashing swords, running, and sparring as if desperate in their preparation to retrieve Mya and in apprehension of impending war.

I'd been practicing as well, with minor success, just no downpours that would put a dent into a fire of any size. Charlie and I also trained with Mocha. She knew my father already, so we showed her his belongings to learn to bring a message to him when the time came. A long shot, but we practiced anyway, feeling adrift.

That night, Dev, Daniel, and I sat together at dinner. We ate in near silence, each of us absorbed in our own thoughts. I understood what I needed to say, to put into motion, but doing it felt like giving up on my father. Admitting he was lost to us.

I chewed a green vegetable, something we didn't have back home, the name forgotten. It made no difference. I couldn't taste it anyway. I swallowed thickly. "We should leave for Terra tomorrow. We've wasted enough time."

Daniel leaned across the table to hold my hand. "You sure?" His eyes met mine, the dark circles beneath reflecting how hard these last few weeks had been on him.

"I'm sure. Dev—you'll tell Erikson and Hugo? They'd probably love to see their families."

He nodded, absently stirring the veggies on his plate.

"I've gathered some Caelum soldiers to go with us," I continued. "We're not going to risk trouble on the road to Terra." I gave Daniel a pointed look.

"I've spoken to some as well. I'll finish gathering supplies. We'll be ready at sunrise." He squeezed my hand in reassurance.

A wave of butterflies took flight in my belly. I now thought of Caelum as my home. Leaving somehow seemed as if I were abandoning the people with someone untrustworthy to captain the ship. Even with my misgivings, traveling to Terra still felt like the right choice. I couldn't leave this only up to Daniel—I needed to plead our case to King Dryden in person.

"I'll inform Graftonberg, so he doesn't hunt us down for stealing troops and supplies." I hated that I had to beg for his permission. I'd have to be subtle and somehow convince him we're doing him a favor.

Dev stood and put a hand on my shoulder. "You're a good woman, Cate. Thanks for taking this one for the team." His lips held a teasing grin. It was nice to find a little humor in something. Even if it was partly at my expense.

"You can repay me later," I shot back.

The boardroom sat empty, but I suppose that wasn't a surprise, given it was after dinner time. Baron Graftonberg was probably off somewhere sipping port wine with Roy and a gaggle of onlookers. With the assistance of the steward, I found him in a sitting room and held back a grin at the accuracy of my prediction.

The baron sat in an overstuffed chair, swirling his burgundy-colored drink and guffawing with another man—count something or other. We'd been introduced once, and I immediately spotted him as a Graftonberg crony, promptly forgetting his name. His rheumy eyes belied how often he partook of the spirits he now gulped. I inwardly smiled as he coughed and sputtered his drink when catching sight of me.

"Princess," the count said, bowing awkwardly, revealing a bald spot in his thinning brown hair.

I ignored him and turned to the baron, taking a seat without being asked. "Daniel and I wanted your opinion on something."

Graftonberg straightened in his cognac-colored leather chair, preening in front of his friends. Roy took the seat next to mine. I avoided eye contact. He'd initiated unwanted advances a few too many times, suggesting the Caelum people would find him more suitable than Daniel. Once he'd cornered me in a secluded corridor and… let's just say I wasn't sure what would have happened if a maid hadn't interrupted. The guy made my skin crawl, well on his way to becoming Jowly Jr.

"We think," I continued, directing my gaze to the baron, "that King Dryden can be of assistance once Daniel and I tell him that Princess Mya is being held captive. He'll jump at the chance to rescue her, sparing no expense."

"The princess has been captured?" Roy asked, leaning forward.

"She tagged along with Daniel to the peace treaty."

His sandy brows lowered in confusion. "Why would she do that?"

"You'll have to ask her." We were getting off track. "We'll need some men to accompany us to Terra so we can request King Dryden's help. When the Terrans rescue Mya, they'll find Lucas and Father. A win for all of us."

Graftonberg tapped his chin as if in contemplation. Like it was a hard decision, the pompous—

"When would you leave?" he asked.

"The sooner the better." I smiled sweetly. "Would you feel comfortable watching over the kingdom while we're gone?"

The count laughed while the baron narrowed his eyes. "I'm perfectly capable—"

"Of course you are. I wanted to consult with you first."

"You should leave at sunrise. The quicker King Dryden is notified, the faster we'll have an answer." He gulped his drink and set it with a clunk on the end table.

"I appreciate it, Baron. We have much to prepare. I'll be off."

I closed the door behind me and strode down the corridor. Dev was right. Appeal to his pride. So predictable.

The next morning, we departed with fifty Caelum soldiers, Daniel, his small crew, and me atop North. We rode all day until we reached Bandit's Hole. A cute town, despite its name, with a lovely inn and barns to house the horses.

"So far, so good," I told Daniel as we dismounted.

"Don't jinx it. In theory, I've used all the bad luck."

"One can hope."

He pulled me around the corner of the barn and took me in his arms. His lips met mine in a soft, comforting kiss that sent tingles down my spine. "I've been wanting to do that all day. So. Many.

People nearby." He punctuated his words with kisses. Poor Daniel, destined to one day be king, but such an introvert at heart. Not unlike me. Both of us thrust into roles that didn't come naturally.

I wound my fingers tighter behind his neck, pressing myself to him. "I agree. Too many." I kissed him back with fervor, shutting the rest of the world away, at least for a few moments.

His forehead pressed against mine. "Thank you."

"For what? Being an excellent kisser?" I had since gotten over my concerns I'd had in that department after our first kiss.

He stepped away, lips tilted up. "For being my… what do you call it? My *person*. The one I always want to share my news—good or bad. You're who I think of first thing in the morning, when I drift off to sleep, and long into the night in my dreams. You *are* my dream." He gently tucked a lock of hair behind my ear. "Thank you for keeping me sane. For helping me through this."

He'd been strong for me. I'd been beside myself about my father, yet he'd lost Mya and carried the weight of returning home without her. It felt good to know I managed to shoulder some of the burden for him. "It's a two-way street. You've been there for me, too."

He let out a short laugh. "I don't understand that first part, but I think I catch your overall meaning. Come on, let's go inside."

We checked in, but before we could retire to the dining room for dinner, a slim, balding man approached, dressed in the tailored red coat of the hotel staff.

"Your Highnesses." He bowed. "May I speak to you for a moment?"

We consented, and he led us to an office. He cleared his throat. "We've had some unusual sightings as of late, and I wanted you to be aware."

"Unusual how?" Daniel placed a palm on the desk's polished wood surface and leaned forward.

"Animals. Ones we don't usually see in these parts. They're eating livestock, stealing chickens, that sort of thing. A man was killed up the road by something big—a cat, maybe."

Daniel glanced at me, not sure how much we wanted to reveal

about the large swath of land the Embers had burned, displacing wildlife south.

"I've heard the reports," I said. "You have enough men to guard the livestock?"

He bit his lip. "I believe they're starting sentry shifts."

I nodded my approval. "Thank you—"

"Byers," he replied. "I manage the inn. I've been warning the travelers."

"Good work. Keep us posted."

We started for the door, but Daniel pivoted. "We would enjoy some dinner in the dining room this evening. Table for two."

After cleaning up, we sat in the cozy space in an intimate corner, a candle flickering between us. The others ate outdoors from a buffet the inn provided.

"Thought we could use a little more time together." Daniel's knee brushed against mine under the table.

"It's perfect. I'm happy you thought of it. Sometimes I get so caught up in everything else."

"Me too." His eyes glittered in the candlelight. "We need to do this more often."

A waiter set goblets of water in front of us, asking for our order. The selection was small, but after a day in the saddle, the food sounded mouthwatering.

"I hadn't realized the animal problem had ventured this far south," Daniel said after the man left.

"Wonder if that fire burned out of control."

"Must have. We were already seeing weird migration patterns. I told you about the drundles?" He traced a fold in the tablecloth.

"Yup. And the tree leopard that wanted you for dinner." I hoped to not come across one on our trip. There were still so many creatures I wasn't familiar with here. But a giant toothy cat? I'd get the idea pretty fast.

"I was flattered by the invitation but would much rather dine with you." He sent me one of those knee-wobble-inducing smiles.

"It is nice to forget about things for a while." I brushed his fingers with mine. "No prying eyes—"

"Pompous barons," he continued.

"Jowly. He makes me lose my appetite." Hopefully, he wouldn't do anything too rash while we were gone.

When the food came, I forgot the baron and ate more than I had in weeks. Perhaps it was having Daniel across from me, the calm in the storm, or my stomach catching up with me. I gazed longingly at a piece of bread, still half-eaten on Daniel's plate. He glanced at the crust that held my attention. Before I could snatch the roll, he swiped it up and pretended to pop it into his mouth. Instead, he fed me the bite, his eyes crinkling in the corners while I licked the butter from my lips.

"Let's get more," he said.

"And dessert." I resisted the urge to slide my finger through the remaining sauce on my plate and lick it clean.

After dinner we climbed the steps to our rooms together, both of us stuffed—me regretting the last bite of fruit cobbler. It felt so good to be normal, almost like a real date. To put our problems aside for the night and enjoy each other. If we lived back home, we could go to the movies, Taco Tuesday, and share mochas at the local coffee shop afterward. That life. Sometimes I ached for it, then I remembered not quite fitting in, always wanting something more. That something was here. My purpose. My love… my prince.

We gathered outside the barn, the dawn sky a brilliant orange to the east. My shoulders relaxed with the restful night's sleep, feather pillow, and full belly, which all contributed to my optimism. Perhaps it was also Daniel and his positivity that we'd have a clear ride to Terra the next few days. Everything lay on the line for us to convince his father. My shoulders tensed at imagining Daniel telling the king about Mya. *One day at a time*. We can worry about Dryden when we get there.

Astride North, I rode up next to Daniel. "I think we're ready."

The soldiers sat high on their mounts, surrounding us in the small courtyard. Dev gave me a nod from the rear of the pack.

"Say the word," Daniel said.

I opened my mouth to speak when a townsman rushed toward us, stealing the words. "Help," he called, stumbling into the center of the group, the horses jittering backward. "There's a pack of boars headed into town."

"Boars don't travel in packs." Daniel rubbed the back of his neck. "The fires," he mumbled under his breath.

"Which way?" I asked.

He pointed northeast. "Headed right down the middle of the road earlier."

"Split up. Half go warn the townspeople, the others find the boars." I nodded reassuringly to the man. "Looks like you'll eat well tonight."

The soldiers scattered, which would delay our trek, but the Caelum people needed to see a leader who cared about their welfare. I turned to Daniel, who remained by my side. "I didn't know you had boar here. Finally, an animal I know something about."

He raised his brows. "Really. Been boar hunting before, have you?"

"Sure, all the time," I replied airily.

"You alright here?" Daniel patted North's flank. "I'm going to do some actual hunting."

"I'll wait for you in the barn." I blew him a kiss, then headed into the large structure behind the inn.

A few horses remained from those staying at the lodge, the stable otherwise eerily quiet. The scent of hay mixed with stalls needing to be mucked out was now familiar. A few short months ago, I'd never even ridden a horse. After depositing North in a stall, I slumped onto a bench along one side. A sheep bleated somewhere in the stillness. The stablemen must have gone in search of the boar. It was nice to be alone without anyone's heavy expectations. I tilted my head against the wall and stretched out my legs. Dawn had come early, and a quick nap would be perfect. Horses lightly stomped their hooves, a fresh breeze floated through the open door, and my eyes fluttered closed.

North's whinnying startled me awake. A pig-like animal stared at me not ten feet away, larger than any boar I'd seen in the Portland Zoo. Its bristly hair stood on end like raggedy black toothbrush bristles.

"Easy, boy."

It snorted, snout glistening with unidentifiable wetness. If the scariness of its enormous canines wasn't enough, the ick factor added another level to the situation. I needed a weapon. The hay rakes hung on the opposite wall out of reach. Next to me sat a feed bucket half-full of oats. Do boars eat oats? I had no idea, and this thing stood several feet taller than any back home.

"You hungry?" I slid the pail from against the wall, wincing at the scraping sound it made along the rough-hewn barn floor. If I dumped the food here, the animal would move too close, impeding my escape. Flinging the grain might startle the beast, causing it to charge. Slowly, I stood with the pail. It watched me warily. Just a couple of steps and I'd have a clear path to the door.

It lowered its head, its eyes turning angry. How I knew the animal was mad, I wasn't sure, but those black eyes definitely meant business. Before I could rethink it, I upended the bucket, and the oats streamed onto the floor. The boar took a step forward and sniffed the grain. *Please eat it.* Sure enough, that wet snout buried itself in the pile, allowing me time to creep toward the entrance. But when I turned, the exit was blocked. An entire herd of boar trotted in my direction, perhaps hearing their comrade noisily eating.

I was trapped.

CHAPTER 31
DANIEL

It had been a goose chase of a morning. Two hours later, we'd warned the townspeople of the pack of boars, but so far nobody had trapped or killed a single one. There had been a few sightings, though only at a distance. I appreciated Cate's soft-heartedness for her people, but we needed to focus and proceed to Terra, even if I dreaded it. Nerves jolted into my belly. I wasn't sure who I feared telling more about Mya—Mother or Father.

My horse trotted toward the barn, probably assuming he was headed to food and rest. Instead, I walked him to the paddock. I had instructed a few men to round up everyone else and meet here.

The stable yard stood empty. A tingle of unease led me to search for Cate. I'd left her here, thinking she was safe. We'd been gone so long, she might have snuck back to the inn for a rest and snack. I started that way when I heard a squeal. *Not the human variety.* Slowly turning, I tried to determine which direction it had come.

Quiet.

Then shuffling from the barn. Horses?

A grunt.

That was no equine. I rushed to the entrance. Inside, a group of boars crowded around something on the floor. All I had to do was shut the door and they'd be captured. I smiled to myself, but just as I pulled the handle, Cate spoke.

"Little help here?"

I blinked, searching the stable yard once more.

"Up here."

The barn's few windows left the space dim. In the shadows above the snuffling animals, Cate sat in the loft. I could see her dilemma—the boars packed the only exit.

Several grunted and the mass of wild pigs shifted, growing restless. One squealed as another butted against it. A stream of oats hailed down from the rafters. Cate held a bucket aloft.

"I'm almost out of food." Her face flickered with both concern and humor. We'd chased these guys all over town, and all Cate did was feed the poor bastards.

"I'll be right back. Don't go anywhere." I held up my palm in the universal "stay there" sign, even though she obviously wasn't moving.

Some of the men filed into the stable yard, and I directed them to find more food—oats—whatever they could get their hands on. I opened the paddock gate and ensured that all our horses were led away from the area. The last thing we needed was a spooked gelding causing a boar stampede.

Buckets of grain, some sort of leftover slop from the kitchens, and a ham bone arrived.

"Alright, who brought the bone?" I held it up.

A baby-faced soldier slowly raised his hand. "I thought they ate anything?"

Maybe they did, but a bit morbid, even for me. We constructed a food trail to the paddock with a generous pile in the enclosure.

When I returned to the stable, the herd had become restless, rooting and shoving one another. After my eyes adjusted, I could make out Cate sitting with her knees pulled to her chin, the skirt of her blue riding habit spread around her.

"Nice of you to come back." She gave me a wry smile.

"Patience, Princess."

She shoved a stray hair behind her ear and grinned. "Don't be so pushy, *Prince*."

We successfully led the animals into the paddock with only one dicey moment when a particularly large female showed more interest in me than the food. Eventually, they were all secured, and I made my way back to the barn.

Cate stepped from the final rung of the ladder, and I pulled her to me, her honey and lavender shampoo filling my senses. She smelled like home. Not Terra. A place reserved just for us.

"You outsmarted them," I said.

"If that were true, I wouldn't have needed rescuing." She kissed my cheek. "Let's get out of here."

Several days later, we approached Terra Castle, the rest of our trip uneventful. The ivy-covered stone towers peaked over the four-meter walls rimming the perimeter. The palace drew out countless mixed emotions bottled up so tight the glass might shatter. Pine scent washed over me the way only childhood smells could evoke memories of games of hide and seek, swordplay, and riding lessons. Other images grew darker as we rode through the gates. Father transferring power into me—electric energy leaving me breathless in the dirt until I did something correct, the look of disappointment crossing his features, or more so, the sadness in my mother's eyes.

"Daniel."

I turned to see Cate searching my face. The sun shone on her hair, turning the strands around her cheeks a golden honey. Having her by my side soothed my nerves with the knowledge I wouldn't be forced to confront him alone. Yet it felt selfish, subjecting her to his wrath to ease my way.

"You okay?" She squeezed my shoulder.

"Yeah. Why?"

"I've been talking to you, but you're a million miles away," she said, her words soft. I could feel her concern. She knew enough about my past to understand and was also familiar with the weight of expectations from her own family. And the kingdoms.

I stepped from my horse. "I'm fine." *A lie.* "And I'm glad you're here." *The truth.*

We passed our mounts to a groom, but before venturing into the castle, I couldn't help but check on Raven. He stood safely in the barn and nudged me with his nose through the bars of the stall. Cate handed me an apple from a nearby barrel, his favorite. "How are you feeling, boy?" I entered the enclosure and examined his legs, relieved to find them bandage-free and sound. "He looks good."

Cate leaned against the door and a brief wave of contentment rushed through me, radiating from both of us. We may be facing what seemed like insurmountable challenges, but at least we had each other.

"Ready?" she asked.

We interlocked fingers and strode into the house side-by-side. Staff discreetly informed me of the location of both my parents, who unsurprisingly were not together. I glanced at Cate. "Let's tell Mother first."

She nodded, and we headed up the stairs to the yellow sitting room, the same place we spoke last when she agreed to help ensure my escape. I hoped there hadn't been repercussions for deceiving the king. There'd never been evidence that he'd laid a hand on her, but my trust didn't go far.

Queen Lila sat with a book in her lap, staring out the expansive window into the east garden. My arrival shouldn't be a surprise; someone would have informed her by now. At the sound of my footsteps, she turned, her face lighting up. I crossed the room to hug her, searching for her feelings to discover if she knew about Mya. Only happiness at seeing me emanated from her.

So, she didn't know then. The realization tumbled into my gut, rolling with guilt. Selfishly, I'd hoped the news had leaked and I wouldn't have to be the messenger.

"Daniel." She drew me in. "I thought you might stay in Caelum a bit longer." She turned to find Cate approaching. "And what a surprise. So happy to see you, dear."

We all took a seat. The feminine room always made me uncomfortable, the spindly-legged chairs too fragile. I exhaled, the pregnant pause sending my nerves crackling. Mother peered around me to look through the doorway. "And Mya? The guards told me they didn't see her. Did she not come with you?"

"She's not here." I laced my fingers together, then unlaced them. "Things didn't go as planned with the peace treaty."

"Oh? We've heard little here. Your father has been waiting for a report."

"We wanted to tell him in person," Cate said.

I could feel Mother's anxiety rising. Cate stayed steady, calm even. She held it together because she knew how difficult this was for me.

The story unfolded. How Mya followed us, the trap set by the Embers scorching the land, their lack of interest in peace, and finally the account Dev gave me of her capture. My throat tightened as her anguish seeped into the room like a dense fog. Tears filled her eyes, and she didn't know what to do with her hands, fluttering to the hollow of her neck, temple, then lap.

"I failed her. I'm sorry." I wanted Mother to hold me and tell me everything would be okay. But in reality, it was my support she needed.

"What could have possessed her to do such a thing? She snuck out of Caelum Castle and followed you?" Her bewilderment mirrored mine when I discovered Mya tagging behind us.

"I think she's been feeling ignored. Useless. She wants more to do than plan parties."

Mother's chin raised. "Well, of course she does." She stood and went to the window. "So, they have her. She's out there somewhere. With them." She turned back. "What do they want from us? What's the ransom?"

"We haven't heard. They have my father, too." Cate sat rigidly straight, holding it together like the leader she was born to be.

Mother sank into her chair and looked to Cate. "You'll make rain. Then we'll go in and save Mya. And King Aldridge." Her head swiveled between us. "That will be the plan, correct?" She smiled weakly. "Your rain. That's the answer."

CHAPTER 32 **LUCAS**

The next morning, I trudged to the fields with the same group of prisoners. We failed to pass by the king, which made me wonder if they'd moved him elsewhere or if he was even still alive. Bex, the lanky guy I met yesterday, worked several rows over, his tall frame hunched over while tilling unwanted crabgrass with a hoe. The men next to me didn't make eye contact, ignoring my whispered efforts to gain information. If Mya fared better, she'd never let me live it down, and so far, surely, she was in the lead.

After the noon break, my body ached everywhere. Too many days in the pit had softened it. I wheedled my way to Bex's row and bent to pick a weed to throw in the burn pile. He grunted but didn't say much.

"So, Bex," I whispered. "What's with the food shortage? Is it the drought?"

"They store what they can." One shoulder lifted.

"And let the people go hungry?"

He snorted. "The prisoners, yeah. They're trying to raise an enormous army. I heard they want to quadruple their farming in the next ten years."

I plucked another weed, my spine creaking. "Where are they getting more men for an army?"

He looked behind him. "Things are going on here."

"What things?"

He leaned in closer.

"Hey! You there," an Ember shouted. "I've warned you before." The man marched over and brutally knocked Bex to the ground before I realized what was happening. The Ember, armed with a metal stick, hit Bex across the back, then stooped and pulled him up by the arm. He stumbled again. The chain attached to each ankle only gave so much leeway.

"Let's go." The man dragged Bex forward to the middle of where we worked and ordered him to take off his shirt. "This is what happens with a second offense," the Ember, a menacing fellow with eyes too small for his face, called. "And you," he pointed at me. "You've now had your one chance. Don't want to hear we aren't generous." He pushed poor Bex, who appeared as if he might throw up onto a mound of dirt while I watched in horror.

The metal rod in the Ember's hand began to glow hot. The iron hovered near Bex's shoulder blade, then came down in a long swipe, leaving a fifteen-centimeter line, red and puckering at the edges. His echoing wail sent a shudder through me. The acrid smell of burned flesh wafted through the huddle of prisoners. The monster branded him like livestock. Guilt gnawed at my insides, the fire burning a hole through my conscience. It should have been me. I'm the one who put Bex in jeopardy.

This place. I needed out. If we banded together, we might stand a chance, but this is how they kept us in line. No fraternizing. No planning. No sharing of secrets. Would they be this harsh on Mya? Worry buried itself under my skin. The thought of her vibrancy snuffed out by the Embers winnowed into my thoughts, leaving me thinking of her with every strike of the hoe.

Perhaps they'd underestimate her. If she could stay alive, she might be our best source of intel. The real question was, what would we do with the information we found?

The Embers had us on a tight leash—literally—I pulled at the chains at my feet. The fact that my survival might rely on King Dryden, the original definition of snake-in-the-grass, sunk my mood lower. I wouldn't put my trust in the Terran king, even if my life depended on it. And apparently, it did.

I'd keep searching. There had to be a way out, though escaping without Mya wasn't an option, which made it more difficult when the only time we were together was locked up in a jail cell.

The rest of the day dragged. Bex wouldn't meet my eye, which was probably for the best because even conveying an apology by mouthing "sorry" might lead to more trouble. It didn't stop the sick guilt in my stomach. At least it replaced the hunger.

When I returned, Mya had already slumped on her cot. I'd hoped she'd have a triumphant smile plastered across her face, but instead, tears welled in her eyes. I crossed the small room and sat next to her. The guard clanged the door shut, and I waited for his footsteps to fade before turning to her.

"What happened? Did they hurt you?" Worry sprung new, my thoughts from the field tumbling over one another.

"No—I'm fine. It's…" Tears spilled over her flushed cheeks.

I put an arm around her, and she buried her face in my shoulder and sobbed. She'd been so strong until now, making me wonder what caused the break. I patted her back like an awkward fool, which prompted her to burrow deeper, and I held her tight. She wrapped her arms about me until we both clutched one another.

I couldn't remember the last time someone held me. She felt warm, and soft in all the right places—a heady mixture of comfort and longing. The hug—at least for me—began to turn into something more. Awareness of her body against me, where our legs touched, and the heat of her breath on my neck led to a warmth that seeped into my hollow bones. My fingers slid through long, dark hair, silky and smooth. A heart fluttered quick like a rabbit's—mine or hers, I wasn't sure.

I drew away, our faces centimeters apart. The tears had stopped, her eyes now deep pools of blue, cheeks flushed, pink lips parted, daring me to kiss them. To take advantage of her in this vulnerable state wouldn't be right. Before I could detach myself, those lips were on mine. Soft, tentative, and warm.

I kissed her back.

I couldn't help it. Our predicament had drawn us together like two souls on a life raft adrift at sea. Her combination of strength and vulnerability enticed me more than I'd been willing to admit. Palms drifted along my sides, and I drew her closer, fisting her hair and releasing. Something in the back of my head reminded me that I should stop. She was hurting. Yet… Her nails slid down my spine, sending a shiver through me. Finally, a thought stopped me cold… this was Daniel's sister.

I pulled away, scooting back on the cot. "I'm sorry." Why did I always choose such complicated girls to kiss? Ones I somehow believed needed an apology after we finished?

"You are?" She touched her mouth, now perfectly swollen, with light fingertips.

"For taking advantage," I clarified.

Those kissable lips quirked up. "I'm not."

She had the kind of confidence befitting of her rank. Still, she'd been upset about something. Our surroundings brought everything back into focus. The Embers—what had they done to her? I stood and paced the small cell to create space between us. "What happened today?"

"Maybe we should talk about what happened just now?" She tapped her fingers on the edge of the cot.

Not going to happen—my heart drummed in my chest—not at the moment, anyway. Other topics, such as what the Embers were up to, were more important. She was smart, beautiful, brave—all things I found attractive, but I hadn't thought about someone else like that since Cate, and it felt… kind of good… kind of strange. And Mya being Daniel's sister. That didn't sit right. I needed to extricate myself from him and Cate for closure, not join the family. Though I was getting ahead of myself. It was just one kiss. A series of kisses. Fantastic. Kisses.

"Lucas?"

"Yeah?"

"You drifted off there."

"Are you avoiding telling me why you were upset?" I countered, having no intention of discussing anything else.

She bit her lip. "I found out some stuff today."

I sat on my bed, focus returning.

"Stuff I wish I never knew. You're right. I want to forget... pretend it's not happening." Her features clouded, once again fighting tears. She took a deep breath, then exhaled. "They sent me to a different area, not sure why. Maybe I wasn't very good at handling unruly toddlers. It was a giant room with rows and rows of beds filled with..." She scrubbed her face with her hands.

"What was there?" I leaned forward.

"Girls. Pregnant girls. Some were in labor, others already with babies. Most weren't Embers. They were from Caelum and Terra."

Were these the kidnapped girls? "Teenagers?"

Mya nodded, a rogue tear streaking down her cheek.

Bex's words came back to me: *They're trying to raise an enormous army.* My hand flew to my mouth in utter disbelief at the Embers' vileness.

"It's a baby factory," Mya whispered.

CHAPTER 33
CATE

"Absolutely not," Daniel responded to his mother. "We're not risking her life. We already learned the hard way with Mya and King Aldridge, did we not?"

I didn't blame his mom. She believed it would be easy-peasy: Cate sends buckets of rain from the sky then—poof. No more fire and the soldiers storm in and rescue everyone. Obviously, it's the buckets of water part where the problem lies. I sent a sprinkle into a six-foot area around me and Daniel, but there's a vast difference between a drizzle and enough to incapacitate the Ember's flames. Not to mention we'd have to go into *their* stronghold, blind to where they kept the prisoners. If they were even alive. My insides bottomed out at the thought.

While Queen Lila and Daniel argued quietly in the corner, I roamed the room, lost in reflection. This was like The Great Battle all over again. Cate the savior. Cate the prophesied one.

I thought I had more time.

Years even. Now that Alana was gone, I had to figure this out alone. Otherwise, the blood of Mya, Lucas, and Father would fall on my hands.

"She's not going, and that's final," Daniel shouted.

"Cate." The queen turned to me, tears streaming down her cheeks. "Please help us."

I'd only ever seen her composed. Now the pain of losing her child etched across her features. Her emotion, so raw, forced the vice-like pressure to turn another crank on my conscience.

"I'll do whatever I can." A noncommittal, political answer, and I hated myself for it. "I'm sorry. We need to see King Dryden." I fled the room, clenching my fingers into fists to keep them from shaking.

Daniel appeared at my side. "You can't make decisions for me," I whisper-shouted.

"But, Cate—"

I put my hand on his chest. "Let's decide together. Besides, I'd rather not leave Graftonberg in charge, and if anything happens to me, then I worry about what will become of Caelum. So, I agree. For now, I'll stay home. Even though it kills me to see your mom like that. Just don't be so bossy, okay?"

He placed his hand next to me on the wall, blocking me in, his face drawing close. "You are your own boss," he whispered. "I trust you. And I love you with every fiber of my being. But please…" The concern in his eyes bored into mine, making me feel cherished instead of managed. "Let me protect you."

His lips found me, gentle and caressing. When we pulled apart, I nudged my forehead to his. "Okay." I took his hand, and I gave him a rueful smile. "Especially now that we're going to see your father."

He stepped away and groaned. "Can we skip this part?"

"Nope. Pretty much why we're here. We need his army."

King Dryden sat at his desk in his office, the same room that fateful night I'd discovered his plot to use me. The lightning—apparently of my own making—had hit the wall of windows, which now gleamed shiny and new behind him. The study, L-shaped with a seating area out of sight, must have held someone else because his focus was split between us and the other side of the space.

We stepped farther into the room. A man in ragged brown clothes, with hollowed cheeks and a thin frame, stood at attention, hands clasped behind his back.

"Daniel. Catherine. Someone has already informed me of your arrival." The king's brows knitted together. "Nice of you to stop by after visiting with your mother." The sarcasm in his tone wasn't hard to miss.

Daniel took another step. "We have news."

King Dryden steepled his fingers over the glossy wood desk. "Apparently, this young man does as well. He's a captured soldier sent home with a message and won't speak to anyone but me."

The man must be carrying the hostage ransom information. My heart jumped that he might have news of my father and Lucas. I glanced over at Daniel, whose jaw tensed. We should be the ones to tell him about Mya, not a stranger. "Sir," I said. "Could we talk to you alone for a moment?"

"Isn't that interesting? I was just going to ask you to leave while I hear what this man has to say."

"Father—"

"Now, now, Daniel. You've done enough for Caelum-Terran relations. I don't need to bend over for this girl. You already have."

Anger bubbled, making me want to smack the king's pompous expression from his face. At least he now openly showed his disdain instead of attempting to trick me. That ship had long since sailed, and he knew it. I took a deep breath. Because the king could sense my emotions, I needed to remain calm to appear strong. How had Daniel managed to maintain the mask his whole life?

Daniel and I exchange looks. He glanced over at the Terran in tattered clothes and shrugged. "Mya's been kidnapped," Daniel blurted.

King Dryden stilled, his smug expression fading. His disconcerting eyes shifted to me. "You let them come into your castle grounds and take her? What kind of inept security do you have?"

Not enough, I thought, remembering the men in the woods not too long ago. I knew better than to respond.

Daniel quickly relayed the full story, explaining that Mya had followed him to the peace treaty. I couldn't sense feelings like him or his father, but even I could tell Daniel wasn't able to hold his emotions together, his voice a raspy tremble at times.

"Stupid girl." King Dryden hit his desk with his fist. "And you." He glared at Daniel. "You should have turned back with your sister the moment she arrived."

He'd said as much to me in private. I'd tried to assuage his guilt by reminding him that Mya made her own decision, but nothing would convince him.

"We believe they have my father as well." I tried to move the attention away from Mya and Daniel.

"And now the Embers have the upper hand." He leaned back in his chair. "Against both kingdoms. I assume that's why you're here, Princess. To ask for my help?"

"And to inform you in person," I said.

"How magnanimous of you. Traveling all this way to tell a man his daughter is a captive of the enemy." There was that sarcasm again. "Let's hear this young man's story, shall we?"

All faces turned to the emaciated Terran, his attention shifting uncomfortably from the floor back to us. Dryden should give him a chair and food before he passed out. He looked so malnourished my first instinct was to feed him.

"I'm to relay a message." He rocked from foot to foot, eyes darting from me to the king.

"Spit it out, soldier," Dryden said, his dark brows slashing downward.

Sweat trickled down the man's temple. "The Embers will safely deliver Mya. If you join them with the Terran army to overtake Caelum."

My head swam. The backs of my knees tingled, my heart a bass drum in my ears. I stumbled to a chair and sat across from the king before a full panic attack ensued. I wanted to believe he wouldn't ally with the Embers, but it might be the perfect opportunity for him to finally rid himself of my kingdom once and for all.

"If you agree," the man went on, his shoulders slumping. "I'm to return to them with the message within two weeks."

"Is that all?" King Dryden asked.

"Yes, Your Highness."

The soldier was dismissed, and Daniel slumped beside me. My stomach churned, and I dug my fingers into the arms of the chair. "You can't do it," I said.

The king leaned forward. "Can't I?"

"Father. Be serious. You'd be increasing your enemy—giving them access to bordering lands.

"Growing one adversary. Destroying another?"

"We are not your opponent," I said, my voice shaking. "Not anymore."

"Who would be easier to defeat in the end? Caelum or the Embers? As king, I have to look out for my people."

"Partnering with them?" Daniel asked. "You can't be serious. You're baiting us. What is it you really want?"

"Am I? You're correct about one thing. I always want something. I wish I had my son back."

"I'm right here," Daniel ground out.

"You're one of them." His head tilted to me.

Daniel paused to take a breath. I could tell he was trying to even his emotions. "We can all live in peace. There doesn't have to be an *us* and *them*. Everyone is tired of war. Let's get Mya back—your offspring that *actually* is missing—and stop fighting."

"What do you propose?" King Dryden cocked his head in mock interest.

"An army from both Caelum and Terra, working together," Daniel said.

"Just go in there. Storm their city. That's the plan?" He raised a brow. "They'll know we're coming. I want insurance—Caelum must provide double the army as us. Ten battalions."

Graftonberg would never agree. He wanted to let my father rot with the Embers and grab the crown for himself.

"One more thing." Dryden placed his hands on the desk, leaning forward. "Princess Catherine will lead the soldiers. And it better rain."

CHAPTER 34
LUCAS

Mya's words settled. They seeped into the cracks that I tried to block so I wouldn't go mad from the horror of the enemy, of the things people did for power. The pieces fell into place. For whatever reason—something to do with genetics—the Embers never had trouble conceiving, unlike the Caelumites and Terrans. Because of this, over hundreds of years, they'd outnumbered us, even though we were faster and more skilled.

Already too many tried to scrape together a living on poorly kept lands worsened by drought, yet they continued to populate. It was true—they were playing the long game. Their only hope of beating us was by sheer numbers. They were raising an army. Kidnapping girls from the border towns and impregnating them to eventually turn the children into soldiers or slaves. How many years had this been going on? My stomach turned, the smell of the meager meal someone had slid into the cell worsening the bile building in my throat.

"How are they? The girls. Are they treated—" I couldn't bring myself to say more. Their conditions, no matter how bad or good, wouldn't make up for what the Embers had done to them.

The pain in Mya's eyes conveyed her answer. "Some seem to have accepted it. They want to hold their baby, or are protective of the unborn, stroking their bellies. But others…" She lay down, staring up at the ceiling. "I helped one today. Her name was Lily, and she was in labor. I don't know why they put me there. I've never seen anyone have a baby. Maybe they did it as a warning. Anyway, Lily had given up. She didn't want to push anymore, and she didn't want it born into their hands. She screamed and cried for hours, saying she'd rather die than give them her child. Then she just stopped. She didn't make a sound and all she did was stare, practically not blinking. Watched out the single little window in the corner of the room."

"What happened to her?"

"The baby was born. She wouldn't look at it. They gave it to another new mother to nurse. I cleaned it off—did you know babies come out covered in goop? It was so tiny. One of his little hands gripped my finger. It wouldn't let go when I gave him over." She lay on her side, facing the wall. "And one day, that innocent baby will be an Ember soldier. Someone we will have to kill."

I squeezed my eyes shut, staving off the madness. Something was missing from their makeup to leave them without a conscience. Would that child grow up as one of them, or was he redeemable? Were any of them?

The next morning, a guard roused us by clanging his stick on the bars. "Hurry up. We need you right now," he said. The Ember returned moments after I'd laced my boots to steer me out the door. They clasped irons to my legs, but didn't connect the chains to the other prisoners as usual. Some already followed a group of Embers down the street.

"Let's go." One shoved me from behind.

The smell of smoke, common in Ember City, infiltrated my lungs, the air a hazy gray. A blaze had caught the roof of three buildings and threatened more. Here in the heart of the city, some structures were made of stone, but all the roofs were wood, presumably due to lack of know-how in stonemasonry and architecture. Or perhaps to save time. Men clung to ladders and tossed water from pails onto the flames.

Someone handed me two buckets. "Go get more. Pump's in the courtyard."

Two streets over, I found the square and zeroed in on the cage, unsure if I hoped to see King Aldridge or not. It sat empty, though two Embers shoved him toward it. They must release him occasionally to relieve himself. He collapsed to the floor of the enclosure, his back slumped. Someone had given him a blanket which he laid over his legs. Once the guards left, I took advantage of the chaos of men running to fetch water, many of them prisoners like me, and raced to the king.

He moved to the edge of the cage to reach me, his knuckles white on the bars, swaying where he stood. "Who escaped?" he croaked. "Daniel?"

"As far as I know, he made it out. I haven't seen him here." I kept the obvious other plausible reason for his absence—his death—unspoken. "And Mya's here."

His brow crinkled. "Who?"

"Princess Mya," I emphasized her title.

"What the devil would she be here for? Old Dryden let her out of his sight?"

No wonder her presence confused him. It *was* hard to believe. "She snuck out and came with Daniel. She may be our ticket out of here, given the Terran king will want to save her. I've been assigned to keep an eye on her, so presumably they want to use her as ransom."

"They'll barter her against us. And Dryden will agree." His green eyes dulled.

I'd underestimated how dishonorable King Dryden could be, my only prior worry was whether he'd abandon his daughter. Now I realized he'd use this position to his advantage against Caelum. Something King Aldridge understood immediately. "Daniel won't go along with it," I said, forcing conviction into my voice. "Cate will convince him."

He grunted. "If they have a choice."

"You there!" A burly Ember stomped toward me. "The water pump is that way." He pointed to the side of the courtyard. I was lucky to avoid a beating. One last glance at the king showed him slumped against his enclosure, the hope drifting out of him.

I filled my buckets and returned to the fire, which was no closer to being contained than before. Living this way was madness. With pumps every few blocks, both prisoners and townspeople arrived from various directions, sloshing containers and rushing to the fire. The spigots must connect to wells. No one had figured out pipes for running water in homes or even a hose. I handed off my pail to those climbing the ladders, thankful I hadn't been assigned the dangerous job of teetering over the blaze.

With fresh buckets, I headed back to the courtyard, hoping to speak with King Aldridge again. A slight girl who struggled with a burlap bag turned out of sight around a corner. *Grace!* I dashed toward her, glancing behind to ensure no one was watching. I caught up to her easily, even with manacles clanging and chains hindering my normal stride.

She stopped in front of a door on a side street, fumbling with the oversized sack and the knob. She had the same dark strip of cloth wrapped around her upper arm as Mya, which must denote prisoner status for the women. I put a hand on her shoulder to stop her from entering. "Grace," I whispered.

She flinched, her reaction exaggerated. *Oh, Grace, what have they done to you?* She turned, her back stiff, then softened upon recognizing me.

"They got you too," she said, her eyes roving over my face.

I was happy to see her alive, but now that I knew what happened here, my worries only ratcheted. "Are you okay?" Of course she wasn't, but she seemed to understand what I meant.

"More or less." A wobbly half smile surfaced.

"Have they…" I couldn't finish the sentence.

She blanched. "Not yet. But probably soon."

I told her about the princess and that King Dryden would come.

She glowered. "He won't lift a finger for us. He might barter for his daughter. But the rest of us?"

Her words rang with truth. "We're planning an escape," I blurted. *Were we?* "Tell me where you're staying."

She did, although I wasn't familiar with the area. Maybe Mya would know.

"We'll find a way," I assured her, more confidently than I felt. Grace and Aldridge both had voiced the thoughts I'd been trying to suppress. Relying solely on Dryden meant trouble. I had never hoped for Daniel's survival more than now. Though I shouldn't count Cate out. She might be our only hope.

"Or Princess Catherine," I said, knowing Grace would have seen King Aldridge in the courtyard. "She'll come through." Once again, everything rested on poor Cate's shoulders. She must be going out of her mind with her father captured. Though what did she know of leading an army? The last time she made rain, it nearly killed her. I pictured her pale face in the infirmary bed as I'd said goodbye, IV tubing snaking up her arm.

"I've got to go." She shifted the bag higher on her shoulder. "Delivering laundry. That's where I work."

"Watch for us," I called, but after the words escaped, I wondered why I'd spoken them. We had no escape plan. It was almost as if speaking it would *will* it into reality. Everything came back to the same problem. I might be able to get away, but I had Mya and now Grace to watch over. And what of all the other girls? I'd stay alert for opportunities and tell Mya to do the same.

There was a line at the water pump. The king eyed me from his enclosure, but I did not approach again. When I arrived at the fire, Bex was being forced up the ladder, his chains clanging and sliding across the rungs. The metal ladder's top end rested directly against the burning overhang of the roof.

"Don't do it." I slid up next to him with my containers.

"Not much choice." He grabbed a bucket with one hand and ascended.

Sparks flew, one landing on my sleeve. I batted it out and backed away. Bex reached near the top, not able to go farther due to the inferno. He poured the pail, extinguishing the nearest flames. A sigh of relief escaped, and I started to leave for more water, but a crash sent me spinning on my heel.

Part of the roof had caved in, the inferno erupting higher. Bex's ladder skidded into the blaze. His tunic caught fire, then his hair. The ladder swayed, then slid as he tried to keep his balance. Adrenaline and fear pumped through me as I ran to steady it. Everything happened as if in slow motion, every detail of Bex's horrified expression etching into my brain, yet too fast for me to stop the plummet. The ladder tumbled to the ground, a flaming Bex with it. One look at his awkward angle told me it was too late. I swallowed thickly, tears burning behind my eyes.

Bex was dead.

CHAPTER 35
DANIEL

"I can't believe him." I paced the old nursery floor on the fourth level where we collected ourselves after the disastrous meeting with Father.

Cate idly rocked a wooden horse, lost in contemplation. "Hmm?"

"He's worse than I thought."

She pressed her lips together. "You haven't seen him clearly before now."

I scraped a hand through my hair. Was that true? Probably. He wasn't entirely bad, and that was the problem. Every villain has a light side. My father was convinced he'd made the best choice for Terra. He just doesn't care at what cost. Ruthlessness was the only way he knew how to rule.

There had to be a better way. One where Caelum and Terra lived in peace. One where Cate and I would not be at odds.

"He's putting Terra's needs first." I wasn't willing for Cate to believe my father was unredeemable. Or maybe it was me who wasn't ready to accept it. "As a king should do."

She straightened from her slumped position. "Really? And is that what you'll do when you're king? Terra first?" The hurt in her eyes felt like a jab to the stomach.

"No—I mean… sometimes." I was digging myself a huge hole. But what did she expect? That Caelum was always the priority?

Her mouth hung open a moment, then closed into a firm line. "I don't know what to say to you right now." She stomped out the door, slamming it behind her.

I sunk into a chair. This wasn't the time to be fighting. But what did she want? Completely deny my entire kingdom to be with her?

A knock sounded. *Good, she's returned to apologize.* Only it was Emily's blonde head who peaked through. *Great*. All I needed was a tongue-lashing from yet another woman.

"May I come in? I couldn't help overhearing some of your conversation. I was next door." She stepped inside without waiting for my response.

I wearily gestured to the seat beside me. When she sat, her sage-green skirts took up most of the chair.

"If you'd asked my opinion instead of going behind my back, I could have told you this would happen. But you didn't." She tapped her fingers on the side table. Pinky, fourth, third, index... repeat. I'd forgotten about that nervous habit of hers. She might seem confident, but conversing no longer felt as natural as breathing as it once did. I'd failed a lot of people lately. Terrans, my father, Emily. Cate. Yet it seemed impossible to appease them all.

"It's complicated," I muttered.

"But why?" Her focus turned to the window. "Why did you choose *her*?"

"Love," I answered, not hesitating. "What you and I had was friendship. And convenience. But with Cate..."

"What? With Cate what?" She lasered in return, blue eyes flashing.

"It's like my whole world shifts, and she's at the center. I can't imagine life without her."

Her brows creased. "Isn't that dangerous, though? Sounds as if the future king of Terra is at the beck and call of the Caelum princess. How can your people trust you to have their best interests? Because doing what's best for Caelum, doesn't always match with us."

I sighed heavily, tired of this day. Tired of more problems. "I don't need this right now."

Her fingers started tapping again. "I think you do."

It was my turn to stare out the mullioned window into the garden.

She stood and leaned over me, demanding my attention. "And when you figure it out," she whispered in my ear. "I'll be here." Her lips brushed against my cheek, softer than I expected. She smelled of vanilla and pastries. Her face remained inches away, azure eyes scouring.

The door swung open. I jockeyed to see around Emily. Cate stood there, her features frozen in shock. She turned on her heel and fled—déjà vu from the last time in Terra.

"Cate! Wait." I jumped up, struggling to push Emily and her enormous skirts aside, ignoring her indignant hand on hip, as I raced into the hall.

The castle corridor stretched empty into the distance each way, closed doors along both walls. She likely hadn't had time to reach the stairwell at the end leading to her room one floor down. "Cate?"

Silence.

"Please. Let's talk about this. It's not what you think." It strangely echoed our last fight. Hopefully, she trusted me more now. Except Emily was her Achilles heel. She would have laughed it off if it was anyone else.

"Give her some time." Emily came up beside me. "She just needs to cool off. You've never given her a reason not to trust you, right?"

"Uh… yeah. Right." I scrubbed my face, past mistakes hanging thick in the air. "Cate!"

"You want to sit and talk some more? Catch up? Apologize for barging into my room a few weeks ago when I was half naked?" Her voice echoed loudly in the empty hall. Cate could be one door down for all I knew.

"Later," I bit out. Where had she gone? Not for the first time, I wondered why my ancestors made this place so enormous.

"You're not going to say you're sorry?" She pursed her lips. "Does that mean you're not?" Her mouth curled up coyly.

"I apologize. It was *clearly* a mistake." I stomped off to search, leaving Emily standing there, her expression like a cat in cream.

"See you at dinner," she called.

I ignored her.

After opening what seemed like every door in the hallway, I finally admitted defeat and trudged to my room. She'd talk when she was ready. Emily's reminder of the evening meal sent me washing up and changing. It always amazed me the number of shirts that hung in the wardrobe waiting for the prodigal prince to inevitably return. Clothes never mattered to me. I put on what people expected me to wear, end of story. At random, I snatched items from the closet.

Cate must have packed a gown, or one was left here from her prior visit, because she radiated in deep purple when she entered the dining room twenty minutes later. Her long hair was swept into a complicated style on the top of her head, her cheeks pink. On closer inspection, the blush, contrived by makeup, hid the paleness underneath. She faked her calm admirably, smiling and nodding, even to Emily's parents, the Duke and Duchess of Earlington, whom I knew she despised. On the way here, Cate had teased Dev that one day he'd be a duke and had sung a silly song, apparently once popular in America. It had stuck in everyone's mind, leaving us all singing a round of *The Duke of Earl*. I smudged away a grin when I greeted them.

Emily sidled up next to her parents. "Nice to see you again, Daniel." She put on a believable show as well, all innocence and dimples.

I bowed over her hand politely, sneaking a glance at Cate, who averted her gaze, and pasted a wide smile to greet others at the table full of father's advisors, generals, noblemen, and their wives. Tonight's "festivities" would number close to thirty guests.

We sat in assigned seats, per custom, arranged by my father, no doubt. Cate and I were not placed together. I was at the foot next to my mother and strategically positioned alongside Emily. Father, at the head, with Cate on his right as a supposed "honored guest." All smoke and mirrors around here. Some things never changed.

Polite conversation ensued, along with plate after plate of food. I'd missed Hildy's cooking and tucked in, doing my best to ignore Emily. Mother and I spoke of banal topics such as her roses in the garden. Emily resorted to tugging on my sleeve.

"Daniel," Mother warned. "I've occupied enough of your attention." Her well-timed look, all too familiar, and one only a mother can give, urged me to behave. Ever the gracious hostess, she knew slighting Emily in front of all these guests would be in poor taste.

To avoid a scene, I fixed a pleasant smile and turned to her.

"I must tell you about our new foal," she said. Then proceeded to talk the rest of dinner, laughing, touching my arm, and commenting on every dish. "Your cook has outdone herself tonight. These are all your favorites, right?"

Hildy had made me a welcome-home supper with all the best bits. Apparently, everyone in Terra was trying to woo me to stay. My gaze strayed down the table to Cate, who was making a valiant effort at small talk. She hated these things. And it must be worse watching Emily flirt so shamelessly. I only hoped it didn't trigger a panic attack. Social functions ratcheted her anxiety. I focused on her emotions, weeding out the others until I felt her. It came easily, tuning everybody out until it was only her.

Annoyance. Tension. Anger—probably directed at me. Or at Father. But she stayed in control, her expression placid, hands steady. She was a marvel. So new to this world, to leadership, yet she carried herself with poise.

"Daniel," Emily said. "You didn't answer me. These are your favorite foods, are they not?"

I turned, finding her solemn eyes searching mine. "Yeah. They are." I looked away, unable to hold her gaze.

"Everyone misses you," she kept her voice low. "We all want our Terran prince back. You can't keep doing this. One foot in Caelum, the other here. What's best for them doesn't always work for us. Don't force unity no one wants. Your father knows this."

I wanted to dismiss her, but she echoed my deepest worries. Thoughts I tried to bury and pretend didn't exist. How much were my views swayed by my time in Caelum? By loving Cate?

Dessert arrived and King Dryden clinked his glass, sending my attention down the table. "Everyone. Thank you all for coming." He set down his goblet. "I have a few announcements."

I sat straighter, my spine tightening. Cate and I hadn't yet decided if we were agreeing with his plan. Is that what this was about?

"Princess Catherine and Prince Daniel have relayed some news with their visit." He paused for effect. "King Aldridge has been captured."

Silence blanketed the room, followed by whispers and murmurings traveling down the table like wildfire. We hadn't even told the Caelum people. Once again, my father overstepped.

"You may be wondering where my daughter is tonight. We've been keeping this under wraps for reasons that will become apparent," he went on.

I started to regret how much I'd eaten, the food now a leaden ball in my stomach, while I waited to hear my father's announcement. Faces would soon turn to me with varying degrees of pity or horror that I'd allowed my sister to be captured. I picked up my water cup to wet the sandy dryness in my throat.

"Mya has been working as a spy," the king said matter-of-factly, as if the proclamation was predictable that his only daughter, known for her dancing skills, was a Terran undercover operative.

I almost sprayed water from my mouth, and a coughing fit burst through my lungs. The man had no shame in lying, his face perfectly composed. Cate's surprise flashed before schooling her features. All other eyes remained on the king.

"She's let herself become captured by the enemy for intel, knowing I would be working with Caelum to bring her home. I'm sure her intelligence will prove invaluable."

More murmurings from around the table.

"Catherine has agreed to supply double the soldiers that Terrans provide. And of course, our little rainmaker will be present to ensure everyone's safety."

Cate's expression remained as still as a summer lake. Did she go behind my back and agree to this without my input? We could have found another way… somehow.

Father raised his glass. "To Princess Catherine. The Concealed!"

I lifted my cup, forced to play along. Cate would hate being reminded of the prophecy with her code name. She remained ramrod straight with a plastered smile I knew to be fake. She was either miserable or extremely angry. I didn't bother to sense her emotions. My bet was on both.

CHAPTER 36
CATE

All eyes had swiveled as that snake, King Dryden, toasted me as their savior. He'd snared me in his plans, leaving me no choice. I could announce that it nearly killed me the last time I made water and had absolutely no idea if I could do it again. Or how Mya didn't listen to anyone's warning and got herself captured. Mya was no more a spy than Austin Powers. But saying any of those things would weaken relations between our kingdoms. I needed the people's confidence, especially if I took over the reins from Father. I swallowed thickly. *Temporarily*. I couldn't bear to think in permanent terms because that would mean we had failed.

I didn't do failure. Not anymore.

I should make a speech. Something to convey self-assurance and poise, but my mind whirred like a hummingbird, racing from thought to thought. It kept flitting from the looming problem of the impossibility of producing enough rain to shield our soldiers, to how I'd convince Graftonberg to supply an army. I cursed Father under my breath for his choice of regent. He may have sealed his own fate.

Once everyone returned to eating their desserts, the king tilted toward me. He had to sense my anger, along with confusion and frustration. Of course, he still didn't know I was aware of his secret superpower. I tried to control my emotions, but come on! I was an American teenager at heart, not a cold-hearted ruler.

"You'll see my method is best," he whispered, his cologne twisting my stomach. "You'll have to raise an army either way—to rescue your father, or against the Embers and Terrans, if you don't meet my requests. At least if you side with me, you can keep your kingdom." He paused. Waited for me to look up from the fork I stirred my uneaten dessert with. "For now."

I wanted to take my goblet and splash water on his face like in the movies. Wash the smug expression away. Instead, I calmly folded the napkin in my lap and set it on the table.

"What a lovely dinner. I have much planning to do." I stood, smiling at my dining companions. "Have a good evening."

Tradition would next have the men and women separate. The males talked over important matters while the females gossiped. I wasn't going along with that farce tonight. If Dryden wanted me as their savior, then I certainly wouldn't be relegated to needlepoint.

I exited the room, careful to keep my shoulders back and not trip over the hem of my full-length gown. I needed it to appear as if I was too busy to be in their company. In actuality, I'd return to my room with nothing more to do than sulk. Hiding from Daniel earlier to process seeing him with Emily hadn't resolved anything. Is this what my parents went through? Would I always wonder if he'd prioritize Terra at the cost of Caelum? His defense of King Dryden had been the last straw.

I arrived at my suite without incident, though half expected Daniel to intercept me. Maybe he was still with Emily. Did the girl have no shame? Hovering over him in that chair, her chest in his face. I flopped into a wingback, surveying the space with its cozy window seat pillows and warm rugs. The last time I stayed in this room, I'd left in a flood of tears to Caelum. Let's hope history won't repeat itself.

I could still picture Daniel's flubbed apology. Where he stood, where I collapsed to the floor sobbing. A misunderstanding, but ultimately, our issues arose from his inability to stand up to his father. And… here we were again. This place was toxic. Had we learned nothing?

Last time we hadn't trusted each other. I'd lost my trust—and my head—today, but I knew one mistake I wouldn't repeat. This time, we'd talk it out. Yes, I had run, but I'd never leave the kingdom without speaking with him first. If he chose to back King Dryden, and my heart ached at the thought, then he'd have to explain it to me clearly.

And if that were true… we'd part ways. We had to.

Dryden threatened to attack Caelum, siding with the Embers. If Daniel approved, that was proof enough that we could never work.

I wanted to cry, to throw something across the room. Feel anything. Instead, there was only numbness. Too much had been piled at my feet. Perhaps it was shock. Or maturity. I didn't have time to fall apart. The problem of raising an army without permission and creating precipitation without Alana's help needed solving. Possibly without Daniel either. Dread crawled up my spine. I paced the bedroom, then, too cooped up in this space with so many bad memories, headed outdoors.

The garden, lit by twinkling lights, led to more nostalgia about the time Daniel taught me to dance, instead of clarity. I sat on the edge of the fountain, letting my fingers drift through the water. The liquid—so elusive to me—but just an object of beauty here among the greenery. Yet it could save so many lives.

The crunch of pea gravel alerted me to someone approaching. Daniel strode around the bend. He hadn't seen me, completely absorbed in his own world. The lights cast shadows across his face, accentuating his strong jawline, though shielding his expression.

"Hi," I said softly. "Looking for me?"

His gait stalled. "I came out here to think."

It should have hurt, but the numbness persisted. What was going through his head? How he'd made a mistake and really belonged with Emily? That King Dryden was the best ruler in the entire universe?

"Well, I was here first." *Good one, Cate. That's solving our issues.*

He glanced around as if lost in his own garden. We hadn't been this unsure with each other in a long time.

"You wanna sit?" I patted the stone next to me.

"Yeah, I do. You're not avoiding me anymore?"

"I guess not."

He sat, and I raked the gravel back and forth with the toe of my shoe. He should apologize—explain himself—yet he remained silent. *This is going well.*

Finally tired of waiting, I spoke, "Does this mean you're Terran again?"

"I've always been Terran," he said. "Because I'm with you doesn't make it less true. I can't deny my kingdom just to be with you."

"*Just* to be with me," I deadpanned.

He stood again. "I have duties. I'll be king one day."

"You're just now figuring this out?" My heart pounded in my ears, the numbness wearing off with the sharp reality that I might lose him.

"No. Maybe." He rubbed the nape of his neck. "It feels different. Being here."

"I thought we'd work together. Do what's best for both kingdoms."

"Yeah, but who decides what's best? What if what is good for one isn't for the other?"

My throat suddenly felt too swollen to speak. "You really believe that?" I whispered. I felt sick, but my voice returned strong in a wave of rage, "I would never." I stood and pointed my finger at his chest. "I would *never* put the Terran people at risk for Caelum's gain. And if you would even think of doing that. Well… I guess I never knew you at all."

I wanted to run. Every muscle itched to leave and wallow. But I wouldn't repeat those mistakes. I stood my ground and let him speak.

His answer wasn't what I expected. "Maybe I don't know myself." He turned away as if to depart.

"Wait." I clutched his sleeve. "I deserve more explanation than that."

His spine still faced me, stiff and proud, motionless. "What if… what if I don't see clearly when I'm with you? What if I'm betraying Terra and don't even realize it?"

I didn't know how to respond.

"You hate my father," he said.

"I thought you did too." I raised my hands in exasperation and moved so I could read his expression.

His shoulders slumped. "I do. I do. It's just… I love him too." His eyes, watery, shone in the fairy lights.

"Okay," I put a hand on his arm, "that doesn't mean you have to agree with what he says or does."

"I don't. And I'd never approve of Terra going to war with Caelum again. But I understand that he wants the fewest casualties for our people. And that means having you there."

"I can't make it rain!" His nonsensical answers cut through the remaining numbing ice like a pickaxe.

"He doesn't know that."

"What happened to protecting me? Shielding me and all that crap."

"Nothing happened. I haven't changed my mind. You shouldn't go. I'm just saying that I understand him. He's putting Terra first. I need..." He stared at the nearby roses, closed into tight buds for the evening. "I need some space to make sure I'm not being run over."

"By who—me or your father? Or Emily? Because it seems pretty clear from my point of view."

"A little time." He stepped farther away.

"Well, you better figure it out, because I might not be able to make so much as a dew drop if you're not around." It made me sick to admit it. My crutch. It had felt so seductively good to rely on him.

I slumped back on the fountain's edge. Tears burned behind my lids. "I don't understand. As soon as we step on Terra Castle grounds, you become his lackey."

He turned and looked at me. Really looked, as if my face had the answers he wanted. "I don't want to be *anyone's* lackey." His voice was soft, barely above a whisper.

"That's what love is." I knuckled away a tear. "I need you. And you need me. We're a partnership. This isn't you. I don't know what someone said to convince you otherwise, but we can do anything if we work together, including finding a path to peace. It's you and me against the world, remember?"

"I guess I'm just wondering why we have to be against everyone."

It wasn't what I meant, and he should have recognized that. "Look, I'll try to see your father's side. I will." Compromise. Isn't that what couples did? Even if it entailed compromising with a dictator?

"I want a little space to be certain I understand my choices. Think everything through to be sure no one is clouding my judgment," he said.

No one like me, I thought, but couldn't form the words to say it aloud.

I found myself nodding. "So, I'll figure out how to raise a Caelum army. And deal with the water issue, I guess."

"Here's the thing," he sighed heavily. "Father asked me to stay here. He doesn't want to risk both his heirs."

Another tear escaped. The biting pain in my stomach throbbed as if he'd punched me. "And what did you say?"

CHAPTER 37 **LUCAS**

A crowd gathered around Bex's body. I snatched someone's still-full bucket and poured it over him, extinguishing the flames.

"Who was it?" someone asked.

"His name was Bex," I replied. "And he deserved better." Despite the fire, coldness settled deep into my chest. An icy decision that one day the Embers would pay for their deeds.

The fire blazed on. Eager to escape the scene, I snatched more containers and trudged to the water pumps. By the time I returned, the body had been moved. Bex should have a respectful burial, but more likely, they threw him into a burning building. The coldness in my bones intensified.

We worked all day on the fire, finally containing it, sizzling out the final flame. I tried to ignore the image of Bex's broken form and concentrate on the task, yet every time I returned to the site, I couldn't shake the picture imprinted in my head.

They let us bathe at the water pump, generously providing soap. A change of clothes waited for me in the cell. Mya hadn't arrived, and I changed quickly, grateful to have some of the smell of ash and smoke off my body.

Though there was no clock to determine the time, our dinner came and the light through our meager window dimmed. Still no Mya. Unease squirmed under my skin. Did they change their minds and leave her to the fate of the other girls? Perhaps they didn't care if unspeakable things happened to her anymore. It would be the ultimate revenge—to impregnate the daughter of your adversary with a child destined to grow up to be an enemy. Rowan kept us together so I could protect her, yet I hadn't seen him recently. The other Embers might have taken matters into their own hands.

The door to our cell rattled. Mya entered, backlit by an Ember's lantern. I rushed over, stopping myself short of throwing my arms around her. "You okay? Did they hurt you?"

"I'm fine. Just tired." She lay her head on my chest. "Exhausted. There was a girl in labor. She asked me to stay with her and they let me. I held her hand, fetched water, that sort of thing. But the midwife—something happened, and she left. So, I delivered the baby."

"They had *you* do it?"

She wrapped her arms around me. "There was no one else. It was… bloody. And amazing. Sad—I don't know, I just want to go to sleep."

She wasn't making much sense, so I guided her to the bed and helped her with her shoes, covering her with the threadbare blanket. I'd thought we might discuss options for escape tonight—Bex's charred body fresh in my mind. It would have to wait until tomorrow. How long would they hold off before they decided to make Mya or Grace another broodmare?

We needed out.

The next morning, we both woke early after tossing and turning most of the night. "Hey, you alright?" I asked.

She sat on her cot, staring listlessly at the floor. I moved next to her, and she lay her cheek on my shoulder. Which felt… nice. Too nice. "We have to get out of here," I whispered.

"I know." She buried her face in my tunic. "How?"

That was the question that needed an answer. "I don't think we can break out of this jail together, so we should look for opportunities when you might be able to slip away and meet up."

Her head flew from my shoulder. "Today?"

"I wish, but we need more time to plan. Watch for lapses in the guard, something that happens regularly. I'd love to get Grace out too." Adding another person would make escaping more difficult, but I couldn't live with myself if we left her.

"I think I saw her yesterday. Someone called out her name. She delivers laundry."

"That's her. I talked to her too."

Her brow furrowed. "How?"

I explained about the fire, the king, and meeting Grace. She gasped, her hand flying to her mouth the moment she learned of Bex's fate.

"You're right. We have to escape. It could have been you on that ladder." She leaned against the wall. "You know, Grace might be useful. If she's delivering laundry, she'll be more familiar with this place than us."

The cell doors clanged. Time to go. "You're brilliant," I whispered. "Good luck today."

Her eyes shone with hope, something I hadn't seen. Her sparkle buoyed my spirits even as the chains clamped onto my legs, and I was attached to the prisoner in front and behind. There would be no chance of escape while we were connected. Once in the fields, we were left with just the chain between our ankles. Not optimal, but I'd make do. At least Mya and Grace had no such restraints.

Today we traveled to the farmland again. Some men from another prison group had already started labor with bags of grain. They worked in threes. A Terran prisoner prepped the hole, a Caelumite dropped in a seed, and another Terran covered it up. A flock of crows gathered nearby, hoping to unearth newly planted kernels. Their presence felt ominous, a morphing black blanket coating patches of field.

The Embers disconnected us from each other, and we were tasked with the same job as the others. We were short Terrans, so I had to use a hoe rather than manipulate the earth. For the first time, I wished to possess the Terran ability. Using wind would just blow dust everywhere.

I wiped the sweat from my brow, the sun now high. The birds continued to follow, and I purposefully failed to bury a seed so a raven would have it instead. This little guy hopped along behind like a pet. The Embers tried to make Caelumites shoo the flock away, but the birds were drawn to us rather than intimidated.

Finally, we were allowed a break to drink from the stream. The water ran through some brambles and trees—young forest growth that had burned in the past and grown partially back, likely thriving from the brook, and one of the few patches of green around this place. Movement in the brush caught my attention. Gray. A flash of orange. Could it be? My breath hitched. Molly's head peered out from behind a bush. I covered the cry of relief at seeing her alive with a cough. She must have escaped the dragons and realized I would be taken here. I hesitated at the stream while the others started to return to work.

I could leave.

On my signal, she'd fly over, I'd hop on, and we'd be gone before anyone stopped us. The thought tumbled in my head, leaving me almost giddy with the idea. It only took a few moments of elation before the selfish thoughts sent my conscience flaring. I wouldn't abandon the girls. Subtly, I lifted my palm, indicating I needed her to wait. I wasn't sure how long Molly could stay undetected, but we weren't ready. As much as I wanted to throw my arms around her, she would have to remain out of sight until the plan came together.

Mya arrived before me tonight. I drew her in and held her, ignoring her surprised expression. "Molly's here," I whispered in her ear.

She waited until the guard left, then said, "How? Where?"

I explained what I knew and told her about our mission with the other dragons, a story I hadn't previously shared. "We have a ride if we manage to escape."

"How many can Molly carry? You, me, Grace… the king."

I'd been thinking about King Aldridge all day. He should have been my first priority, yet he would be the most difficult to rescue. We'd have to steal the key to the cage, that or return for him.

"I'm not sure how to free him." I paced the cell, keeping my voice low. "Grace might know where to find the key—she's been around more than us. They also let him out at least once a day for a trip to the loo."

"Talking to her will be an issue." Mya tested the bars, absently ensuring they were locked. "I saw her today, but when I tried to get her attention, she startled like a rabbit and hopped away. I'll have to try again."

We were running out of time. Mya must feel the same. Before I could reassure her, she strode over and placed her fingers to my lips. "We're going to be okay. I'll find a way tomorrow."

It had been forever since someone encouraged me. That task usually fell on my shoulders. The reverse was strange but nice, and I needed it more than I'd realized.

"I'm glad you're here." I leaned into her touch, her fingers sliding to my cheek.

Her lips tipped up. "I'm not."

I smiled, pulling her hand away and kissing her palm.

Her lashes fluttered. "Maybe I am a little happy to be stuck with you."

"Exactly. I'm a real catch." My usual deflection of feelings with humor naturally fell into place.

She took a step back. "Are you? Because I kind of thought you might be unavailable."

"Oh, I'm quite single, Princess." I gave a stupid little bow. I really was ridiculous.

She folded her arms in front of her. "Emotionally unavailable."

I stood up straight. "Oh? Who told you that?"

"Are you still in love with Cate?"

I froze, silliness evaporating. The first thing that came to mind was —*always*. I didn't say it aloud. Because was it still true? I'd hardly thought of her since being locked up with Mya. "I'm not sure I want to have this conversation." I sat and rubbed my sweaty palms on the blanket.

"And there's my answer." Her eyes held disappointment, but her jaw set proudly.

A long silence fell between us until I spoke, "Would it help if I said that this is the first time I've wanted to stop?"

She uncrossed her arms. Crossed them again. "Yeah, I guess it would." She huffed a breath. "A little."

"That's why I was sorry I kissed you. It wasn't fair."

"No, it wasn't. But honestly," she bit her lip. "It wasn't fair to you, either. I knew you still loved Cate. I kissed you anyway."

"It was a nice kiss." I grinned.

"Only nice?" She flopped backward on the cot.

"Excuse me. Sublime. Your lips are like clouds, like pillows… cloud—um—pillows." I'm truly an idiot, but it worked because she giggled. "I could talk about your kisses all day, but next time, I'd rather enjoy them in a better environment. Perhaps without the bars? Shall we return to discussing our escape route?"

She smiled. "Let's."

CHAPTER 38
DANIEL

A tear drifted down Cate's cheek. I hated seeing it. Hated hurting her. Emily's comments had me confused, a mixture of opinions tugging me in two directions at once. I ignored them at first, ignored *her*, but the words tunneled into my brain, unshakeable. I'd hardly thought of Terra and my duty for months. Cate and I both wanted peace, but we hadn't fully imagined what that would look like. I needed room to figure it out—to make sure spending so much time in Caelum hadn't swayed me.

But space wasn't a luxury we could afford. I'd told Father I would never abandon Cate, and nothing would stop me from accompanying her to war, or to hell and back, for that matter. Would I love a vacation from our plight to sort myself out? Of course. Sometimes life doesn't work that way.

"What happened to I'll always shield you? You'll always be there for me?" Cate's voice was just above a whisper.

I scrubbed my face. "It's all coming out wrong. As usual. You know I always say the wrong thing when I'm flustered." I took her hand. "I will be going with you to get your father and Mya back."

"But you said you needed space…"

"I have every intention of being there." I was confusing her. Confusing myself. *Ugh. Why is this so hard?*

Cate stood, her lips held in a thin line. "We're wasting time. I need to be in a good place mentally to practice, and we should organize the Terran army, then head back to Caelum and figure out how to raise one with my people twice as large."

"Let's meet in the morning. We won't get much done tonight, anyway." I wanted to better understand my swirling thoughts before we talked again.

She left without saying goodbye. How strange it was to feel so far apart from her. A tiny voice inside wondered if it *was* possible she unknowingly manipulated me. My father did—he was the master at exploitation—was I playing into his hands? Then there was Emily. We'd known each other our entire lives. She also had ulterior motives —to keep me from Cate. Was there truth in her conniving words? Was I truly abandoning Terra?

Footsteps sounded and relief coursed through me at the thought of Cate returning. I hadn't really wanted to send her away, but was afraid of saying something else dumb while my thoughts were so scattered. Emily rounded the bend, the twinkling garden lights illuminating her pale-pink gown.

"We didn't finish our conversation earlier," she said.

"You gave me some things to think about." I gestured for her to sit, then joined her. "Can I talk with my old friend Emily? Not the girl I hurt?"

Her head went back in surprise. "I've always been your friend. That's why it hurt so much."

"I didn't mean to cause you pain. I'm sorry it did. That was never my intention."

Her finger tapping started up again. "I should have talked to you before you left for England and told you my feelings had changed. You were so annoyed that you had to go, it surprised me that you fell in love."

"Me too." A half smile escaped.

"And I'm protective of you. Besides Dev, I'm your oldest friend."

That was true. She'd been a big part of my life. Up until recently. I sighed. "It seems like everyone wants something from me. If I do one thing, it hurts someone else and vice versa."

"And what do *you* want?" She put her warm hand on my knee.

"Peace."

"At what cost to Terra?"

"Why does there have to be a cost? The Caelumites—most of them are good people. So are Terrans. Can't we forgive past grievances? We've fought together in a war. Isn't it time to stop fighting each other?"

"They stole our land," she said quietly. "Half of my father's property was taken by them. Shouldn't we be able to fight for what's ours?"

"That was over a century ago."

She held up her hands. "So that's it? They win?"

"We're not going to solve this today. Besides, Mya is in the hands of the real enemy. I should be focused on bringing her back."

"And that's what the king is doing. Forcing Caelum's hand to help her."

"Or is he using Mya as a bargaining chip for his gain?"

"Terra's gain." She gave a small shrug.

"Really?" My voice hiked. I stood, towering over her. "You think it's okay to gamble with Mya's life like that?"

Her cheeks pinkened. "No. I mean, sometimes as ruler you have to make hard choices. That's what your father did."

I'd wanted to understand my own mind better. The conversation with Emily enlightened me, though not in the way she'd intended. Terra needed a leader who didn't disregard the life of his daughter. Someone who cared about others, about fairness. Father wasn't able to distinguish which he loved more, Terra, or his own power. It had become twisted in his head, and he'd almost tangled me with him.

It's natural that Emily would have difficulty overcoming the bias of her father, King Dryden's lackey. The Duke of Earlington had spewed hate for Caelum in front of his daughter her entire life. Perhaps she wasn't the correct person to act as an advisor, though if I intended peace between the two kingdoms, discovering the deep-rooted prejudices would aid in deciding a way forward.

"Thanks for your insights. I'm headed to bed." I patted her shoulder and left without a backward glance, heading straight for Cate's room. When she answered the door, her brows elevated in skeptical surprise.

"I'm sorry." I rested my head on the doorframe. "I'm being an idiot again."

She opened it wider, beckoning me in, her expression flat.

I entered and sat in the chair she offered. "Can we pretend today never happened?"

She remained standing, staring at the floor. "I wish."

"How about ignoring what I said—yes, I needed a minute to get my head on straight—and now it is. We're getting your father, Mya, and Lucas back. Together. My father is power hungry, and just because I'm not on his side doesn't make me not on Terra's.

"And Emily?"

"She's brainwashed by the duke," I answered without hesitation.

"Hmm?" Cate put a hand on her hip. "It was her father who wanted her to kiss you?"

"Oh, that." I felt my neck redden. "No, that was her. But I didn't enjoy it. And it was only on the cheek."

She took the seat across from me, her purple gown spreading around her with elegance. "Well," she said primly. "I'd love to kiss and make up, but we have a war to plan."

After a few hours, we came up with a strategy. The next morning, I went in search of Dev. He'd lead the Terran army, my father tucked safely in Terra Castle, per usual since both his heirs were in danger. Cate and I would leave today and meet up with the Terrans in two weeks at a rendezvous point. It would take time for us to travel and gather the soldiers needed. Not to mention the issue of swaying Graftonberg.

I met with Father in the breakfast room to inform him of my departure and intention to support Cate. I laid out my points, explaining I needed to represent the monarchy in this battle. He agreed begrudgingly to assist Dev in gathering the army.

The king sat in front of his untouched food and leaned back in his chair. "The people won't understand. They respect you—want to see you on the throne someday."

"Not if I'm a cowardly prince. One who lets his sister rot in enemy hands."

"I could order you to stay." He sipped his juice as if his decision would be made on a whim.

"You could. But you won't."

He took a bite of eggs, focusing on his plate. "We're done here."

I started for the exit, but before I left, he said quietly, "Bring Mya back for us, son."

Without turning, I said, "I will."

Next was Mother. Her pain and worry hit me before I even entered the room. Cate stood by my side for this meeting. We all hugged. Cate cried with her, and their emotions, thick and heavy, were liable to pull me under. I fought the burning tears threatening to spill down my cheeks, knowing it was my turn to be strong for them.

"Take care of him." Mother squeezed Cate's hand. "And you." She turned to me. "Do the same for her."

"I promise," I said. And I meant it with every ounce of my soul.

In some ways, I wished we could have crept out before these two meetings, but that would be the coward's way. The emotional toll of Cate's and Mother's feelings left me drained. We needed the closure. A chance to say goodbye because I might not be returning. This time, nothing would come between me and saving Mya. Even if it meant my downfall.

CHAPTER 39
CATE

After one last hug with Queen Lila, Daniel and I were on our way to Caelum. This road was becoming tedious. As much as I loved North, I'd kill for my beat-up sedan back home in Oregon. Maybe one day we could build a train between the kingdoms. Isolation fueled distrust between the two peoples, sustained by animosity from old stories of wicked deeds, wars, and the hatred fed by each generation holding a grudge and expanding the tales. If they spent more time with one another, they'd understand how many similarities they share.

The only positive point from the war with the Embers was the truce between Caelum and Terra—the soldiers working together against a common enemy. The building blocks of trust had been laid, but it wouldn't take much to topple them.

We traveled with the Caelum men who accompanied us to Terra Castle. Daniel, astride Raven, now healthy enough for the trip, rode next to me. We tentatively mended our dispute, him humble, and me attempting to understand the dilemma of being King Dryden's son.

As the journey wore on, the pressure I placed on myself mounted, and I alternated between despondency and anxiety. We traveled with nothing to occupy me but the weight of those relying on my shaky water abilities—my father, Lucas, and Mya's lives dependent on me, along with the army we would raise. The spinning fears wouldn't cease, a constant companion that soon escalated. One would think a panic attack should materialize on a battlefield, or at the sight of King Dryden's steely gaze. Instead, my spiraling thoughts, when allowed the chance to run free, left me most vulnerable, tumbling into an abyss of my own making.

The clip-clop of horses' hooves rang in my ears. Rushing pain filled my chest, and my breath turned erratic. My vision clouded, the wide road stretching ahead, a path to destruction. I swayed in my saddle, pulling North to a stop.

Daniel discreetly signaled to the soldiers to provide us space, his voice a faint echo in a tunnel, the men's faces a blur of concern as they crowded away. I slid from North's back, stumbling to the side of the road, my body folding in on itself until I collapsed, head between my knees. I was faintly aware of Daniel's touch, but it did little to ease the explosive pain in my chest. There wasn't enough oxygen in the air—I was slowly being smothered. The first (and second, and third), time I'd experienced the agony, I thought I was dying—that my heart would surely give out. After some experience, and coping techniques shared by a therapist, I learned to find my way out of the horror, though I wasn't there yet, not by a long shot.

Instead of imagining my father's torture, Lucas bleeding alone in a cell, and me failing to produce a drop of rain, I tried to focus on the hard ground beneath me and the smell of pine from Daniel's steady presence. My pulse pounded on, aching under my ribs. If I could only get my brain to snatch a statistic out of the depths, rather than concentrating on my heart's erratic rhythm. *Trains.* I had been thinking about them. Here, on this route. It's in there somewhere... *Nearly a thousand people die yearly from train-related accidents in the US.*

I traced the dusty earth, my fingers scraping until it lodged beneath my nails. *Number of people dying in avalanches each year in America? Twenty-eight.* The sensation of being buried alive loosened, the weight on my chest lightening. I took a deep breath; the oxygen feeding my lungs and chasing away the numbness tingling across my cheeks. Daniel sat beside me, and I leaned into his strength. "I'm sorry," I whispered.

He combed his fingers through my hair. "I feel so helpless. I want to do something. Fight something. But you've got it all locked up in there." His thumb caressed my temple.

"There's nothing to battle but me." I cast him a wan smile.

"Your color's coming back. You better?"

I'd been told I turned white as snow when an attack came on, but I had never been coherent enough to check in the mirror. "Yeah, I think so." At least I didn't feel the need to come up with any more statistics. Daniel continued to play with my hair, and I let the soothing tingle on my scalp take over. "That helps, thank you." I tilted into his touch.

"No rush. We're making good time for once," he said. "They'll wait." He nodded to the soldiers who had separated into two groups, flanking the road fifty yards up and back on the route.

I shifted to better see his face, the sunlight through the trees dappling his mahogany hair, those sky-blue eyes staring warmly into mine. "What if we can't rescue them? What if *I* can't rescue them?"

His brows knitted. "This isn't entirely on your shoulders. Those loyal men standing over there certainly don't think so. We have well-trained soldiers on both sides. We'll get them out. Whether it's sunny or a downpour."

"You guys have any meteorologists around here? Maybe we can time it just right." His perplexed expression made me smile. "Weather people?"

"Ah, no. I'm afraid we aren't so good at predicting rain."

I smirked, remembering the number of times in Portland I left my umbrella at the house because of an unreliable weather report. "We aren't that great at home either."

"Seriously, Cate. We're in this together. I'm sorry I ever made you doubt that."

"Because *you* doubted it."

"I suppose you're right. As usual, I explained it all wrong. I never would have stayed in Terra. But I *do* understand why my father wanted me home. Both his heirs are in jeopardy."

"I guess," I grudgingly admitted. "Maybe I'm a little biased against him. Ok, a lot."

He nodded. "You should be. But if we're going to make peace, we'll have to figure out how to compromise with him sometimes."

I arched my brows. "But not on this. You're staying with me." I reached up and brushed an errant hair from his brow. "Always."

His lips moved toward mine. "Always." I met him in a soft, hesitant kiss, sliding my fingers up his arm.

"I love you," he whispered, kissing my forehead, then moving lower behind my ear, sending shivers colliding across my chest. He drew me in, deepening our embrace. The warmth—the heat—enveloped me and banished the shadows.

Our knees collided, clamoring to move closer. I pulled away and laughed, finally taking in my surroundings. The soldiers weren't quick enough to swivel to keep me from seeing their stares. We were partially canopied by tree branches, but still very much out in the open on a well-traveled road. "We better go."

"As long as you're feeling up to it? I could kiss you again just to be sure." He flashed a mischievous smile.

"That's one tactic my therapist never mentioned." I hauled myself to my feet, brushing away the dust from my gown. I wore my pants under my dress so I wouldn't have to ride sidesaddle. Not the most princess-like behavior, but with days on the road, nobody wanted to be stalled by propriety.

We mounted our horses and continued the journey. My tornado thoughts calmed to a category one hurricane, more typical for me. When we stopped for breaks, I snuck away with Daniel, not for more make-out sessions—sadly—but for attempts at waterworks. Multiple trials of Daniel transferring his energy to me did not help, and we decided my power alone would eventually produce results. I didn't want the soldiers to know how much I struggled. The lack of safety in wandering far without escort led to little practice on the road. And very little success.

As we approached Caelum Castle, a falcon circled overhead, diving toward North and me. "It's Mocha," I exclaimed.

"Who?"

In the recent chaos, I hadn't had time to tell Daniel about her. I wrapped a thick cloth from the saddlebag over my arm and held it out. She landed perfectly, bobbing her head for her usual treat.

"We'll have to wait until we get back to the castle," I told her. She held out her foot, presenting a paper attached. I carefully removed it and unrolled the tiny scroll. The three words on the sheet sent a shiver skittering down my spine.

Please hurry home.

"What is it?" Daniel asked, likely sensing the dread in my emotions and leaning closer.

I handed him the parchment. He tried not to act concerned, but I didn't miss the flash of apprehension cross his features. "Have a pencil?"

The contents of my saddlebag stirred under my fingers until I found the pencil at the bottom next to my hard-bound journal. After I passed it to him, he wrote on the other side of the scrap and returned it.

Almost there.

"That's your profound note?" I asked, huffing a small laugh.

He shrugged. "It's true, isn't it?"

The castle loomed in the distance. We'd be riding into the stables in fifteen minutes. I tied the paper onto Mocha. "At least it will be good practice. Off you go, girl." She soared into the air, gliding, then pumping her powerful wings upward toward the mews.

My thoughts whirred, examining and discarding each possibility. Father was back. The dragons have come. The Embers invaded. I'm to dress up for a giant ball tonight thrown by Graftonberg. The latter option was most probable. Just like him to want to celebrate the king's capture, extending his power.

We rode into the stables. "Anything special going on?" I asked a groom, a freckle-faced teenager.

"Not that I know of," he said.

Daniel and I exchanged looks of relief.

"Oh, wait," the stable hand said, "almost forgot. There's some sort of big announcement tomorrow. In Neva."

Neva was the closest town to us, and one of the biggest in Caelum. The city had a symbiotic relationship with the castle and royals, trading goods and providing workers.

"What kind?" Daniel prodded.

The young man shrugged. "Who knows? The baron organized it. I'm to help ready the horses in the morning."

We exchanged yet another look, this one wary. After taking care of our mounts, we checked in with Charlie, who was relieved we'd made it home in time before the assembly tomorrow.

"It's not my place to say," Charlie's gaze flickered to the ground, "but I thought you should be there. King Aldridge would want it."

"Thanks for the message. I appreciate you looking after me." I gave his arm a reassuring squeeze. "I'll be there."

We headed inside to find Graftonberg, locating him in his usual sitting room surrounded by cronies, including Roy, the ever-dutiful son. They swirled mulled wine in elaborate gold goblets—ones I'd never even seen my father use—their smug faces congratulating themselves on the life they suddenly inherited within the castle. I wondered how many of them had moved in already.

"Ah, look who's back." The baron smirked and held up his glass to the both of us. "And where is the Terran army you promised?" His eyes roamed the space as if soldiers would appear out of thin air.

There were eight in the room. The count—I really needed to learn his name—Roy, Hanson, a soft-spoken prominent landowner I'd met with my father who did not seem to belong with this group, and the others I didn't recognize. They all had one thing in common: their eyes were fixed on Daniel and me.

"They're assembling as we speak. We plan to meet at the bluff in ten days," Daniel said while he took another step into the room.

"Who's we? You and who else?" the count asked, taking another drink from his goblet.

Daniel and I needed to tread carefully here. "I'll be going with the small band of Caelum soldiers we used for protection to travel to Terra," Daniel said.

"And the princess?" Jowly leaned forward.

I wanted to tell him it was none of his business, but I supposed since he was the regent, he should be informed. I smiled demurely, at least I hoped it was demure. Judging from his narrowed lids, it probably came out more snarky than sweet. "I'll be going to battle."

I watched for his reaction. Daniel and I were curious if he'd want me to stay—to manipulate me like King Dryden wanted—or if sending me to war would clear the path for his ambitions to rule. We actually had a side bet going, the winner procuring the other's favorite dessert from the kitchens this evening. I figured the baron would hope to get me out of the way.

For once, Graftonberg kept his expression neutral. Perhaps because if I left, it would be a win-win for him. "And the danger? Are you concerned?" he asked.

"Of course she is," Daniel answered for me. "But I'll keep her safe."

Roy chimed in, a smirk plastered across his doughy features, "Like you did your sister?"

Daniel's hand clenched at his side. He probably wanted to punch the guy. *Join the club*. "She'll have the Terran army behind her," he said.

"They going to build her a shield out of weeds?" Roy asked.

My mouth dropped at his sarcasm and frank animosity toward the prince. The power was traveling to his head, which raised my suspicion that the Graftonbergs plotted to become the next rulers of Caelum. But they were starting a fight with the wrong girl. Before Daniel threw Roy out the window—and we were on the third floor—I cut in, "Play nice, boys. I'll be fine." I strode the rest of the way into their circle and took the remaining open seat across from the baron. "I heard something about a gathering in Neva tomorrow?"

"Yes. We intend to announce your father's capture. It's been kept a secret far too long," Graftonberg said, his voice falsely grave. "I will tell them the king's wishes—that I'll be regent."

"You planned to do this without me?"

"We don't need you there." His gaze leveled.

"All the same, I'd like to be present. It would reassure the kingdom we're united, don't you think? I can say a few words, encourage the people. Let them know the Terrans are assisting in the king's rescue."

He examined me warily, presumably trying to decide if I could be trusted. He'd obviously hoped to make this announcement on his own and cast me off as an absentee princess. On the other hand, if I granted him my support, especially before leaving on a dangerous mission, this would strengthen his position. It would seal his claim to the throne if I were killed. A shiver snaked across my chest at the thought.

Graftonberg turned to his entourage, seeking counsel. Roy held his lips in a lopsided purse, while the count nodded in approval.

"Your support would be helpful. Thank you," the baron said.

The relative stiffness in his jowls revealed his reluctance to thank me, but we were still in the cordial phase of our dislike for one another. At least with an audience present. We exchanged a few details, including riding into town together, then exited the room.

"I'll have to check the silver when they leave. *If* they ever leave," I told Daniel when we were out of earshot, down the corridor.

He raised his brows adorably. "You're speaking American again."

I giggled. "It means they're likely to steal stuff from the castle. Did you see those goblets?"

"Ah. They've made themselves at home, haven't they?"

"The mice will play."

He smiled as we turned the corner to our favorite sitting room adjacent to my father's office. "I know this one. While the cat's away."

"Exactly." I slumped into a chair. "How many of Graftonberg's boys club are going to move in, I wonder."

"Too many." He sat next to me, popping a cracker in his mouth. A Caelum charcuterie board, consisting of pickled vegetables, meats, and fruit, had been left for us. "Your father pulled one over on you with that regent thing."

He really had, and the thought weighed heavy with the knowledge he might be gone forever. "I couldn't talk him out of it." The pattern on the carpet weaved in and out of my vision like a kaleidoscope under my glassy focus. I blinked away the burn of tears, not ready to explore what would happen if we didn't save him. We'd skirted around the topic for days. Daniel scooted his chair closer to mine and took my hand, watching me until I tore my gaze from the floor. He remained silent, patiently waiting for me to tell him my thoughts.

"Why do you think the Embers sent a ransom for Mya to King

Dryden, but we've heard nothing here in Caelum for my father?" I worked hard to keep my voice steady.

"It could be any number of reasons."

"I'm afraid I know the answer." I swallowed through the thick closure of my throat, finally ready to form the words that my mind kept returning to. "Because he's already dead."

CHAPTER 40
DANIEL

We rode out the next morning, Graftonberg and Cate in the lead, me feeling like a third wheel. It should strengthen the Caelum people's confidence to have the Terran prince here supporting King Aldridge's rescue, but the baron had delegated me to the rear of this makeshift parade into the city. My ego could withstand the blow, though I'd rather be near Cate to better read her emotions and those around her. So far, the baron and his comrades felt a mix of animosity, curiosity, and reverence toward her. Alana's prophecy and the deluge from The Great Battle left room for awe, even if they did want to steal the kingdom out from under her.

I worked to reassure Cate last night that her father was still alive. Unfortunately, I'd been wondering the same and I'm not sure I convinced either of us. The Embers were unpredictable, their surveillance spotty, yet sometimes eerily accurate. They might realize that Graftonberg enjoyed his new role and wouldn't save King Aldridge, and as much as it pained me, they clearly suspected my father was more likely to betray the Caelumites, not only to rescue his daughter but to gain more power for himself.

Along the route, the Caelum people came out in full force. A grandstand had been set up in a field outside of town where thousands gathered. With so many soldiers not returning from the mission, word had spread that news might be relayed today. Their delight at seeing Cate

in the parade couldn't be missed, with small children pointing and waving, broad smiles drawn on the adults' faces. A few even shyly grinned at me when I passed. Some probably didn't know I was the prince, though Caelum's newspapers had apparently printed more than one image of me.

"Welcome," the baron announced from the stage.

I dismounted and climbed the steps to stand next to Cate. Tension rolled off her in waves. The few times I'd heard her speak publicly, she was actually quite talented and far too critical of herself. For a moment, I became distracted by the blush in her cheeks, the slope of her nose, and the long lashes fluttering. I wanted to pull her into my arms and soothe the frayed edges, but a thousand pairs of eyes stared up at us, so I edged near enough that our shoulders brushed.

"Thank you all for attending," Graftonberg continued. "I have a grave announcement. On a mission to forge a peace treaty with the Embers," he paused dramatically, "King Aldridge was captured."

Murmurings erupted, growing into a buzzing hive of whispers and dismay. Cate stood stock-still next to me, her face placid. Beneath the surface, emotions roiled—concern for her father, apprehension of the crowd's reaction, and anxiety for the speech to come. Our whole plan hinged on her performance, and she knew it.

"The king has put me in charge as regent until Princess Catherine has reached her year citizenship in Caelum. I will lead this kingdom with all the solemn wisdom you would expect as King Aldridge's top advisor these past years. We are a great people…"

I tuned him out at this point as he extolled the Caelumites, himself, and the future. He exuded Pompous Windbag, and I wasn't sure if the crowd bought it, if not for Cate and me standing dutifully behind. He droned on and on as the audience shifted from foot to foot, with parents shushing bored children.

Cate stepped forward to stand directly beside Graftonberg. She put a hand on the baron's arm when he paused for a breath and called out, "Isn't it wonderful we have someone who cares so much about Caelum as our regent?"

The response: a lackluster clap.

"Thank you for coming today and showing support for me and my father. I've grown attached to this kingdom and will do everything in my power to protect it. My father is the heart and soul of Caelum, and I've seen firsthand the number of sacrifices he has made. He isn't up in the castle hosting fancy dinners every night. He's in his office pouring over strategies with generals, fortifying our borders, and ultimately, he sacrificed himself at a peace treaty for the good of the kingdom. Unfortunately, we've learned we can't trust the Embers. They will never make peace with us. So, we must claim what is ours and get our king back!"

The crowd shouted and cheered, followed by a wave of chatter. I could feel their distaste for the Embers, with threads of hate weaving and wrapping itself through the masses. I tried to block the emotion, but the overpowering strength forced itself into me. Their feelings were black and sour and seeped into my skin like a sickness. I turned my focus onto Cate instead. Her nerves jittered on edge, but I also detected pride—in her people, and herself for standing up for what was right.

"In fact," Cate raised her voice. "I plan to lead a group with Prince Daniel and the Terrans." Cate's words marched on, not pausing to let the baron barge his way into her speech. "And they'll be backed by the best soldiers in the world—the Caelum army. We're getting our king back and showing the Embers who's in charge!"

Since I knew her announcement was coming, my gaze shifted to the baron. Only the side of his face was visible—the jowls dropping in momentary shock.

Cate continued, "Let's give credit to Baron Graftonberg, who is exercising great lengths to bring my father home." She started clapping, and I joined, exactly as we'd plotted. It fed the baron's ego and drowned him out before he could protest. His mouth finally closed in a tight smile. Cate looped her arm through his, waved to the crowd, and guided him off stage.

The somber tones of the reverse parade through the Neva streets oscillated with tension. The crowds had mostly dispersed, but the few who remained wore conflicted expressions. They wanted to support Cate, with a few shouting, "Long live the king!" However, no one wished for war. Their emotions were tumultuous—concern for loved ones who might be sent to battle, for their captured king, and Cate, who saved them once—but could she do it again?

Cate had brought candy in her saddle bag and tossed it to the children, which did little to improve the mood of their parents. King Aldridge was popular here in Neva, and the uncertainty of his capture left them uneasy. The baron stewed in silence on our trip through town, seething on the inside.

Once we cleared the city, Graftonberg turned his wrath on Cate. I rode up next to them in case she needed interference.

"I told you." His jowls reddened. "We are not losing more Caelum men. Aldridge made his choice."

"Convenient, isn't it?" Cate replied. "That you don't want to retrieve the one person who can usurp your power? I did you a favor back there. If the people find out you are unwilling to rescue their king, they'll turn on you."

"Princess," his tone turned mocking, "your father doesn't *want* to be rescued."

"That's a lie." Cate's anger flared.

"Is it?" the baron asked, looking down his nose. "Before he departed for this debacle of a peace treaty, we had lengthy conversations preparing for the possibility he wouldn't return. His only wish was to keep his precious daughter safe and the kingdom intact."

The thing about reading emotions and using them to detect lies is that experienced liars aren't nervous when they tell a falsehood. It's all routine. Like having a normal conversation. The baron was angry and frustrated, no doubt, but that telltale blip of nerves that gave so many away didn't present itself. Unfortunately, I suspected he was a practiced fabricator, and his words did have a ring of truth. King Aldridge *would* have made plans with his regent.

Graftonberg continued, "He knows we can't afford to lose more men. The borders aren't shored up. We've struggled with Ember attacks. Frankly, Princess, after the last battle, we don't have the army to send."

CHAPTER 41
CATE

How could there not be enough soldiers? He must be lying. My father had never indicated to me we'd run out of men. And he wanted to be rescued, didn't he? I thought back to the strategy meetings before he left. Sometimes they would shoo me away, yet I *had* heard him and his advisors discussing their losses from The Great Battle. *And* of border unrest. Father assured me it was nothing. *Skirmishes,* he'd called them. Maybe because he never expected to have to raise an army to march on our enemy so quickly. He believed I'd bought them time.

That's why Father wanted the peace treaty. Not just to get Lucas back, but because he fully understood we were vulnerable. My belly panged with hurt that he didn't tell me. Was he embarrassed, or wasn't I important enough to inform? I swallowed the lump forming in my throat. I would *not* cry in front of Graftonberg.

Did King Dryden know we didn't possess the soldiers to match his request? Terrans might have taken fewer losses, The Great Battle on Caelum territory, not Terran. This would make us the weaker kingdom. Goosebumps prickled along my arms. The deal with Dryden just became an even worse agreement than I thought.

I didn't respond to the baron because I wasn't sure how. I'd blundered—made an agreement with someone who shouldn't be trusted—my own boyfriend's father. I glanced at Daniel riding beside me.

Resentment bubbled beneath my skin. I tamped it down, knowing he'd feel it. Although I could always say it was directed toward King Dryden. Or Graftonberg. Because those feelings simmered somewhere in the turmoil, and he wouldn't be able to tell the difference. Resenting Daniel for not being able to sway his father didn't help the situation. He'd stepped up to the edge of Dryden's treachery and walked away. Not as quickly as I would have hoped, but he still chose the right path —to save the kingdom of Caelum *and* his sister. Yet now, the plan teetered in precarious danger.

I finally gained the composure to speak to the baron, swallowing my pride. "It appears I've announced an army, so we'll have to raise it. Where will we find enough soldiers?"

"Foolish girl. You'll leave us unprotected for an invasion."

I couldn't share that we had no choice because King Dryden could turn against us, and an assault would come from the Terrans, not Embers. Not with Daniel next to me. Not with his sister in danger. The Caelum people will be unprotected regardless of the choice we make.

"We'll speak with Colonel Dixon." Graftonberg shifted in his saddle, his girth not suited for riding.

"I've some ideas as well," Daniel said.

The baron snorted. "I bet you do."

"Cate and I can talk about it when we arrive at the castle, since it appears you won't be receptive to anything I say."

"And why would that be, Prince? Your father tries to inch the border closer to absorb more and more of our lands every year. He promotes hatred of our people. We would have peace in our kingdoms if it weren't for him."

For once, I agreed with the baron. Could it be possible he wasn't as bad as I originally thought? Then I remembered Roy, the cronies and their golden goblets, and his complete distaste for me and all things female. To give him a modicum of credit, he did love the kingdom, but he also loved power. And the love of power always corrupts.

"And what about you spewing all that vitriol?" Daniel responded. "It works both ways, Graftonberg."

"Let's just call a truce." I couldn't believe I was siding with Jowly, but arguing wasn't helping our situation. "How soon can we get a meeting with Colonel Dixon?"

"This evening. He's stationed a few hours away. I'll send a messenger." He set his mouth in a grim line.

We arrived from the tense journey and finally separated from the baron. Daniel led me to the gardens to a stone bench for some solitude, the same seat Alana had taught me to feel the energy at sunrise. I couldn't believe she was gone. So many lives… just extinguished. I was tired. Tired of the deaths, the infighting, the war. My bedroom back in Oregon with the pink bedspread and well-worn novels stacked haphazardly on the shelf beckoned. Where my biggest problems were not being invited to prom or working a long shift at my parents' store. I dabbed the wetness collecting at the creases of my eyes.

Daniel sat beside me in silent support, his warm leg nestled by mine. He'd been so quiet today, except for the outburst against Graftonberg earlier. "You okay?" I asked.

"Me? What about you?" The pads of his fingers gently swiped away a tear from my cheek.

He already knew—could feel my anguish. Not for the first time, I wondered how difficult it must be to sense others' emotions. "How are we going to fix this?" I asked.

"We'll meet with the colonel and find out what we're working with. And I didn't want to say this in front of the baron, but perhaps we don't disclose how many soldiers Caelum contributes to my father. What he doesn't know, won't hurt him. By the time we get Mya and King Aldridge back, it won't make a difference."

It might be difficult to keep that secret from Dryden, but I liked the idea. "We still need every person we can summon."

"True. But we have a weapon you aren't thinking about."

"What's that?"

One side of his mouth turned up in a half smile. "Not what. Who. *You're* our weapon."

"But—"

"You already showed me you can produce rain when we're close to each other. Let's practice."

He pulled me up off the bench only for me to sit right back down, shaking away his hand on my arm. "My emotions are all over the place. I… can't." Everything felt too raw.

He moved closer to me, his features softening. "I *know* you are struggling."

"Stop reading me," I snapped. Anger bubbled, grappling against my better judgment, and threatened to erupt.

Anger toward King Dryden and the chokehold relationship he had on Daniel, and at myself for not handling both of them more effectively, flooded to the surface. Anger at Alana, who never should have agreed to participate in the mission that took her life. I felt selfish, making her death only about losing my mentor, instead of the loss of goodwill she promoted within both kingdoms. The turmoil and bitter thoughts swirled into a downward spiral, despite my efforts to fight it.

"Cate, I'm going to give you some tough love." Daniel stared into the distance, signaling an uncomfortable topic. He struggled with eye contact, probably due to growing up with Dryden. I didn't blame him; I had difficulty meeting the king's gaze, too. "I know you're angry and hurting—at the world, me included. It's time to turn it around. We only have a week to figure this out before we're riding into Ember territory. No more feeling sorry for yourself. No more *I can't*."

He bit his lip, now watching my reaction, waiting for me to fall apart. Strangely, the fog cleared. He was correct—I couldn't continue as Cate, the girl who worried too much. Cate, who was unable to control her power. I would always have anxiety—it was part of my make-up—but it shouldn't rule my life. Alana prophesied I would defeat the enemy. That I'd unite the kingdoms. Neither had happened yet. The Great Battle wasn't enough.

Almost killing myself wasn't enough.

My job was not over.

"You're right," I said quietly. "And I *am* mad at you. It's irrational, and I hate it because I also love you, but you're linked to your father and he's made a bad situation even worse, capitalizing on our vulnerable position. I have no idea how we'll reconcile with him once this is all over. And it *will* be over. I'm going to do this. And I hate to admit it, at least for now, I need you."

Hurt reflected in his eyes. "Why do you hate to admit it?"

I tore away my hand from his. "Because I want to stand on my own two feet. That's what strong girls do back home, you know."

His expression remained impassive. "Why? Your American ideas are hard to wrap my head around. Just because you lean on someone, doesn't mean you're not still strong. We're in this together, remember? I have no doubt you'll be a warrior soon, yielding water like a goddess. And you will do it without me."

I sighed, shifting into him. "Sometimes I wish I knew what *you're* feeling. I just told you I was mad at you, that I didn't want to need you, and you sit there, cool as a cucumber."

His gaze returned to the horizon. "I'm angry at my father. And a bit frustrated with you for blaming me. I hate it too. But we can't let our kingdoms pull us apart." He turned to me again. "I'm sorry. Neither of us is perfect."

I buried my head into the crook of his neck. "Thank you for being honest with me. We'll get through it." He felt solid and warm, his embrace grounding, reminding me to be grateful for his support.

I closed my eyes and relished the sensation. Our love wrapped around us, the energy binding us. Becoming tangible in the way I only feel when we're together. It gave me the confidence to try again. To believe in myself.

Deep breaths. In. Out. Feel the water in the air, the moisture clinging to the grass from last night's dew.

The rain came. Not a sprinkle, but fat drops, pelting our heads. I squeezed my lids shut, gripped Daniel, and focused on expanding my reach, stretching out farther and farther. My mind floated, sensing the energy curling through the field and beyond until only the faintest whisper was detectable at the outer reaches. Finally, I pulled away from our embrace and watched, a hand still on Daniel, acting as a touchstone. The downpour advanced to include the castle and trailed into the valley, swelling to three football fields in size.

He gifted me with a wobbly smile. "I knew you could do it." His eyes were wet, and not from the rain. "I'm so proud of you, Cate."

We kissed, his lips sweet, then insistent. We let the water drip between us, soaking our clothing and cooling our skin, the warmth of each other enough that we never wanted it to end.

The rain gradually diminished, and we traipsed back to the castle to change. Our fingers interlocked; Daniel steadied me on the now muddy grass. My clothes and shoes were ruined, though I hardly cared.

"Next, we need to practice seeing how far apart we can be." He squeezed my hand.

"Hey! Let me bask in my glory—*our* glory, for a while first. Besides, we should clean up to talk to this Colonel Dixon."

"You've never met him?"

"I don't remember. There are always a ton of people that come and talk to my father… I mean, there *were* a lot of people." I swallowed the scratchiness rising in my throat. I couldn't think about that now.

"You okay discussing what you're capable of with the colonel? He'll need to be informed for strategy purposes."

"Let's meet him first. Especially since he's Graftonberg's choice."

Roy, Count What's-His-Name, the baron, and a stocky man in military uniform convened at the conference table. I hated this room. Nothing good ever happened here. The round table, much too large for our small gathering, forced us to cluster to one side.

Daniel pulled out my chair, then sat beside me. "Gentleman." He inclined his head. "And you must be Colonel Dixon."

He nodded once in affirmation. A burn scar puckered across his cheek.

"I assume Baron Graftonberg filled you in?" I asked.

"Let me be frank, Princess Catherine. We're not in good shape. Deserters, lost lives, injuries—they all add up to weakened defenses." His gruff tone matched his demeanor.

My stomach churned. Maybe he would refuse to lead the army to save my father. And what of Lucas and Mya?

"The baron here thinks we should call it off. I understand you made an announcement today. We could quietly shift plans and not gather the soldiers. Eventually inform the people that the king was unable to be rescued."

My heart pounded an unsteady rhythm at his words. "But we're not going to do that, are we?" My voice came breathier than I'd like. Probably because my lungs felt as if a vice squeezed them, cranking tighter with each breath.

He tapped his fingers on the wood table. "We are not. I've known your father for years. We're going after him."

"Colonel," the baron said, "I thought you agreed."

"I did no such thing." He leveled a matter-of-fact stare.

Graftonberg's jowls shaded pink. "I will not let this castle go unprotected."

"The castle, or you?" Colonel Dixon asked.

Roy stood, pushing back his chair. "That's out of line."

"The colonel has a point," Daniel said. "You're protecting your own hides and care little about your king's."

Roy let out a sarcastic laugh. "Kind of like your father."

Sympathy surged for Daniel. He'd never escape King Dryden's shadow. I couldn't even defend him because in this case, Roy had it dead on.

"We're not discussing him," Daniel snapped.

Graftonberg slammed his fist on the table. "Enough. My instructions came direct from Aldridge."

"That he conveniently didn't share with anyone else," Daniel said.

I was tired of the fighting. We were wasting more time. I wanted my father back, and Lucas and Mya, too. "I'll make it rain," I said quietly. Silence settled over the space. "We can take fewer troops, and I will protect them. There's a chance I won't be able to shield a huge army, anyway."

The colonel nodded gravely. "Clear the room. Just me and the princess stay."

Daniel gave me a questioning look, and I spoke up, "The prince can remain. You might want him here for this conversation."

"I am the regent," Graftonberg blustered.

The count was the first to step toward the door. "Let's go, gentlemen. I know when I'm not welcome. I'm sure the colonel will fill us in later."

Roy and the baron followed suit, but not before Jowly gave me a final glare with his beady eyes.

The colonel's expression softened when the others left. The scar pulled one eye downward when he relaxed his face. "Will we be putting your life in danger for you to produce this water?"

Very few were aware of what happened at The Great Battle—my heart stopping, the need for resuscitation. The fact that Colonel Dixon knew meant he must have been in my father's confidence. Even the baron wasn't fully aware. I was touched that he worried. Usually, I struggled to decipher if people cared about me, the person or me, the *prophecy*. Daniel squeezed my knee under the table.

"I probably can't cause the same storm as The Battle, but I think I can cover a couple hundred yards. And..." My cheeks grew warm. "Prince Daniel has to be near me."

"You mean, you don't want to be separated? I'm sorry, Your Highness, this is war, and the best place for the prince's talents might not be next to you." To his credit, he appeared remorseful. He could have easily taken the snide route.

"She means," Daniel replied, "her power works better when we're together."

He squinted at us, his bushy salt-and-pepper brows descending. "I've never heard of that. How close do you need to be?"

He had a point. No one seems to have ever seen anything like it. We're an anomaly. "We'll be working on distance," I said. "Currently, touching works best."

The colonel nodded, taking it in stride as just another piece in the puzzle to work out in our strategy to defeat the Embers. "And it doesn't jeopardize your safety?"

"I-I don't think so." There's no telling how my nerves will react when in peril. I might forget my training and instead pour my own energy into the rain, endangering my life. And more frightening, it's possible I won't be able to stop until I've completely depleted myself.

Even so, I was willing to take the risk.

Again, he accepted my answer, trusting I would handle it, and moved on. "We leave in a week. I'll gather the troops and be back in five days. We'll talk strategy when I return."

I stood and took Daniel's hand. "Let's get to work."

CHAPTER 42
LUCAS

Mya trudged into the cell the next day, and as soon as the guard closed the door and footsteps receded down the corridor, she raced to my cot, her face alive with excitement. "I managed to talk to Grace, and you're never going to believe this. She knows where they hide the key for King Aldridge's cage."

"What do you mean, where? Don't you mean who?" Surely, it's on a keychain in some guard's pocket.

"You know how you saw them returning the king to the enclosure from his walkabout? A couple of days ago, Grace was delivering towels when they brought Aldridge out. They keep the key in a drawer. She watched him remove it and put it back. The room is locked, but Grace has a master for a ton of places, including *that* room."

"I've been trying to figure out if there was a certain schedule when he's out of the cage to plan our rescue around that time, but now we don't have to. If we release him ourselves, that'll mean fewer guards."

"How will you escape your job in the fields?"

"I have an idea. Are you still working with laboring mothers, or are you on babysitting duty?"

Mya's mouth turned down. "The kids. They're awful. I swear I put out five fires the little ruffians started today when they couldn't control their tempers."

"Perfect."

She scoffed. "Not really. I'd rather be digging dirt all day with you."

It was the first time I wondered what kind of Terran powers Mya had over the earth. I had trouble imagining her playing in the mud. "Can you sneak away to talk to Grace?"

She tapped her bottom lip, which drew my attention to its pink fullness. *Now is not the time for distractions.* "When she brings the laundry in, I'll figure out a way. Even if I let the place burn down."

I grinned. "That's the idea."

The next day was just like the others. I planted seeds, helped move irrigation pipes, and sneakily fed my crow friend, all with a grumbling stomach. Our plan was dependent on the three of us, with Mya updating Grace today. After a quick cleanup at the water pump, I trudged back to my cell, exhausted, but hopeful.

Mya sat on her cot, her black hair in disarray, strands escaping from her bun in streamers across her forehead, shiny with perspiration. Yet she never looked lovelier—cheeks flushed, eyes holding a glint of achievement. "We're all set. Grace is in."

"Tomorrow?" I asked, sitting on my bed opposite her.

She nodded. "Grace is scared to death but determined to get out of here, too. She's seen the baby factory." Mya paused, the weight of the Embers' vileness hanging between us. After a few moments, she tilted her head. "I like Grace. At first, I thought you were crazy to bring her into this, but you were right. She has a backbone in there. She'll pull through."

"I think so too." It felt good to know someone else was on our side. My ego would have me be the hero and perform all the rescuing, but for our plan to work, it would take the three of us. "So, tomorrow at noon?"

"Yup. I'll start the show." Mya leaned forward. "So, what's the first thing you want to eat when we get out of here?"

I laughed. "Haven't we been through this?"

A shoulder tipped up. "What can I say? I have a one-track mind."

"Tell me yours again, then." I longed for my mom's stew, but the memory lingered just beneath the skin, too raw to share again. The idea of home dangled tantalizingly close, hope propelling it in my circling thoughts, forcing me to bat it away to avoid the distraction.

Mya dreamily described her cook Hildy's famous pastries. Dimples flashed in her pink cheeks, ones I'd never noticed before. They must only show themselves when something was truly worthy. It made me want to earn that dimple. She deserved to be happy, and I wondered if she was content in Terra. King Dryden's shadow loomed over that castle like a dense fog.

"Do you think things will change between you and your father when you get home?" I blurted, interrupting her reverie over buttery crispiness.

Her sculpted brows angled downward. "How so?"

"Will he treat you like a fragile girl who was captured or a strong woman who held her own?"

Her lashes fluttered, gaze drifting to the floor. I'd made her uncomfortable.

"Probably the first. I'm used to it." She shrugged and lifted her attention back to me. "Women have to find their own ways to be powerful. We incite more changes than men understand—than my father realizes. And, even though she's sort of a sore subject between us, I think Cate is going to change things for girls here. She's modern, but everybody loves her for saving us. I don't blame you for loving her, too. Half the men in both kingdoms likely do." She smiled faintly. "In a weird way, I'm attracted to you *because* you admire her. It means you prefer your women with backbone."

I hadn't spent much time pondering my tastes in females, though Mya was on to something. "Just so you know, I haven't been thinking about her," I admitted. "My mind's been on you. I'm out in those fields wondering what you're doing. Praying that no one is taking advantage of you. And sometimes..." The tips of my ears started to burn. "Sometimes I think about our kiss." My natural tendency was to add a joke, maybe something like how anything was better than digging in the dirt like a Terran, but I restrained the impulse. She deserved more than my stupid deflections.

"You do?" Her radiant blue irises held mine.

I nodded slowly, then moved to sit beside her, making sure to not make any sudden movements, as if it might scare her away. "May I find out if it's as good as I remembered?"

Her head tilted ever so slightly in invitation, those gorgeous eyes drifting closed. I brushed my fingers along her jaw, her skin smooth and cool. Leaning closer, so I could feel her breath, I touched her lips to mine. More powerful than the last time, perhaps because there was no guilt to contend with, a jolt of desire bolted through my belly. I held back, keeping the kiss slow and languorous, cupping her face gently. She scooted nearer, and my palms trailed down her neck, now warm to the touch.

A rattle at the cell gate had us jumping apart. "Don't make me separate you two," a gruff man said, carrying our dinner. He slid them under the bars. "Mealtime."

I stood, grabbed the trays, and handed her the food, bringing mine back to my cot. Taking a bite of dried meat, I whispered, "I'm not sorry anymore."

A small smile lifted her swollen lips. "Neither am I."

Sweat dripped down my spine as the sun beat overhead. It should be nearly noon, and if all goes well, I'll be recalled from field duty. Earlier, I'd caught a glimpse of Molly and subtly motioned her to stay put. Hopefully, she understood my message. Closer proximity would aid communication, though that was entirely too risky.

The day wore on. And on. Something must have gone wrong. Mya was supposed to tell Grace to wait for us at the rendezvous point. If she informed her but couldn't complete the rest of the plan, then Grace could be risking everything by abandoning her duties for no reason. Unease grew. I told myself they were smart girls, and if the setup went awry, they'd figure it out and try tomorrow, but it didn't stop the sense of foreboding.

Every day that passed put everyone at risk. How long should we expect them to keep the king in a cage? I could only assume they were waiting for a ransom deal. Or that Aldridge acted as an insurance policy for future demands.

The Embers in charge finally called an end to the evening. The clanging of the chains with each step back to the jail rang with both dread and anticipation. Would Mya be there? Had she been punished? I searched for signs of upheaval from our planned distraction, but the Ember townspeople moved as they typically did, trudging to their homes after a day's work.

The cell sat empty when I arrived, and I reminded myself that Mya wasn't always the first one back. Still, it didn't prevent the knot in my stomach from twisting tighter. This was all my idea. If something happened to them, it was *my fault.* Yet what choice did we have? Attempt escape and accept the repercussions of failure, or risk the girls being placed into the baby factory while further threatening the king's execution. Every moment, every second, could mean the difference between life and death. The Embers' tactics were sickening. The guilt, the despair, the uselessness of my situation seeped into my flesh until my pacing ceased and I slumped on the cot with my head between my knees.

Footsteps in the corridor had me popping up to the bars. Mya, worrying her lip, traversed the stone hallway with a guard on her heels. The door jangled open after I stepped back into the room, the Ember eyeing me with distrust. It clanged shut again, and we waited until the clomping of his boots receded to huddle together on her bed.

"Is Grace all right?" I whispered.

"She's fine." Mya pushed an errant lock behind her ear. "I managed to talk my way into retrieving a clean set of rags and rushed to tell her. No one noticed her absence. That we know of, anyway."

"What happened? Are you okay?" I searched her face for distress and found none.

"At first, I was stationed with the mothers instead of children. I convinced them to send me away as a babysitter. When I tormented a little boy into starting a fire, not my finest moment, by the way, someone else rushed to put it out. Tomorrow, I'll have to take one of the kids to a place where we can be alone."

The idea was for Mya to coax a child to start a blaze, so the prisoners would be pulled from the field to extinguish it like last week. I'd go to the pump to get water, Grace would hand me the key, Mya would meet us at a rendezvous point, and in the chaos, we'd escape with the king. Many things could go wrong, obviously, like Mya not being able to start the fire, but the real danger would be leaving. Grace had plotted a path through alleys and empty houses to reach the outskirts of town, her master key and laundry knowledge essential to our plan.

I took in a deep breath and blew it out. "How are you going to manage it tomorrow? They might not be so accommodating to let you work with the kids. Why'd they even allow you to switch jobs today?"

She pursed her lips in contemplation. "I'm good at convincing people. It'll be fine."

"We can't stay in limbo based on the whims of the Embers. It's too dangerous for Grace. And you."

Her eyes snapped. "I *said* I would do it and I will." She stood, pacing the small space, her fists clenched.

I wasn't sure if she was angry at me or them. "I'm not discounting you. I am just trying to plan accordingly. Decide if we need to adjust."

"Well, we don't." Her glare shot daggers across the room.

This was the first time I'd seen the family temper. I figured it must be hiding in there somewhere, but much preferred consoling with kisses than dodging barbs. Holding my tongue would be the smart move, though I couldn't quite bring myself to do it. "Listen here, Princess. I realize you feel as if you have it all under control, but if you don't mind, I'd like to reassess. Grace's life shouldn't be on the line due to your ego."

"My—"

"Yup. You heard me. E—Go."

She crossed her arms. "I so do not want to be trapped in here with you."

With this attitude of hers? Neither did I. "The feeling's mutual. Glad I found out you take after the rest of your family now, before I'm in too deep."

A pink flush crept up her neck and into her cheeks. She flounced over to her bed, pointed at mine to get me to move, and flopped down, turning toward the wall. Our meal slid under the bars, though neither of us moved to eat. We stewed in silence, until I finally decided to retrieve my food, violently chewing the hard piece of dried meat provided. Mya covered her ears to block the sounds of my overly noisy eating. I'm sure it offended her princess sensibilities. I didn't much care.

We stayed silent for the better part of an hour. Would I have liked her to be the first to speak? I would. But I needed to know if we were proceeding as planned. "So, we're still a go for tomorrow?" I asked.

Silence. Even though she was quiet, I knew she wasn't sleeping. I'd grown accustomed to the cadence of her soft, deep breaths during the night. "Mya."

"Yes. As discussed," she hissed, still facing the wall.

"You should eat. It might be a while before we find food when we're on the run."

She sat up slowly. To my surprise, tears streaked her cheeks.

"I thought you were mad," I said.

"I am." She swiped away the wetness with the edge of the blanket. "But I also understand why you might not believe I can handle myself tomorrow. There's something I haven't told you. Something only my brother knows about me." She hesitated, biting her lip the way she did when nervous.

"It isn't my ego. I can… persuade people to do things." She kept her voice low to avoid being overheard.

I chuckled. "I know that's a talent of yours, but if that were true, we'd be out of this jail."

"The guards have one job. To keep us locked up tight. I can't change their minds completely. It works more when someone hasn't… committed."

I sighed. "I'm fairly adept with words myself, Mya, but you don't see me claiming—"

"It's my power," she blurted. "You can't tell anyone. I'm able to change people's feelings. Make them believe something is a good idea."

"You what?" I exploded, then realized I might draw the guard if I wasn't quieter.

She manipulates thoughts? I couldn't stop the first thing that popped selfishly into my head. Had she used it on me?

CHAPTER 43
LUCAS

Mya twisted and untwisted the corner of the blanket. "I know what you're thinking."

That she's been manipulating me all this time? That my feelings aren't actually real?

She continued, "You're wondering how it works. If it even does. Silly Mya and her delusions of grandeur."

"That's actually not what I was thinking. I don't take you for a liar."

"What then? What do you want to know?"

I wanted to prod and find out how this affected our relationship, but the whole idea made me feel small. As if I had to beg for her attention. Like I hadn't known my own mind when I decided to kiss her. Ultimately, I wasn't ready for her answer about us. Instead, I asked, "Can you turn it on and off?"

"Ohh…" Her tone indicated she knew what I'd been thinking despite my efforts to avoid the topic.

"Yeah," I deadpanned, waiting for her to continue.

"I only use it sometimes. And not on you. I promise." She stared at me with those gorgeous eyes, now brimming with worry that I wouldn't believe her.

Maybe because I didn't want to accept that she'd influenced me, or perhaps she was working her magic at this very moment, but I did believe her. I nodded once. "Okay. Let's move on. Tell me all about this power, and we'll devise all the ways it will help us get out of here."

The next morning, when the chains clamped to my ankles, butterflies whirred to life. Yesterday's nerves left me jittery and tired, and today I still couldn't tamp them down. Mya and I talked long into the night about contingency plans and how she would wheedle her way out to locate a better place to start the fire. She'd pack flammable objects in her apron pockets and would ensure one of the particularly ornery children became so dirty that she would have to take him outside to clean. Then she would convince the child to stray into a nearby building and annoy him enough to ignite the blaze. She had already scouted out the location, which appeared empty when she'd peered inside yesterday. We hoped the fire would rage sufficient to pull us from the field, while still tame enough, at least at first, for Mya and the kid to escape.

The flock of ravens hopped behind me, my bird friend in the lead. I'd been sneaking them seeds for days now. They'd taken to following me overhead on the way back to the jail, and I hoped they would today.

Several hours later, a man sprinted toward us from the direction of town. Mya came through! I blew out a breath to ease my jitters and attacked the soil with my hoe.

"What's going on?" an Ember guard asked once the huffing man arrived.

He put his hands on his knees, strands of blond hair falling into his eyes, and I listened for news of the fire. "There's an army approaching," he gasped between breaths. "Both Caelum and Terran. Rowan said to lock up the prisoners. Take 'em to their cells."

My jaw dropped. A rescue. King Dryden actually came through?

But what about the plan?

If I was locked up, then it would all be for nothing. We could wait for our soldiers, but they might not win. Which would leave us in the same position—as prisoners. The chaos of battle would be a perfect distraction, coupled with the fire that Mya hopefully started.

Our ankle chains were once again joined, further decreasing the odds of escape. The guards forced us to march at double speed toward town. At the edge of the city, we met another Ember soldier, this one strapped with a sword and hilted daggers. "Change of plans. There's a fire, just outside the square. We need the prisoners' help while we assemble the troops. Send them over and grab buckets on your way."

Mya did it! The timing couldn't be more perfect. We'd escape, then meet the army and retreat with them, or join the fight and save those captured, depending on how many soldiers arrived from our side. Otherwise, we'd figure out a plan to return for the others and stop the Embers for good.

The fire blazed, already encompassing three houses, one alley over from the courtyard. Flames licked the sky, the air filling with sooty smoke. I wondered if we didn't extinguish it, how much of the city would burn. As soon as they detached my chains from the next prisoner, I hurried to an empty bucket, eager to leave.

"Hold on." A man's meaty hand grabbed my shoulder. "You're going up the ladder."

Bex's body, engulfed in flames, flashed. "I-I'm afraid of heights. Dizziness." I shook my head. "I'll fall up there. Faint dead away."

The Ember's broad brow tilted closer. "You'll climb, or be unconscious for other reasons. Now." He pointed a sausage-like finger to the fire.

Several ladders stood empty, and I chose the one farthest from the highest flame. A container of water already sat at the base. The chains clanked against the rungs as I struggled to keep my balance while holding the heavy bucket. Liquid sloshed onto my shirt, though I welcomed the coolness across my chest because each step brought the heat closer. Heights didn't particularly bother me, but I was no fan of fire, especially when the roof I leaned against could collapse at any moment. Plus, every minute the girls waited, loitering in the square, or hiding out in the room with the key, hoping the enemy didn't enter, would be equally dangerous for them. I heaved myself up far enough to throw the water onto the flames, then scrambled back down.

The same Ember stood at the base and thrust another full bucket into my hands. Once again, I ascended, dumped the liquid, then descended. The process repeated itself over and over. The fire blazed on, with no apparent improvement. Each time I hoped to take my pail and escape, there was always someone there to hand me more. The flames edged closer with every climb. I poured the water directly onto the rungs for better protection instead of the roof. The image of Bex's body, neck angled in death, had imprinted itself in sickening clarity, and played in my mind on a loop.

My next trip down, I huffed and gasped. "The smoke," I wheezed, blinking rapidly.

"Back you go." Another prisoner practically shoved me up the ladder. No one wanted this job, and they'd do anything to avoid it, even betray a comrade.

On the descent, I grasped my neck, hiccupped a choked breath, then collapsed onto the ground when I reached the final rung.

"Hey. Get up." A boot kicked my ribs, and pain shot into my chest.

I didn't let up with the ruse, clutching my shirt and writhing in the dirt. "A break," I whispered.

The Ember who struck me rolled his eyes and ushered someone else up the ladder, not bothering to wait on me and my fake poor constitution. As soon as he turned his back, I crawled to an empty pail, checked over my shoulder to find no one watching, then snuck away toward the courtyard.

A quick scan of the area revealed pandemonium. People scurried with buckets, women held children's hands, ushering them into the relative safety of homes, and soldiers strapped on weapons while they rushed in disarray to join the fight at the town's outskirts. The king still sat in his cage, which was exactly where we currently wanted him.

Mya and Grace weren't in the courtyard. They must be waiting in the room with the key. Grace instructed me to enter the last door on the right. I strode confidently toward the building, acting as if I was supposed to be headed in that direction instead of the pump. It would be more believable without the chains on my ankles.

No one stopped me. I turned the knob. Locked.

I knocked softly, praying the girls were inside. No window framed the outside, and the entrance lacked a peephole. A scrape sounded from the interior, followed by the door cracking. One of Mya's blue eyes peered out, and she ushered me in. My shoulders relaxed in relief.

"What took you so long?" she whisper-hissed as soon as the door shut. Grace stood directly behind, her face a mask of worry.

"No time to explain. The Terran and Caelum army arrived. Have you heard?"

Mya placed a hand on her hip. "Hasn't everyone? It's a madhouse out there with soldiers running everywhere. We've been so worried they would find us. All the prisoners are being locked back up. They're going to notice we're missing, and soon."

If they hadn't already. "You have the key?"

Grace pulled it out of her apron pocket and handed it to me.

"You girls head out first. Grace, you still on for the meeting spot?"

She nodded. "Down the alley on the left. A partly burned abandoned house." She gave me a tentative smile. "It should be a good starting place."

"I'm glad you're with us," I said. "Thank you for your help."

I lifted a foot, which would only stretch a handsbreadth because of my bindings. "Anything in here that might get these off?" The small space held a few dusty cabinets, a table and two chairs, but otherwise stood empty.

Mya shook her head. "You're stuck with them for now."

Disappointing, but I'd manage. I learned to adjust my gait with the chains after the long hours in the field, so it could be worse.

The girls filed out, skirting the edge of the courtyard, while I watched through a narrow crack. No one seemed to pay them any mind and fortunately, they didn't wear shackles. They'd removed their dark cloth armbands, denoting their prisoner status. Once they turned the corner, I scrutinized the square for guards watching King Aldridge. The soldiers had vanished, with only one visible manning the pump, his back facing me. Best not to squander the opportunity. I stepped outside, adrenaline screaming through every heartbeat.

Around twenty meters stood between me and the king, the steel bars glinting in the sunlight. I searched the air for my raven friends. The sky was empty, save for the billowing smoke. I scanned the roofs, dark shadows lining the peaks. On closer inspection, they weren't actually shadows, rather my feathered friends. I lifted my arm and the flock rose, a sea of black wings, so many they nearly blocked out the sun. My bird buddy had recruited friends—a massive swarm of them. I dropped my arm in one swift movement, and they dove low into the courtyard. Under the cover of the distraction, I started toward the enclosure.

The king must not have noticed me, because he still drooped against the cage's wall, his face not visible from this angle. Attempting to act natural, I strode to the center of the square, even though my gait hitched with the constriction of my bindings. Ravens swooped in and out of the people dashing to collect water. No one paid attention to me with so many birds dive bombing the area.

King Aldridge's usually neatly trimmed beard had grown ragged and long over his haggard, thin face, his eyes still closed. Forearms protruded from his filthy uniform, which sagged on his emaciated frame. They'd been starving him. The man I'd known since I was a boy, who took over as a father figure when mine died, was hardly recognizable. I pushed the bubbling outrage and shock away and focused on our escape.

The lock hung in front, a thick iron contraption. I fingered the matching key. "King," I whispered. He didn't move. I slid the key into the hole, and it turned with a satisfying click. The bolt pulled off easily, but the door's hinges squealed in protest at opening. King Aldridge remained motionless.

I scrambled inside the space, hardly big enough for the two of us, and placed my palm on his shoulder.

Nothing.

A clammy sweat blanketed my skin. Am I too late? I slid my fingers up his neck to feel his pulse, jostling him with my other hand. His eyes fluttered open, rimmed blue-black with fatigue. "King," I whispered. "I've come to rescue you."

"Have you now?" a deep voice boomed from behind.

The guard from across the square stood outside the enclosure, dagger drawn, palm flickering with flames. I slowly raised my hands and straightened. My gaze flickered to the remainder of the courtyard. Bucket-carrying men and women paid us no mind, and no other armed soldiers appeared. The flock of ravens had mostly cleared.

I warily watched the man. I'd not seen him before; he wasn't one of the Embers who accompanied us to the fields. He almost seemed friendly with curly blond hair and rounded cheeks. If it wasn't for the fire sparking from his fingers and the glint of the raised blade.

"Let's go," he gestured for me to step out of the cage.

This decision could change the trajectory of my life. Either it ended here with a knife in my chest, or I could rescue Caelum's king. I thought of the fighting happening outside of town. If I left King Aldridge behind and exited this enclosure, would my allies make it here and release him? I couldn't take that risk.

Before I could move, a bird dove straight for the Ember's face. He batted at it, swinging wildly. Using the distraction, I slammed into him, knocking us both into the dirt, the fall reverberating through my bones. His hand seared my shoulder, the pain licking across my back, but I rolled away, catching the wrist holding the knife. I wrenched it backward until it fell with a thump beside me. Without hesitating, I snatched it up and plunged the dagger into his chest. Pulling out the blade, I slashed his neck for good measure, wiped it on his tunic, then tucked it into my belt, doing my best to ignore the man's still-open, lifeless blue eyes.

The king hadn't moved, remaining slumped against the side of the cage, watching.

"Sir, we've got to go."

He used the bars as support to stand, his muscles atrophied and weak. Each slow movement was excruciating to watch. At any second someone would notice the Ember at my feet, blood pooling beneath him. I slipped my arm around him, and we hobbled toward the alley. A last glance behind showed a flash of prisoners' eyes quickly turning to resume their task.

"This way," I ushered him forward as if I had been here a million times when, in actuality, I'd never seen this dirty lane. I strained to peer ahead to find the burnt-out building. We wouldn't make it if the backstreet stretched far. The smell of urine, smoke, and something unidentifiably rancid wafted in the air.

"Almost there." King Aldridge leaned heavily on me. They must have been hardly feeding him, because he'd lost at least a stone, though still heavy enough to slow us down. He hadn't spoken, making me wonder if he was even coherent.

Finally, the structure came into view. The front façade was intact but blackened with soot, and would shield us from onlookers. Fortunately, glass was in short supply, so very few houses possessed windows except for small, elevated rectangular vent-like openings too high for anyone to stare through. We burst through the door, and the girls were both inside. Mya sat on an old crate while Grace stood near the wall, rushing forward to help with the king when we entered.

Mya placed a finger over her lips, then scooted the box closer to let the king sit. "The walls are thin," she whispered. "There are children and a mother next door."

I took a moment to exhale some of the tension from my body. Step one: complete. We had hoped to continue our escape, but with King Aldridge's condition, we might need to stall until nightfall, when we could travel more slowly. Though once they discovered he's missing, a manhunt would commence. We risked becoming sitting ducks the longer we waited.

I kneeled beside him and whispered, "Are you okay?"

His haggard face sagged, his normally bright, green eyes, glassy. He required food and water, and I had none.

He nodded slowly. "Thank… you," he croaked.

"It's my honor, sir."

Mya bent next to us and held out a waterskin. She smiled ruefully. "We have to carry them at all times when babysitting to put out the flames."

The king's eyes widened with recognition.

She grinned. "You're right, I shouldn't be here, but I am. Lucas has been watching out for me. I'm Mya, by the way, sir. We've met, but only at formal occasions."

His lips turned up in the barest of smiles. He took the container, letting water slide down his throat. She handed him a few nuts, which he chewed slowly.

She stood and gave King Aldridge some space. "They'll be looking for us soon."

"There's another hideout down the way," Grace said. "We need to get further from the square."

"How far?" Mya asked, eying the king.

"About five minutes?"

We shouldn't go together. Aldridge would slow them down. Besides, two girls, a guy in chains, and a king who's been on display for the last several weeks would be too conspicuous. "Tell me where."

Grace explained the route, and I reiterated Molly's hiding place. I tore the hem of my shirt, handing the scrap to Mya. "Show it to Molly, then tell her what happened. She'll protect you."

"How much will she understand?" Grace crinkled her nose. She always was a nay-sayer about my dragon.

"She'll do all right. Don't forget to call her by her name." I smirked.

Grace's shoulders eased ever so slightly. "I will." A small smile escaped. "Gretna the Great, was it?"

"Funny." I rolled my eyes. "We'll come as quick as we can. If it becomes dangerous, have Molly take you someplace safe, then send her back for us."

"I don't want to leave you," Mya whispered, her soft voice calling like a siren. I ached to stay with them, but they'd be safer on their own.

"We'll see each other soon." I leaned in and brushed her cheek with my lips. I wanted to linger, but tore myself away. "Grace. You remember your knife skills?"

She nodded and gravely took the dagger I handed her, stolen off the Ember in the courtyard.

They peered through a crack in the door, then exited quietly. Every part of me yearned to leave with them. I could only pray that if someone came upon them, Mya would talk her way out of it. Her skill, which originally led to feelings of betrayal and uncertainty, now left me with hope.

I turned to King Aldridge, who sat straighter on his crate. He finished the water Mya had given him in one gulp. "I'm ready." He set the container down.

"Let's give it a few more minutes," I replied. It would allow the girls a head start and time for the food and drink to strengthen him.

"There's fighting outside the city," I said.

Aldridge raised a brow. "Dryden actually bothered to rescue his daughter?"

"The army might be ours. I imagine the people want you back."

He shrugged. "Perhaps. I left Graftonberg in charge, so doubtful."

"Why would you do that?" The baron wouldn't be my first choice. Or tenth for that matter.

"Safer for Cate if no one attempts to save me. She'll eventually take over, and we can't afford to lose more soldiers fighting for me."

"But Graftonberg is a…"

"Pompous blowhard. I know."

I chuckled. King Aldridge had never indicated that he didn't like the man before.

The king stood, though his movements remained slow. "Shall we go?"

I opened the door a crack and peered through. I could only see in one direction without sticking my head out all the way, but best I could tell, the alley remained empty. I creaked it open fully. "Let's go," I whispered.

We stepped outside, my nerves wound tight. The narrow lane felt claustrophobic. Grace had described a cut-through in a burned-out warehouse as our next stop, which, when reached, would allow us to traverse a large area without being seen. According to her instructions, we still had two more streets to cross before we arrived.

The king stumbled, righting himself. "I need a moment." His face shaded gray. I didn't have to tell him we didn't have a moment—he knew the risk of delay.

Another bird—a falcon this time—glided through the space between structures and landed on Aldridge's shoulder. He grimaced at the talons digging through his tattered uniform. At first, I thought it was Blade, but this bird was smaller.

"Cate's here." He held out his arm for the creature to sidestep across it, leaning against me for support. "It's hers. I gave it to her before we left."

I froze at his words, fear spiking. She shouldn't have come. My thoughts spun—wondering if she could use her powers without hurting herself, protective instincts flaring.

"Take a piece of my uniform. We'll tie it." He gestured to the emblems sewn to his chest.

I found his unique crest and tore it away, taking a strip of fabric with it, then fastened it to the bird's leg. Aldridge dropped his arm, and the falcon flapped her wings, disappearing into the smoky air above. I caught him just as a leg buckled beneath him. "Okay?"

He nodded, his skin ashen.

"Cate has a falcon now? Feels like a lifetime since I've been in Caelum." And I wanted nothing more than to return.

He only grunted in response, encouraging my silence. Thoughts of home pressured my gait, but the king couldn't keep my pace. We trudged on until coming to an intersection.

A group of Embers raced down the alley toward us. "There!" one of them shouted. Several more emerged from the other direction.

We were caught.

CHAPTER 44
DANIEL

Colonel Dixon came through on his promise to assemble as many soldiers as he could and still leave the Caelum people somewhat protected. Not enough men to destroy the enemy, but perhaps with Cate, we'd succeed as a rescue operation. Father also provided the promised Terrans, and they awaited us at the appointed meeting spot, a day's ride from Caelum Castle.

Cate and I had practiced nonstop the last week. The rain diminished significantly with distractions or each time we lost contact. She shared her struggles with a group of Caelum soldiers, no longer able to keep it a secret. We placed her in various scenarios: in the midst of hand-to-hand combat, riding, or defending herself with either a sword or knife. Her fighting skills had improved, but she couldn't yet hold her power while wielding weapons. Fortunately, there was a lag between her distraction and the rain halting, so the water didn't stop completely if she regained focus quickly. Presumably, this was because the moisture had already gathered, but more than a minute or two of diversion led to a dry spell.

Her anxiety ratcheted with each hiccup, causing another full-blown panic attack that required a trip to the infirmary and a sedative to lower her soaring heart rate. Despite all these obstacles, her progress marched on. I was in awe of her. A few soldiers poorly hid their frustration that she couldn't flip the water on with a switch, but I knew

how difficult it was for her, how much she'd toiled and exhausted her body to learn. She would give everything of herself to save even one. It was beautiful. Heartbreaking.

Terrifying.

"You okay?" A week later, Cate rode North next to me, the sunlight dappling her honey-brown hair.

"Sure. Of course. You?" I asked.

"Nothin' to worry about." She grinned, her lips too tight to be convincing. "How much longer?"

"We'll be outside The Camp in around an hour."

Mocha circled above, and Cate beckoned her. She showed the falcon a piece of cloth that had been King Aldridge's and sent her off again, even though it would be a long shot to locate him. She'd insisted on bringing her with us, while I hid my doubts. Maybe it was the Terran in me. I didn't connect with birds, and her usefulness seemed questionable at best. I suspected the true reason for Mocha's presence might simply be that she soothed Cate's nerves. And if that were the case, I fully supported the falcon.

Fire had ravaged the forest, the path we traveled, a wasteland. The first time I'd journeyed this far north, it sickened me to see the crimes the Embers had committed against our world. Though we wouldn't eliminate the enemy on this mission, I ached for that day.

Anxiousness riled in my belly. This operation could all be for nothing if the captives were dead. The Embers had already established they couldn't be trusted. For the millionth time, guilt at leaving Mya pierced my conscience.

Colonel Dixon rode up beside us. "I'm surprised they haven't launched an ambush. This close to the city, the Embers had to have seen the troops. I'm assuming they sent scouts forward to prepare. Be on guard." His gaze landed on both of us. "And stay together," his voice a grim reminder of our plight.

Battle was chaotic. Keeping track of another person increases vulnerability. Men were assigned to shield us, though I'd been a part of enough conflicts to understand the risks.

We planned to approach the city as close as we could and send a smaller group to infiltrate and find the captured. Although they might outnumber us, the Embers' only power was fire. That, and their enormous size. They were also skilled in swordplay, having been trained since childhood. And so had we. Cate, and by proxy me, were the key to our success. Even if we succeeded in hampering the enemy with water, we still journeyed directly into the hornet's nest. Casualties were eminent.

I reached across our mounts for Cate's hand. We'd practiced on the journey for Raven and North to become accustomed to riding so close. We would need to stay on horseback as long as possible. Gripping each other meant only having one hand to fight. Raven did well doubled with Cate, but we discarded the option because if she rode in front, it hampered my ability to use my sword, and behind she was more vulnerable with nothing protecting her back.

We traveled in the midst of a thousand allies of Terrans and Caelumites. The wave of alarm took mere moments to reach us in a ripple of warnings.

The Embers emerged to meet our army outside their city. Cate squeezed my hand, our gazes locking. The light breeze and warmth were more suited for a picnic in a meadow rather than battle, sunlight giving Cate's gold-flecked irises a green glow. Shouts and clangs of swords echoed through the air, breaking the spell.

They were upon us.

The first drops of rain came within minutes. Cate's countenance remained serene, and I knew, at least for the moment, she was able to tune everything out except the energy flowing around her. The water started above us, then spread across the battlefield. The Embers had not yet reached our central pocket of protection. As long as our troops held the line, we would be safe. We'd halted our horses but needed to advance closer to the city, both for infiltration and coverage of the battle with Cate's water when she entered The Camp to find the captives.

"Look," she pointed upward. "Mocha's back already." She extended her arm for the bird to land, noticing something tied to her leg. I pulled it off, allowing her to concentrate on the water, then held the blue cloth up with a recognizable emblem sewn into it.

"Cate. I think your father's alive."

Her mouth stretched into a wide smile, momentarily oblivious to the oncoming Embers. "He's alive," she repeated. She nodded a few times, as if saying it to herself, launched Mocha back into the sky, then returned her focus to the task.

The rain soaked into our uniforms, dripping from our faces and horses' manes. The ground muddied, turning treacherous and slippery.

"Forward!" shouted the colonel.

Our march to Ember City progressed in stops and starts. All the while, I gripped Cate's hand like a lifeline. A second wave of Ember soldiers halted our advance. They arrived in a sea of brown and must have been organizing themselves in town before meeting the other troops. The enemy now outnumbered us ten to one. Cates's worry swelled. I erected my emotion shield, her fears threatening to overwhelm me. Our army tightened, ensuring their safety within Cate's circle of rain.

"We'll have to take a group through," the colonel motioned forward. "We could fight all day and still not make it to the city."

"King Aldridge is in there." I held up the cloth.

"All the more reason. It's time." His grim determination boosted my morale.

The soldiers chosen for the operations knew the signal. We would leave Colonel Dixon behind to lead the battle, placing me in charge of our smaller group. I had led missions in the past, and the responsibility always weighed heavily to not only succeed, but return with everyone alive.

Dev rode up beside me. "We're doing this?"

"Now or never. You sure about coming?" He'd volunteered to join us before we had left Caelum. "It won't be easy."

He grinned. "That's why I'll be there."

Still surrounded by a screen of soldiers both on foot and horseback, we fought our way through the battle. I had my sword poised in my non-dominant hand. I'd trained all my life to be ambidextrous, while Cate needed her right side to defend herself with any accuracy. Our fingers locked together, a steadying touchstone in the chaos. The rain poured on, decreasing visibility, but rendering the Ember's flames nearly useless.

An Ember crashed through the line protecting us, the tip of his sword aimed straight for Cate. I jerked Raven's head, attempting to maneuver myself to block the blow, but I was too late. Her grip slipped from mine to grasp her weapon with two hands. The sound of metal-on-metal clanged, their swords clashing. The Ember's face filled with rage as he hammered his blade toward her again.

I leapt from Raven to the wet ground, rounding behind the man. He twisted, seeing movement out of the corner of his eyes, and shifted his weapon to me. I blocked the blow which reverberated through my body, then shoved him. His feet, unsteady in the mud, sent him lurching sideways into North, who shimmied nervously. Cate's seat held, though the man's blade sliced into her ankle. Before he could inflict more damage, I sank my sword deep into his back. He collapsed at my feet, but I hardly noticed with all my attention turning to Cate.

She gripped her leg, red seeping from between her fingers. I opened myself enough to feel her pain, sharp and pulsing, before closing again to avoid distraction. Heart racing, I rushed forward to examine the wound. She waved me off.

"It's fine. Let's keep moving." She yanked a cloth from her saddlebag, and I helped wrap the injury, sliding my fingers across her shaking hands.

"Good enough." Her cheeks had paled to a translucent white, illuminated by the sun filtering through the clouds.

The sun. Rain no longer dripped down our faces. I searched the battlefield to find telltale orange flames erupting from the palms of Embers. The wetness helped quell the effects, but underestimating the fire could prove deadly.

Cate's hand, cold and sticky from blood, grasped mine once I mounted Raven. Her panic at seeing the rays of light glinting in long slivers across the sea of fighting men pounded in my mind.

"It's going to be all right. Let's start again," I assured her. "Deep breaths. Just like we practiced."

Her shoulders rose and fell. A drop splashed on the crown of my head. Then another. No sooner had the downpour started than a second Ember broke through the shield. This one I struck down before he reached us. Our line suffered damage, creating a jagged hole where two Caelum soldiers once protected us. Cate's lips formed a grim band when we skirted around the downed men, but the rain continued.

"We're going to have to barrel through," I shouted. Most of the Embers were on foot. Our protection was half mounted, the others fighting from below. Our progress was too slow; we gained a few feet, halted to fight, then progressed a little farther. If we left our surrounding guard behind and pressed on to the city with only those on horseback, only fifteen of us would remain.

I checked with Cate, and she agreed, her face a stoic mask. Only her eyes gave away her fear. The strain of carrying the rain left her taut as a tightrope, the rest of us balancing on her string of survival.

My heels dug into Raven's side, coordinating with Cate and North. Almost immediately, we swerved to avoid another mounted Ember, surprising him with our sudden movement. Our hands slipped apart. Cate gave me a reassuring glance. We'd practiced this. The ring of rain would become smaller, but if she concentrated, it would continue to fall as long as we stayed close. The realities of the battle differed from the staged war on the fields of Caelum Castle, yet she held steady.

I crushed an advancing Ember's head with a stray rock, using my power to keep my sword arm free. Dev dodged a flying arrow before the Caelumites rushed their winds forward, deflecting the rest of the oncoming weapons. In battle against Caelum soldiers, arrows were rarely employed, as Caelumites usually rendered them useless. I glanced behind. The Embers had caught us off guard. Several downed allies with protruding arrows lay in the mud, the conflict closing in around them.

The winds drove the rain in sheets into the faces of the enemy, marring their vision. We increased our speed to a near full gallop as we raced across the field, mowing down anyone in our path. A lucky sword strike hit a Caelumite in our front guard. He toppled from his horse, forcing North to vault over him. Cate's eyes closed momentarily, but we continued on. Another glance back showed the others still engaged in the fight, caught in Cate's storm. No one pursued our small band.

We finally broke through, riding across the muddy plain. If only there was more to hide behind, but the land had long ago been burnt, then burned again, until almost nothing remained. A few skeleton trees stood, lone talismans marking the past.

None of us had actually seen Ember City; we only knew the general direction. The farther we ventured, the less likely Cate could hold the rain over the battlefield. No one chased us, which demonstrated the Embers' disorganization. They'd probably thought we wouldn't be dumb enough to enter their lair, though they should have expected it after capturing royalty from both sides. Or… perhaps they did, and we were entering a trap.

Smoke plumed to the west. "That way," I called.

I peeked behind—we had traveled about a kilometer from the battle, which now bloomed with fires. Cate's range had already failed. The Embers met us too far outside of town. Even if Cate and I touched, the water likely wouldn't reach our soldiers. We hadn't counted on this distance, and now we left the army vulnerable.

Cate turned in her saddle, her features collapsing in despair. "I should go back."

"It will take too much time. Speed is the best thing we can offer them now, and our greatest chance of surviving in there," I pointed forward, "is with you."

The city loomed in front of us, a jumble of run-down buildings. The Embers had cultivated trees and bushes on the outskirts. Coming closer, we found an orchard, surprisingly intact. Cate ended the rain to conceal our approach and to take a much-needed break.

"Let's stop here. We'll hide the horses in the trees and go in on foot," I said.

We dismounted and pulled out rough-hewn brown clothes from our saddle bags as a disguise. The acrid smell of smoke from a fire within the city singed our nostrils. Cate pulled a sack-like dress over her riding attire to cover them and donned a bonnet to shield her face.

"You ready?" Dev asked, his worn costume causing me to flash a smile, knowing he always appeared at the height of fashion, somehow even managing it in his Terran uniform, now covered by a tan tunic and loose pants.

"Yeah, you?" I searched his emotions. Nerves, yes, but loyalty, confidence, and determination filled his thoughts. I couldn't ask for a better friend.

"Ready as I'll ever be." He cocked a half grin.

"Let's go, then." Cate moved forward.

We crept through the trees, and the smoke thickened. When the buildings came into view, we stopped short.

Cate's mouth hinged open. "The city's on fire."

CHAPTER 45
CATE

We skirted the city's rim to find a safe entry point, with most of the eastern and northern borders in flames. The chaos pulsed at a frenetic tempo as we entered. The men had mostly abandoned the tightly packed houses, shacks, and warehouses to fight, likely unaware that their homes were burning. We expected to have to sneak in, but nobody gave us any notice. Moving in groups of three while leaving one man with the horses, Dev, Daniel, and I journeyed together. The plan was to locate a jail—if such a thing existed here. They must permit prisoners outside; otherwise, Mocha wouldn't have returned with my father's emblem.

Daniel brushed the side of my hand in reassurance, and that familiar tingle floated through me. My feelings wavered between the guilt of dragging him into this mission and gratefulness for his presence.

The layout of the rambling city weaved in a maze of dilapidated structures and alleys. People had either locked themselves in their houses to avoid the fight or ran to the fires, bucket in hand. We dodged flames and zigzagged through the streets toward the center of town.

"What if they're in one of those?" I pointed to a building with a half-collapsed roof.

"Too valuable as hostages," Dev replied. "The Embers would move them elsewhere."

"Yeah, if they know what's going on here. The prison guards may all be fighting."

Daniel shook his head. "I'm with Dev. They wouldn't leave them alone."

Yet the uneasy feeling persisted. It didn't feel right. Why was the town burning? Our army certainly didn't start the fire, although it would have been a smart strategy. The smoke billowed, immersing us in a toxic haze. Surely their fighters would notice and send men back to help combat the blaze, which would give our soldiers a better chance, though the arrival of more Embers into the city would be disastrous for our plan to free the captives.

"Hurry," I huffed through the smog, despite barely keeping up with their long strides. Daniel and Dev weren't advancing with the super speed gained by energy to avoid becoming conspicuous among the enemy. I'd progressed moderately with this ability, but compared to Daniel, it felt like I was riding the tiny tricycle in Mario Cart, while he had a Formula One racer.

"You there," a gruff voice called out.

I caught Daniel's eye. Should we run or keep up the ruse of being Embers minding our own business? Daniel gave the slightest of reassuring nods and turned slowly. Dev and I followed suit.

A man stood in the lane, club in one hand, a metal pail in the other. "Where are your buckets?"

"We were just gettin' them." Dev's feet shuffled, his gaze remaining steady on the Ember.

I focused on slackening the rigidity of my stance.

"You're going the wrong direction. Burrowers, eh?" the Ember replied.

I had no idea what he was talking about. I could only assume it meant hiding instead of helping with the fire.

"Burrowers?" Dev said. "We'd never do that. What are you, the burrow police?"

The man dropped his bucket, slapping the club in his hand. "Not from around here, are ya?"

"Of course we are." I took a small step forward to convey confidence, the exact opposite of my instincts.

"Then you'd know there are always people like me assigned to stop the burrowers." He glared at us and pulled a string from around his neck that hid under his shirt. A whistle dangled from the end.

Before he could blow it, the three of us came to a simultaneous decision and took off in the opposite direction, the shrill sound of trilling echoing down the lane.

Footsteps pounded behind, and more whistles sounded out of nowhere from all directions, raising the alarm. Up ahead, a burning home had collapsed into the alley, blocking our way. We were trapped.

I slowly turned, hands up, like I was in a cop show—did they even raise their hands here in surrender? A quick glance showed Dev and Daniel following suit.

"What now?" I whispered.

"Wait and see," Daniel said. "Go along with it for the moment."

"They might lead us right to the jail," Dev muttered.

"Being locked up won't do us much good," I retorted under my breath. Our choices were limited to fighting against… one, two, four, seven… now ten men. Didn't they have anything better to do than bother with us? Though now that I examined them more carefully, their soot-covered clothes and faces indicated they'd come from fighting the fires.

"Rowan's in the square," one of them said. "Bring them there."

A bulky, balding man grabbed my upper arm, his tight grip reminding me of the first time I'd encountered an Ember after a party in England. That life floated through my memory in wisps too elusive to catch.

They shoved us through town, winding our way south into areas intact and safe from the fires. We looped north after a time, to the heart of the city, once again drawing nearer to the blaze.

A courtyard, about half the size of a football field, was the first open space we'd seen not crammed with dilapidated buildings. Men and women lined up behind a pump with buckets, some hobbling with a twelve-inch chain between their ankles. I hunted for signs of anyone we knew.

Daniel's hand gripped my forearm. "Cate."

I scanned his face, which had gone slack. My captor shoved me forward, directing my gaze to the rear of the square. Father and Lucas alive… surrounded by Embers.

Though our situation was bleak, I could only muster intense relief at seeing them. A giant of a man with closely cropped hair held my father, whose arms were tied behind his back. Lucas, also restrained, stood nearby, a group of twenty Embers with swords or daggers at the ready surrounding them. Mya wasn't among them, which left more questions than answers.

Our entourage propelled Dev, Daniel, and me toward my father and Lucas. The king's frame had shrunk. My heart ached to see his face dirty, beard lengthened, and cheekbones gaunt. Those green eyes, so similar to mine, held sadness—grief at seeing me in the arms of the enemy. Reality began to sink in. The Embers had everyone—my father, me, Lucas, Daniel, and presumably Mya. The only two safe rulers were King Dryden and Graftonberg. And neither was fit to run a democratic kingdom.

"Found these burrowers," our captor with the club told the tall Ember gripping my father.

"Can't you see I'm bus—" The man holding the king met my gaze. I ducked my head, letting the bonnet shadow my face.

"Well, look who we have here. You know who you've got, Stevens?" He grinned, his smile eerily handsome, showing off gleaming white teeth.

"It's the princess and her prince." He smirked. "Come here to save your father? You could've stayed safe, holed up in your castle, and left the king here. Now there's no one to continue the Caelum line. And the Terrans are in no better shape." His attention turned to Daniel. "Your father apparently decided against our deal. I took him for a smarter man than that."

Daniel chose not to respond, his jaw tightening.

It was Dev who spoke, "And who are you, may we ask, since you're so intelligent?"

The surrounding men chuckled. "It appears my surveillance is better than yours. Rowan. Elected leader of the Embers." His stare dared us to challenge him.

"In your imagination," Daniel shot back. "Embers don't have elections. There hasn't been a leader in over a hundred years, and that guy only lasted a few months."

A few more sniggers rippled across the courtyard.

Rowan's mouth turned up in a half smile. "You always were a few steps behind, Prince. No matter." He focused his gaze to me. "It looks like I'm in an interesting position, Cate."

My preferred name on his lips sounded sharp and bitter. He didn't deserve the privilege of using it.

"How so?" I raised my chin, making sure he knew I wasn't afraid of him, lie that it was. Every part of me wanted to snatch the knife from my boot and defend myself. I held off, mostly because of Rowan's glinting sword and his tight grip on my father. They hadn't checked us for weapons, thinking we were just Ember deserters at the time. I silently prayed they'd forget.

"We could use some help putting out these fires." Rowan tilted his head to the east, where billows of smoke careened upward.

"And if I won't?"

He raised the blade to the king's throat. "Don't try me."

I looked to Daniel. Did he have a plan to get us out of this mess? If I complied, maybe some of the men would disperse from the square, improving our odds of escape. For the first time, my gaze fell to Lucas. I'd seen him, of course, but had been focused on the man who now held steel against my father's neck. He had also lost weight, his jawline sharp, diminishing his boyish appearance. He gave me a slight nod, a warning that Rowan would make good on his threat.

I reached for Daniel's hand. If I was going to produce rain, then it needed to travel farther than I'd ever managed. I closed my eyes, savoring his touch—the warm pressure of each finger on my palm—then moved outward to sense the gentle energy humming around us. I pictured the burning city, the wasteland between it and the battle, and our men fighting for their lives. Visualized the liquid coalescing, clouds swelling and crashing together in dark undulating masses, chased by sheets of water drenching it all.

Cool wetness sprinkled across my nose, followed by fat drops, then buckets. My clothes soon stuck to me, the skirt heavy and encasing. I stretched my mind to the circling energy, then let it soar to the battlefield. If I chose to help the Embers with their fire, I would bring on an army of Terrans and Caelumites.

I opened my eyes to find Lucas staring with a soft smile, water collecting and darkening his lashes.

You okay? he mouthed.

I nodded. *You?*

He glanced back and forth at our captors and shrugged, the strain around his hollow eyes evident. Lucas, who always pretended that even the worst situations were manageable, couldn't hide the trouble we faced. Regardless of whether our troops come or not, it might be too late. Daniel watched our exchange, his expression troubled, and I knew it was more than jealousy. He too worried we wouldn't make it out. I squeezed his hand in false reassurance.

Rowan dropped the sword from my father's neck; a thin scarlet line remained. Rivulets of blood striped his skin and smudged pink in the rain. "You shouldn't have come, Cate," the king said, his slumping shoulders defeatist, which made me wonder what they'd done to him to accept this loss.

"I don't regret it," I replied, my throat clogging. The energy wavered with my emotions, and I fluttered my eyes closed to concentrate. If these were my last words to my father, I wanted them to count, even if it scattered my focus and shattered my heart to think this might be the end. My powers were too closely linked to my feelings. I'd worked hard to sever the tie, but I still wasn't completely capable of removing the bond. Instead, today I would use it to my advantage.

"I love you," I cried, my lids flying open to see Father's grieving expression. Tears mixed with rain streamed down my cheeks.

"I love you too." He stood a mere ten feet away, yet unreachable, surrounded by guards, Rowan's grip tight around his bicep, his bindings still in place.

"It's not over," Daniel said, probably more for my benefit than the Embers'.

"I know," I whispered. Except I didn't. It was hopeless. My grasp on the energy was slipping. I poured myself, my feelings, my *soul* into it, the water reaching a fever pitch as if it might drown us all.

Rowan spoke, shouting over the downpour, "Keep it up until we hear the fires are under control." He pointed at several guards. "Go take reports." Two left. "Stevens, return to patrol. She's not going anywhere." The fingers embedded into my upper arm released.

"How often do you burn down your own city?" Daniel asked. "Seems like you should invest in more stone."

I'd wondered the same thing. The structures centrally were mostly rock, except for the roofs, but on the outskirts, the buildings were predominantly wood. Perhaps they didn't have stone masons or expertise to construct it.

"This was arson," Rowan said. "We didn't start it."

Daniel chuckled. "And how would you know?"

"Because someone spotted your sister leaving a burning building."

Mya was alive. Daniel's fingers tightened around mine.

"Maybe she didn't want to be burned alive. Seems sensible enough." Daniel shifted closer to me, though a guard still pinned one of his arms behind his back.

"She hasn't been seen since," Rowan said.

Hope flared. Lucas's mouth quirked before he smoothed his features.

Rowan's bored expression grated my nerves. "Don't worry. We'll find her."

"Mya?" Dev asked. "She's an expert in camouflage. You'll never see her again."

Surely Dev was bluffing. She'd stand out as a princess in whatever she wore.

"What do you think, lover boy?" Rowan turned to Lucas. "If she's really gone, then your usefulness is over." He smirked at Daniel. "You hear that, Prince? Your sister and the knight have been bunking together. How do you like that?"

"I think I trust Mya more than you."

"And him? You trust him?" He gestured to Lucas.

Daniel's hand slackened, then re-tightened. "I do."

Lucas's expression remained unreadable.

"Back in the pit for you," Rowan called. "Or we can finish you all off now."

My power wavered. "What are you waiting for?" My voice came

out low and guttural in the effort to sustain the rain. I almost longed for the return of the dismissed guard to help hold me up.

"For you, of course. Once the fire is gone, not a lot of reason to keep you alive."

"Daniel's worth something," I replied. "King Dryden will make a bargain." The least I could do was to save him. Not much hope for the rest of us.

I couldn't hold out much longer. My knees wobbled. I tried to focus on the tie with Daniel, each finger's pressure on mine. His pinky tapped once, twice, three times.

A signal.

In a flash, our touch slipped, and his captor fell to the ground, the man's throat slit from the dagger Daniel procured from beneath his clothes. I scrambled to pull one out of my boot, shakily preparing to stab anyone who came near.

Shouts rented the air, coupled with the pounding of running feet splashing through puddles. Colonel Dixon, with a group of at least a hundred soldiers, streamed into the courtyard, a soggy flood of blue and green uniforms with more trailing behind, battling in the streets.

Chaos ensued, bodies slamming into one another, swords whistling, men falling. I stood in the middle, dagger raised, while metal and flesh clashed around me, all the while keeping the rain pouring. Our men's best defense.

"Princess," a voice boomed.

My face lifted to find Rowan with the sword at my father's throat once again. "Stop the water," he commanded.

More Embers teemed into the courtyard from all directions, engulfing our soldiers. If the rain stopped, we wouldn't stand a chance. Daniel fought nearby, protecting me with a weapon he must have taken from an Ember. One charged toward me, and he stepped in, downing the man with a quick thrust. The Ember's angry eyes turned to shock when the steel ran him through. Daniel didn't hesitate, moving on to the next at lightning speed. Lucas was also now free, blowing sheets of rain into the surrounding enemy in a cyclone. He planted his feet at the center of the storm, fury and desperation etched across his features.

My father stood proudly, neck extended, the blade tight against his skin while streams of water slid down the metal. His determined eyes stared into me, seeming to plead with me to hold strong. "Don't stop," he whispered, almost too quiet to hear. Yet it echoed in my head as if he'd screamed it.

Anguish ripped through me. I searched for anyone to take on Rowan, but everyone else fought for their lives.

Except for me. They were all protecting me.

And I had to protect them.

"If that's your answer." Rowen's muscles tightened as he prepared to pull the sword across Father's throat.

I hesitated, unsure. Father nodded, the sharp edge cutting his skin. He was choosing to sacrifice himself. One person to save many.

"No!" I lunged forward, dagger pitched toward Rowan. But I was too far away. The blade sliced through my father.

CHAPTER 46
CATE

Blood.

It pulsed with the artery, bubbling over his tattered uniform until he collapsed. Crimson pooled around him, puddling as fast as the water washed it away.

"Father!"

I wanted to help—staunch the bleeding—do anything to heal him. My racing thoughts circled, panic crushing against my ribs. He needed help. I tripped forward, hovering over him. The clash of a sword rang inches from my ear, yet it echoed as if in a tunnel. Reality finally triggered. I'd seen the wound, and it would haunt me forever. *It was too late.* Agony and grief poured from my core, the water radiating like it hadn't since The Great Battle. My dagger wobbled, and I stood from my kneeling position. In a daze, I scanned the fighters, the king's killer nowhere in sight.

"Retreat!" I called. "Retreat!"

Every part of my body trembled, pieces of soul puddling into the dirt next to the king. We had to get out. I couldn't hold any longer. We'd rescued Lucas. And my father was… dead.

The word lodged in my brain on repeat.

Dead.

Dead.

The king was *dead*.

Daniel grabbed my hand, and we bolted through the courtyard. Every ounce of my strength focused on maintaining the storm and placing one foot in front of the other. My own energy mixed with the atmosphere's, my body dragged down by out-of-control emotions. Daniel stabbed an Ember blocking our path. Scarlet bloomed across his chest.

So much red.

I tore my gaze away to see Lucas headed in the other direction. "Lucas!" I screamed. I couldn't lose someone else.

He stopped, his eyes wide with a moment of indecision. "I'll find you later," he called. "Mya!"

He must know where she was hiding. All that nonsense Dev spouted obviously wasn't true. She'd never been inconspicuous in her life. She needed Lucas. More than I did. Even though I ached to call him back. To keep him by my side, though I wasn't sure who would be protecting who.

Daniel's steps hitched. He wanted to follow.

"Trust Lucas," I assured him. "Let's go." I didn't think we'd make it out of here if we deviated to help him.

We raced through the maze of a city, our course taking us toward the battlefield instead of the orchard where our horses waited, herded by hordes of Embers. We would have to double back later.

Finally, we broke through the depressing buildings. The Ember army greeted us with lines of soldiers as far as the eye could see. A trap. They funneled the escaping soldiers out of town to their awaiting army.

"Split up!" the colonel called. "Go round. Get out however you can and meet up at the point."

Worry swirled deep in my gut. Things were grim when it was every man for himself.

"The orchard," I shouted, searching for the others. Two from our team veered left. "Where's Dev?"

Daniel spun, his hand unclasping from mine. "Dev!"

I couldn't take any more losses. We rushed back the way we came, dodging others rushing in every direction. "Dev!" I screamed. A sandy-haired man sat in the dirt facing away from us, leaning against a door. He turned just enough for me to see his profile. "Daniel, over here!"

I hunched over Dev, finding blood seeping from his thigh.

"Just got to bandage it up." He smiled weakly.

I tore the apron from my dress and kneeled to use the strings as a tourniquet, my heart beating in my throat. The gash, deep, at an angle that appeared to be from a glancing blow, oozed purple-red.

Daniel gently pushed my fingers away. "Cate," he held his palm up. The rain had stopped. "Focus. I'll take care of him."

I hadn't even noticed. I felt like a circus juggler caught in the middle of the knife-throwing danger act. All the balls were tumbling around me.

I put my hand on Daniel's shoulder, turning from him and Dev, my knife ready to strike. The area had emptied, turning eerily quiet, the silence pressing upon us. Our group had all searched for other ways out, and the Ember soldiers followed. I imagined eyes watching through darkened cracks and crannies, prepared to sound the alarm. The Ember army waited outside the city like a spider web, ready to catch anyone stumbling into its path. I had no desire to be the fly, and it was only a matter of time before some re-entered the town.

The rain once again fell. It had been dry too long—every moment counted when our men were in peril. Seconds ticked by, each one an eternity.

"Just leave me," Dev grunted.

"Shut up, Dev," I retorted. "We're not leaving you."

"Bossy, Princess. And you're making the ground muddy. Can't a guy get a nice dry place to sit?"

Relieved to hear him joking, my shoulders relaxed a fraction.

"Well, hurry—" The sounds of splashing footsteps stopped my words. An Ember turned the corner, steps from us. I didn't hesitate. Whether due to training, fear, or self-preservation, my body launched into motion. I lurched toward him and plunged my knife into his heart before he could react. The man fell, taking my dagger with him. I stooped to yank it out, Daniel now hovering close.

"I got it." I swiped the knife clean, working to compartmentalize my feelings. The blood… it ran everywhere. I suppressed the reeling memories of my father's body.

"Ready?" I asked, sheathing my blade. My mind would shut down soon—we had to escape before my thoughts spiraled. *I just killed a man.* I squeezed my eyes tight, remembering the others who had died at my hand. My skin itched to escape—to wash the blood and pain away. But I could never scrub this day from my memory.

Daniel helped Dev up, and we headed toward the orchard. Dev slowed us, but I couldn't bear to leave him behind, so we hobbled on together. We passed soggy, charred remains of buildings, some half standing, while others were intact, the fire jumping its way across town. My water had extinguished the flames. Women and children pulled blackened beams and debris into the street in a matter-of-fact manner, as if this was normal life for them.

Behind, we heard a group of Ember soldiers turning the corner. "May we help?" I asked a woman with soot smeared across her cheeks. Without waiting for an answer, we ducked into the structure with a gaping hole in the roof. Ash-filled puddles pocked the floor. I snatched up a broom and started to sweep water along the dirt-packed ground toward the door, careful to remain hidden.

The woman's mousy hair sat lifelessly on her slumped shoulders, the sack-like brown dress hanging on her skeleton frame. Seemingly exhausted, she didn't even question who we were.

"Thank you," she said, her voice hoarse from the smoke.

I knew little of the Ember women. Did they possess the same powers? Was their life the sad existence I expected it to be? By her downtrodden appearance and sparse living conditions, I suspected all was not well in The Camp.

One room encompassed the entire house. Two beds were shoved against each wall. A corner kitchen on my right consisted of a small countertop, woodstove, and basin with a bucket next to it. On my left, sat a couple of chairs on a partially burned jute rug.

"You're welcome." I smiled, though she only stared back listlessly.

"Time to go," Daniel said, grabbing a charred piece of wood from the floor. He'd been working on clearing the place of larger debris while I swept.

As I followed him out, the woman's face haunted me. I wanted her story. To understand her, and how she fit the picture of our enemy. I would ask Daniel about the Ember women after our escape.

The rain had lightened to a sprinkle, forcing me to concentrate, shoving the woman's plight into the back of my mind.

We finally reached the orchard. Here in the trees felt safer, less exposed. To safely avoid the Ember army, we would have to cut a wide swath outside of town.

North greeted me. Relief at finding our horses safe boosted morale. The other groups had already left, our three horses the only ones remaining. Three would be less conspicuous, though we'd be easily outnumbered if we ran into trouble.

Dev's leg soaked his uniform with blood. It bloomed further when he mounted, the rain only partially rinsing the red seeping from the wound. He noticed my watchful eyes on his pale skin, his grimace doing little to ease my concern.

"Tie him to his horse," I told Daniel.

He took one look at Dev and reached for the rope wrapped around Raven's pommel. Dev winced when the binding tightened over his thighs, though he didn't complain. Daniel in turn, flinched at Dev's pain.

Meanwhile, exhaustion depleted my reserves. I'd been supplementing the energy with my own again. My jelly-like legs heaved into the saddle. At this rate, I'd have to be tied soon, so I wouldn't fall off too.

"We're going northeast instead of south," Daniel said.

"We'll be out of range." I couldn't cover the whole area with water if we veered farther off course.

"You've done enough." He put his hand on my arm.

"I can do it," I gritted out while my body ached to stop. If I could save even one more…

"Cate." He waited for me to look at him. "It's done."

The weight of his words sent tears welling in relief.

It's done.

I sagged into North's neck to hide the rain mixed with tears streaming down my face. It was over. I'd accomplished everything I could. And it would never be enough.

My father was dead.

CHAPTER 47
LUCAS

Cate's stricken face when she witnessed King Aldridge's fall, would forever be imprinted on my brain. She'd stood there frozen, then hunched over her father, unaware of Rowan's sword ready to strike her down. I'd wrenched my way free, taking advantage of my guard's distraction in the pandemonium, and barely wrestled the blade from him in time to intercept Rowan's blow. She'd been moments from following the king into the dirt.

The chaos that ensued allowed escape. Rowan slipped away—the coward—finding the danger too great. Later, Cate's frightened eyes bored into me when I'd announced my intentions to go after Mya. My protective instincts lured me to her, but she had Daniel. The other girls needed me more. The pull to Mya and my promise to her spurred me west toward the meeting point with Molly.

I finally reached the grounds where I'd spent days planting seeds, not without harrowing moments on the way. Cate's rain persisted except for a brief ill-timed respite while I fought a group of three Embers, earning a burn on my arm, which oozed clear fluid from angry red skin.

The fields stood empty as I raced to the stream, still hampered by my chains, praying I'd find the girls safe with Molly in the copse of trees. When she heard me approach, Molly's long neck stretched forward. Next came Mya's dark hair, flying free, wet strands framing pink cheeks and a brilliant smile, those dimples making a timely appearance. Grace hovered behind her.

I threw myself into Mya, savoring the feel of her arms snaking around my middle, heart thumping at her touch. The relief her safety brought burned beneath my closed lids. My fingers traveled over her shoulders, neck, and cheeks, ensuring she wasn't hurt. Finally, I pulled away.

"You really know how to start a fire." I grinned at her.

She laughed, that dimple showing, making my chest swell.

"And Grace. We wouldn't have escaped without your knowledge of the city."

"You're welcome." She tilted her head and mock-curtsied.

There was that cheeky girl I'd met in the tavern so long ago. I patted Molly, who nuzzled my hand. A check of her side where Leo injured her showed it had nearly healed.

"Where's the king?" Grace asked softly.

"Dead," I answered, clearing the clog in my throat. The man had been like a father to me, but I couldn't dwell on his loss with more important matters pending. I bypassed their shocked expressions. They'd been with him only the hour before, and we had been so close to getting out. I wouldn't allow his death to go to waste—he'd want us to escape.

"You two climb on Molly. She'll hold me with her talons." I actually wasn't sure how far the dragon could carry the three of us, but at least we'd travel farther from the city. My chains wouldn't allow me to ride astride, so I indicated for her to grasp me with her feet. Her claws jabbing me in my sides would be uncomfortable, though she'd be gentler than Leo. And nearly anything would be better than enduring the pit. At this point, if caught, Rowan would be generous to place me in the hole—more likely I'd suffer the same fate as the king.

The girls climbed on without complaint while I rubbed under Molly's chin. "I missed you. Don't know how you got away, but I'm so glad you're here. Okay, ready? Let's head south." I pointed toward Quorum. Molly's wings flapped and she hovered several feet before latching hold of me.

We flew through the rain, and over the Ember army, who awaited the escaping Caelum and Terran soldiers like a cat ready to pounce on mice. It wasn't long before we soared out of the storm. By my calculation, the flight to Quorum would be around five hours. I suspected Molly would require breaks, but she admirably flew, knowing exactly where we were headed. It was time to bring Grace home.

Darkness had settled when we arrived and found a patch of grass for landing. I dropped Mya off at the inn, promising to meet her soon. Grace ran ahead to the tavern, bursting open the door. Warmth spilled from within, a rectangle welcome mat of light cast onto the ground outside.

I leaned against the doorframe. My last time here had been the heart-wrenching scene with her father when we believed Grace was lost to us. Now John's ruddy face collapsed in on itself, like a deflating souffle, as he unapologetically held out his arms and cried. Grace threw herself into his chest, wrapping her thin limbs around his waist.

"I thought you were gone," John choked out.

Grace's response came out muffled, "I was."

They broke apart, and Grace gestured for me to enter. The tavern, closed for the night, still smelled of cooking meats and ale. My stomach grumbled.

"Lucas saved me," she said. "And you're never going to believe this—my accomplice to escape was the princess, Mya." A grin appled her cheeks.

John's brow crinkled. "The Terran?"

She nodded. "I know. She's actually nice."

Her father ran a hand over her shoulder as if he were checking to make sure she was real. "Did they hurt you? The Embers?" He didn't wait for her answer; instead, turned to me. "Did they?"

"Your daughter is well. She avoided… the worst of it." Now was not the time to tell how narrowly she missed those horrors. "She's very brave and played an integral part in our escape."

Grace's smile shaded rose. "And I rode a dragon here."

John took a step backward, his face paling. "Perhaps we should sit down for this."

"Actually, sir." I cleared my throat. "I should be getting back to the princess. I was wondering if you could help me with a few things?"

I walked freely for the first time in weeks toward the inn. John had removed the ankle shackles and provided a meal for Mya and me. Two covered steaming plates of meat pie, mashed potatoes, and juneberry tarts balanced in my arms. John couldn't stop looking at Grace, not quite believing she'd made it home alive. I'd told him she had some great knife skills outside the kitchen and should consider training all the ladies in town. We'd been too stuck in our ways here in Caelum—it was time to teach women and girls how to defend themselves.

I creaked open the door to the Royal Inn. The same worn but clean appearance greeted me with the lingering scent of wood polish. The innkeeper directed me toward my room and opened it for me. As soon as he left, I crossed the hall to Mya's room.

When I knocked, dinner in hand, she appeared with wet hair and a new gown, this one Caelum blue and only slightly better fitting than the brown sack she'd previously worn. The color, which the Terran princess likely never wore, brought out the aqua in her eyes, which sparkled at my appearance.

"You have food!" She ushered me inside, discarding all propriety. A small table sat in the corner where I placed her plate.

"Where's yours?" she asked.

"In my room." I shrugged, not wanting to presume. "Plus, you've obviously bathed and I—"

"Go wash up. I'll nibble on this roll while you're gone. Then come back and we'll eat. We've been talking about food for weeks. We should enjoy it together."

Her willingness to wait surprised me, though I couldn't say it made me unhappy. "I'll hurry." I slipped out the door and took the quickest possible bath, grateful that the innkeeper also left me clean clothes. I couldn't believe how much a man could miss soap.

Finally, I snatched up my plate and joined Mya. She greeted me with a mouth full of food but tried to hide it by guiltily swallowing. "Sorry. One bite turned into two..."

Half of her savory pie remained and a few potatoes. Her tart still sat intact. "Can't blame you. I'm absolutely starving."

We ate mostly in silence, with little moans and exclamations of how delicious everything tasted. I didn't care that the meat was wumbeast, and the pastry had gone lukewarm. I savored every mouthful, and when the time came for dessert, both of us grinned at each other like schoolchildren on Christmas morning. The tart, sweet taste of juneberries burst in my mouth with the first bite. Mya's smile returned, purple staining her teeth. That was the trouble with them—worse than a huckleberry, they had serious staying power. Neither of us cared.

With the last morsel devoured, Mya said, "Tell me what happened with the king. And… Cate must have been somewhere with all that rain—did you see her?" Ebony lashes shadowed her cheeks with those final words. Cate's presence still loomed between us.

I unraveled the story of King Aldridge, and how we were caught, Cate and Daniel arriving in the courtyard, and ultimately, his death because Cate refused to stop the rain.

"That must have been horrible for her." Mya wiped away a stray tear. "To make that decision—choose between the army and the king—and see your own father murdered. But why? Why didn't she stop? The king is always the number one priority."

Her empathy was admirable, but King Dryden had brainwashed her. "Living in Terra too long, I see," I said lightly. I couldn't really be mad at her. His influence was all she'd ever known. I continued, "Aldridge didn't want her to stop. He wouldn't have lived with himself if all those men died to save him. Besides, Rowan would have killed him either way. It was our only chance of escape."

"Then what happened?"

"Everything at once. They'd failed to de-arm Cate, Daniel, and Dev, so those three pulled out knives. I took advantage of the confusion with the Caelum and Terran army streaming in. Then we all just… dispersed. Melted into the city the best we could."

There had been that moment when Cate needed to go one way and me the other. I'd felt the tug of duty to her—to protect her—but it dissipated. My focus flipped to Mya. I'd been out of my mind with worry that the girls hadn't reached Molly, or been discovered, or the million other things that could have gone wrong. Cate and Daniel presumably had a plan. Was I worried they didn't make it out? Of course. We each had our jobs to complete that morning. Mine had been Mya and Grace. And from the way Mya looked at me just now... she definitely surpassed job status.

I wanted there to be a crumb on her lip so I could do that whole, *You have something right... here,* thing and brush it off gently as an excuse to touch her. Painfully for me, she'd licked every flake of pastry from the corner of her pink lips, then dabbed daintily like a princess, not someone who had devoured the meal like a wumbeast. I couldn't blame her. I'd done the same, and if she hadn't been present, I would have finished in half the time.

"So, what's the plan from here?" Mya asked.

Was she asking about us? Because I ached to know if she thought we were a jail-house fling or something more. Continuing our relationship would be problematic, especially because of her father. A topic that wasn't discussed in our prison cell.

Mya cocked her head, making me realize I hadn't responded. "How are we getting home?" she asked, enunciating each word.

Ah. Of course. She wanted to go home, not clarify our relationship. "Terra or Caelum?" I offered. I'd love to return to Caelum first, though she might feel the need to reunite with her parents.

"Oh, I assumed Caelum." Her cheeks pinkened. "Unless you don't want me to go?"

We could possibly both be wondering if we had a future together, but were too nervous to broach the subject. "I'd like to check in there, yes." I folded the hand towel I had been using as a napkin and placed it on the table. "Daniel hopefully will have returned with Cate. If we take Molly, we'll beat them both."

Her eyes widened.

"Unless you want horses, we can probably find some here," I added quickly.

"No," she stopped me. "I'm surprised you trust me enough to keep riding her."

I snorted. "Why wouldn't I? You're capable."

A small smile escaped her lips. "I think you're the first male to ever believe me capable."

"You've been hanging out with the wrong guys, then."

She nodded slowly. "I have."

I leaned in when her eyes flitted to my mouth. She smelled of lavender as I hovered near her, not quite touching before closing the distance. Soft and gentle, we relaxed into each other. It was a kiss filled with relief and promise, our questions melting away. We both wanted this—the here and now, but the spark of something more spurred us on. Unlike any girl I've known, her confidence was intoxicating, yet her willingness to grow, improve, and be more is what made me not want to let go.

I scooted my chair closer, slid my palm across her smooth cheek, then buried it in her dark hair, which waved freely down her shoulders. A gasp escaped her when my lips moved to just below her ear. She wrapped a hand behind my neck and pulled me tighter, her nails digging ever so slightly into my skin. I sighed into her, then slowly detangled myself, remaining centimeters apart.

"I like this better without the bars." I circled a finger around the pad of her thumb.

"Me too." She worried her lip. "What are we going to do?" she whispered, her eyes troubled.

This time, I knew we were both anxious about the same thing. Caelumites and Terrans don't mix. Her father—the scariest person around—would not approve. And I still had duties in Caelum.

"I've not been here. How did Cate and Daniel manage?"

She huffed a laugh. "Not well."

My protective instincts perked. "Why? Are they not together?"

"No, they are." She sighed and leaned back in her chair. "Daniel was in Caelum pretty much the entire time you were gone. But he's wanted in Terra too. He does a lot of good for the people, even if it's just helping soldiers train. His presence… is needed. And I missed him. Both as a brother and a buffer for my father. I don't claim to have as much influence as him, but my absence will be noticed. It's a difficult balance, and many aren't ready to accept friendlier terms between the kingdoms."

"I can see that." I crossed my arms and thought of all the Terrans I wasn't interested in reconciling with.

Her lips thinned. "Exactly."

"I want to try," I said, running a hand through my still-damp hair in frustration. This chasm between the realms had gone on long enough. "And—" I exhaled. "I really like you. Of course, you're beautiful—so beautiful—but it's what's in here." I fisted my chest. "I don't care that you are a princess, or that every male in the room wants you. I just care that you have an enormous heart. And you make me laugh. And you're kind."

"Okay. I'm going to get a huge ego," she stopped me, placing her palm on my hand. "I'll go to Caelum, and we'll send a message to Father that I'm safe. And then… we'll figure it out from there."

"I like that plan. And you can catch up with your brother."

She nodded, the heady air in the room deflated. There were no guarantees that Daniel and Cate would make it home.

I stood, pushing my chair back. "Early start tomorrow. It'll still be a few days before we reach Caelum. I'll buy supplies in the morning and meet you here with breakfast."

I leaned down for one last lingering kiss. "Goodnight."

Her lips curled. "I'll be ready."

CHAPTER 48
DANIEL

We escaped.

Instead of surrounding the city, the Embers waited for our troops to exit the way most of them entered—through the battlefield on the south side. There were a few nerve-wracking moments, the route circuitous and extended a day farther east than we intended, but we finally arrived at the designated meeting point two days south.

Colonel Dixon stood amongst a gathering of soldiers as we rode up. "Colonel," I called.

Relief crossed his features before his leadership mask was restored, as if he never doubted our return. He strode over while we dismounted.

"Mya and Lucas?" I asked. A quick glance around camp showed no sign of them.

He shook his head. "Haven't seen them."

"How many casualties?" I switched gears from brother to soldier. Cate sidled next to me, holding North's reins.

"Don't know yet. They've been trickling in. I arrived about six hours ago and a group was already here. I dispatched the first Terrans to inform your father. I'd hoped to delay the news to the baron until we knew more." Unspoken was that he'd been waiting to find out if we survived. "Which way are you headed?" he asked.

I glanced at Dev, who leaned against his horse, sweat trickling down his temple. Dev's leg had swelled puffy and red around the wound, and we still had multiple days' ride. Either kingdom's castle was essentially equidistant from here. "We'll go to Caelum." It made the most sense. Cate needed me, and she had to be present during the transition of power and for King Aldridge's funeral.

Cate had hardly spoken since leaving The Camp. Both her parents were now dead. She must be feeling adrift in this world, especially when she had a loving family who lived in America. Her emotions read flat, an indicator of falling into shock. I'd felt it before from others, most commonly after losing someone close or after a battle filled with casualties. We'd always known we might not rescue the king, but reality sat differently. Cate would be queen. Even if the baron remained her regent for the next year, eventually she would lead her kingdom. First would come a funeral, then a coronation to plan soon after. So many changes for her.

Cate stepped forward. "Colonel, can you remain here a couple more days to wait for the rest of the survivors? We'll stay the night, then take a group to Caelum Castle. And is there a medic?"

"Yes, Ma'am. Will do." His mouth formed a thin line, his scar tugging at one corner. "The medic hasn't made it back."

I wondered how many more were alive. Most had likely been routed away from their horses, making it easier for the Embers to hunt them down. If they survived, they'd be at least two days behind when traveling by foot.

After we'd settled in a makeshift camp for a well-deserved sleep, I scooted next to Dev. His sallow skin tinged yellow in the firelight. "You going to be able to ride back?"

He grimaced. "Don't have much choice, do I?"

"You could wait for the medic. He'll have medication—antibiotics. I'm worried your wound is infected."

"Did you meet him?" Dev asked.

"Who?"

"The healer," he ground out. "Couldn't win a fight with a kitten. That guy's not coming back."

Another weight hefted onto my shoulders. "All right. Get some sleep."

The morning came too soon, all of us exhausted from lack of rest. I helped Dev mount again, tying him to his horse so if he fell asleep, he wouldn't fall off. We'd changed the bandage, packed fresh ones, and crossed our fingers he wouldn't worsen.

We rode for days in near silence, Dev too sick and feverish for conversation, Cate withdrawn and glassy-eyed. I tried to coax words from her, but she remained stoic. At night, she let me fold her in my arms by the fire, though taking turns as watchman allowed for little sleep. We traveled with a band of other Caelum soldiers who discretely gave enough space for privacy, while still keeping close guard. They too were somber, and either lost comrades or wondered if their friends trailed somewhere behind us.

Cate's hair straggled from its braid, wisps clinging to her damp forehead. Normally she'd brush them away and dry herself with a cloth, but she seemed oblivious.

"Please talk to me," I said.

She swallowed, her neck muscles working past the perpetual lump in her throat. She still hadn't cried and needed to. "Let's just get home." She didn't even look at me.

"Cate. This has been going on too long. Please."

She finally turned to me, her jaw set. "I need to be strong. This is the only way I know how right now."

"You realize it's not your fault."

Her eyes flashed with anger, the first emotion I'd seen or felt from her in days. "How is it not? I didn't stop the rain. The leader warned me, and I didn't do it."

"And what, let hundreds of men die for one? You had no way of predicting what would happen."

"I should have." Her pain, no longer shielded from me, dipped so dark it practically coated my tongue with bitterness. She dug her knees into North's side and cantered forward to the group of soldiers ahead.

"She needs time," Dev said, his words slow and deliberate, eyes fever-bright.

"Unfortunately, she doesn't have the luxury. We'll be at Caelum Castle tomorrow, and she'll be the new unofficial queen."

"Yeah, but it's just us right now. Let her be."

"It's hard not being able to help her. Fix it somehow."

"Sorry, mate. Being there is enough." This was the most Dev had spoken on the entire journey home, the toll it took evidenced by his sagging body. He'd always had my back. Just like I had his and Cate's. It didn't matter that he had been silent until now. He was right, being there was enough.

A few minutes later, Dev's eyes closed, slumping over his horse's neck awkwardly. This wasn't just a light snooze. Something was wrong, and despite the ropes, there was a possibility of him falling and being dragged. My heart lunged into my throat.

"Dev!"

No answer.

I reached over and grabbed the reins of his horse, then lurched off Raven to halt Dev's mount. His skin was hot, sticky, and entirely too pale. Several soldiers rode up behind and we hauled him from the saddle, undoing the knots, laying him carefully on the trail.

I checked his heart—a fast, fluttering rhythm, his chest still rising and falling. His bandage needed changing. I pulled it away, wincing at the foul odor, to find yellow pus lingering with bloody red tissue. The side of the wound gaped wide.

He needed medicine. We had to get him to Caelum as fast as possible. "Find materials for a gurney. He's done riding." It would slow us down, but we'd manage. A blanket and two branches later, we rotated carrying him. Cate hovered, her anxiety now palpable. All it took for her to snap out of herself was someone else to worry about. Her selflessness would serve her well as queen, though potentially wear her down.

We came to a small village with an apothecary. An old man provided herbs for a poultice and offered to care for him, but the healers at the castle were more capable, so we continued on. We did procure a rickety wagon for Dev, who tossed and turned, no longer aware of his surroundings.

Cate rode up beside us. "He doesn't look good." Her demeanor had changed from wooden to alert. She slid off North and leaned in to touch him through the cart's bars, checking for a pulse. "It's too fast." Her worried gaze met mine. "We need to hurry."

The ruts in the road and the dilapidated wagon did not pair well. Yet we were only about an hour from the castle. *Come on, Dev, we've got to make it.* Each pothole and divot left me cringing at Dev's jostling body.

It was my turn for melancholy. I still remained uncertain if Mya made it out alive. King Aldridge's death had crushed Cate. I didn't always agree with the man, but he helped keep my father in check. Cate must now lead a new country and deal with King Dryden's machinations.

She ripped a piece of blood-stained bandage from Dev, then called for Mocha, who had been circling overhead for hours. She pulled on the leather glove and drew out some treats for the bird from her saddlebag. Not that Mocha needed it. She'd been hunting for days, eating better than us.

When the falcon landed on her arm, she wrapped the bandage scrap around Mocha's leg and gave her the home signal. It no doubt reminded Cate of the uniform fragment of her father's. Her grief washed over me, emotions raging out of check. Mocha took off and gracefully flew toward the castle. At least they would be prepared for our arrival, although they wouldn't know who was injured. It would be best to convey the news regarding the king in person.

After around a half hour, the road turned curvy, and the ruts deepened. I examined Dev from my horse, his eyes now closed. He'd stopped thrashing about and held eerily still. Unease snaked up my spine, leaving my scalp prickling.

"Stop," I called, launching from Raven to reach him. "I don't think he's breathing."

CHAPTER 49
CATE

My own breath snapped in my chest, an anchor snagging against the bottom of the sea. We were so close, only thirty minutes from the castle, yet it might be too late. I slid from North and raced to Daniel where he'd climbed into the wagon and hovered over Dev. Daniel's broad shoulders shielded me from seeing Dev. "Does he have a pulse?"

"I don't know. I can't feel it." Daniel's voice thrummed with panic.

My stomach coiled with worry. He needed Dev by his side, his oldest friend.

Hoofbeats sounded down the lane, their riders obscured by a bend in the road. I'd learned earlier this month that Embers weren't hesitant to stray this close to the castle and braced for an attack.

"Daniel, someone's coming," I called.

His hands worked furiously to unbutton Dev's jacket for better access, the collar too high on his neck. He was oblivious to anything else but his friend's well-being.

His wide eyes caught mine, sweat beading along his brow. I pulled out my dagger and held tight to North's reins to ensure she didn't bolt. I wished there was time to mount again, but at any moment they'd come around the bend. Our small band of soldiers all remained on high alert. A flash of blue filled me with relief. A group of Caelum soldiers rode toward us, at least five, with the red medic armband. I purposely did not specify who was hurt in the message Mocha carried, hoping they would believe it might be my father and make extra preparations. I never expected them to meet us on the road.

"Over here," I called.

"Found a pulse," Daniel cried. "It's barely there."

He scrambled from the cart to allow the healers inside. They'd brought bandages, the blue IV mixture, sedatives, and pain medication. Soon we were back on route, Daniel and I exchanging relieved looks. Dev wasn't out of the woods yet, but at least he was getting treatment. A medic sat on each side of him to monitor his vitals for the rest of the trip. No one asked about the king, likely in deference to me, and I didn't offer the information.

We rode on, my mind swirling with worry for Dev mixed with visions of my father's sliced throat, his body toppling toward me on repeat. So much blood. Sticky, red, oozing. Everywhere. The realities of war seeped into my bones, leaving me brittle and cold. I couldn't avoid talking about my father, but clung to those few more minutes of delay like a lifeline.

We rode into the courtyard, grooms racing to take care of our mounts. Graftonberg, Roy, and the count exited the castle, acting like a trio of royalty, their jewels glittering in the afternoon sun.

I dismounted, waiting for the baron to approach. A cluster of soldiers and servants lined the drive at our arrival. I cleared my throat, making sure Daniel was at my side. My heart thumped an unsteady rhythm as I prepared to give the dreaded announcement. "King Aldridge has died," I called.

Everyone's right hand rose to their chest, a Caelum tradition of honoring the dead. To my astonishment, all the people in the courtyard moved en masse to one knee, even the baron and Daniel, bowing their heads. I started to kneel, but Daniel whispered, "Stay."

"Long live the queen!" the baron shouted.

"Long live the queen!" echoed throughout the grounds.

Tears pricked my eyes, the reality of my father's death and the ramifications of it sinking deeper into my soul. Instinct took over. "Thank you," I murmured. "We have injured with us. We should all proceed into the castle."

They stood and awaited my procession through the doors, my shoulders sagging with relief once away from onlookers.

I trudged into the conference room, knowing the baron would want a full update. We relayed what we could, Daniel stepping in to explain the events leading up to my father's death. Had I told the tale, I likely would have confessed my part in his demise, taking the blame. If I had only found another way—just stopped the rain for a few minutes—he would still be alive.

A knock interrupted us. The door burst open. Mya tumbled through, followed by Lucas. Daniel and I leapt out of our seats. Mya flew into Daniel's arms, and I squeezed Lucas, his clean uniform smelling of wool and soap. We'd only known each other a short time, but our history was embedded into my skin like a tattoo. He was part of the reason I came to this world. My first memories here would forever intertwine with him, and it felt as though an eternity had passed since we'd seen each other.

"I missed you so much." I squeezed him a little harder, then stepped away. "When did you make it back?"

We all started talking over one another. Daniel slapped Lucas on the back in one of those bro-greetings, then Lucas pulled him in for a hug, while I embraced Mya.

"Looks like we're done for now," the baron said, standing up to leave. "We've been briefed already by Princess Mya and Lucas."

Daniel's brows scrunched in confusion. "You knew my sister was alive and didn't bother to tell me?"

Graftonberg gave him a heavy stare. "We matched up your stories. I needed to make sure we weren't missing anything."

Anger boiled in my chest. "Just get out." I pointed to the exit.

They left, heads held high, despite their deception. Graftonberg was the one who couldn't be trusted, not us. One more knock against him. And I'd been counting.

The next few days snailed in a sluggish haze. A depressingly small number of Caelum soldiers trickled in from our mission. Colonel Dixon had not returned, likely awaiting stragglers. The longer he was delayed, the more I feared for his safety. In the infirmary, Dev turned a corner, and the healers expected him to make a full recovery.

Another bright spot was Lucas and Mya. Daniel switched from anger to relief that she was safe, though still not fully forgiving her for trailing after them in the first place. One day, I stumbled upon them in the corridor. Mya's back was against the wall, Lucas's lips hovering over hers, his expression so tender it made my heart pang. A tinge of something—not quite jealousy—was quickly replaced with the joy of seeing him happy, and the knowledge that our friendship could return without the worry of anything else between us... namely that one kiss we'd shared.

I turned on my heel before they noticed me and headed straight to Daniel to convey the news. To my surprise, he laughed, the first I'd heard in a long time.

"Do you know something I don't?" I asked.

"Only that my sister always gets her way." He grinned. "I've suspected she admired Lucas for quite some time."

"Oooh. *Admired*. So fancy."

He rolled his eyes. "I haven't been living in America for the last eighteen years."

"Right. You're too princely." My lips quirked.

He pulled me into an embrace. "It's good to see your smile. Even a small one."

I sighed against him. "This has been hard. And I know I need to rein Graftonberg in... I'm just..."

"Grieving?" He rubbed my back. "We won't let the baron do anything too drastic. I've been keeping an eye on him."

I committed myself to watch him closer as well. Daniel couldn't always be here. Another problem we'd deal with later.

Arrangements for my father's funeral were top of everyone's mind, and I let the preparations go on without me. I'd never planned a funeral, much less a royal one. Everyone was quick to offer their condolences, and I became used to the automatic replies, thanking them for their kindness. Some would recall a particularly generous anecdote of him, which would make my eyes burn and nose tingle until I took a moment to tell myself that a queen didn't cry.

Although, to be honest, I wasn't sure that was the truth. The only example I could think of in my world was Queen Elizabeth, known for her stiff upper lip. Fashioning myself to someone I'd only ever witnessed as elderly before she died maybe wasn't the best role model. Daniel's mother had also hidden her emotions—perhaps out of habit of keeping them from her husband—which didn't help me decide how to act, either. In the end, I concluded my tears were private, my grief private, and I would stay strong for the kingdom. Already deemed too young and still not meeting the qualification to reign without a regent, I wanted to avoid rumors flying that I was too emotional to lead.

Every day leading up to the funeral was more difficult, causing me to retract further into myself. There would be no strategy meeting over my father's secret weakness for tea and scones, no more stories of his childhood or of my mother. Mention of my mom had been scarce, a painful topic he preferred to avoid. He admitted in one of our afternoon meetings that he never should have accused her of being a traitor, banishing her to a cabin, only for her to die giving birth. It was his greatest mistake, and he had lived with the guilt daily. At least he would be free of those demons.

The day of the funeral arrived. Emma dressed me, the gown a navy blue, and coated in sparkling beads and seed pearls the color of a deep night sky. The multiple layers and weight constricted my movements, giving me the sensation of walking underwater. She attached a diamond tiara to my intricate up-do, my mother's favorite, and worn when I danced with my father at the Terran ball. So much has happened since then.

The elaborate carriage ride to Neva passed in a blur, the baron sitting at my side while I brushed the velvet cushion, my fingers trailing back and forth across its blue knap. The softness was soothing, like stroking a cat. Protocol dictated that Daniel travel farther up in the procession. People lined the entire route from the castle to the funeral site, tossing roses at us. My father's ceremonial coffin lay empty, covered in lavish flowers, and rode behind on an elaborate platform. We would probably never recover his body. I suppressed thinking about how, later today, they would bury the hollow box on castle grounds.

We stopped outside the city, where arrangements had been made for the ceremony. When I stepped out of the carriage, the wave of attendees stretched as far as I could see. Families with children perched on shoulders, elderly with canes, and all shapes and sizes must have traveled from the entire kingdom to be here.

Set slightly apart, King Dryden and Queen Lila sat in front. No one told me they were coming. As much as I wanted to dislike everything about Daniel's father, attending the funeral was a generous gesture. A political move or an olive branch? Now it appeared I'd have my boyfriend's parents staying at the castle when all I craved was to crawl back into bed.

The baron and I stepped onto the dais. Colonel Dixon acted as my personal guard after arriving with a group of soldiers two days prior. Lucas stood off to one side, his presence comforting. Graftonberg exalted my father in his speech, lamenting that he had to act as my regent for the next nine months instead of turning the kingdom over to me. I imagined both Daniel and King Dryden could detect that lie, though it didn't exactly take special powers to do so.

Finally. My turn. My brain found it difficult to process the sheer numbers that would listen to me speak.

Be vulnerable.

Be strong.

Be their queen.

Someone handed me a megaphone of sorts, amplified by a technology unique to Caelum that I didn't fully understand. Caelumites in the crowd were assigned to direct the sound through the air so that everyone could hear.

Heat crept up my torso and neck, flushing my cheeks, as my pulse stampeded against my ribs, the dress suffocating. I took in a shallow breath. Since my father's death, I'd been too deep in my shell to experience anxiety, too numb to notice. Seeing the number of faces paying their respects to their king was nearly my undoing.

I waited for the lump in my throat to melt, then spoke, "Thank you for coming. I know a number of you traveled to be here, and I can't tell you how much your support means to me. I, like you, miss King Aldridge. He was a tremendous leader. But many of you don't know he was also a great father. We—" my voice faltered. "We didn't get enough time together. He was learning his role as a parent, and… we were learning each other. We used to have tactical meetings in his office and shared tea and scones. He always stole the last biscuit." A few chuckles echoed through the audience. "King Aldridge never did anything by halves, always stretched to produce his best, and most of the time succeeded. And importantly, he sought to ready me for this day. To teach me about Caelum, the kingdom I have grown to love, to instruct me in battle strategy, and prepare me to one day be queen. He was an incredible man."

I paused, taking in another breath. "His last moments were to sacrifice himself for his men. The sword that slit his throat belonged to the Embers' new leader."

Murmurs erupted from the crowd. Everyone always wanted the particulars of death, no matter how gory. Sick as it was, I needed them to hear. To fuel their anger against the Embers, the fire that also burned in me. The flame flickered to life after being encased in grief these last few weeks.

"You heard correctly. They have a leader, and I've seen with my own eyes the authority he carries over the Embers."

I raised my chin. "As is customary, in one month I will be crowned Caelum's queen. Under law, I'll have a regent, but mark my words, I will still protect this kingdom with my life. My priority will be defeating the Embers so we can live in peace. I will fulfill the prophecy. I promise you that."

"Long live the queen!" somebody shouted. It echoed, rippling through the crowd like an ocean's wave, giving me strength. I caught King Dryden's eye and held it. His gaze usually unsettled me, but today it was different. He wouldn't be pushing me around any longer. Neither would the baron. The people's support flowed through me. They needed a strong leader. Someone to replace my father, and I would live up to the task.

I didn't have a choice.

Back at the castle, I watched my father's casket lower into the ground alongside an intimate group. I erected that icy wall again, holding my head high when all I wanted to do was collapse next to the burial site. Tell him how sorry I was. Have one last conversation. But he wasn't there. His body was with the enemy.

This grave was empty.

I greeted everyone graciously while a condolence line formed. Finally, my feet aching, and my neck strained from the dress that must weigh fifteen pounds, I arrived at my suite for a rest before dinner. It would be another stately affair, King Dryden sure to be present.

I draped myself over the sofa, exhausted, both emotionally and physically, my limbs wilting into the cushions. A knock, followed by Emma, had me wincing at the interruption.

"Sorry to bother you, ma'am." She curtsied, as usual. I couldn't stop her formality, even after we'd saved one another's lives when the Ember entered this very room those months ago. "This came for you. He said it was urgent."

"Who?" I sat up and took the package from her, about the size of a paperback novel.

"A soldier. One of ours who just made it back from Ember City."

"Has anyone else checked this out?" My thoughts flashed to a bomb or anthrax—modern problems in America—not here.

Emma shook her head. "I don't think so…"

Something felt off, yet I wanted to know the contents and certainly didn't need Graftonberg involved.

My fingers, suddenly damp, slid along the edge of the paper. It peeled back to reveal a small box. Apprehension prodded me to move it off my lap. I set it next to me on the sofa. Emma hovered—she'd probably always be protective of me, and vice versa.

I slowly edged up one side of the lid. Inside sat a phone. A *modern* phone. It was so strange to see it here, my mind could barely process it. Like when an airplane accidentally makes it through edits into a movie set in medieval England. I turned it over in my hands and time stopped, my heart, my body, paralyzed. I would know the case anywhere, so often sitting on the chipped kitchen counter back home, imprinted with a picture of the ocean. My mom's favorite place. A note stuck to a crack at the bottom of the box. I pulled it out with shaky fingers.

Read the texts

With trembling hands, I turned on the power to the phone. I knew the password numbers by heart—my dad's birthday. The display lit up, the wallpaper a snapshot of the four of us at my high school graduation. We were so happy. Me in my cap and gown. Jack, four at the time, in an adorable polka-dot tie, Mom and Dad looking on proudly. An unread text sat at the message icon. I pressed to open it.

A picture flashed on the screen. In the background were the oak cabinets of my kitchen in Oregon. A gasp escaped. With a single image, my two worlds collided into one nightmare. I recognized Rowan's face. The same cocky expression spread across his features as when he killed the king. He gripped a knife, wedged against my little brother's neck. The veins in Rowan's hand, the way he held the dagger, his widespread stance, all a flashback to my father's death.

The red… the blood pooling and seeping everywhere on that fateful day arose—the memory, an unwanted daily companion. Jack's face was tear-stained—those big brown eyes I missed so much pleaded for help.

COME FIND US HERE, OR HE DIES. YOU HAVE TWO WEEKS.

Heir of Earth and Sky will continue in Book Three

Make sure to join our Discord
(https://discord.gg/5RccXhNgGb)
so you never miss a release!

THANK YOU FOR READING THE CAPTURED

We hope you enjoyed it as much as we enjoyed bringing it to you. We just wanted to take a moment to encourage you to review the book. Follow this link: **The Captured** to be directed to the book's Amazon product page to leave your review.

Every review helps further the author's reach and, ultimately, helps them continue writing fantastic books for us all to enjoy.

Also in series:

The Concealed

The Captured

Want to discuss our books with other readers and even the authors?

JOIN THE AETHON DISCORD!

You can also join our non-spam mailing list by visiting www.subscribepage.com/AethonReadersGroup and never miss out on future releases. You'll also receive three full books completely Free as our thanks to you.

Don't forget to follow us on socials to never miss a new release!

Facebook | Instagram | Twitter | Website

take the place of an innocent and Marcus to protect the king – they're forced to trust one another with their lives. Now inescapably entrenched in the gory, duplicitous world of the blood trials, feelings long-buried surface, blurring the lines between duty and honor, love and loyalty. But Marcus carries a devastating secret–one that could destroy the foundations of Dru's world... **Don't miss this adult romantasy debut combining the second-chance romance of *Heartless Hunter* by Kristen Ciccarelli with the deadly trials of *Gladiator*. With their lives and their hearts on the line, will love be enough to thwart the might of the Imperium?**

GET TRIAL OF BRONZE AND BLOOD NOW!

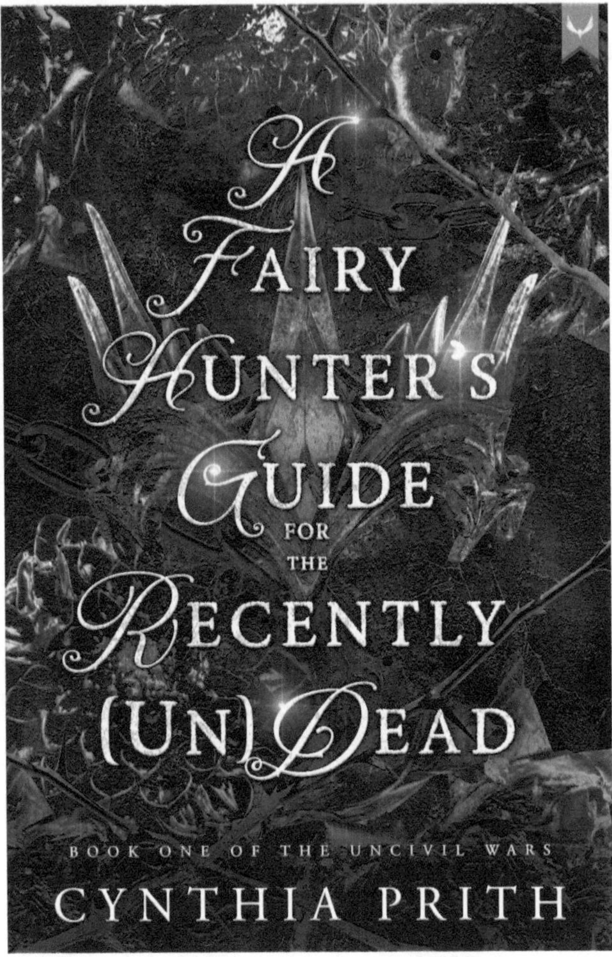

A fairy hunter desperate to save herself. A blighted knight hunting for his freedom. A looming war. Unexpectedly resurrected, Gwendolyn finds herself kidnapped by her mortal enemy: the fae. A distressing prospect considering her monster-hunting mother trained her to eradicate them. Worse, a bargain has been struck with the fairy lord on her behalf, and Gwendolyn knows too well that such deals always come with a terrible price. Trapped in the fairy lord's glittering court each night and banished back to her own world upon waking, Gwendolyn must find the terms of her bargain quickly if she hopes to survive and outsmart him. Yet, despite her inherited hatred of fae, the fairy lord is not without his charms. Gwendolyn struggles to resist his allure when every time they meet, he offers her anything she could ever wish—a bargain that would no doubt cost her entire soul in trade. She soon discovers the only creature in this twisted realm she can truly trust is a man as trapped as herself; a blighted knight made from the pieces of a hundred failed heroes. Cursed down to his literal bones, he cannot help but hunt her on his master's orders. Despite this, Gwendolyn's heart aches for him, his situation so very like her own. She knows, despite his insistence that she cannot trust him, that if she were to break his curse, they might actually stand a chance of fighting their way out together... **Don't miss this Romantasy debut where the monster hunting vibes of *VAN HELSING* meet the glamorous ballrooms of *BRIDGERTON*, in the Victorian style of Emily Wilde's *ENCYCLOPAEDIA OF FAIRIES*. Perfect for fans of *The Labyrinth*, *A Court of Mist and Fury*, and *Queen of Roses*.**

ACKNOWLEDGMENTS

My first thank you must go to my readers! Thank you to everyone who has messaged or encouraged me along the way or simply enjoyed *The Concealed* enough to pick up *The Captured*. Some days, I have to remind myself that real people are turning those pages and loving my stories, and I'm truly humbled. Reviews are the best way to support an author, and I would be so thankful if you took a few moments to do so. I'm excited to continue the journey with you all to book three.

A huge thank you to Aethon Books, Rhett Bruno and Steve Beaulieu for their continued support. Thank you to editors Kalene Williams and Jennifer Ehrhardt for a fantastic job polishing this manuscript. I'm grateful to Blue Nose Audio who created another amazing audiobook, this time with two fantastic narrators: Amanda Leigh Cobb and Joe Jameson. I am so lucky to have them!

To Wednesday night critique group—or as we like to refer to ourselves fondly—The Little Writing Group that Could. We've done it together, and I wouldn't have it any other way! Thank you to Darren, Dorene, Parris, Melissa, and Jenna. I truly believe I wouldn't be here without you, and *The Concealed* manuscript would be somewhere collecting dust, half-finished. My beta readers were incredibly helpful for *The Captured* development. Thanks to Jade, Fatima, Rebecca Weber, and Petunia Fish. And of course, special thanks to my daughter Claire and husband Michael for reading early manuscripts (more than once), giving advice when I doubted, and talking through the rocky points. This book is so much better because of you.

Speaking of family, as always, I credit my parents for giving me the confidence at a young age to try new things, even if they are difficult. Becoming a published author definitely qualifies! My husband has taken on so much more around the house and with the kids—thank goodness he knows how to do algebra because I sure don't remember. Thank you for stepping up to allow me to pursue this dream. And to my lovely daughters for all their support. Claire, my brainstormer and book lover, and Brooke, my quiet supporter who is always in my corner. I couldn't ask for more. Lastly, thank you, God, the ultimate supporter. You are the true reason for my blessings.

ABOUT THE AUTHOR

SK is a physician by day and reading-obsessed by night. She lives in sunny Arizona with her husband and two daughters, where you might find her planning the next great family vacation, experimenting with a new recipe, or spending way too much on fancy coffee and tea.

Website:
https://skhortonauthor.com

SK Horton newsletter signup:
https://dashboard.mailerlite.com/forms/896549/118888234667213917/share

www.ingramcontent.com/pod-product-compliance
Lightning Source LLC
Chambersburg PA
CBHW020457310726
48979CB00016B/2696/J

9781964505169